# SHADOWS OF REACH

# SHADOWS OF REACH

## TROY DENNING

BASED ON THE BESTSELLING VIDEO GAME FOR XBOX

GALLERY BOOKS

New York   London   Toronto   Sydney   New Delhi

# G 10

Gallery Books
An Imprint of Simon & Schuster, Inc.
1230 Avenue of the Americas
New York, NY 10020

First Gallery Books trade paperback edition October 2020

GALLERY BOOKS and colophon are registered trademarks of Simon & Schuster, Inc.

For information about special discounts for bulk purchases, please contact Simon & Schuster Special Sales at 1-866-506-1949 or business@simonandschuster.com.

The Simon & Schuster Speakers Bureau can bring authors to your live event. For more information or to book an event, contact the Simon & Schuster Speakers Bureau at 1-866-248-3049 or visit our website at www.simonspeakers.com.

10   9   8   7

Library of Congress Cataloging-in-Publication Data

Names: Denning, Troy, author.
Title: Shadows of reach / Troy Denning.
Other titles: At head of title: Halo
Description: Gallery Books trade paperback edition. | New York : Gallery Books, 2020. | Series: Halo | "Based on the bestselling video game for Xbox"
Identifiers: LCCN 2020028886 (print) | LCCN 2020028887 (ebook) | ISBN 9781982143619 (trade paperback) | ISBN 9781982143633 (ebook)
Subjects: LCSH: Halo (Video game)—Fiction. | GSAFD: Science fiction.
Classification: LCC PS3554.E5345 S53 2020 (print) | LCC PS3554.E5345 (ebook) | DDC 813/.54—dc23
LC record available at https://lccn.loc.gov/2020028886
LC ebook record available at https://lccn.loc.gov/2020028887

ISBN 978-1-9821-4361-9
ISBN 978-1-9821-4363-3 (ebook)

*For Elliot Courant*

# HISTORIAN'S NOTE

This story takes place in October 2559, a year after the events of *Halo 5: Guardians*, as the AI Cortana retreats into the Domain, then resurrects a host of Forerunner Guardians and uses them to impose martial law on interstellar civilizations across the Orion Arm of the Milky Way Galaxy.

# CHAPTER ONE

0217 hours, October 7, 2559 (military calendar)
UNSC Owl Insertion Craft *Special Delivery*
Insertion Run, Continent Eposz, Planet Reach

The situation monitor on the forward bulkhead remained in blackout mode, waiting for the Owl's hull temperature to drop far enough to deploy the nose cameras. It didn't matter. John-117 had inserted onto dozens of glassed worlds during his thirty-four-year combat career, and he knew what to expect: a blanket of silver-limned clouds hanging over vast sweeps of heat-fused ground. Mats of lichen and algae starting to take hold in scattered pockets of dust and mud. Black-bottomed ponds licking at mirror-smooth shores, spider-veined river systems draining into half-empty seas . . . and not much else.

The Covenant was gone now, save for a few holdout factions still clinging to their hatred of humanity or a lost hope of transcendence. But during the war, the aliens had rained monsoons of hot plasma down on hundreds of worlds, burning soil and melting bedrock, boiling oceans and filling the air with superheated vapor. Any creature that had escaped instant incineration had suffocated on superheated smoke, or seared away its feet fleeing over molten ground, or emerged from hiding to eventually starve while wandering barren expanses of ash-impregnated lechatelierite.

Nothing survived a Covenant plasma bombardment. John knew that.

But this was Reach, the closest thing to a home he and his fellow Spartan-IIs could remember, and he wanted to see for himself how it was faring these days.

He *needed* to.

Operation: WOLFE was supposed to be a simple mission, just a two-kilometer descent into the ruins of CASTLE Base to recover the assets Dr. Catherine Halsey needed to save galactic civilization, again, from a rogue AI.

Cortana.

Two years ago, Cortana had been *John's* AI, residing in his Mjolnir armor, connected to his mind through a port in the back of his skull. And she—

Damn. It was happening again.

John could hardly think of Cortana's name without finding himself in a battle against his own thoughts, replaying the entire incident in his mind and wondering what he might have done differently. It wasn't a bad neural lace or hypnotic suggestion or anything like that—he was just . . .

He checked his heads-up display for the GO TIME.

ETA twenty-seven minutes. Enough of a window to get himself sorted and focused. John had known before their last battle together that Cortana was descending into the final stages of "rampancy"—a sort of inevitable AI schizophrenia—as her mind literally outgrew its neural matrix after seven years of existence. But with the fate of humanity hanging in the balance, he had allowed Cortana to infiltrate the control systems of a primordial enemy vessel, sacrificing herself so he could destroy a devastating weapon threatening Earth. And it had worked.

Until Cortana returned from the dead.

Things had really gone off the rails then, and John had made some decisions he regretted. Worse, he had dragged the rest of Blue Team into the mess along with him, going AWOL to uncover the mystery of Cortana's rebirth and rescue her . . . from what? Herself?

Transformed by residing for a year in an ancient quantum information repository known as the Domain, Cortana had returned more intellectually capable than ever, with a host of long-hidden, massive "Guardians" at her disposal. She had wasted no time issuing an ultimatum to every world in the Orion arm of the galaxy: accept her rule and live in peace, or defy her and suffer the brutal consequences.

John's second-in-command, Fred-104, called it peace-through-menace, but that was an understatement. The Guardians were so powerful they could neutralize entire worlds and knock fleets out of orbit, killing thousands—or even hundreds of thousands—when huge vessels crashed down on the towns and cities below. And Cortana had also corrupted an army of human AIs into aligning with and spying for her. Now interstellar civilization was sinking into a nightmarish surveillance state, with the situation worsening each day.

And John could not help feeling responsible. Had he ordered Cortana to stand down when her deterioration began to accelerate, she would never have been drawn into the Domain . . . but he would never have destroyed that Forerunner weapon. . . .

It was all just going in circles.

There had been no good choices, in any event—John knew that. He had done the best he could under such terrible circumstances . . . right up until he disobeyed orders and went AWOL, and had to be doggedly hunted down by his superiors and fellow Spartans. Someday there was going to be a reckoning for that decision. Just not now.

Now he had a job to do.

John checked the ETA. Twenty-five minutes. Still plenty of time.

But during the previous day's pre-drop threat sweep, the *Special Delivery*'s mothership—an *Eclipse*-class prowler named *Bucephalus*—had picked up some surface chatter suggesting there was a low-intensity conflict under way in the Arany Basin. It hadn't been much, just a few transmissions as one group of humans warned another about an enemy patrol, followed a few minutes later by a trio of heat flares that could have been anything from plasma strikes to missile detonations. There had probably been more to the battle, of course, but the *Bucephalus*'s instruments weren't sensitive enough to pick up small- and medium-arms fire from orbit. Just the artillery.

John and the other Spartan-IIs had grown to maturity on Reach, so he'd always paid special attention to any mention of it in the intelligence reports routed past him over the years. He knew that not much had happened on the planet since the Covenant plasma bombardment. A handful of salvagers—both human and alien—had started to visit Reach after the glass cooled, and two years ago, a small colony of rehab pioneers had set up somewhere on the continent of Eposz.

The Arany Basin was located on Eposz, so it seemed likely that the conflict involved the rehab pioneers somehow. But even that was not a certainty. The intelligence reports had grown extremely rare after Cortana issued her ultimatum, and the few John *had* seen did not refer to Reach. The fight could be between anybody—two salvage companies, the rehab pioneers and a salvage company, different rehab factions, or a hundred other possibilities.

All John knew for sure was that the conflict location was good news, because Blue Team had no intention of entering the Arany Basin. Sure, he would have liked to check on the pioneers and see how they were doing. Reach was the only home he could remember, and he would have liked some reassurance that it was in good hands.

But that wasn't the mission.

"Two minutes."

John let his gaze drop to the woman who had spoken, a steady-eyed crew chief in the jump seat beneath the situation monitor.

Dressed in the black insertion suit of a marine special operations flight crew, Stella Mukai had a round face, Newsakan features, and a warm, no-nonsense manner that seemed equal parts den mother and drill sergeant. On her sleeve, she wore the flat black rocker and triple chevrons of a chief petty officer—a rank just two steps below John's own rank of master chief petty officer.

The ETA in John's heads-up display still read twenty-five minutes, so he asked, "Two minutes until what, Chief Mukai?"

Mukai pointed above her head, and John realized she had caught him staring at the blank situation monitor.

"Until the nose cameras deploy," she said. "But you won't see much at this time of night. With the cloud cover over Eposz, the surface glass is going to be about as reflective as a dust nebula."

"What a shame," Fred-104 said over his voicemitter. He was seated directly across the green-lit troop bay from John, secured in place by an oversize titanium-alloy crash harness designed especially for Spartans. "A state-of-the-art insertion craft like this, and nobody thinks to install an infrared enhancement package?"

Mukai's brow shot up at the remark—*every* Owl had an infrared enhancement package—and she cast an admonishing glare in Fred's direction. The *Special Delivery* was her baby, and nobody told a crew chief how to run her boat—not even a Spartan-II wearing four hundred kilos of GEN3 Mjolnir power armor.

Fred pretended not to notice Mukai's reaction, tipping his helmet back so that the faceplate was angled up toward the monitor. It wasn't a bad strategy, giving the crew chief a chance to cool off without backing down. Fred could be smart like that, patient but unyielding. It was one of the qualities that made him such an effective soldier—even if he still seemed a bit irritated by the UNSC's response to some of Blue Team's actions during the Cortana event.

Linda-058 sat next to Fred, her own faceplate directed slightly toward the deck. Her hands were resting on her thighs, palms up, and she seemed to be almost floating in her seat, her body upright and motionless as the Owl bounced and shuddered toward the surface of Reach. She was only about half present, John knew. Her attention was focused inward on a quiet mind, her external perceptions tickling over her like a moth's feet. She liked to say that meditation was her best combat asset, the secret to making an impossible shot with the sky falling on top of her—or to lying motionless for days, waiting for the target to show itself. John didn't know about that. He tended to fall asleep when he tried to still his thoughts, and he didn't do motionless. But there was no arguing with the results. Linda was the best sniper in the United Nations Space Command.

The fourth member of Blue Team, Kelly-087, sat on John's side of the troop bay, in the seat to his left. Her hands were grasping her shoulder restraints, and her dome-faced helmet was moving in time to the music he knew was blasting inside her headgear. Kelly had developed a sudden fondness for twentieth-century "rock" bands a year ago, after the Cortana event. John suspected the driving beats and rebellious lyrics were Kelly's own version of meditation, a way to smother the extraneous thoughts and doubts that filled a soldier's mind before an action began.

John's stomach grew heavy as the *Special Delivery* decreased its angle of attack and began to decelerate. The nose cameras deployed and went active, and the situation monitor switched from blackout mode to a dark-as-night external view.

The ETA on John's HUD dropped to twenty-three minutes. Mukai was still glaring at Fred, who was still pretending not to notice. Clearly he was in need of tactical support.

"Chief Mukai, it would be helpful to get a look at what's happening down there," John said. "I'd appreciate consideration of Spartan-104's suggestion to use infrared enhancement."

"That was a suggestion?" The crew chief continued to stare at Fred. "Funny. All *I* heard was a smartass lieutenant telling me how to run my bird."

Fred finally dropped his gaze to Mukai. "Sorry, Chief. I'll be clearer the next time I make such a request."

Mukai nodded. "I'd appreciate that . . . sir."

Special operations teams were tight-knit units where rank took a back seat to functionality and cohesion, so by acknowledging Fred's commission, Mukai was tacitly accepting his truce offer. John felt proud of himself. If the Spartans ever ran out of enemies, maybe he could transfer to the Diplomatic Corps.

Negotiate peace treaties or something.

Mukai spoke into her headset, and the situation monitor blossomed with color. A blotchy blue field filled the screen, slowly drifting downward as the *Special Delivery* descended over the polar snowfields toward the green circle of Big Crater Bay. Ringing the southern edge of the bay was a wide indigo crescent where a mud beach separated the water from the endless orange sweep of the Eposz glasslands.

The glasslands still showed orange because lechatelierite cooled from the top down, its surface solidifying into a vitreous blanket that kept heat from radiating into the air. The ground beneath could stay molten for a year, and remain hot to the touch for a decade. And the beach existed because much of the liquid that had been vaporized during the Covenant's plasma bombardment had not yet returned to the oceans. Most of the planet's water continued to hang in the atmosphere in vast banks of fog and clouds, or to lie trapped on the glass in giant lakes and ash bogs.

A crimson dot flared into existence on the monitor, expanding rapidly against the indigo ring that surrounded Big Crater Bay. The hot spot was located on the northern boundary of the beach, about where the Babd Catha Ice Shelf had once ended. Reach still had plenty of geothermal activity, so the heat blossom could have been a geyser or volcano erupting just as the *Special Delivery* passed overhead.

Yeah, sure.

Kelly stopped rocking her helmet and turned her bulbous faceplate toward the monitor. "They *are* seeing this in the cockpit," she said. "Right?"

Mukai craned her neck around to look up at the display.

"Count on it." The dot swelled into a button-sized blur, then divided into five points and continued to expand. Mukai's eyes widened, and she looked back to Kelly. "Trust me. They have buzzers."

Rather than distract the pilots by asking for a report, John synced his HUD to the *Special Delivery*'s combat information system and saw the open-bottomed triangles of five airborne bandits. The configuration—a staggered polygon—had been favored by reconnaissance flights since the dawn of orbital combat. A MS31 designator code floated beneath each of the five symbols.

"They're Seraphs," John said. "All Morsam-pattern."

"And that's a good thing?" Fred asked.

One of the Covenant's most durable space fighters, Seraphs could be found in the fleets of Covenant splinter groups ranging from Kig-Yar pirate bands to the Banished to the Servants of the Abiding Truth. They were a bit graceless and ungainly in atmospheric flight, but fast, energy-shielded, and heavily armed.

"Well," Mukai said, "at least they're not Phaetons."

Fred looked toward her. "You're a real ray of sunshine."

Phaeton exoatmospheric fighters were Forerunner craft designed a thousand centuries before—and still technologically far beyond anything in the UNSC fleet. Produced from self-assembling blocks of smartmatter, they weren't all that sturdy. But they *were* well-armed, with long-range mass cannons and self-guiding pulse missiles. They could even teleport short distances to evade enemy fire. But the most alarming thing? They were usually attached to one of Cortana's Guardian Custodes. So, when Phaetons were in the area, fighting wasn't an option. The only viable tactic was to retreat and hope for a safe escape.

The heat blossoms continued to expand on the situation monitor. The Spartans all hated this part of the mission—being helpless passengers at the mercy of someone else's skill. But there was an art to flying Owls, and Major Van Houte was twice the pilot any of them were, with a long history of successful insertions under conditions far worse than these.

But there were still five Seraphs coming—and they were obviously aware of the *Special Delivery*'s presence.

"Relax, Spartans," Mukai said. "Those Seraphs might know we're here, but they don't know *where* we are. There's a difference."

"Thanks," Fred said. "Now I feel better."

"As cool as a comet," Kelly added. "I can't even remember the last time an insertion went off as planned."

John could. It had been nine years ago, at the height of the Covenant War, when they landed on the ice moon Umagena to capture the insurrectionist traitor Hector Nyeto. The target hadn't been there, but the insertion had gone off without a hitch. And the fact that he could still remember it . . . well, John certainly couldn't recall all of the insertions that had gone *wrong* since then.

He went back to waiting for the sound of cannon strikes.

The *Special Delivery* had left orbit over Reach's northern pole, where the frigid temperatures just about guaranteed that there would be no inhabitants on the ground to notice the flame trail and hear the unavoidable sonic boom as the Owl dropped through the upper levels of the planet's atmosphere. The insertion plan called for the craft to slow from hypersonic to supersonic velocity as it traveled south across the remnants of the Babd Catha Ice Shelf. As it crossed Big Crater Bay, it would slow from supersonic to subsonic, which would make it far more difficult to detect and locate. Unfortunately, the Seraphs had been lurking on the north side of the bay and had no doubt spotted the Owl while it was still above the ice shelf, traveling at hypersonic speed and generating a lot of noise and flame.

But the bay was coming up fast. John could already see it in the situation monitor, and the Seraphs would still have to climb fifteen kilometers before they reached interception altitude. By the time they did that, the Owl would be across the bay and traveling at subsonic velocity, and by then it would be a ghost in the dark.

Or so he hoped. The Owl was made to sneak, not fight. It carried six Argent V missiles internally and a retractable 370mm autocannon under the chin, and nothing else. It might be able to chase an infantry platoon out of a drop zone, but against shielded fighter-interceptors like Seraphs, its only defense was to avoid and evade.

The Seraph symbols on John's HUD began to arc out in a starburst pattern, trying to array themselves in a broad circle so they could triangulate on the *Special Delivery*'s flame trail. It was a foolish maneuver. By the time they fixed a vector, the Owl would be much too far ahead to catch . . .

Unless the Seraphs weren't trying to make the interception.

John studied the top of the situation monitor, looking for the thermal blooms of approaching craft. The blue blotches of the polar snowfields had been completely replaced by the green circle of Big Crater Bay and, along the top edge, the orange sweep of the Eposz glasslands. But there were no more heat blossoms—at least, not that the *Special Delivery*'s nose cameras could resolve.

The crisp voice of the Owl's copilot, First Lieutenant Maks Chapov, sounded over the internal comm net. "Master Chief, how would you feel about losing the digging equipment?"

John glanced toward the rear of the troop cabin, where the team's downsized excavation equipment sat secured to the deck. Positioned side by side and facing aft for speedy unloading, the two machines—a four-boom drilling jumbo and a two-kiloliter load-haul-dump wagon with a heavily loaded cargo shelf on the back—were barely four meters long and two meters wide. But they were powered by Toroidal Magnetic Confinement Device compact fusion reactors and equipped with heavy-duty hydrostatic transmissions, so they were as heavy as full-size armored personnel carriers. If it came down to dodging Seraph fire, the *Special Delivery* was going to have all the agility of a resupply pod.

"Why would I need to?" John replied.

"Major Van Houte doesn't like the Seraph deployment," Chapov said.

A hotshot flier who had transferred into the crew after a Phaeton mass cannon took out the *Special Delivery*'s last copilot, Maks Chapov had unusual skill and quick reflexes that were the perfect complement to Eznik Van Houte's vast experience and bottomless bag of tricks. At least, that was how the captain of the UNSC *Infinity*, Thomas Lasky, had explained the pairing to John—though it seemed more likely that Lasky was just trying to leaven a young pilot's aggression with the wisdom of an old veteran.

"They're not trying to intercept us," Chapov continued. "The major thinks they could be a tracking flight."

"I think he could be right," John said. "What's that have to do with my excavation equipment?"

"If the tracking flight is vectoring in a wing of interceptors, I'll need a light boat to get us out of here in one piece."

"Any indication that's what the enemy is doing?" John asked. "Or who they are?"

"There's some long-range comm chatter," Chapov said. "In Jiralhanae."

"That's not good," Fred said.

Only two of the major Covenant splinter groups were dominated by Jiralhanae, a huge pseudo-ursine species that had supplied the Covenant with many of its most ferocious warriors. The first was an army of religious zealots known as the Keepers of the One Freedom. The second was a horde of mercenary raiders called simply the Banished. Both were bad news, and both employed Jiralhanae pack-attack tactics that made their fliers among the most feared enemies of UNSC fighter squadrons.

"Yeah, not good," Chapov said. "And it gets worse. The tracking flight launched from the coordinates of SWORD Base."

Fred groaned, Kelly let her chin drop, and even Linda broke her meditation long enough to look toward the situation monitor. The Keepers and the Banished were both obsessive salvagers of Forerunner artifacts, and years earlier a Forerunner vessel had been discovered buried under the ice near SWORD Base. The UNSC had attempted to destroy both the vessel and the surrounding installation when Reach fell, but the Covenant plasma bombardment had prevented anyone from actually confirming a successful demolition. So it was possible that enough of the vessel remained to explain the presence of ex-Covenant salvagers.

It just didn't mesh with why the Jiralhanae had launched a tracking flight instead of an interception mission.

John continued to watch both the situation monitor and the combat information system synced to his HUD. Neither display showed a fighter cadre vectoring across Big Crater Bay at intercept velocity, but that didn't mean they weren't coming. Orbital combat control systems were not an option for stealth insertions, because a communications stream would reveal the insertion craft's presence—and sometimes its exact location. So the *Special Delivery* was limited to its own instruments, which could only detect threats approaching from below the horizon.

John couldn't recall the formula for determining the distance-to-horizon, and he didn't need to. The question had barely occurred to him before his Mjolnir's onboard computer, linked directly to his mind via a neural lace implanted at the base of his skull, calculated the answer and displayed the information on his HUD. Cortana used to do that—answer his question before he could ask it.

DETECTION LIMIT 489 KILOMETERS

AT ALTITUDE 15,305 METERS

MINIMUM TIME TO INTERCEPTION

2:24 MINUTES/SECONDS

ASSUMING CRAFT FLYING DIRECTLY

TOWARD EACH OTHER AT MACH 5

Mach 5 was about as fast as an interceptor could fly and have any reasonable hope of reacting to a target's evasive maneuvers, so there was no need to second-guess the parameters the onboard computer had chosen. Once an enemy craft appeared on the horizon, the *Special*

*Delivery* would have two and a half minutes to react, and probably a lot longer than that, since chances were small that the two craft would be flying directly at each other. It wasn't a lot of time, but it was still almost twice as long as the Spartans would need to unfix and dump the excavation machines.

Which made Chapov's question a bit premature.

"Lieutenant Chapov," John said. "What aren't you telling me?"

"I don't understand, Master Chief."

"You were at the mission briefing," John said. "You *do* recall that the assets we're trying to retrieve are hidden in Dr. Halsey's lab at the *bottom* of CASTLE Base?"

"I remember."

"And you also remember that what's above CASTLE Base right now is essentially a big rubble pit?"

A lieutenant was superior in rank to a master chief, so strictly speaking, John was being a bit insubordinate by interrogating Chapov this way. But respect was an earned commodity in any military unit, and that was especially true in special operations, where junior officers were expected to show senior enlisted personnel the deference they deserved. And after three decades on the front lines, leading Spartans against humanity's most dangerous enemies, John had earned the right to speak to a young hotshot copilot any way he felt necessary.

Besides, CASTLE Base was located two kilometers underneath what was once Menachite Mountain, which had been reduced to a ten-kilometer-wide detritus field during the Covenant attack on Reach. So the success of the mission depended on making retrieval as simple as possible—and on the vault where the assets were stored still being intact, of course. But Dr. Halsey had promised John that the vault was strong enough to withstand the collapse of CASTLE Base, and she was rarely wrong.

Especially when she was risking the lives of her Spartans.

After a short pause, Chapov said, "I do, Master Chief."

"Then why are you telling me to dump my excavation equipment?"

John asked. "Do you expect Blue Team to dig out the entrance to CASTLE Base by hand?"

"I haven't told you to dump the excavation machines." Chapov's tone was resolute and unintimidated. "Not yet."

"*Yet?*" John said. He was aware of his mythical status in the UNSC, and he liked that Chapov was willing to stand up to him anyway. But that didn't mean he was going to let the kid off easy. "Lieutenant, do you understand the stakes here? Dr. Halsey needs what's in her lab to stop Cortana. Aborting this mission is *not* an option."

"Which is why I'm asking you to think about the excavation equipment," Chapov said. "If we get shot down, Blue Team won't be digging out anything."

John checked the combat information system in his HUD again. There weren't any interceptors in view, and the tracking flight had fallen so far behind that it was barely on the display. But the *Special Delivery* had descended to ten thousand meters, which meant the distance-to-horizon was only 361 kilometers. An attacking Seraph could be close enough to open fire in a little less than two minutes.

Still plenty of time.

"Lieutenant Chapov, what aren't you telling me?" John asked again. "And this time, don't dodge the question."

"There's nothing to tell," Chapov said. "We don't like the way this feels. That's all."

"Glad to hear I'm not alone in that," Kelly said. "If there's a tracking flight, there are bound to be interceptors."

"Exactly," Chapov said. "We can't see them yet, but with that chatter we heard earlier . . ."

"You're worried about an interceptor flight coming up from Arany Basin," John said. Located in the plains east of the Highland Mountains where Menachite Mountain and CASTLE Base were located, Arany Basin was a vast lowland adjacent to their planned flight path. "Because it isn't that far off our course."

"It's a concern," Van Houte said, joining in. Over the Owl's internal comm net, his voice sounded raspy and almost brittle. "But we should be fine."

"Should be? Or will be?" John didn't know whether it would even be possible to dig out the entrance to CASTLE Base by hand, but Chapov was right about one thing—they would have no chance of success if they didn't make it to the landing site.

"There are no guarantees, Master Chief," Van Houte said. "You know that."

"All too well," John said. "But when someone asks me to think about an equipment dump, I'd like to know why."

"My fault," Van Houte said. "Lieutenant Chapov isn't accustomed to a pilot who thinks out loud."

"And?"

"And I said we could be in trouble if a flight of interceptors launches from the basin."

John looked at the situation monitor again. Only a thin crescent of water remained, its green glow slowly dropping out of view as the *Special Delivery* approached the south side of Big Crater Bay. The insertion plan called for the Owl to slow to subsonic speed before it crossed the shoreline and started over land, but the combat information system indicated it was still traveling at almost Mach 5. Clearly Van Houte was modifying the insertion plan to stay ahead of the tracking flight.

But at that kind of velocity, the Owl would be generating so much friction heat and sonic energy that any Seraphs coming from the Arany Basin wouldn't need to be vectored in. They would just be able to follow their own thermal detectors.

"We'll need sixty seconds to unfix the equipment," John said over the internal comm net. "And we can't dump it at this velocity."

"Have some faith, Master Chief," Van Houte said. "I still have a trick or two left."

John wasn't sure he believed the major. But beneath the situation monitor, Chief Mukai was sitting in her jump seat with her head cocked, studying him with a bored expression that suggested she could not believe the legendary John-117 was worried about a few stray Seraphs. It was an act, of course, but he took her point. Eznik Van Houte had been flying insertion craft as long as John had been fighting the Covenant, and he would let them know when the time came to worry.

"Sorry, Major. Just apprising you."

"No need to apologize," Van Houte said. "I'd be nervous too if some crackerjack copilot started asking what equipment I could dump."

"Sorry, sir." Chapov sounded resentful, not apologetic. "I must have mistaken your muttering for a directive."

"No worries, Lieutenant. You'll learn soon . . ." Van Houte let the sentence trail off, and when he spoke again, it was in an indistinct mumble. "Well . . . didn't expect . . ."

John felt his weight pushing against the crash harness as the *Special Delivery* changed course. On the situation monitor, the last green sliver of water slid off the bottom edge as Big Crater Bay passed completely out of view behind them, and the indigo crescent of its muddy southern beach began to creep down the right side of the display. The Owl was veering southeast, *toward* the Arany Basin. The combat information system showed it dropping through six thousand meters, but still traveling at Mach 5.

Van Houte wasn't modifying the insertion plan—he was trashing it. John watched his HUD for some indication of the problem, but saw nothing. Of course, the Owl had descended to fifty-five hundred meters, which put its detection limit at . . .

He found himself waiting for his Mjolnir's onboard computer to provide the answer. It was connected to his mind through the same neural lace that Cortana had used, but it was not nearly as efficient. That was only to be expected. After Cortana had corrupted so many smart AIs, the UNSC now avoided using them, substituting less capable "dumb" AIs whenever possible. And someone aboard the

*Infinity*—probably Captain Lasky himself—didn't want the Spartans taking even *that* much of a chance. Although their GEN3 operating systems were partitioned to prevent an AI—even a smart one—from interfering with the Mjolnir's functionality, on this mission they carried only upgraded versions of the same onboard computers that had supported their Mark IV prototypes thirty years earlier.

A half second later, the answer appeared on John's HUD.

He still expected to hear her voice as a part of it. No matter how efficient his computer was, it didn't fill the void left by Cortana's absence. That hadn't changed, and John doubted it ever would.

DETECTION LIMIT 288 KILOMETERS

AT ALTITUDE 5,462 METERS

MINIMUM TIME TO INTERCEPTION

1:24 MINUTES/SECONDS

ASSUMING CRAFT FLYING DIRECTLY

TOWARD EACH OTHER AT MACH 5

Depending on where the trouble was coming from, Blue Team would have only about a minute and a half to dump the excavation machines. But that didn't much matter, because at Mach 5, the Owl would be ripped apart as soon as Chief Mukai dropped the rear loading hatch.

"Arm decoys," Van Houte said.

"At *this* speed?" Chapov's voice broke an octave high. "We'll disintegrate the second we open—"

"When I need your opinion, Lieutenant, I'll ask for it." Van Houte delivered the rebuke so calmly that John wasn't quite sure it was intended that way. "Arm the decoys, please. I'll tell you when to open the doors."

"Aye," Chapov muttered. "Arming decoys."

The indigo beach vanished from the situation monitor, yielding to the mottled orange sweep of the warmer lechatelierite. John saw no indication of an approaching threat, but his HUD showed their altitude continuing to drop rapidly. If Van Houte didn't pull up soon, there was going to be a very large crater in the Eposz glasslands.

Knowing better than to distract the pilots midmaneuver, John looked to Mukai—and found her riding easy in her jump seat, smirking at Fred with her hands resting in her lap. Whatever Van Houte was doing, it wasn't the first time.

Mukai noticed John watching her and smiled. She tugged at the straps of her crash harness, making sure the quick-release buckles were securely fastened, then waved a finger at all four Spartans.

"Make sure your harnesses are locked down," she said. "It's going to get rough."

"Could we know why?" Kelly asked.

"Because it's better than being shot down," Mukai said. "Okay?"

"Seems reasonable," Fred said. He bumped Linda's shoulder. "You catch that?"

Linda remained steady as a mountain. "A quiet mind is an alert mind."

"So that's a yes," Fred said. He looked across the troop bay toward John. "Any hints from the cockpit?"

To guard against overloading the avionics systems, only the team leader had the capability of syncing into the cockpit feeds. John checked his HUD and found the feed as uninformative as before—though he did note that the Owl's detection limit had dropped to 260 kilometers.

"No idea."

"Sorry to keep you in the dark for so long," Van Houte said over the internal comm net. "We had maneuvers to plan."

"If you're still planning," John said, "we can wait."

"We're used to waiting," Fred added. "We're infantry."

"No need," Van Houte said. "I can fill you in while Lieutenant Chapov disables the missile ignitions."

"What?!" Chapov screeched the question.

"Disable the ignition systems on all six missiles," Van Houte said. "Must I give you every order twice?"

"Of course not, sir. Disabling ignition systems on all six Argents."

"Thank you, Lieutenant," Van Houte said. "Now, Master Chief?"

"Yes, sir?"

"You may have noticed that I've abandoned our insertion plan."

"I had, Major," John said. "I assume you have a good reason."

"I'm afraid so. As we were crossing Big Crater Bay, I noticed some beyond-the-horizon launch flares."

"Ah," John said. "Given the tracking flight we picked up, weren't we expecting that?"

"Not from the direction of New Miskolc, we weren't," Van Houte said. "They'd have been in visual range just about the time we reached our objective at Menachite Mountain."

"That would've complicated things," Fred remarked.

"Not that badly," Van Houte said. "But there was a second set of launch flares."

"Let me guess," John said. "From Mohács?"

"Oddly not," Van Houte said. "It was closer to the Szarvas Regeneration and Salvage Facility."

"They're trying to box us in, then?" Kelly asked, completely unfazed. "How are their chances?"

"That depends on how many launches I didn't see," Van Houte said. "So far, we have flights launching from the ruins of two UNSC sites—SWORD Base and the Szarvas salvage yards—and an urban center where I'm fairly sure there would have been some UNSC administrative facilities."

John understood Van Houte's concern. Reach had once been a vital support world to the UNSC, a supplier of vast amounts of war materiel and home to more bases than John could name. Given the low-intensity conflict in the Arany Basin, it was beginning to sound like there was an entire horde of raiders foraging the planet's old UNSC installations.

That was hardly surprising, given the vast amounts of military hardware that had been abandoned during the Reach bombardment. But it *did* make John rethink the enemy's likely identity. The Banished and the Keepers of the One Freedom loved to forage Forerunner sites, but neither group had much interest in UNSC technology—certainly not enough to launch a continental-scale salvage operation. Both organizations were predominately alien, and human equipment just wasn't that valuable to them.

"What about the Highland Mountains?" John asked. The greatest concentration of bases was in that location, including the Reach Military Complex where the Spartans had been billeted during their training as children. "Especially around—"

"I would have mentioned CASTLE Base," Van Houte said. "But that doesn't mean anything. If I happened to be looking the other way, or they launched while we were still on the far side of the bay, or there was a ridge of mountains in just the right place—"

"Understood," John said. "We could have a dozen flights coming straight at us and not know it."

"Probably not a dozen," Van Houte said. "But more than a few."

John glanced across at Fred. He wasn't about to abort, not when Dr. Halsey was counting on them to retrieve what she needed to end Cortana's despotic reign. But if the alternative was getting shot down . . .

"Getting complicated fast." Fred shrugged. "What else is new?"

"It won't be complicated for long," Van Houte said. "We'll be fine once we disappear."

John didn't see the *Special Delivery* going sensor-invisible anytime soon. At their speed, even the Owl's fused-carbon phenolic laminate skin could not shed heat fast enough to "disappear." The craft would light up like a torch on even the most primitive thermal-imaging system.

The sound of alert buzzers came over the internal comm net.

"Finally." The buzzers fell silent, and Van Houte's voice dropped to a mutter. "They . . . long enough."

John resisted the temptation to ask who had taken long enough and checked the combat information system on his HUD. He found a flight of Seraphs approaching from the direction of the Szarvas Regeneration and Salvage Facility. The display listed their range as 508 kilometers, well beyond the Owl's detection limit—which he found puzzling, until he noticed the Seraphs' altitude and realized they were still climbing in an effort to maximize their own detection ranges.

So the enemy didn't have an orbital combat control system either. The Seraphs would be using their onboard sensor systems to hunt down the *Special Delivery*—which John might have found comforting, had the Owl not been dropping below 4,500 meters altitude at Mach 5, trailing a sonic wave that had to sound like an artillery barrage to anyone approaching from the right vector.

"You were beginning to worry me," Van Houte whispered. "Now, where are the rest of you?"

"Sir?" Chapov asked. "Are you talking to me?"

"Are you piloting a Seraph, Lieutenant?"

"Of course not."

"Then I'm not talking to you," Van Houte said. "How are my missiles coming?"

"Disabling the ignition system on the sixth Argent now."

"Good." Van Houte's voice lowered to a whisper again. "We're going to be dropping them any—"

The alert buzzers sounded, and two more Seraph flights appeared on the combat information display on John's HUD. The first was the tracking flight that had originally spotted them, now approaching from the direction of SWORD Base at Mach 10. The second was an entire squadron of ten additional Seraphs, approaching from New Miskolc at Mach 9. Both flights were diving down from altitudes of slightly less than 10,000 meters, being vectored in by the high-flying interceptors from Szarvas. They would need to decelerate soon or risk overshooting the *Special Delivery*.

"Lieutenant," Van Houte said, "is that last missile ready yet?"

"N-negative." Chapov sounded irritated. "I mistyped the override code."

"Imagine that." Van Houte chuckled. "Relax, son. We're in no big hurry."

It didn't look that way to John. Now that the enemy had the *Special Delivery* in sensor range, all three flights were diving to attack altitude, and over the Owl's internal comm net, he could hear proximity alarms sounding off in the cockpit.

He wondered how long it would be before the shooting started, and the answer appeared on his HUD.

ESTIMATED TIME TO INITIAL ENGAGEMENT:

83 SECONDS

It was almost the same as the minimum time to interception the computer had displayed the last time John checked. But with the combat information system providing vectors and locations for the enemy craft, the computer now had the data to refine its estimates. John just wished he knew why Van Houte sounded so damn calm with interception flights arriving from three directions.

The proximity alarms sounded again, and more Seraph designators appeared in John's HUD, coming from the direction of Fenyot Basin. That kind of hurt—Fenyot Basin had been a favorite training site for the Spartans, and John didn't like to think of a bunch of Jiralhanae raiders bashing around the hoodoo maze where he and his comrades used to play monthlong games of sniper elimination and stealth tag.

The alarms suddenly fell silent, and Van Houte said, "Prepare for vanishing maneuver."

"Vanishing maneuver?" Linda had finally removed her hands from her thighs and was looking forward, toward the cockpit. "I have never heard of such a thing."

"My own invention," Van Houte said. "Insert like a fireball, vanish like a ghost. Chief Mukai will tell you what to do."

"Man the firing ports?" Fred asked.

Van Houte broke out laughing. "Good one, Spartan."

"Who's joking?"

"You are," Mukai said. She reached up to the collar of her black insertion suit and thumbed up the cooling system. "If we open the firing ports at this speed, those interceptors won't *need* to shoot us down."

As she spoke, the *Special Delivery* suddenly nosed up and slid into a wingover, then dropped back into its dive . . . facing backward. The Owl's rear hatch, which had only a thin layer of ablative heat shielding, began to take the brunt of the air friction, and the interior of the troop bay shot up fifty degrees. The skinsuit inside John's Mjolnir activated its cooling circuits, and he began to understand Van Houte's plan.

Every planet in the galaxy was bombarded by a constant rain of meteors, sometimes large enough to become bolides and explode into a brilliant burst of light and fragments. If Van Houte could time his "vanishing maneuver" just right, he might be able to fool the Seraphs into believing they had been tracking such a fireball, then use the Owl's stealth capabilities to slip away in a rain of decoys and un-ignited missiles as it dropped to subsonic speed.

"Prepare for deceleration." Mukai pressed a valve on her lapel, and her pants ballooned as her suit began to squeeze her legs and hips to keep the blood from pooling in her lower extremities. "High-g protocol."

John tightened his belly and legs, then watched in astonishment as the situation monitor overheated and sparked into blackness. Below it, Mukai's face grew pink and sweaty, then quickly grew dry and red as her sweat evaporated. He looked aft, over the back ends of the excavation machines, and saw the Owl's loading hatch paling from steel blue to ash gray. A circle in the middle started to glow white and expand.

"Major, you're about to melt through—"

"Tell me something I *don't* know, Master—"

The transmission ended in a blast of static; then John was thrown against the side of his harness as the *Special Delivery* fired its main engines and began to decelerate. John's Mjolnir initiated automatic g-force protocols, using its hydrostatic gel layer to keep his blood in his torso and head.

The excavation machines strained against their mooring chains, the tremendous g-forces lifting them toward the rear hatch. The hoisting winches and haulage buckets stacked on the cargo platform on the back of the load-haul-dump wagon began to strain against the high-tensile net holding them in place. John checked the combat information display on his HUD and saw that the Owl was pulling twenty-one g's in deceleration. A loud pop sounded from the forward bulkhead.

"Whoa!" Mukai's outburst was answered by a metallic ping and a long sonorous peal, and she cried, "Cheap . . . Imberian . . . crap!"

She fell silent, and John found the soles of her boots bobbing up and down in front of him. She was still strapped into her crash harness, but three of the jump seat's mounting brackets had failed, splitting along the fastener slots and pulling off the bulkhead bolts. Her arms were draped over the sides of the chair, limp and swinging in the green light, and it seemed apparent she had blacked out after her exclamation.

John's HUD showed twenty-three g's, and the *Special Delivery*'s engines were still firing. He and the other Spartans could handle another fifteen g's before they had to worry about blacking out, but it was a wonder the pilots were still conscious.

The last mounting bracket on Mukai's jump seat pulled away from the bulkhead, a long split opening between the fastener slots. In another breath, she was going to pull free and fly toward the back of the troop bay.

John extended an arm to catch her, as did Fred and Kelly, but when the flange finally failed, it was Linda who plucked Mukai out of the air and clamped her tight to her Mjolnir's breastplate. Even with powered armor, Linda's arms shook with the effort of keeping the chief from flying free.

Van Houte's voice sounded over the Owl's comm channel. "Launch . . . decoys."

John checked the combat information display and saw that the *Special Delivery* had decelerated to Mach 2.5. Protocol dictated that decoy doors remained closed at anything above Mach 2, but he assumed Van Houte knew the Owl's actual tolerances far better than he did.

At least he hoped so.

"Lieu . . . tenant?" Van Houte's voice was strained, as it should have been. The combat information display showed the deceleration force hovering at twenty-five g's. "Oh . . . hell. Launching. . . ."

The *Special Delivery* shook violently, and its nose began to slue back and forth as air pushed into the decoy bays and Van Houte fought to retain control. Two sharp clangs sounded aft. John looked back to see the rear section of the drilling jumbo lifting off the deck, a pair of broken D rings dangling from its mooring chains.

Midmaneuver or not, he had to warn the pilot.

"Major—"

"Dropping . . . missiles."

The *Special Delivery* pitched and wobbled as a thousands-of-kilometers-per-hour wind entered the open missile bays from the wrong direction. The drilling jumbo slammed down on its rear tires, then began to buck wildly as the deck rose and fell beneath it.

"Cut thrust!" John shouted. "Cut—"

Van Houte killed the drives, but the *Special Delivery*'s nose had already come up again. The deck rose beneath the jumbo. The heavy machine slid aft and crashed into the loading hatch. The entire Owl shuddered, and the port safety bolts snapped free and ricocheted off Linda's armor. A wedge of darkness appeared along the far edge of the loading hatch; then a shrill whistle filled the troop bay, and a two-thousand-kilometers-per-hour wind tried to rip the Spartans out of their crash harnesses.

Linda still gripped Mukai, clutching the chief to her breast like a baby.

Sirens and alarms blared inside John's helmet, and the combat information system flashed so many warnings in his HUD that his faceplate looked like a lightning storm inside.

"What's happening back there?!" Van Houte demanded. The craft banked to starboard, pushing the jumbo into the loading hatch even harder. "It feels like I'm flying a Warthog . . . with a flat tire!"

"Loose cargo." John hit the emergency release on his crash harness. "Cease banking."

"Not an option." The Owl's nose began to rise. "We need to come around and shed speed *now*."

There was nothing but a hydraulic cylinder securing the port side of the loading hatch, and it was no match for the weight of the drilling jumbo. The cylinder began to extend, and the wedge of darkness continued to expand, and the hatch itself started to deform.

"Affirmative." John pushed the crash harness up and out of the way. "Attempting to secure the cargo, but the loading hatch is already taking damage."

"No choice," Van Houte said. "We disappear *now*, or we have a squadron of Seraphs designating us as their destination."

John stepped toward the runaway jumbo and found the rest of Blue Team following his lead. After three decades fighting side by side, it often seemed his fellow Spartans knew what he wanted before he opened his mouth to transmit it. He reached for a tie-down hook and found Kelly already holding the chain attached to it. On the other side of the vehicle, Fred had the tie-down hook, while Linda was securing a half-conscious Mukai in the crash harness Fred had just abandoned.

The Owl's nose came up steeply, and even the sound-dampening traction soles on the bottoms of their sabatons were not enough to keep the heavy jumbo from dragging them aft. John's HUD was now showing the *Special Delivery*'s speed in kilometers per hour instead of

Machs, which meant the craft had dropped below the speed of sound on Reach. It was probably already flying in stealth mode.

John reset his feet and pulled hard against the heavy jumbo. Next to him, Kelly dropped to her rear and braced a foot against the cargo platform on the back of the load-haul-dump machine. She was spun sideways as the jumbo continued to push into the hatch, and the hatch continued to deform.

"Cease . . . climbing," John said.

"Not an option," Van Houte said. "We've got hills. *Big* hills."

The safety bolts on the starboard side of the hatchway popped free and clattered off the LHD; then the wind slipped behind the hatch panel and tore it completely open, forcing the Owl's tail down. The nose pitched upward almost vertically, and the jumbo shot toward the gaping hatch, its locked tires skidding down the slip-resistant deck as though gliding on ice.

"Let it go!" John released the drilling jumbo, then grabbed for the collar of Kelly's armor and dived for the starboard side of the troop bay. "Secure yourselves!"

He hooked his arm through a crash harness and felt the Mjolnir's force-multiplying circuits react, securing him and Kelly in place as the jumbo shot out through the hatch—then reached the end of its front tie-downs.

The back end of the machine rocked upward and hit the upper threshold of the hatchway, and that was the only thing that kept it from snapping the front chains and plummeting out of the Owl and into the night. John checked the motion tracker in his HUD and found Fred and Linda secure on the other side of the troop bay, with Mukai still tucked safely into Fred's crash harness.

But the drilling jumbo was far from secure. It was now hanging halfway out the open hatch, still attached to the deck by its forward tie-down chains, rocking back and forth on its frame as the unrelenting wind tried to tear it free. Beneath it, the damaged hatch panel was catching the air, keeping the Owl pitched upward like a rocket plane climbing for orbit—except that it *wasn't* climbing. The engines remained quiet, and any attempt to power them up would fill the troop bay with hot efflux.

John noted the altitude in his HUD. The Owl was at two thousand meters and dropping—which was pretty amazing, considering there were mountains to either side rising to twenty-five hundred meters. The only good news was that he didn't see any Seraphs following them in—though that was probably only because the mountains were hiding their sensor signatures.

"Put us down," John said. "No engines."

"No engines, no problem," said Chapov. The copilot had seemingly recovered from his blackout and was now flying the Owl. "But you have about ten seconds to get back into your crash harnesses."

"And I wouldn't be late," Van Houte added. "Lieutenant Chapov may be a hotshot, but even he can't work miracles."

Kelly was drawing herself back into her seat. John did the same, then looked across the troop bay to see Fred and Linda already pulling their harnesses down. An Owl's troop bay was designed to carry up to ten Spartans along each side, so there were plenty of empty spots, even with Mukai still in Fred's original seat.

John's harness locked into place with three seconds to spare. "We're ready."

"Good," Chapov said.

A deafening clang sounded from the Owl's tail; then John saw the loading ramp fly up and launch the drilling jumbo forward. In the next instant, his seat bucked so hard he rose into his crash harness and felt the shoulder bars bend. The jumbo hit the end of its last mooring chains and decelerated rapidly as they broke, skidding forward across the nonslip deck and shattering the situation monitor hanging on the forward bulkhead—then tipping toward John's side of the bay.

He thought the *Special Delivery* had gone into a side roll until he realized he was still sitting upright, that he was being thrown against the wall behind him, and he brought both hands up to prevent the jumbo from smashing him and Kelly. Somehow Chapov had landed the crippled Owl on its belly, and now it was plowing through the glass, level, fishtailing, and quickly decelerating.

"Brace yourselves!" Chapov warned.

John thought there must be a cliff or ravine coming. Instead, he heard a series of quarter-second hisses as Chapov used the attitude thrusters to bring the Owl under control, and then a single long *whoooosh* as the nose dropped and the craft finally slammed to a full stop.

For a moment no one spoke. John's view across the bay was blocked by the drilling jumbo. He carefully pushed it back onto all four wheels, and heard Mukai give a small, startled cry as it crashed back to the deck. Thankfully, she was still alive and conscious again.

Then Chapov's voice sounded over the intercom, relaxed, cocky, and unhurried.

"Ladies and gentlemen, on behalf of the pilot and crew of the *Special Delivery*, welcome to Reach. The time is 0241 military standard. I suggest you collect your weapons and equipment and exit the craft as quickly as possible. We have company on the way."

# CHAPTER TWO

0241 hours, October 7, 2559 (military calendar)
UNSC Owl Insertion Craft *Special Delivery*
Vadász Dombok, Continent Eposz, Planet Reach

It was so dark outside the Owl's hatchway that even the fused-mode night-vision system in John's Mjolnir helmet couldn't gather enough light to provide an unmediated image. The terrain appeared inside his faceplate as a digitally rendered outline in green, with the illusion of volume provided by areas of shading and highlighting. The result was something like an impressionist painting, an interplay of light and shadow that suggested the *Special Delivery* had ended its flight on a long, broad terrace clinging to the side of a moderately steep ridge. Directly behind the Owl, framed by its loading hatch, lay a narrow, snaking furrow of scintillation that could only be its crash path. To the left hung a curving darkness that promised a bottomless abyss—but which might deliver nothing more than a shallow ravine.

Knowing there was still a fair amount of thermal radiation rising from the planet's glassed ground, John had his onboard computer adjust the NVS input toward near-infrared. The image immediately grew crisper and more colorful, with the ground now represented by subtly fluctuating bands of orange and pink, the air in calm blue, and the clouds overhead a boiling mass of yellow and green. The crooked furrow of the Owl's crash path resolved as a hot crimson trough filled with jagged shards of broken lechatelierite, stretching for a kilometer and a half behind them.

John leaned a little farther out of the hatchway and performed a quick scan of the sky, checking for inbound Seraphs and still wondering whether they belonged to the Banished or the Keepers—or maybe even to some new horde of Jiralhanae scavengers that he had not heard of. That was the trouble with this Pax Cortana. She was clamping down on interstellar civilization with an iron fist, and the harder she squeezed, the more insurgents she was going to have shooting out between her fingers.

When John saw no crimson halos blossoming above, he extended an arm behind him, pointing toward the weapons locker where his motion detector told him that the other Spartans were already gathering their weapons and equipment.

"Blue Team, adjust your NVS to near-infrared—you'll be able to see better out here," John said. "Linda, you're overwatch. Make sure you have plenty of ammunition for the S5."

"Always."

Linda slipped past and sped down the ramp, a fully packed load-hauling harness slung over one shoulder. She carried a standard MA40 assault rifle—the most recent addition to the line, which featured the storied MA37—in one hand and a customized SRS99-S5 AM sniper rifle in the other. The sniper rifle had been manufactured to special tolerances for the Misriah Armory's competitive shooting team, which made it less than ideal as a field weapon—its unique parts were hard to replace on a mission, where dirt and grime and hard shocks were impossible to avoid. But Linda treated the thing like a baby. She even had a name for it—Nornfang, in honor of the Norns of Norse mythology, who wove the fate of all things in the cosmos—and she claimed it increased her effective range by two hundred meters.

So John had never questioned whether the trade-off was worthwhile. It had to be, or Linda wouldn't be carrying it.

At the bottom of the ramp, she turned right and climbed out of the crash furrow, then started across the terrace toward the slope, her feet slipping every now and again where the dust lay just right on the glassy surface. The hill crest was about six hundred meters above her, a long ridgelike summit that was almost too close for sniper work, since it would be within range of some of the enemy's common longarms.

John watched until she started to climb, so he would have some idea of where she was placing her sniper's nest, then looked toward the front of the troop bay. Mukai was pulling equipment out of the forward lockers at a furious pace. Fred and Kelly were already geared up, their weapons affixed to the mounts on the back of their armor, their torsos and waists engirdled by slap-mount harnesses strung with hard-sided cargo pouches.

"Fred, you and Chief Mukai unload the excavation equipment and get ready to move out—fast."

Fred's LED flashed green on the team status bar inside John's helmet; an instant later, Chapov's voice sounded over the comm net.

"Don't set the SDD yet."

In the *Special Delivery*'s case, the self-destruct device was a fist-sized block of an explosive called octanitrocubane. It was a downgrade from the Fury tactical nukes that most stealth craft had carried during the Covenant War, when FLEETCOM hadn't minded a little collateral damage if it meant destroying a nearby enemy vessel. But octanitrocubane was still powerful stuff. A small quantity would disintegrate the Owl so completely that even its nanoblack biopolymer coating would be unidentifiable.

"Affirmative," John said. "Problem?"

"Nothing to worry about," Van Houte said. His voice sounded strained. "I'll handle the SDD from here. Just make sure you're clear before those Seraphs find us."

John was already starting down the loading ramp. "What about you and Lieutenant Chapov?"

"I'll be fine," Chapov said. "But Major Van Houte is—"

"Still in command of this bird," Van Houte interrupted. "Evacuate and move out."

"Don't tempt me," Chapov said.

"That's an order, Lieutenant."

"Sorry, sir," Chapov said. "But I can't obey that order until I confirm you haven't suffered a traumatic head injury. Your judgment could be compromised."

"Do I sound like I have a head injury?"

"Impossible to tell," Chapov said. "We'll have to extract you first."

"Help is coming." John was starting to like Chapov. The kid might be arrogant, but he was determined. "Kelly, join me up front."

"I'll bring your gear, shall I?"

"Affirmative." If a flight of Seraphs showed up while they were still trying to extract the pilots, there wouldn't be time to go back for anything. "Thanks."

John stepped off the ramp and started forward. The Owl had made a hard landing rather than actually crashing, so its tail and wings were still attached. But it had broken through the vitreous ground crust and cut a trough through the sandy substratum, creating a waist-deep channel still glowing orange with thermal bleed-off.

He clambered over the wing and found the nose of the *Special Delivery* buried beneath a shelf of lechatelierite, with jagged plates of the glassy stuff leaning against the fuselage along both sides. That Chapov had somehow kept the craft from catching a wingtip as it plowed the long furrow was impressive—John doubted that he himself could have done it, even with his enhanced reflexes.

John tossed a few random pieces of lechatelierite aside, then dropped to his knees and peered into the darkness next to the *Special Delivery*. The nose was jammed tight into a cramped cavity between the vitreous crust and the sand-bed beneath. The cockpit area was so flooded with residual heat that all he saw was a red fog, and he could not get a clear image no matter how he tried to balance his night vision's fused-mode technology.

He activated his external helmet lamps and crawled into the cavity. The Owl had a double-cockpit design, so the copilot's seat was located above and behind the pilot's, with a separate bubble canopy covering each. Both pilots had tried to raise their canopies so they could evacuate, but the shelf of lechatelierite had prevented the pilot's from rising more than a few centimeters.

The copilot's canopy had risen about half a meter because the cavity had been opened larger and higher over his cockpit. Chapov's upper body was visible on the near side of the craft, his arms splayed against the side as he struggled to pull himself free.

As John approached, Chapov gave up and squinted into the light through his helmet's transparent faceplate. "I tried for a belly landing," he said. "But with all that weight hanging out of an open hatch—"

"No one's complaining, Lieutenant."

John rose to a crouch, pressing his shoulders against the cavity ceiling, and shined his light into the cockpit. Chapov's flight suit was still partially inflated, bulging around his hips and preventing him from pulling free.

"Cover your face."

"What?"

John rapped a knuckle against the aluminum oxynitride canopy. "This could shatter your faceplate when it breaks."

John grabbed the bottom lip of the canopy with both hands, and Chapov buried his face in his arms and looked away. Transparent aluminum was actually a polycrystalline ceramic rather than a metal, and it did not bend in the slightest when John began to pull. So he braced his feet against the side of the Owl and tried harder. The force-multiplying circuits in his armor activated, and he felt the Mjolnir adding its power to his strength.

The hull dimpled beneath his boots, but the space between the canopy and the rim of the cockpit did not expand.

"Don't be crazy," Kelly said. She placed their gear on top of the Owl's wing, then ducked under the lechatelierite beside him. "That stuff is designed to stop plasma cannon rounds. You can't break it alone."

"Now you tell me." John shifted forward, folding himself nearly double in the cramped cavity, and waited as Kelly arranged herself next to him. "Say when."

"When."

They pulled together . . . and suddenly dropped into the sand as a crescent of canopy snapped off in their hands. Chapov immediately rolled onto his chest and slipped out of the copilot's cockpit, then squatted at John's feet, shining a wristlamp into the confined space next to Van Houte.

"You'll never extract the major in the same way." The eyes behind Chapov's faceplate were gray-blue, the nose narrow, and the mouth wide with thin lips. "There's no room to get in there, unless you start digging."

"No time for digging," Van Houte said over the comm. "Just let me know when you're clear of the SDD blast radius."

"No. We'll find another way." John rolled to his knees and peered over Chapov's shoulder. There was maybe a head's width of cavity between the Owl's nose and a wall of sandstone bedrock, and the canopy was pressed tight against a meter-thick ceiling of lechatelierite. "Blue Four, sitrep?"

"I'm still climbing the ridge," Linda said. "But I see no inbound Seraphs yet."

"Let us know if that changes."

Linda's status light winked green, then Van Houte was on the comm again.

"Don't you dare risk the mission to extract me," he said. "It's my mistake that put me here, and I'm happy to—"

"What mistake?" John asked. He sat back on his haunches, then looked back at Kelly and shook his helmet. Chapov was right: there was no time to dig a cavity large enough to extract the major. "We're on the ground, alive and with our equipment intact."

"I decelerated too hard," Van Houte said. "That caused an equipment failure, endangering the craft and the mission."

"You did what you had to." As John spoke, Chapov dropped his chin—no doubt thinking of the deceleration tolerances Van Houte had exceeded. Ignoring him, John added, "And I don't see any Seraphs strafing us."

"Yet," Van Houte said. "Move out. That's an order, Master Chief."

"Sorry, Major," John said. "You got us to the ground, so it's my mission now."

He was referring to a long-established ONI protocol: once a mission reached the ground, command passed from the flight commander to the leader of the special forces team.

John pointed Chapov toward the rear of the Owl. "Join up with Fred and Chief Mukai. Maybe you can drive one of the excavation machines."

"Of course," Chapov said. He stepped close and switched off his comm mic, then spoke in a low voice through his helmet voicemitter. "But you *do* know the major exceeded g-tolerances, right? If he'd given the yoke to me earlier—"

"We'd have been splattered all over the glass," John interrupted, also speaking only through his voicemitter. "You blacked out."

"But I *wouldn't* have, if we had stayed inside tolerances," Chapov insisted. "The equipment wouldn't have come loose either."

"And we'd have had a dozen Seraphs chewing our tail. Instead, they're still behind us searching for bolide debris." John pointed again toward the back of the Owl. "The major made a good call. Go."

Chapov hesitated, his narrowed eyes hinting at distress more than resentment. It was clear he had more to say, but now was hardly the time—and John wasn't sure it ever would be. It was a bad idea to second-guess a seasoned superior.

HALO: SHADOWS OF REACH

*"Now,* Lieutenant."

Chapov's faceplate grew gray and opaque as he activated its night-vision mode. "Right away, Master Chief. Sorry."

He spun on his heel and scrambled onto the Owl's wing, and finally John understood. It hadn't been Van Houte at the yoke when the maimed Owl came down—it had been his hotshot copilot, and Chapov felt like he had let the team down. Maybe he wasn't quite thinking of it that way yet, but he eventually would. That was why he was trying to convince John that the hard landing hadn't been his fault. Because, really, Chapov was trying to convince himself.

John switched back to the comm net. "And, Lieutenant?"

Chapov stopped on top of the wing, but didn't turn around. "Yes, Master Chief?"

"This is nobody's fault," John said. "You made an incredible landing under the circumstances. Anybody else would have had us spread out across ten kilometers of glass."

Chapov paused a moment, then said: "Maybe only five kilometers. Major Van Houte is a pretty decent pilot himself."

The roar-scrape-crunch of steel ripping into glassy ground sounded somewhere beyond the Owl as Chapov hopped off the wing and started toward the loading ramp. John switched off his external lamps and watched through his NVS as Chief Mukai pushed the LHD's excavation bucket into the wall of the crash furrow, using it to cut a ramp out of the trough. Fred was up on top of the lechatelierite, standing off to one side and waving her forward.

"Blue Two, is the drilling jumbo operational?"

Fred nodded without looking away from her work. "Affirmative. Are you thinking what I am?"

"Probably," John said. "Have Lieutenant Chapov bring the jumbo forward. Blue Four?"

"Setting up on the ridge now," Linda replied. "I have confirmed sixteen—now eighteen—bandits over the decoy impact zone. Nothing coming our way yet."

"Good," John said. "Can you identify the search pattern?"

"Expanding grid, I think," Linda said. "Definitely systematic."

"Acknowledged," John said. Systematic suggested Keepers of the One Freedom—or at least not Banished. He knew from UNSC intel that the Banished tended to be more unpredictable and random in their approach, since they were led by a mob of chieftains competing to win the favor of a fierce Jiralhanae warlord named Atriox. The Keepers were more organized and rigid in their structure, with a strict chain of command and a religious doctrine dedicated to joining the ancient Forerunners in divine transcendence—akin to what drove the Covenant during the war. "That gives us some idea of what to expect—and how much time we have."

"But there is a problem with your plan," Linda said. "The terrain down there is as dark as a grave—until you activate your lamps."

"Even *under* the glass?" John asked.

"It is just a pinpoint, like a star through fog," Linda said. "I doubt the Seraphs can see it from so far away. But if you ignite the plasma drills—"

"They'll shine us up like an emergency beacon," Kelly finished. "So yeah, that won't work."

"You see?" Van Houte said. "You need to put the mission first, Master Chief."

"I know that."

The scraping sound stopped as the LHD finished the ramp and climbed out of the crash furrow. Mukai started up the slope toward the top of the ridge—then abruptly started toward the nose of the Owl.

"Cut a line a little in front of the cockpit." She had attached her flip-down night-vision visor to her helmet. "It doesn't need to be deep—just enough to give me some bite."

"What are you thinking?" John asked.

"That you're wasting time," Mukai said. The LHD was already rolling past the Owl. "No offense."

"None taken," John said. He wasn't sure whether the LHD could break up a meter-thick blanket of lechatelierite, but Mukai probably was. Like everyone on the mission, she had been cross-trained on the excavation equipment, and as a crew chief she would consider it a point of honor to learn the specifications of both machines by heart. "I should've known better than to ask."

"It's okay, Master Chief," Mukai said. "You'll learn."

John chuckled at that.

"Blue Two," he said, "you and Chapov collect the gelignite bins and find a route over that ridge. Blue Three, you're still with me, on shotgun."

A pair of status lights winked green. John and Kelly grabbed their gear off the wing and slapped their weapons and load-hauling harnesses onto their Mjolnir's magnetic mounts, then climbed onto the Owl's fuselage. By then, Mukai was thirty meters in front of the downed craft, swinging the LHD around in preparation for her rescue attempt. The vehicle was remarkably silent for such a powerful machine, its TMCD compact fusion reactor making no sound at all and its hydrostatic transmission humming quietly as it approached.

Kelly loaded her M45E tactical shotgun with plastic-saboted strike rounds, then led the way off the fuselage onto the smooth expanse of lechatelierite terrace. Here and there, the plasma-fused ground was covered by a thin layer of dried mud—the result of seven years of post-glassing dustfall—and walking on it was like crossing a silk-draped ice rink. They stopped four paces later, guessing that would be about a pace in front of the Owl's nose, and faced away from the waiting LHD.

"Can we risk some helmet lamps?" Kelly asked. "I'd hate to shoot someone's foot."

"Blue Four?" John asked.

"You may as well," Linda replied. "The bandit formations are starting to loosen up and expand their search grid."

She did not need to explain her thinking. It wouldn't be long before a pair of Seraphs overflew the landing site, and when that happened, there would be no hiding the *Special Delivery* from their thermal sensors. John activated his helmet lamps and shined them on the ground a couple of paces in front of Kelly, and she did the same.

John checked his motion tracker to be sure Fred and Chapov were safely outside Kelly's ricochet arc and, not seeing their designators, assumed they were still inside the Owl's troop bay, collecting the drilling jumbo and gelignite bins.

"Fire at will."

"Take cover," Kelly said. "Firing."

She pulled the trigger, sending a flurry of eight-gauge slugs into the ground about a meter in front of the Owl's nose. A curtain of dust and glass shards rose as high as their knees, but John could see the fire was proving even more effective than necessary. Capable of blowing a hole through a Warthog's engine block, the steel rounds were punching a third of a meter down into the lechatelierite, creating an uneven, fracture-lined trench. As Mukai had suggested, it would give the teeth on the bottom side of the LHD's two-kiloliter bucket plenty to bite.

Van Houte's voice sounded over the comm net. "I'm starting to see cracks above me. Am I to take it that Chief Mukai's crazy plan is working?"

"My plans are never crazy," Mukai said. "You can set the SDD for fifteen minutes."

"Belay that," John said. "Can you link it to your comm unit?"

"I can," Van Houte confirmed.

"Then do it. Let's give them something to worry about when they start chasing us."

"Always wise," Van Houte said. "Just be sure you make a clean extraction. The comm option comes with an automatic deadman switch."

Kelly stopped firing and reloaded. John took the opportunity to pace the length of the trench, then stepped to one end and motioned the LHD forward. Three steps was three meters, and the LHD's bucket was only two meters wide.

"Does all that quiet time mean we're clear to evacuate?" Fred asked.

"Do you have the gelignite?" John asked. "And the detonators?"

"You have to ask?" Fred replied. "Who leaves the fun stuff behind?"

"Then you're clear."

"And I suggest you hurry," Linda said. "I make three bandits coming our way. I can't tell if they've seen you yet, but I am sure they will."

"That's only to be expected," Kelly said. She took her place at the other end of the trench and shined her helmet lamps into it. "Why *wouldn't* a flight of Seraphs pass over at just the wrong moment?"

Fred and Chapov appeared on John's motion tracker as they brought the drilling jumbo into the crash furrow and headed for the ramp Mukai had cut. Then the LHD's bucket was dropping down between John and Kelly, and all his attention was on the bottom edge as it dug into the trench. The steel teeth bit deep, launching conchoidal shards into the air, but it wasn't the way LHDs were designed to work.

LHDs were made to scoop up loose stone and haul it away, not tear it out of the living bedrock. But Mukai knew how to get the most out of any machine. She gunned the engine hard, pushing the vehicle forward until the front tires rose off the ground and spun in the dark air.

"Hit it again," Mukai said. "It's coming loose. I can feel—"

Kelly was already firing, planting the first rounds at John's end of the trench and working her way back. His shields flashed as two slugs ricocheted into him and deflected into the night, but a web of finger-width cracks fanned back toward the Owl, and the LHD dropped onto its front tires again.

After that, the lechatelierite broke up almost instantly under Mukai's assault, shattering into hundreds of chunks that the excavation machine scooped up and lifted out of the way. The resulting pit was not quite a meter deep, with a floor covered in glass nuggets ranging from the size of a fist to that of a flight helmet.

"You're close," Van Houte said from inside his cockpit. "I can see your lamps."

"The bandits can too," Linda said. "They're dropping in for a strafing run, six o'clock on the Owl."

"They're coming up the valley?" Fred sounded almost happy about the prospect. "Relax—we've got this."

"We do?" Chapov asked.

"How about *I've* got this," Fred said. "You take cover under the jumbo."

"The one with four bins of gelignite strapped to it?" Chapov asked. "*That* jumbo?"

"Affirmative." John didn't know what Fred had planned—and there wasn't time to ask. "Chief Mukai, I'll finish up. Dump that load of glass and get the LHD out of here."

"On it."

John jumped into the pit Mukai had excavated. "And when the Seraphs open fire—"

"*On it.*" Mukai had been Special Forces her entire career. She didn't need John to tell her when to take cover.

Kelly jumped into the pit beside John, and they began to throw and kick glass chunks out of the way. When they finished, there were only a few centimeters of ash-clouded lechatelierite between them and the Owl, and Kelly began to fire strike rounds into it. The slugs penetrated and, robbed of most of their energy, bounced harmlessly off the pilot's canopy.

"Be ready," Fred commed. "Opening fire now."

"You?"

"*Them,*" Fred said. "But no worries. I'm always ready."

Plasma bolts began to streak down out of the darkness, filling the night with flashes of crimson heat, burning through the Owl's fuselage armor, melting long furrows into the vitreous ground to both sides of the pit. John and Kelly dropped to their bellies and continued to dig, using their gauntlets to smash the last lechatelierite nubs away from the canopy so Van Houte could raise it and escape.

A bolt burned through the copilot's broken canopy; then John's shields flared and failed as two more glanced off him. Kelly rolled off the Owl and dropped into the narrow gap between its nose and the lechatelierite crust alongside it.

"You can open fire anytime now," she commed. "Please do."

"This is a mining machine," Fred said. "Not an anti-aircraft turret."

Finally realizing what Fred was planning to do, John rolled into the gap on his side of the Owl, then switched off his helmet lamps and peered under its wing, back along the fuselage. The drilling jumbo was a bright, fuzzy block of red in his NVS, with a small puddle of dim red—Chapov—lying between its tires. The Seraph flight was a stack of tiny yellow lunate shapes spitting crimson dashes of brilliance down at the *Special Delivery*, the lead craft's fire already stitching across the glassy terrace beyond the Owl's buried nose, the second craft's fire just starting to burn strike scars into the sand behind it.

And Fred was an orange Mjolnir-shaped bulk standing on the operator's platform at the rear of the jumbo, his helmet tipped back to watch the approaching Seraphs. The drill booms were fully extended and pointed at the sky, and his hands were on the controls, twisting and turning as he adjusted the positions of the emitter nozzles, trying to keep them arranged in a tight fan as he positioned them in front of the oncoming fighter craft.

It wasn't the worst idea Fred had ever had.

Fred depressed the thumb switches on the ends of the two handgrips he was holding, and a pair of blue plasma beams shot skyward from the center drill heads. John's view of what happened next was blocked by the Owl's wing, but the strafing ended in a heartbeat. The heavens flashed gold and screamed with metal-drum thunder, and then there were flaming pieces of fighter craft falling all around.

Fred was already grabbing the second set of handgrips. He hit the thumb switches and sent another pair of plasma beams up into the darkness, this time from the drill heads on either end of the fan. The flashes were smaller this time, and spaced a few breaths apart, and a Seraph went spiraling toward the ridge missing a quarter of its hull and vanished in a sharp, glass-shaking clap.

The third Seraph arced away in the opposite direction, wobbling wildly as the pilot struggled to retain control after a wild evasion maneuver. John lost sight of it as it arced over the ravine, but as he climbed out of the narrow gap where he had taken cover, he heard the distant crunch of a hard landing.

"Nice timing, Blue Two," John said. He checked his team's status display and found all Spartan LEDs green. His Mjolnir wasn't linked to the *Special Delivery*'s crew, so he couldn't confirm their status automatically. "Condition jumbo?"

"A little chewed up, but mobile," Fred replied. "Down one boom and lost part of a bin."

"Part of a *gelignite* bin?" Chapov asked. Clearly he had come through the attack in one piece. "How are we not a crater in the sand?"

"Good question," Fred said. In fact, the nitrocubane-enhanced gelignite that the UNSC used was one of the most stable explosives available, which was why it had been selected for this mission. It could be burned without detonating, so it didn't seem all that surprising that it could take a plasma strike. "Now, get up here and drive this thing. I'll scout a route on foot."

"Chief Mukai, status you and LHD?" asked John.

"Both unharmed," she reported. "So far."

"Then get over the ridge as fast as you can," he said. "Don't wait for anything. Blue Four?"

"The enemy is maneuvering to approach from across the ravine," Linda said. "That seems very cautious. Perhaps they think our plasma drill is a new kind of anti-aircraft weapon?"

So definitely not Banished. That faction would have come racing en masse, each Seraph trying to beat the others to the prize and steal the glory.

A clatter sounded behind John. He reactivated his helmet lamps and saw the pilot's canopy rising as Eznik Van Houte climbed out of the cockpit. Like Chapov, the major wore a flight suit still bulging around his hips with retained high-g inflation pressure. His weathered face was not visible behind his gray faceplate, but John could picture his tired brown eyes and bushy gray mustache.

"Hold this." Van Houte passed John a buckle-on survival belt packed with magazine pouches, ration packs, and a hydration flask, then reached into the cockpit and withdrew an old MA2B bullpup assault rifle dating from the days of the Insurrection. "And this."

John checked one of the magazines and found it loaded with penetrators—.390 rounds with copper jackets around depleted uranium cores. The major was a man who believed in putting holes in what he hit.

Recalling that Chapov had been unable to retrieve his own survival belt when he evacuated, John gave the copilot's canopy a gentle upward push. The electric motor engaged and, with no lechatelierite ceiling to cause resistance, finished lifting the canopy.

Kelly reached in from the other side and withdrew Chapov's survival belt, along with an MA5B bullpup assault rifle. It was a solid choice for a pilot's emergency weapon, short enough to fit into the cockpit scabbard but with decent range and a suppressor-adapted barrel that made it ideal for stealth fighting.

"Blue Three, catch up with the LHD," John said over the comm. "Help Chief Mukai get over the hill. Major Van Houte, with me."

Kelly's status LED flashed green. Van Houte buckled on his survival belt, then took his MA2B and started back toward the access ramp Mukai had excavated earlier.

John extended an arm to block his way. "Sorry, Major, we're in a hurry." He lowered his arm to knee height, his elbow bent at ninety degrees. "Climb aboard."

"You want to *carry* me?"

"Yes, sir," John said. "Preferably conscious."

Van Houte gave a short laugh, then stepped over John's arm, sitting in the crook of his elbow. "But the mission comes first," he said. "If I start to slow you down—"

"You won't."

John deactivated his helmet lamps and pulled Van Houte tight to his chest, then sprang out of the crash furrow onto the glassy terrace. He glanced back across the ravine and saw engine flares the size of fingertips approaching in a five-across line. Behind that line was another, and behind the second still another. He did not take the time to look for a fourth line or a fifth, because once you reached overkill, your tactics didn't change.

John pulled two frag grenades off his load harness and depressed the priming switches, then waited as the first line of engine flares drew steadily closer. They were already in strafing range, but seemed to be more interested in reconnoitering the crash site than attacking it.

"Shouldn't we be running by now?" Van Houte asked.

"We will be."

John continued to wait, watching as the first line of Seraphs approached. In his NVS, they looked like big yellow disks with a stream of crimson efflux shooting out between their forked tails. Their plasma cannons remained cold and dark, a sign that, on this pass at least, they were intent on identifying the mysterious weapon that had destroyed two of their fellow craft rather than killing anyone on the ground.

And that was just fine with John.

He tossed the grenades into the crash furrow, about ten meters behind the downed Owl, and remained where he was.

"Now?"

"Not safe yet."

"*Safe?*" Van Houte spoke the word as if he had never heard it before. "We're Special—"

The grenades detonated, creating a cluster of blinding flashes that washed out the thermal elements of John's night vision and left him staring at a white faceplate.

Linda's voice came over the comm. "Move now, Blue Leader." A green waypoint appeared in the white fog inside his faceplate. "The first rank is breaking formation."

John sprinted across the glassy terrace. The washout drained from his faceplate, and he found himself starting up the yellow-orange slope toward the top of the ridge. Progress was slow. For every three steps up, he slid one step back, the soles of his sabatons slipping on the thin mud-cake that covered the smooth slope. The drilling jumbo was five hundred meters above him and to the right, just preparing to crest a low saddle in the ridge. The LHD was two hundred meters below it and even farther to the right, angling toward the same saddle from the opposite direction. Fred and Kelly were a short distance ahead of the two vehicles, using their Mjolnir's superior fused-mode night vision to find the route.

Vehicles and Spartans alike were glowing crimson inside John's faceplate—and they would be just as visible to the thermal sensors in the approaching Seraphs.

"We need diversions," John commed. "Anything to keep the enemy from focusing on us."

Three status LEDs winked green, and Linda's S5 sniper rifle began to boom. John saw four muzzle flashes behind the waypoint in his HUD, perhaps fifty meters below the ridge crest, but did not look back to see if she had hit anything.

She *had*. The only question was whether four rounds of Linda's special ammunition—titanium-jacketed high-velocity armor-piercing 14.5mm depleted uranium—would be powerful enough to punch through a Seraph's energy shielding. John was betting that they would, but it really didn't matter. What counted was that the enemy pilots would see their shields flickering and realize they were under attack. Then they would start to think about who was hitting them and with what, and *that* would give John and the rest of the team enough time to get over the ridge.

He took two more frag grenades off his load harness, depressing the primer switches and holding them in the same hand—then heard the screech of warping metal and looked over to see the large green sickle of half a Seraph hull lying thirty meters to his left. John started across the slope toward it.

"Wait." Van Houte pointed up the slope toward the ridge. The light-gathering night-vision system in his pilot's helmet was not as flexible as the dual-mode system in John's Mjolnir, but it was good enough to indicate the top of the ridge. "We're supposed to be going that way."

"This won't take long," John said. "I just want to confirm something."

Linda's rifle began booming again, and he glanced over to see the second rank of Seraphs peeling off above the ravine. One of them was trailing hot fumes, and another was wobbling. Clearly, her special HVAP rounds *were* capable of piercing Seraph shields.

"Blue Leader," Fred commed, "*uphill.*"

"Need a minute."

"A minute?" Kelly asked. "Are you mad?"

John looked away from his footing long enough to see the third rank of Seraphs approaching. The crimson dots of their plasma cannons were already glowing bright along the front edges of their disks.

"Distract them."

He tossed the grenades in his free hand down the slope and reached for two more. There was no chance of damaging a Seraph with frag grenades, of course, but they were good decoys. In the pitch dark below Reach's heavy cloud cover, the multiple detonations would create hot spots that looked like ground-to-air missile launches to a thermal imaging system—and *that* would reduce his targeting priority to just about zero.

The grenades exploded; as expected, a line of plasma bolts

streamed across the ravine toward their dwindling fireballs. John depressed the primer switches on the next two grenades. These were his last, but there was no sense saving ordnance when using it was the best way to avoid getting killed.

He heard another series of detonations—two, then two more—as Fred and Kelly tossed their own grenades, then glimpsed more streams of plasma converging on their fireballs.

No enemy fire was directed at him though, and he reached the Seraph debris he had noticed a few seconds earlier. It was slightly less than half a craft, a sliver shaped like a waning moon, about fifteen meters long. He could hear the self-mending hull squealing and sizzling as it struggled to close a breach that could never be repaired, and even his helmet filters could not keep out the acrid stench of burning fuel rod propellant and boiled Jiralhanae blood.

John tossed his last two grenades as far down the slope as he could, then activated his helmet lamps and ran the beam over the top of the Seraph's dark crimson hull. He saw recessed sensor dishes, plates of extra armor over systems-control nodes, three separate integrated antennas, the seams of a still-sealed boarding hatch . . . and a blood-red emblem consisting of a broken, inverted triangle with a pair of black blades extending from each side.

"Oh, hell," Van Houte said, pointing at the emblem. He was still riding in the crook of John's left arm. "Is that—"

Linda's rifle began to boom from the ridge again, then more grenade detonations sounded from across the slope behind him.

"Blue Leader," Fred commed, "we need you up here *now*."

A peal of gelignite thunder rumbled across the slope, so powerful it shook the glass beneath John's feet.

But this time the aliens were not fooled. A wall of plasma bolts burned into the slope below and began to climb upward. John glanced across the ravine to see the fourth wave of Seraphs approaching, their weapons blazing and their formation tight.

"Blow it," John said.

Van Houte's gaze was still fixed on the emblem on the Seraph's hull. "What?"

"The *Special Delivery*." John sprinted for the ridge crest. It was only two hundred meters away, but it might as well have been twenty kilometers. "Blow it—"

"Wait," Linda said. "I'll tell you when."

"Uh . . . sure," Van Houte said. "But that emblem—"

Plasma fire began to chew at John's heels, filling the air with shards of glass and smoke. He would have dodged, but he was just as likely to step into the path of a plasma bolt as out of it. So he just ran.

The crest was only a hundred meters away now. Five more seconds and—

*"Now,"* Linda said.

"Execute," Van Houte said.

A compression wave hit John from behind, nearly knocking him off his feet and pushing him up the slope an extra five meters. But the plasma fire stopped. The entire ridge trembled beneath the impact of crashing Seraphs, and John's faceplate fogged red on both sides with heat wash.

"Execute?" John asked. Verbal trigger words were supposed to be complicated codes that someone could not use mistakenly in the course of normal communications. *"That* was your SDD activation code?"

"It worked, right?" Van Houte craned his neck, looking past John's shoulder toward the Seraph debris they had just left. "That Seraph emblem, wasn't it—"

"Yeah," John said. "It was Banished."

# CHAPTER THREE

Even with the Phantom's exterior task lamps flooding the crater with light, there was little for Castor to see—only a sandstone basin forty meters across, tiny particles of heat-fused silica glittering in its soot-streaked bed. Keeper pilots of three different species policed it an arm's length apart, the beams of their handlamps searching for answers lost to the power of the blast. Ribbons of nanolaminate hull plating lay scattered about the crater rim, all that remained of the Seraphs that had been above the unidentified insertion craft when it self-destructed.

Castor did not like unidentified. Unidentified meant danger.

He had encountered this kind of destruction before, as a chieftain commanding a battle pack during the War of Annihilation, and later as a *dokab* leading the Keepers of the One Freedom against the heretics of the United Nations Space Command, and he knew it to be an asset-denial tactic used by human military forces. This first observation was troubling in its own right, but there were others.

The second observation was that, during the chase across what the

— 51 —

humans called Big Crater Bay, his Keeper pilots had found it difficult to tell whether they were pursuing an insertion craft or a fireball. The new arrivals had tried to camouflage their approach, and camouflage suggested secret intent.

A third observation was that the blast had been hot and all-devouring, the kind that disintegrated a craft so thoroughly it could not be identified or reverse-engineered. Almost always, such explosions were meant to protect secret technology.

A fourth observation was that the crater was about the size of a UNSC Pelican, and the UNSC's Office of Naval Intelligence used stealth versions of Pelicans called Owls to insert small units on secret missions.

And taken as a whole, all that secrecy could only mean that there was a human special operations team on Reach. What Castor did not know was who they were and whether they had come to interfere with his quest. But he intended to find out.

A young Jiralhanae pilot appeared outside the Phantom, at the foot of the loading ramp. Wearing the blue-and-gold harness of a captain-deacon, he was tall and broad across the shoulders, but still thin in the middle. His fur was the same mottled gray as Castor's lost war-brother Orsun, and his tusks had a familiar curl that always made looking upon him a bittersweet experience.

The youth crossed his arms over his chest and knelt, an overly formal gesture that only served to remind Castor that this warrior was a pale shadow of his father.

But compared to Orsun, most warriors were.

"Krelis, can you not see I await your report?" Castor asked, trying to be patient with the untimely fawning. "Rise and speak."

"As you will." Krelis lowered his arms and drew himself to his full height. Standing a little over three meters, the youth was even more imposing than had been his father. "It is an hour since the infidels crossed the ridge with their Sky Slicers and you commanded us to end pursuit."

Castor felt his tusks grind at the use of a human temporal unit. He had long since accepted the wisdom of using human names and measurements in a galactic region filled with their human colonies. But here on Reach, where the Covenant had won one of its greatest victories, such accommodations were a bitter reminder of the Covenant's ultimate defeat.

"I ask the *dokab* to withdraw his command," Krelis continued, "that I may finish what I began."

"So you can lose *another* seven craft?" The question came from Castor's right, where the Sangheili blademaster Inslaan 'Gadogai stood at his side. "The Keepers cannot afford such courage."

Krelis opened his lips in a sneer, revealing the bright, sharp fangs of his age. "When an *izlar* insults me, he would be wise to do it wearing armor."

"Armor?" 'Gadogai pulled his plasma sword off his belt and stepped out of the troop bay. "Why would I need armor to insult *you*?"

"Hold," Castor said.

When 'Gadogai ignored him and started down the loading ramp, Castor grabbed the Sangheili by the shoulder and stopped him. It was not a risk he enjoyed taking, for he had been warned that 'Gadogai had a short temper. But Krelis was Orsun's only surviving son, and Castor would not betray his dead war-brother by allowing the last of his line to die a pointless and shameful death.

"Krelis does not know who you are, Blademaster," Castor continued. "Grant me the favor of accepting his apology."

"If you insist." 'Gadogai allowed himself to be drawn back into the troop bay. "Killing him would be little sport, anyway."

"It is not I who will be killed, nor I who will apologize," Krelis said, starting up the ramp. "It is that four-jawed *kiniji*. It was my honor—"

"No." Castor stepped forward, placing himself between the young pilot and 'Gadogai. "No one doubts your courage, Captain-Deacon. But the blademaster is right about losing more Seraphs—as veterans of the Silent Shadow usually are in such matters."

Krelis's eyes widened, and he stopped in his tracks. "You command me to apologize?"

"You would be doing the Keepers a great service." Castor needed to give Krelis an honorable excuse so the other pilots in his wing would continue to follow him. "There is no time to train your replacement."

Krelis gnashed his tusks, but he heeded Castor's not-so-subtle warning about the outcome and advanced no farther. "As you will, then."

Castor turned sideways on the ramp, allowing Krelis and 'Gadogai a clear view to each other. Krelis spread his arms and showed his palms, a symbolic gesture of peace that had the practical effect of proving both hands were empty.

"By command of the Last Dokab," Krelis said, "I offer my apology."

"And for the sake of the Keepers, I accept." 'Gadogai dropped the handle of his plasma sword back onto its belt mount and faced Castor. "But the facts in the field remain the same, Dokab. You no longer have the fighter strength to hold our own against Deukalion and Ballas. If one of the Banished packs attacks you, you lose the strength to fend off the other."

"We should have used our strength when we had it," Krelis said, remaining on the ramp. "Deukalion and Ballas would have been helping us search for the portal instead of testing each other's defenses."

"But we did not," Castor said. "And there is nothing to be won by bemoaning what we did not do in the past."

The last thing he wanted was to explain that the other chieftains did not yet view him as an equal. The Keepers of the One Freedom had joined the Banished a year and a half earlier, six months before the Apparition began to transmit her demands for fealty across the stars, and it had not been an easy union. Castor and the Keepers hoped to hunt the Apparition down and put an end to her blasphemy. In contrast, most of the other Banished chieftains were interested only in consolidating their power and raising their profiles in the horde.

And it did not help that the Banished's leader, Castor's old war-brother Atriox, had been absent for so long. Shortly after welcoming the Keepers into their numbers, Atriox had placed his former mentor, the war chief known as Escharum, in charge and then departed with a powerful assault force on a mission that he claimed would permanently remove all threats to the Banished. While Atriox's old *daskalo* was a fierce and cunning Jiralhanae leader, the lack of the warmaster's unifying presence continued to be felt by all in the Banished. Many wondered where Atriox had gone, and if he would ever come back. Others sought to consolidate the Banished's military strength and holdings under their own protection, perhaps hoping to ingratiate themselves to Atriox upon his return.

All that would change as soon as the Banished found the portal they were seeking on Reach, but it was not Castor's place to remind the other leaders of Atriox's ultimate purpose. 'Gadogai had once warned Castor not to judge his peers by his own standards, and the value of that advice grew clearer to Castor every day. Had he accepted Krelis's suggestion and attempted to impose his will on Deukalion and Ballas, the two chieftains would have united their packs against the Keepers. And then all three factions would have been fighting to control Reach and claim possession of a portal that they had not even found yet.

Castor started down the ramp, but Krelis remained in the middle, leaving him no room to pass.

"There is still time to win dominance," Krelis said. "The Old Packs know nothing of our losses. If we strike Deukalion now, he will yield before Ballas realizes what we have done. By the time he responds, we will have the strength of two packs and be too strong for him to defeat."

"And while we are striking at Deukalion and fending off Ballas," Castor asked, "who will be searching for the portal?"

The Portal under the Mountain was an ancient Forerunner slip-space gateway located somewhere on Reach, most likely on the supercontinent of Eposz. Aside from being a sacred site built by the Forerunners themselves, it would allow the Banished to join Atriox quickly and in great numbers—and finally claim the prize he had been fighting for since his departure.

"The portal will be easier to find when *all* the Banished on Reach are searching for it," Krelis said. "And you still have the strength to make it so, if only you will move boldly."

Castor growled low in his chest. Krelis had all of his father's courage and little of his wisdom. The stakes for finding the portal were far too high for the Keepers to risk igniting a feud amongst the Banished on Reach, even if it was in the hope of uniting them. Castor had seen enough Jiralhanae history to know that was a fool's errand. How could a son of Orsun fail to understand that?

Calming himself, Castor asked, "Krelis, what are my standing commands to the finder of the portal?"

"First, prepare to defend it," Krelis said. "Second, send word to you by messenger only—no transmissions. Third, allow no one to approach who is not . . .'"

Krelis let his answer trail off, and 'Gadogai rattled his mandibles in amusement.

"He is less the slow hatcher than I thought," 'Gadogai said to Castor. He turned to Krelis. "Do you understand why?"

"So one of the other packs doesn't seize it."

"Indeed," Castor said, noting that Krelis had been wise enough to pretend he had not heard 'Gadogai's affront. Perhaps there was hope for the young captain-deacon after all. "If we cannot trust them to search alongside us, what might they do if they find the portal first?"

Krelis's jaw began to work. "But Escharum—"

"Is not here," 'Gadogai said. "And given how Deukalion and Ballas are engaging themselves, it seems clear that your *dokab* is the only chieftain who can be trusted to hold the portal in good faith until he arrives."

Krelis's eyes disappeared beneath his brow fur, and Castor

realized it had finally occurred to the young warrior that 'Gadogai was not of the Faithful. Escharum had assigned the blademaster to the Keepers shortly after Atriox departed on his mission, saying Castor would need the Sangheili's counsel to thrive among the other chieftains. What the war chief had not said was that 'Gadogai would also be Escharum's eyes and ears inside the Keepers—and perhaps even his blade, if Castor tried to betray him. It was an arrangement that had served both sides well, and over the last year Castor had come to consider the Sangheili something of a friend and advisor—even if he found it prudent never to voice his reservations about the Banished's impious ambitions.

After taking a moment to process his realization, Krelis looked back to Castor. "What if there is no portal?"

"Escharum would not command us to find a portal that does not exist," 'Gadogai said.

"Then why are Deukalion and Ballas fighting over a human rehabilitation settlement instead of obeying that command?" Krelis continued to look to Castor as he spoke. "If the portal's existence on this dead world is so certain, why have we found no evidence of it at all? And why do we know so little about where to search for it?"

"It is not yours to worry about those things," 'Gadogai said. "You are a captain-deacon. The only thing you should be concerned with is following—"

"No." Castor was both surprised and pleased by Krelis's pointed questions, and he had no wish to crush the youth's instincts just when he was beginning to show something of his father's stubborn wit. "They are fair questions, Blademaster, and Krelis was not present when we received Atriox's command."

Krelis's eyes grew round. "You speak with Atriox?"

"Now you are questioning your own *dokab*?" 'Gadogai asked.

"Atriox speaks to *us*, through Escharum," Castor said. "I cannot reveal all that he has said, but the warmaster always makes his commands clear."

In truth, Atriox had sent only one command to Castor and 'Gadogai, more than three months earlier. They had been aboard the Keeper flagship, the heavy frigate *Great Light*, discussing how to keep the Banished supplied without drawing the wrath of the Apparition and her Guardians. As they spoke, a buzz had sounded from the wardroom door, and when Castor called "Enter," one of his technical deacons stepped into the cabin holding a portable holopad in her hands.

"I beg forgiveness for interrupting, Dokab." A lithe, brownskinned human with a head shaved on the sides and a fall of tightly curled black hair hanging down her back, she approached without wasting Castor's time by waiting for a summons. "Escharum wishes to speak."

"Escharum?" 'Gadogai repeated. "I hope you stayed out of the scanning cones. There is no need to remind him of the Keeper weakness for humans."

She met 'Gadogai's disdainful glare with the unflinching gaze of a true believer. "He did not see me. I am good at not being seen." She placed the holopad on the table in front of Castor. "It is already linked to the *Great Light*'s entanglement beacon. All you need do is activate it . . . once I am out of the scanning cones, of course."

She shot 'Gadogai a hard glance, then left.

Castor laughed. "I think even if she knew who you were, she would have no fear of you."

"That is but one of the things I dislike about humans," 'Gadogai said. "They lack sense."

Castor placed his thumb over one of the scanning sockets to activate the holopad, and the image of a fierce and grizzled Jiralhanae face appeared over the projection pad. The eyes were set deep under a scarred brow, one red and the other pale white, and the mouth was a wide grim slash that showed neither tusks nor teeth.

HALO: SHADOWS OF REACH

"You wish to speak, War Chief?" Castor touched his fist to his breast. "I am honored."

"My wish is to speak with you and the Sangheili together," Escharum said. "I have no time for repeating myself."

"I am here." 'Gadogai brought his fist to his breast in a manner so casual it made Castor wonder if the Sangheili realized that the sound of his voice had activated the scanning socket on his side of the holopad, and that now his image would be hanging over Escharum's pad next to Castor's. "Proceed at your leisure, Mighty One."

"Then listen well," Escharum said. "Ask the questions you need, but ask them only once. After we have finished, I have other clans to prepare."

Castor took the hint and waved a finger over the scanning socket, instructing the holopad to keep a record of all that passed between him and Escharum. If 'Gadogai did the same, he did not see it. Perhaps the Sangheili knew Escharum so well that he would have no need to return to the conversation to look for nuances of gesture and tone that might clarify his meaning. Or perhaps he would simply remember it all without any need for such practical measures.

"We are listening," Castor said. "There will be no need to repeat yourself."

"I have received a transmission from Atriox," Escharum said. "It was a single message. And a command. He has found the remnants of the slipspace crystal the prophets of the Covenant so desperately sought."

"You are speaking of the Holy Light?" Castor asked. "Atriox has found the Holy Light?"

"Call it what you will," Escharum replied. "It belongs to Atriox and the Banished now."

Castor huffed in surprise, and 'Gadogai let his mandibles open. It was an astonishing revelation that Atriox somehow had in his possession such a powerful Forerunner treasure, capable of deftly manipulating slipspace and allowing passage to locations far too distant for conventional travel. The Covenant had searched for the Holy Light during their war with the humans, hoping that it would grant them access to one of the Sacred Rings, so that they could at last begin the Great Journey and ascend to divinity alongside the Forerunners. But when they finally located the resting place of the crystal on the human world of Reach, it had already been stolen by the infidels and was eventually destroyed during a running battle in the Eridanus system.

"How can that be?" Castor finally asked.

"Not all of the Holy Light was destroyed at Eridanus Secundus," 'Gadogai said. "After the battle, Tartarus sent eight squadrons to search for any remains. He recovered three shards and presented them to the Prophet of Truth in the Inner Sanctum at High Charity."

Tartarus had been the leading chieftain during the final days of the Covenant, a bold Jiralhanae who had single-handedly wrested military control from the Sangheili in an event that had since been called the Great Schism. The recovery of what remained of the Holy Light was doubtless one of many ways that Tartarus had acted as the right hand of the High Prophet of Truth before he perished. Castor started to ask how 'Gadogai could know about the recovery and the fate of the shards, then restrained himself. Even in the short time they had known each other, he had learned enough of the blademaster's history to realize that he was not prone to exaggeration. He had probably witnessed the event in the Inner Sanctum with his own eyes.

"And now Atriox has all three shards," Escharum said.

"All three?" 'Gadogai asked. "Tell me he did not find them in High Charity."

"And if he had?"

"You know the answer," 'Gadogai said. An immense space station that had been the mobile capital city for the entire Covenant, High Charity had been overrun by the Flood in the final days of the war and destroyed in a desperate attempt to prevent the unholy parasite from spreading. If High Charity had survived, it would mean that so had the Flood—a possibility too terrible for Castor to contemplate.

"No," Escharum said. "It was not High Charity. He found them within Truth's ship."

'Gadogai tipped his head first one way, then the other, and finally asked, "The Forerunner Dreadnought is still *there*?"

"Is that not what I just said?" Escharum growled. "Now, hear me well. I do not have much time."

"I am listening," 'Gadogai said.

"As am I."

Castor had no idea where the *there* was that was being spoken of, but he was not going to waste the war chief's time inquiring when he could check with 'Gadogai later. Wherever Atriox had traveled, Castor knew that he had taken the formidable assault carrier *Enduring Conviction* and a vast array of Banished forces and materiel, which told him one thing: the warmaster was deadly serious about whatever he was after.

"Good." Escharum looked away from his holopad, but continued to speak. "Atriox is summoning the clans of the Banished to join him in the war he has been waging, but the only way for us to reach him is to activate the Forerunner slipspace portal hidden on the human world of Reach. We *must* find this portal and activate it. When he sees that the portal is ready, he will use what remains of the slipspace crystal to open it from his end. Then he will come to us and provide us transport to his location."

"You are certain that is the only way, War Chief?" Castor asked. "The Keepers have used slipspace portals before, and—"

Escharum looked back into the holopad. "Those portals do not lead to the Ark, Dokab."

"The Ark?" Castor felt his heart climb for his throat. Like the Holy Light, the Ark was legendary. It was an immense installation far removed from the galactic border, the foundry of the Sacred Rings—and a blessed place to begin the Great Journey. Stanza 212 of the *Psalm of the Journey* described a communications array on the

Ark that was capable of activating all Sacred Rings simultaneously, a hallowed act that would achieve in a single instant what the Covenant had been trying to do over its entire existence—join the ancient Forerunners in divine transcendence by finding and firing their network of Halo rings. All Infidels and Unbelievers would be condemned to Oblivion, and the Faithful would be elevated to the One Freedom of eternal existence beyond life. In an instant.

If Truth had actually made it to the Ark, it meant that the rumors had been accurate. The prophet must have been close to activating the array, and yet, the mere fact that Castor and everyone else were still trapped in their wretched lives was proof enough that he had failed. Now Castor's old war-brother Atriox was calling him to do battle on the sacred Ark.

Had Castor failed to see the Oracle's plan in *that*, he would not have been a Believer.

Once he had recovered from his shock, Castor met Escharum's gaze in the holograph. "As Atriox commands," he said. "The Keepers are happy to answer his summons."

Escharum's grim mouth seemed to rise at the corners, though just for a moment. "I have no doubt," he said. "But first, you must find the portal."

"I fail to understand," Castor said. "Did you not say it was on the human world of Reach?"

"Reach is a large planet, Dokab," Escharum said. "And there are countless places where the portal gateway might be hidden. Its location would have no doubt been lost forever, had Atriox not also found a record of Tartarus referring to the 'Portal under the Mountain.' *This* is our portal."

"There are sure to be many mountains on Reach," Castor said. "Can you tell us no more?"

Escharum's eyes flared. "No. Only that you must go to Reach and find it." He lowered his voice, then continued. "I know only what Atriox put in the transmission, and I have no way to reply or ask questions. Had he known more of the portal's location, we can be certain that he would have included it."

"And when we find this Portal under the Mountain?" Castor asked. Escharum had implied that the Keepers would be sent to the Ark . . . but an implication was not a promise. "The Keepers will travel to the Ark, to do battle at Atriox's side?"

"Along with the Legion of the Corpse-Moon and the Ravaged Tusks, yes." Escharum must have leaned closer to his holopad's scanning socket, because his image suddenly seemed nothing but heavy brows and determined eyes. "Together, your clans will search for the Portal under the Mountain. And when you find it, you will report it to me first. I will meet you there, and together we shall all have the honor of joining Atriox and the Banished on the Ark."

That conversation had taken place more than three months ago, and Castor had not heard from Escharum since. Of course, he was certain that 'Gadogai was reporting their lack of progress to the war chief on a weekly basis, but that hardly mattered—Castor was being less than honest when he told Krelis that Atriox always made his commands clear. For all he and 'Gadogai knew, the warmaster may have already perished in whatever battle he was conducting on the Ark.

It was impossible to know, and the only way to learn the truth was to locate the Portal under the Mountain on the planet Reach. Castor was not done searching—and that was all that Krelis, or any other Keeper, needed to know. He started down the ramp toward the crater, forcing Krelis to retreat backward.

"Be aware, Dokab, that the infidels have longshooters." Though careful to avoid suggesting that Castor should be fearful, Krelis was clearly worried about allowing him to get killed. It was almost touching. "And your armor may not be a defense. Their rounds penetrated the shields of two Seraphs."

"Have you set a perimeter?"

"Yes," Krelis replied. "But I have only pilots, and they have no dark-vision equipment outside their craft."

There was no question of returning to the troop bay. Castor could not allow himself to appear intimidated by the mere possibility of an attack—but more importantly, it was imperative that he personally inspect the crash site. With the probable exception of the Sangheili 'Gadogai, no one else had the experience to interpret the inevitable spoor of a firefight, and he needed to know how much of a threat these humans posed to his quest for the portal. He stopped halfway down the ramp, where his head and torso would be hidden from a sniper on the ridge, then looked back into the troop bay.

"Feodruz, send the Unggoy to sweep the ridge crest," he called. "Have the Kig-Yar search for debris from the interlopers. There will be a reward for anything they find."

A stocky Jiralhanae in full shielded armor appeared in the mouth of the troop bay to acknowledge the order, then began to bark commands into the red dimness behind him. A moment later, ten thigh-high Unggoy in armor and methane tanks charged down the ramp, chirping and hooting into their masks as they squeezed by Castor.

He roared encouragement and waved them on, knowing the gesture would embolden them as they ascended to the ridge crest and swept it for snipers. Because of their small size and lack of physical strength, Unggoy were often treated as no better than slaves by those they served. But Castor had discovered that a little respect earned their unwavering loyalty, and he knew that they would gladly charge a nest of human chatter guns for him. He had seen them do it on several occasions.

A column of five Kig-Yar followed, tapping their breast armor in a show of obedience as they slipped past. With them, Castor remained aloof, merely reminding them that he would pay only for debris from a *human* craft. The thin-snouted saurians had no faith or honor, but they were clever and resourceful, and they could be counted on to remain loyal as long as they were well rewarded—and knew the consequences of betrayal.

Once the Unggoy had vanished into the darkness and the Kig-Yar had begun to search the slope above the crater, Castor motioned Feodruz to follow, then descended the ramp ahead of him with 'Gadogai at his side. Even if the swarm of Unggoy had not persuaded the human sniper to abandon the nest, it would appear that Castor and 'Gadogai were the escorts and Feodruz was in command.

It was a deception that disoriented even Krelis. He glanced toward Feodruz and started to fall in at Castor's side, then seemed to grasp the ploy and went to Feodruz's side instead. He even took care to place himself on the flank toward the ridge, as though trying to shield his superior from a possible attack.

Castor led the small group down into the crater, speaking over his shoulder as he moved. "Show me what you have found so far, Krelis."

"Little that tells us anything," Krelis said. "Only some fused sand and a hole five meters deep. The only thing we know with certainty is that they want us to know nothing about them."

"Which tells us *something*," Castor said. "What have you found outside the crater? There must be tracks and shell casings."

"No shell casings," Krelis said. "And the tracks are difficult to read. I fear the ground has been too churned by our strafing."

"Then there must be blood," 'Gadogai said. "And body parts."

"None that we have found," Krelis said. "But we did find a ramp."

They were in the bottom of the crater now, and it was exactly as Castor had expected, a thin crust of fused silica crunching beneath his boots, a smudgy blanket of soot and ash that betrayed only the tracks of the beings now walking on it. "Show me."

Krelis took the lead and guided them out of the basin into a long trough filled with tracks that were as impossible to read as the young pilot had said. It certainly seemed plausible that there were interloper boot prints in the sand and crushed glass, but if so, they were lost beneath the tracks of Castor's own forces.

But the trough itself was more informative. It was clearly the furrow where the vessel had come down, and even Castor recognized the talent it had taken to land it. A less skilled pilot, and the furrow would have been an impact crater instead.

"How many strikes did the interloper take?" he asked.

"None," Krelis replied. "As reported, we continued to believe it might be a fireball until our first pilots found the crash site. We never fired on it in the air."

"And yet . . ." Castor stopped and looked along the furrow in both directions. Behind them, it ended at the well-lit blast crater. Ahead of him, it vanished into the darkness beyond the range of their lamps. "This was not a safe landing."

"Most likely an equipment failure," 'Gadogai said. "It can happen."

Castor had his doubts. "Did it ever happen to *you?*"

"Of course not. I was Silent Shadow."

"Then why assume it happened to the humans' ONI?" Castor motioned Krelis forward again. "Something strange occurred, for them to crash here."

"Forgive me, Dokab," Krelis said. "But do we care? We know where the humans are going."

"We do?" 'Gadogai asked. "Now, this I must hear."

"It is not complicated," Krelis said. "They have come to defend the human resettlement colony that Deukalion and Ballas are fighting over. The fools have jeopardized the entire portal search."

"Perhaps," Castor said. "Or it may be that fate is finally turning in our favor."

"Always the optimist," 'Gadogai said. "It is no wonder Atriox tolerates your insufferable zeal."

"It is not optimism," Castor said. It saddened him to hear 'Gadogai mocking his faith in such a manner, for it meant that when the Great Journey began, the blademaster would not be one of those walking the Path with him. "It is plain sense. If the interlopers are here to protect their resettlement colony, we have no need to concern ourselves with them. They will not interfere with our search."

"True," 'Gadogai said.

"And the Old Packs will be so battered by fighting the humans that once we *have* found the portal, they will be too weak to attempt seizing it from us."

"True again," 'Gadogai said.

Castor paused, troubled by the reticence he heard in the blademaster's voice. "But you do not seem pleased about it."

"I am only thinking of the Apparition," 'Gadogai said, "and how long it will take her Guardian force to arrive when the fighting grows fierce enough to draw her notice."

Castor's heart clenched. He hadn't thought about the Apparition. Once her Guardians arrived, finding the portal would no longer be possible or important. There would be nothing to do but flee.

After a moment, Krelis asked, "How large can the battle grow? The infidels brought only one insertion craft."

"That we know of, Captain-Deacon." It was Feodruz, speaking from behind Castor, who said this. "How many slipped past without being noticed?"

It was a good question, and one that Castor pondered as Krelis led them another thirty paces into the darkness. At last he veered toward the crash furrow's uphill wall and stopped, then shined his lamp into a small channel that had been cut through the sandstone bedrock and its meter-thick cap of lechatelierite. It was about two paces wide and shoulder-high at the deepest point of the cut, and its bed ascended at a fairly gentle angle onto the glassy slope of the ridge.

"This is the ramp?" Castor asked.

"It is." Krelis stooped and directed his handlamp onto its surface, where the loose ground had been pressed into a long, flat ribbon. About two hands in width, it was crossed at frequent intervals by a zigzagging pattern of divots. "These tire tracks were made by their

Sky Slicer as it climbed toward the ridge. They are probably transporting it to their resettlement colonists to use against Deukalion and Ballas."

"It seems a safe assumption," Castor replied. He took the handlamp from Krelis and moved its beam back and forth across the ramp, examining what looked like claw marks in the sandstone bedrock. "But how did they cut the ramp so quickly?"

"Our pilots saw two separate vehicles on their thermal screens," Krelis said. "Perhaps the second vehicle is some sort of support machine, used to dig emplacements for the—"

A tremendous clatter sounded from the top of the ramp. Instantly they all drew their weapons and whipped their gazes up to find a wide-eyed Kig-Yar shining his own handlamp at the underside of his narrow snout.

"Don't burn! No burn!" The clatter stopped, and the Kig-Yar ran the lamp beam along the length of a long metal arm with a pair of ball-hinges spaced about a meter apart. "You want debris from humans, yes?"

"Yes."

Castor returned his mauler to its carrying mount, then led 'Gadogai and the others up the ramp. He shined his lamp along the metal arm, staring briefly at the melted stub where a plasma round had sheared it off, then moved the beam along the steel sleeve over the two ball joints, and finally came to a meter-long head that looked like some form of human-manufactured plasma cannon.

"The gods will be pleased," Castor said. "As am I."

"Then I will have reward?" asked the Kig-Yar.

"A fine one. Your deacon will see to it when we return to the enclave." Castor glanced toward Feodruz to make certain that his intentions were clear, then said to 'Gadogai, "Do you recognize this? It is not like any anti-aircraft weapon I have ever seen before."

"*Weapon?*" The Kig-Yar cackled. "That is no weapon."

"No?" Castor grabbed the head of the device, then dragged it around so that the end was turned toward him—and found himself looking into an emitter nozzle as big around as his eye. It reminded him of some human machines he had seen many years before, in the tantalite mine on Meridian. "It is part of a drilling machine, is it not?"

"Oh yes. A plasma drill, mining." The Kig-Yar paused, then spoke more thoughtfully. "My clan trade for them all the time, before we join Keepers. I still have reward?"

"Yes. *Two* rewards."

This time, Castor did not bother looking toward Feodruz. Shining his lamp on the ramp, he ran its beam along the claw marks he had noticed in the bedrock earlier.

"And *three* rewards if you can tell me what made those marks."

"Then I am happy Keeper today," the Kig-Yar said. "Those marks from teeth on the digging bucket of hauling machine. Very powerful."

"A digging bucket," Castor repeated. He illuminated the drill head. "And a plasma drill."

"How strange," 'Gadogai said. "Why would someone use an insertion craft to deliver mining equipment?"

It was obvious to Castor that the blademaster already knew the answer—because Castor did too.

"Because they are ONI," he said. "And because they know we are searching for the Portal under the Mountain."

# CHAPTER FOUR

In the dawn rain, the narrow gorge reminded John of the sealed-bobsled courses in the old vids of the Martian Olympics. Its glassy walls rose a hundred meters overhead, and its serpentine channel snaked down a chute so steep and slippery it was often faster to skate-slide than to run. The load-haul-dump machine followed close on his heels, hydroplaning on the wet glass and splashing through plunge pools, hitting walls and making thunder.

The excavation equipment could easily be damaged down here, but at least it wouldn't be strafed. The gorge was too narrow and crooked for a Seraph assault, and even a Banshee would be so busy dodging walls it would be impossible to launch an effective attack. What would happen when they ran out of canyon, John had no idea. They would just have to improvise.

Kelly's voice sounded inside John's helmet. "Hold advance."

She was on point, a hundred meters ahead . . . probably. With all the bends in the gorge, it was hard to maintain consistent spacing. The drilling jumbo trailed the LHD behind John, and Fred followed both. Linda brought up the rear, staying a hundred meters back so she could ambush anyone who dropped into the canyon behind the team.

Everyone was on TEAMCOM, so the equipment drivers should have heard Kelly as clearly as had John. But the LHD continued to advance hard, its tires hissing on the wet glass. John raised his fist, signaling Mukai to follow Kelly's instructions and stop.

"Wait—I'm *trying!*" Mukai said.

"Same here," Chapov added. He was driving the jumbo, with Van Houte standing on the operator's platform beside him. "Wheels are locked, still sliding!"

Chapov's transmission ended in a crash of metal against glass, and John realized the canyon floor had grown so steep that the excavation machines were behaving more like toboggans.

"Do what you can," John said. His own feet threatened to fly out from beneath him each time he tried to slow his descent. "I'll see what the problem is ahead."

"The problem is we've run out of canyon," Kelly said. "Stop those machines *now*—or get off them."

There was a moment of dead air; then Mukai said to Chapov, "You first, *Special* Two. I don't want you sliding into me when I drop my bucket."

"Reasonable," Chapov said. "But I don't have a bucket. Can the stabilizer stands handle it?"

"Only one way to find out," Mukai said. "Drop the rear ones first. Drop them hard."

Two loud crackles sounded as the drilling jumbo's rear stabilizer stands smashed into the canyon floor and began to drag into the lechatelierite. A moment later, two more bangs sounded as Chapov dropped the front stands, and a loud screeching echoed off the walls.

John continued forward, slide-running down the wet glass, then rounded a bend where the gorge grew so narrow he could almost touch both walls at once. The floor fell away in a cascade of knurled lechatelierite, descending a hundred steep meters to the canyon mouth, where Kelly stood silhouetted against the silvery expanse of a vast basin that extended almost as far as the eye could see, clear to a ragged line of olive-gray mountaintops rising from somewhere beyond the pearl-gray horizon.

The scale of the devastation hit John like a cannon round. He had been on glassed worlds before, had seen vast sweeps of farmland shining like a mirror beneath a blanket of lechatelierite. But he had not known what those worlds looked like *before* they were glassed, had not seen in his mind's eye the endless fields of wheat and bambont that had once waved there in the wind, had not felt quite so personally robbed by what the enemy had taken from humanity. Now . . . now he was grateful that the war was over, because with the rage he felt building inside, he was worried that he might have done some things worthy of the "demon" nickname that the Covenant had given to the Spartans.

John began to spring side to side down the canyon, launching sprays of glass each time he slammed his heels down to control his descent. The nearer he drew to Kelly, the more he understood that she was on the edge of an abrupt drop-off—and that the floor of the basin lay hundreds of meters below.

"Don't tell me we're on top of a waterfall," he said, straining to slow himself.

"Obviously, I don't have to." Kelly tipped her head back, looking toward the canyon rim a hundred meters above, then said, "We need a better way out of here."

"Getting out of here isn't the problem. It's what comes next that worries me."

"Yes, there is that," Kelly said. "Getting strafed is no fun."

A tremendous *clang* echoed down the gorge behind them. John whipped his head around and saw the LHD wedged at the top of the cascade, its front wheels off the ground and its bucket jammed into a pocket of bare stone where it had broken through the lechatelierite.

He looked forward again just in time to plant his feet against the uphill side of a knurl, then absorbed the landing in his knees in order to stop. John had descended to within twenty meters of the canyon mouth. One bad step would put him in danger of shooting down the glassy streambed and over the waterfall. He began to pick his way down carefully, kicking his heels into the same footholds Kelly had chipped into the lechatelierite a few minutes earlier.

"*Special* Leader, prep a way to get the equipment out of here," John said, indicating Major Van Houte as pilot of the *Special Delivery*. "Blue Two will help you with setting up any blasting you need to do, but don't execute until I give you the all-clear."

Fred's status LED winked green, but before Van Houte could acknowledge, Chapov was on the channel.

"There's a feeder ravine about three hundred meters back that may be a good way—"

"Tell it to *Special* Leader," John said. Enough was enough. Chapov's enthusiasm had been creeping toward insubordination for the last few hours. He had insisted on driving the jumbo after escaping the crash site, and he always seemed eager to offer his opinion in place of Van Houte's. The time had come to let Chapov know he was trying to impress the wrong guy. "Your commander is in charge of that."

John stopped opposite Kelly. As she had warned, the canyon ended in a sheer precipice, where the stream shot off the edge and dropped more than two hundred meters to the slope below. Over a distance of several kilometers, it descended another thousand meters, then simply disappeared on the floor of the immense basin he had first glimpsed from higher in the canyon. Most of what he could see now was covered in gray lechatelierite, but scattered across the flats were thousands of rippling ponds and hundreds of dark swaths that looked like farm fields cut from beneath the glass.

John raised his visual magnification to maximum and saw that he was at least partially right. The dark swaths were all open ground, much of it tilled and surrounded by cut-block walls of lechatelierite. But the reclaimed fields were either barren or covered in smashed crops, and in some of the larger openings there were heaps of toppled and shattered blocks suggestive of razed villages.

John saw no sign of human rehab pioneers anywhere. But in the center of the basin, several armored vehicles were maneuvering through a set of town-sized ruins and firing plasma bolts at each other. In the rain, his visual enhancement systems could not resolve the image clearly enough for him to make out their affiliation markings. Still, the vehicles on both sides seemed to be floating on boosted gravity drives, and they had the bulky, up-armored hulls typical of Banished combat rigs.

John had his computer send a directional indicator to Kelly, then asked, "What do you make of that?"

"The same thing you do. I have *no* idea."

"Guess."

"If I must." Kelly studied the scene, then finally said, "I noticed something similar earlier."

A directional indicator appeared on John's HUD, and he followed it to a small square of open ground on the near side of the basin. It appeared to be a reclaimed farmstead with a few dozen dismounted figures exchanging electrolaser fire or arcing bright incendiaries of plasma from behind the glass-block walls of several semi-intact buildings. The shapes were still too tiny to identify with certainty, but judging by the body types and the way they moved, they appeared to be primarily Jiralhanae and Kig-Yar—on both sides.

"I can think of only one explanation," Kelly said. "They must be fighting over the spoils."

"Of a rehab colony?" John asked. "The buildings are wrecked and the crops are ruined. What's left?"

"I didn't say it was a *good* explanation." Kelly paused, then said, "But I haven't seen any sign of humans on either side. So I think it's safe to assume the pioneers have fled."

"Or died?"

"Fled," Kelly said. "Those raiders don't appear organized enough to eradicate an entire colony. And rehab pioneers aren't soldiers. They wouldn't stick around to fight."

"Makes sense," John said. "And just as well. A big battle on Reach would have attracted Cortana's attention for sure."

"I wish you wouldn't do that."

"Sorry," John said. Worried about the unknown extent of Cortana's electronic surveillance capabilities, Kelly had developed an aversion to speaking the AI's name. Another thing John had to get used to. "But Reach is a dead system to her. There isn't a repeater station within a hundred kilometers of here."

"That we're *aware* of. Who knows what's hiding in orbit?"

"That's *not* a serious question," John said. "Right?"

"Even the *Infinity* isn't infallible," Kelly said.

The UNSC *Infinity* was now the primary base of resistance to Cortana and her forces, a five-and-a-half-kilometer supercarrier serving as the flagship of the handful of UNSC vessels that Cortana had not yet captured, destroyed, or decommissioned. Currently on-station in a horseshoe orbit designed to keep it within easy support-range of Reach, the *Infinity* was the United Nations Space Command's largest and most advanced vessel, utilizing technology reverse-engineered from Covenant and Forerunner sources.

It was, in short, humanity's last, best hope.

"You really think the signals deck would miss a slipchannel energizing?" John asked. "Or that Lasky wouldn't have countercomms jamming it in a second?"

"I *think* there's no sense taking unnecessary chances," Kelly said. " 'Speak the devil's name and he doth appear' and all that."

John cringed inwardly at the comparison. It couldn't be helped—he wanted to think of Cortana as broken rather than evil, but he understood Kelly's concern. The AI and those aligned with her were monitoring every communication net they could access, including the web of supraluminal links that bound interstellar civilization together. So in the wrong place under the wrong circumstances, speaking her name was literally asking for trouble—and TEAMCOM's encryption was no protection. Cortana was intimately familiar with Spartan cipher routines, and she might even have a universal key that would allow her AI followers to decrypt them in a nanosecond.

"Fair," John said. "The Banished here are surprise enough for one mission."

He called up a pre-glassing map of Reach, then had the computer scale it and superimpose the town of Tököl over the razed area in the center of the basin. As he had suspected, the map's terrain lines across the entire plain were a sharper version of what he saw on the wet glass below, with deeper ravines and more pronounced ridges. But the features were in the right places, and that allowed him to pinpoint his current location: in the mouth of Tárnoc Gorge, atop Tárnoc Falls overlooking the Arany Basin.

John hadn't recognized it thanks to the destruction from the Covenant bombardment, but everyone in Blue Team had been in the same canyon thirty-seven years earlier, during their childhood training. The entire class had been ordered to paint a set of food-dye horns on the flank of every goat in the Bull's Blood wine region without being seen. It had taken three nights, and Blue Team had spent the daylight hours hiding in the network of sandstone slot canyons that cut through the Ujeger Highlands. By the final night, there had been so many locals watching for them that they'd had to extract via a night climb down the Ujeger Cliffs.

But there would be no escaping down the cliffs today—not if they hoped to take the excavation machines to CASTLE Base and complete the mission.

John located the Highland Mountains cordillera on the map, then superimposed them on the ragged gray line of mountaintops rising beyond Arany Basin. Only the tips of the highest peaks were visible, but they had the proper topography and locations.

Except for Menachite Mountain, of course. Where it should have been, there was only a massive empty notch left by the removal of its bulk. The map showed a distance of just over eleven hundred kilometers to the notch, following a route that crossed straight through the southern third of the rehab colony's cluster of farmsteads.

With no satellite net to provide geo-spatial navigation and a heavy cloud cover that prevented celestial navigation, Blue Team would need to rely on dead reckoning and landmark triangulation to find its way to the remnants of CASTLE Base. John fixed a destination point on the notch where Menachite Mountain used to be, then transferred all of the navigation data to his team. Each Spartan's onboard computer would use stride counting and inertial guidance to monitor Blue Team's position. Between the four of them—even fighting and detouring—they ought to be able to consolidate the data and arrive within a hundred meters of the target.

Fred was the first to comment. "At thirty kilometers an hour—"

"We can average forty across the glass," Mukai interrupted. "Perhaps even fifty, if we're not crossing ridges and ravines."

"Fine, let's say forty," Fred said. "That's still a twenty-eight-hour trip. Minimum."

"Twenty-eight is no problem for me," Chapov said. "And if *Special Leader* needs sleep, he can ride in the LHD bucket."

Kelly turned to John and showed her palm, her fingers splayed and curled toward the sky in a silent expression of disbelief. "*Special Leader* isn't going to be the problem, Two."

"Well, it won't be me," Chapov said.

"Nope," Fred said. "It'll be twenty-eight hours of driving across open terrain with enemy fighters overhead."

"Yeah. We need a way to fix that." John looked back toward the duel between the Banished armor. He didn't see much sign of air support, but there were plenty of infantry-sized spikes and bolts flying back and forth between rubble piles—and infantry rarely marched into battle anymore. There were several up-armored Shadow troop carriers parked out of harm's way on either side of what was once the town, along with at least two Phantoms. "And I might know how."

John outlined his strategy. After a long discussion and a couple of improvements, the Spartans began to climb the canyon wall.

It was treacherous because of the rain, and the rim was out of range of the grappleshots mounted on their GEN3 Mjolnir forearms. So they spent a lot of precious time punching and kicking hand- and footholds into the glassed cliffs. Upon reaching the top, John, Kelly, and Linda were planning to continue over Szeged Ridge into Hosszú Völgy—the valley where they had crash-landed the night before—and down into Arany Basin. Assuming they made it that far, they would infiltrate one of the Banished skirmish zones and commandeer a form of transport capable of carrying the excavation machines.

Meanwhile, Fred would return to Tárnoc Gorge to oversee *Special* Crew's defensive preparations and help them fight off attacks until transport arrived. It would be a risky assignment because it would take the rest of Blue Team most of the day just to reach the closest skirmish zone. But if they could hold out until John, Kelly, and Linda returned with suitable transport, it would be a simple matter of taking advantage of the Banished's disarray to relieve *Special* Crew, then proceed to CASTLE Base under enemy colors.

Kelly was the first climber to reach the rim of the gorge—the fastest, as usual. Rather than going over the top, she chipped a firing platform into the glass there and turned around so she could watch the sky behind them. John arrived next, cresting the wall about fifty meters down-canyon from Kelly. He also kicked a platform, creating a shelf that was only about a third of a meter deep before his boots broke through into an airspace. When he began to smash away the lechatelierite in front of his knees and chest, he quickly discovered that the airspace continued all the way up to the canyon rim, creating a fist-wide gap that also extended downward as far as he could see.

The gap, he realized, was due to differential cooling during the plasma bombardment. As the molten silica had run down the canyon wall, it had cooled faster on the outside than on the inside, and that had created a slumping effect leaving the lechatelierite thinner at the top than at the bottom—and opened a gap between the glass and the vertical face it was covering. The void was too small to serve as a fighting position, but it was a reminder to keep an eye out for similar openings as they crossed Arany Basin—both to avoid falling into one, and in case they needed someplace to take cover quickly.

Linda and Fred flashed status green almost simultaneously, indicating they had reached the rim and stomped out their firing platforms. John couldn't see them because they were around a bend, respectively a hundred and a hundred and fifty meters up-canyon. But he knew that as Blue Two, Fred would be watching the western quadrant of sky, above Arany Basin. As Blue Four, Linda would watch the eastern quadrant. Kelly was south, and John was north.

John started with a horizontal scan, sweeping his eyes back and forth in short movements, searching the terrain directly in front of him to locate any craft flying nap-of-the-ground first, then working his way up the slope of the Ujeger Highlands and twenty degrees into the rainy sky to look for higher-flying craft. When he didn't see any, he switched to vertical scanning, running his gaze up and down from the near terrain to the crest of the highlands, then from the crest to twenty degrees above.

He repeated the entire process three times, scanning for five full minutes, before he finally saw a single dark speck crossing a handspan above the horizon. About a quarter the size of a raindrop, it was noticeable only because its horizontal motion made it stand out against the falling rain, and John was fairly certain he would have missed it entirely had it been hovering or diving toward him. He watched it long enough to establish that it was traveling across his frame of reference and not growing any larger. Then, just as it reached the edge of his observation arc, it reversed course and crossed the sky in the opposite direction.

"I have one bogey at twenty degrees high," he reported over TEAMCOM. "It's in a holding pattern between nine o'clock and two."

"Nothing," Fred said.

"I have two bogeys at twenty degrees high," Kelly said. "They're circling between six o'clock and nine."

"Two bogeys at twenty degrees high," Linda said. "Both are circling beyond Szeged Ridge, between six o'clock and three."

"And nothing to the west?" John asked. "Confirm, Blue Two?"

"Confirmed," Fred said. "Whatever's happening in Arany Basin, they're steering clear. Maybe we should've done the cliff descent after all."

"That's a two-hundred-meter down-climb in the rain, with no cover and a hostile flight in a three-sided box block," Kelly remarked. "I'd rather not."

"Those bogeys are quite high for a blocking patrol," Van Houte said. Along with the rest of *Special* Crew, he was still back at the feeder ravine that Chapov had mentioned, excavating the bunker they would be holding until John and the others returned with transport. "It doesn't sound as though they're eager to attack."

"They don't have to be eager," John said. "They just have to be willing."

"I mean, it doesn't sound like they're prepared," Van Houte said. "How far away are they?"

John had his computer run an angle-of-measure assessment, but the fighter craft was so distant it was impossible to determine whether the speck was a Banshee or a Seraph. He chose the reading for Banshees, since it would result in a smaller distance and a more conservative estimate.

"At least a hundred kilometers," John said.

"I estimate the same," Kelly added. "Though it could be two hundred, if I'm looking at Seraphs instead of Banshees."

"I *am* looking at Seraphs," Linda said. As the sniper, she carried superior optics and targeting software. "And I have them at two hundred and two kilometers."

"Ah," said Van Houte. "That explains it."

"Not to me," John said.

"It's a surveillance flight," Van Houte said. "They're just trying to keep track of us."

"You're sure?"

"How is a patrol that far away going to attack anything?" Van Houte asked. "By the time they arrive, you'll have gone to ground and disappeared."

"Or set up an anti-aircraft battery and be waiting," Chapov said. "The major is right. Surveillance is the only thing they can be doing."

"Why the devil would they surveil us?" Kelly asked. "The excavation machines aren't difficult to track. They must know where we are."

"Yeah," Fred said. "And they also know that the last time they tried to strafe us, they lost three-quarters of a squadron."

"Then you think they're waiting for ground troops?" Linda asked. "That makes sense."

"Glad you think so." Fred's voice grew eager. "And if they're going to bring a bunch of Phantoms or Spirits up *here*—"

"Then we're not going down *there*," John finished. "We just need to be sure we're set up in the right place when they arrive."

"What if they bring a larger force than we can handle?" Chapov asked.

"This is no time for jokes," Fred said. "We're trying to plan."

"I'm serious."

"No you aren't," Mukai said. "Spartans, remember?"

John began to consider the plan modifications they would have to make in order to capture their transport in the middle of a ground assault. Eliminating the bulk of the enemy force in a single quick strike would be the key to success.

"The canyon will be a good place for a rockslide ambush," John said. "Start drilling fifty meters from the bunker in both directions—"

"I see what you're planning, Master Chief," Mukai said. "Suck the buggers in and bury them."

"Affirmative," John said. "Blue Two will help you with the charges. The rest of Blue Team will capture transport and disable pursuit."

Blue Team's status LEDs winked green inside John's HUD, but Van Houte was not as quick to agree.

"I see only one problem with that plan," he said. "Those Seraphs aren't waiting on ground troops."

John scowled inside his helmet. "They're waiting on something."

"Yes, us," Van Houte said. "If they were waiting on ground troops, they would be ready to keep us pinned down. Instead, they're up high, trying not to be noticed."

The major had a point. It would take the Seraphs five minutes or so to travel the 202 kilometers from their patrol stations to Tárnoc Gorge, and that could be an eternity in combat.

"So what are they doing?" John asked. He *hated* not understanding his enemy's objective. It was a good way to blow a mission. "Waiting until we move to a less defensible position?"

"You expect me to know what a bunch of aliens are thinking?" Van Houte asked. "I'm just telling you what makes sense from an air commander's perspective."

John knew the principles of tactical air support, but he was accustomed to thinking about them from an infantryman's point of view. For the most part, that came down to calling in strikes when air superiority was friendly, and hiding from them when it was hostile.

"Understood," John replied. "So we see what happens. If they try to pin us down, we break for cover and set up to capture transport here. If they let us go, we continue with the original plan and capture transport in the basin. Thoughts?"

No one spoke for a moment; then Fred finally said, "I think it's the best we can do."

After everyone acknowledged their agreement, John and Kelly clambered over the rim and started across the glassy slope toward Szeged Ridge. Linda would catch up as soon as it grew apparent that her SRS99-S5 antimateriel sniper rifle would not be needed to discourage a strafing run, while Fred would descend into the canyon to help with defensive preparations. That was all according to the original plan, and John could not see a better alternative.

But it bothered him that the enemy might be hanging back simply to surveil them. That suggested not only a disciplined force, but one more interested in determining what Blue Team was doing on Reach than in destroying it—and that kind of restraint was more of a Keeper trait than Banished. So John didn't know how to explain the Banished emblem on the downed Seraph. And he didn't understand why whoever was tracking them wouldn't make the logical assumption—that the Spartans had come to help the rehab pioneers defend themselves.

Linda's voice came over TEAMCOM. "Inbound. Two Seraphs, coming from the north. Four minutes out."

"Anything from the other directions?" John asked.

"Negative."

"So, not a serious attack," Fred said.

"Perhaps they're just trying to get a look," Van Houte said. "From a two-hundred-kilometer standoff, they would have a hard time telling power armor from a vehicle. All they would see is an object indication—and quite an indistinct one, at that."

"Assuming what kind of sensors?" Kelly asked.

"Assuming *any* kind," Van Houte said. "This isn't space, and Seraphs don't have quantum imaging equipment. They're stuck with the same electromagnetic spectrum we are."

John contemplated the ramifications. While the ancient Forerunners had used quantum-scanning sensor systems that even Dr. Halsey claimed not to understand, it was one of the handful of technologies that the Covenant had never been able to properly replicate. The enemy had been limited to exploiting the electromagnetic spectrum in the same two ways the UNSC had: by actively emitting signals and searching for the reflections, or by passively searching for the radiation that all solid bodies emitted merely by existing in a state above absolute zero.

Both methods had limitations, especially when attempting to track and identify objects against a planetary surface. An active signal would bounce off the surrounding terrain, creating background clutter that had to be separated from the intended target. A passive system would need to distinguish between ambient radiation and that coming from the target. In either system, accuracy decreased and computational requirements increased exponentially with distance.

Meaning: at two hundred kilometers against a background of glassed ground, those Seraphs would be doing well to resolve a pinpoint blur. It would be even harder to identify the sensor signature of a target they rarely encountered. If those alien pilots wanted to see what was moving down here, they would need to come in a lot closer.

And that would give John a chance to test their resolve.

Szeged Ridge was only a kilometer away. He and Kelly could cover that distance in ninety seconds and dig in, then arrange a nice little surprise as the Seraphs completed their strafing run.

Assuming they made a strafing run.

"Blue Two, stay up on the rim and help Blue Four make sure they know looking isn't going to be free. Blue Three, we'll dig in behind the ridge. Everyone else, work on getting those excavation machines out of there."

"Then you don't believe they're waiting on ground troops anymore?" Chapov asked.

"That's what I'm trying to find out." John put an edge into his voice. "Are you going to follow orders, Lieutenant, or will I need to explain myself every time I issue a command under movement?"

"Sorry, Master Chief," Chapov said. "I just wanted clarification."

"Clarification is fine. When it's needed."

John and Kelly sprinted across the hillside. The slope was tipped just enough to make running awkward, so they traversed at a slight uphill angle until they crossed a gully and began to ascend straight up to the ridge crest.

"Our two bandits are diving," Linda said.

"Strafing run?" John asked.

"Too early to know."

Linda's status LED flashed green. John checked his HUD and found a time-to-engagement of two minutes, with the crest of the ridge just two hundred meters away. They wouldn't have much time to dig—just smash a trough in the lechatelierite and lie flat.

Kelly was already crossing the ridge. She pulled the shotgun off her magmount and fired five rounds into the top, spraying bits of glass everywhere to create a scrape. Such hastily-made fighting positions were barely deep enough to lie in.

"That one's yours," she said, reloading and moving away.

John angled toward the first scrape and saw that in three spots, the shotgun rounds had penetrated through into a shallow cavity where the molten lechatelierite had flowed down the slope before cooling. It wasn't much, maybe another fifty centimeters, but he'd take what he could get.

He checked his HUD—seventy-five seconds before the Seraphs arrived—then stomped around the edges of the shotgun holes to enlarge his fighting pit.

The cracks of four sniper rounds rolled across the slope, then Linda spoke over TEAMCOM. "Strafing run!"

John kicked away a few last nubs, then grabbed his MA40 off its magmount and dropped to his knees inside the fighting pit. The depth was good, just shallow enough that he could peer over the ridge crest and see the fork-tailed disks of two Seraphs diving toward Tárnoc Gorge. Their plasma cannons were spitting bright red dashes into the rim, and the shields on the lead craft were flickering with overload static.

Linda's SRS99-S5 cracked four more times. The lead's shields went down and a lower cannon began to bleed flames. Two breaths later, a pair of Fred's rockets streaked up from the rim and hit it in the belly. The first strike bounced off and detonated in front of the trailing craft, temporarily hiding it from view. The second punched a hole through the armor and set the lead craft wobbling.

Both Seraphs pulled their noses up and crossed over the canyon toward Szeged Ridge. Linda fired again, and the leader went higher, trailing sparks and smoke as he fled the battle. The other Seraph continued to approach John and Kelly, its plasma cannons stitching twin lines toward their positions. With little more than their rifle muzzles and the crowns of their helmets showing above the ridge crest, it seemed impossible the alien pilot could actually see them—but his targeting was dead-on.

Linda fired again, but if she did any damage, John couldn't see it. He aimed his MA40 into the sky just ahead of the ridge and opened fire, trying to put a wall of bullets into the air for the Seraph to fly into. He heard Kelly's assault rifle rattling and knew she was doing the same.

The Seraph ceased its attack and veered away—though not quickly enough to avoid flying through the gunfire the two Spartans had put up. Its shields flickered and went down, and John saw their rounds sparking against its hull armor.

"Did you see that?" Kelly asked over TEAMCOM.

"Hard to miss." John watched the Seraph climb away over the valley behind them. "He stopped his attack."

"They always do," Fred said, also speaking over TEAMCOM. "Eventually."

"No, this one stopped prematurely," Kelly said. "As soon as we opened fire and revealed our positions, he shut down his cannons."

"Why would he do that?" Fred asked.

"Because he had no wish to hit his targets," Linda said. "You're the one who said this wasn't a serious attack."

"As in 'not trying hard,'" Fred said. "I didn't mean they were faking it."

"But they *did*." John watched the Seraph that had just overflown them climb over the highlands on the opposite side of the valley; it showed no signs of wheeling around for another attack run. "That pilot was more afraid of killing us than of being killed himself."

"Then the Banished can't be trying to stop us," Van Houte said. "They must be hoping to follow us."

"To where?" Fred asked. "CASTLE Base?"

"To wherever we're going," Van Houte said. "It could be that they're only trying to learn what we're doing here on Reach. Or perhaps they hope we'll lead them to a cache of valuable weapons. Who can say?"

"What if they already know why we're here?" asked Chapov.

John didn't bother asking how a Spartan mission could have been compromised. Such a thing was highly unlikely . . . but it had happened before, and there were plenty of ways for it to occur: spies, signal intercepts, eavesdropping devices, intelligence analysis, even lucky guesses. So the possibility, however remote, had to be considered.

"Do you know something we don't?" John returned to scanning the northern quarter of the sky for incoming fighter craft, as the other members of Blue Team would be doing for their own sectors.

"No. I don't have proof, if that's what you're asking."

"But?"

"But . . . this feels like more than a coincidence," Chapov replied. "A flight of Seraphs waiting at SWORD Base when we're inserting overhead—*maybe* that's just a bad break. But flights positioned all over Eposz, ideally located to intercept us?"

"Their positioning wasn't *quite* perfect," Van Houte said. "But it was damn unlucky for us."

"Right. And instead of destroying us, they only force us down," Chapov continued. "Then, after we somehow manage to slip away from the crash site intact, they pretend to strafe us, just so they can take a closer look at what we're doing. I have to say that they're sure acting like they might be worried about destroying something we're carrying."

"Something like a pair of biometric gloves and lenses?" Kelly asked. "Is that what you're suggesting?"

"No," Chapov said. "That's what I'm afraid of."

"That's understandable," John said.

Blue Team was carrying two sets of biometric spoofers, a primary and a backup. Both contained the data they would need to access Dr. Halsey's secret vault in CASTLE Base. Without them, any attempt to bypass the security system would trigger a self-destruct protocol—and incinerate the very assets Blue Team had been sent to retrieve.

And without those critical assets, Cortana might be forever beyond Dr. Halsey's reach.

"It's probably not a realistic fear, though," John continued. "A lot of people aboard *Infinity* were aware of our mission, sure. But the only ones who know about the biometric spoofers are Dr. Halsey, Captain Lasky, and us."

"That we *know* of," Fred said. "Dr. Halsey has played both sides before."

"Only when she had no other choice," Kelly said. "And only because Colonel Ackerson and Admiral Parangosky gave her good reason to."

"Doesn't change the fact that she did it," Fred said. "Or that she could be doing it again."

"Wait," Chapov said. "Those rumors about her working with Covenant splinter groups—they're true?"

"It's all rather complicated," Kelly said. "Don't trouble yourself over it."

"Don't trouble myself?" Chapov echoed. "A known traitor sends us to this godforsaken place to—"

"Dr. Halsey is *not* a traitor," John said. "She's just someone who doesn't let the rules get in her way."

Chapov said nothing for a moment, then asked, "Is Commander Palmer even *aware* of this mission?"

"You don't report to Commander Palmer," John said. He didn't know the answer to Chapov's question, because he had no idea whether Captain Lasky would have felt it necessary to inform Sarah

Palmer, the commander of most Spartan units aboard the *Infinity*. "You report to Major Van Houte, and he works for Dr. Halsey."

"So you see my point?" Chapov said. "We're down here with our asses hanging out and no idea why. We need to assume the worst."

"Dr. Halsey did *not* set us up," John said.

"But someone else might have," Fred said. "The kid has a point. Those Seraphs are eyeing us for a reason."

John ran his gaze around the horizon, watching the distant specks as they watched him right back. He could think of a dozen reasons a flight of Seraphs might want to keep tabs on his unit—but only a couple that involved faking an attack.

Either the Banished wanted something that Blue Team had—such as their biometric spoofers—or they were looking for intelligence, trying to figure out where the Spartans and their companions were going.

Or maybe both reasons were true.

That didn't necessarily mean the Banished were trying to go to the same place as Blue Team or recover Dr. Halsey's assets. But it was a possibility they dared not ignore. Not with what was at stake here.

"Okay, *Special* Two—you win," John said. "We'll assume the worst."

"Really?"

"It's only smart," John said. "Blue Four, you're with us. Blue Two, you and *Special* Crew get those machines up here as quickly as you can. We'll head down Hosszú Völgy into the basin."

Fred's status LED winked green, but Lieutenant Chapov was not as quick to see what John was planning.

"I don't understand," he said. "You're just going to let them follow us?"

"Of course," John said. "That's how you lead someone into an ambush."

# CHAPTER FIVE

The terrain ahead was almost too good to be true. An old irrigation canal left the natural river channel on an outside bend and cut across the glass barrens as straight as a laser beam. The canal was deep enough to hide John and the other Spartans from aerial surveillance, so they would be able to advance unseen most of the way to the enemy-occupied farmstead roughly five kilometers distant. That compound was ringed by a shield barrier and lookout towers, so Blue Team would probably be exposed to at least one observation platform during the final part of their approach. But a simple diversion would buy Fred a couple of seconds to rush forward and fire a rocket into the gunner's platform.

John's only hesitation was that he still wasn't quite sure who the enemy *was* (Banished? Keepers?), so it was hard to predict how the defenders were likely to respond to a shock attack. Still, he had to do something to get rid of the surveillance flight from Tárnoc Gorge. No matter how many Seraphs Blue Team ambushed—having already destroyed two and damaged five since entering Arany Basin—there always seemed to be another ready to take its place. Clearly, this was one fight that wouldn't be won through attrition.

"This target looks like a go," John said over TEAMCOM. "Thoughts?"

He waited in silence, giving the rest of Blue Team time to weigh their responses, scanning meanwhile for signs of an imminent flyover. The Seraphs were still trying to disguise their intentions, swooping in two or three times an hour for halfhearted strafing runs that fooled no one. Either the enemy was trying to protect the biometric spoofers in Blue Team's possession, or they wanted to know the Spartans' ultimate destination.

And it really didn't matter which.

The biometric spoofers' only function was to open Dr. Halsey's secret vault. So if the enemy wanted them, they were probably after the same assets Blue Team was—meaning they probably knew more about those assets than John did. All he had been told was to retrieve a lockbox with an Avar saber imprinted on the lid and the three cryobins secured in the cryogenic portion of the vault—and not to ask questions about any of it. Just follow orders.

And normally, that would have been fine with him. Dr. Halsey had a well-earned reputation for not letting conventional morality impede her research, and cryobins were used to store biological material. As long as Blue Team didn't know what the bins contained, they couldn't be accused of violating military law by obeying an order to recover them.

The lockbox was even more of a mystery. The Avar saber on its lid was the emblem of SWORD Base, and John had heard whispers about an operation that Noble Team had conducted there during the fall of Reach, when Covenant forces were overwhelming the planet. There could be a connection, but given what had been going on at the time, it was hard to see how a lockbox from SWORD Base could have ended up in Dr. Halsey's laboratory—or what it might have to do with stopping Cortana now.

Which would also be fine, if there was no possibility the Banished were after the same assets. Had John known more about the contents of the four containers, he would be in a better position to assess the enemy's intentions.

But none of that changed the problem at hand. To complete the mission, Blue Team had to get its two excavation machines to CASTLE Base. And to do that, they needed to steal a ride and slip away from the surveillance flight harassing them.

After a few moments, Fred spoke over TEAMCOM. "I'm good with go." He was now fifty meters downriver from John, also lying on his belly and peering over the top of the glassy bank. "We've seen seven Phantoms and three Spirits come or go in the last twenty minutes. This has to be a Banished transport base."

"And you think our friends in the Seraphs will just let us steal a transport and fly off?" Kelly asked. She was fifty meters upriver on John's other flank. "I have my doubts."

"I have no doubts," Linda said. She was a hundred meters beyond Kelly, at a bend where *Special* Crew was waiting on the silver-blue riverbed with the excavation machines. "The Unggoy in the lookout towers are not watching the approaches to their base. They're watching the Seraphs circle."

"And that means *what*, exactly?" John asked. He couldn't even *see* the Unggoy lookouts from that distance, but he also didn't have Linda's sniper optics—if she said they were watching the sky, then that was the situation. "That these two groups are hostile to each other?"

"That they're at least suspicious of each other," Linda said. "If they were in communication, the sentries would not be fixated on the sky. They would be watching for *us* on the ground."

"So, it's a perfect setup to lose our tail," Fred said. "I say we slip into the base and blow up a bunch of stuff. The hostiles on the ground will blame the ones in the air and launch a fighter strike. We steal a Phantom, fetch the excavation equipment and *Special* Crew, and disappear in the chaos."

"Why do your plans so often call for blowing stuff up?" Kelly asked.

"I like to make a statement." Fred paused, then grew more serious. "Why? Do you see a problem with that approach?"

"Only that we're reading an awful lot into the skyward gazes of a few Unggoy," Kelly said. "What if they're just bored?"

"No, it's more than that," John said. "Remember those skirmishes we saw in the distance from Tárnoc Gorge? There's a lot of hostile activity down here that we don't understand."

"Which is why we need to be careful about our assumptions," Kelly said.

"True," Linda said. "But those Seraphs haven't strafed us since we moved to within twenty kilometers of this base. They're standing off, and there's a reason."

"And whatever that reason is, we need to take advantage of it," John said. "We don't have enough ammunition to keep shooting at Seraphs every time they fake a strafing run."

"But if we don't fire on them, they'll know we see through their ruse," Linda said. "And then their targeting will improve."

"So we need to change the situation," Fred said. "We either do this now, or we call for support."

Kelly sighed into her helmet comm. With the Banished already on alert, calling for support would be the first move in a battle that escalated into something big enough to draw Cortana's attention. And once that happened, the probability of completing Operation: WOLFE would plummet—as would their chances of returning to the *Infinity* at all. The last time they had drawn Cortana's attention, she had nearly sealed them in a Forerunner cryptum for ten thousand years.

"I see your point," Kelly said. "It *does* seem that boldness is the order of the day."

"Then we're a go," John said. He wasn't taking votes, but every Spartan on Blue Team was an ultra-elite soldier with more than three decades of combat experience. He would have been a fool not to so-licit their input before making the final call. "We'll use Fred's plan."

John outlined how they would execute it; then everyone except Linda—who would remain on overwatch until the rest of Blue Team was in position—slid down the glassy riverbank. The drop to the bed was only fifteen meters—even before the Covenant plasma bombard-ment, the Lapos River had been a flat, braided flow that filled its chan-nel only a few weeks each spring.

Now the river was a smooth-walled viaduct about seventy meters wide, its bottom blanketed by pools of dirty water that drained at ir-regular intervals through cracks and holes in the lechatelierite. Oc-casionally the riverbed was transparent enough to see a subterranean river flowing a couple of meters below the surface. In places, the glass was pitted with craters and holes left over from the Banished invasion. Twice the load-haul-dump machine had dropped a wheel through a thin spot where a mangler spike or high-caliber bullet had caused a shard to flake off underneath.

John stepped over to the drilling jumbo, where Major Van Houte was standing on the operator's platform next to Lieutenant Chapov. "All clear on *Special* Crew's part of the plan?"

"It would be hard not to be," Van Houte said. "Continue down the riverbed well past the canal, and make sure the Seraphs catch a few glimpses of us. We want them to think the mission is continuing right along."

"Right," John said. "But make the glimpses quick and partial. We don't want the hostiles to start wondering why there aren't any Spar-tans with you."

"One question." Chapov waited for John to nod, then asked, "Should we stop before we reach twenty kilometers from the other side of the base? The surveillance flight is bound to make a reconnais-sance run as soon as we clear the standoff distance."

"No need to worry about that, Lieutenant," Mukai said. "This will be over long before we hit twenty kilometers."

"But what if it isn't?" Chapov continued to look at John. "We should have a contingency plan, no?"

"Seems like you just made one," John said. He wasn't sure whether the kid was still trying to impress him, or just didn't understand how fast Spartans moved. He looked back to Van Houte. "Once the fighting starts, take cover someplace with a good view upriver. We'll be coming down the channel, skimming the riverbed and trying not to draw attention. Signal when you see us."

"Affirmative," Van Houte said. "We'll dig in on the south bank."

Kelly and John assumed their usual positions at the head of the column, with the excavation machines in the middle and Fred bringing up the rear. Out here in the glass flats, the only cover was the depth of the river channel, so they were careful to stay fifty meters apart—close enough to support each other, but separated to avoid losing two elements to a single piece of ordnance.

It took only a few minutes to reach the next bend. The glass on the riverbed and both walls grew pocked and soot-starred with the evidence of a recent battle—presumably the one that had driven the rehab pioneers from their farmstead. Mukai and Chapov had to slow down, snaking the excavation machines around the holes and thin spots left by heavy-weapon strikes. Through the larger breaches, John could hear the chortle of flowing water—though he dared not step close enough to peer into the river. The lechatelierite would be too thin at the edges to support a four-hundred-and-fifty-kilogram Spartan.

The battle damage grew heavier as the irrigation canal came into view, and John realized the residents of the farmstead had probably fled their homes and escaped down the canal before being caught and attacked in the river channel.

Kelly went to the south riverbank, where she would not be visible to the circling Seraphs, and took a knee thirty meters from the canal entrance. As John moved up to join her, he noticed a meter-wide water collection trough ahead, cutting across the width of the riverbed and feeding into the canal.

"Are you thinking what I'm thinking?" Kelly asked.

"That the rehab pioneers couldn't have been irrigating much with that canal? What's left of the river is flowing *under* the glass."

"That too. But actually, I was wondering where all the bodies have gone."

John took a more careful look. All signs of blood and gore had been washed away some time ago. But the water-collection trough was filled with shell casings and mangler spikes—no doubt washed into it during major rainfalls, when the water flow would be too heavy to drain away through the crevices in the riverbed. And there appeared to be as much impact-chipping in the lechatelierite as plasma-boring, which meant the rehab pioneers had been equipped with plenty of firearms, and they had fought back hard.

"Maybe the Banished didn't win," John said.

"Then how come the Banished are the ones in the farmstead?" Kelly replied. "It's more likely that some of the pioneers survived and came back for their dead."

"So where are they now?" John pondered the question for only an instant before adding, "Forget I asked. It's not part of the mission."

The drilling jumbo rounded the bend and continued toward the irrigation canal. John and Kelly crossed the riverbed and fell into line between it and the load-haul-dump machine, about twenty-five meters from each. A cluster of blue efflux-points was visible just above the river's south bank, moving back and forth in the distance, so John knew the enemy surveillance flight was theoretically able to see Blue Team and *Special* Crew. At that range, it would be tough for their sensor systems to separate target signatures from the background scatter. But there would be certain anomalies in all the noise that any reasonably experienced pilot would be able to interpret anyway.

In order to keep the pilots confused about those anomalies, John and Kelly approached the irrigation canal moving back and forth to the load-haul-dump machine a few times, taking cover behind it for a moment or two. Fred came up and did the same, and John called Linda forward with a trio of comm clicks.

As they passed the entrance, Kelly and Fred slipped into the canal, where they would be hidden from surveillance. John continued to jog along between the LHD and the drilling jumbo, still moving about to confuse watchers, until the river turned west and he could hide from the Seraphs in the sensor shadow along the south bank.

*Special* Crew continued west with the excavation machines, swerving back and forth across the river channel more than John had expected. The erratic course was not deliberate. The riverbed ahead grew even more battle-damaged, forcing *Special* Crew to weave around a lot of weak spots in the lechatelierite.

The machines were half a kilometer distant before Linda reported that she had resumed overwatch. John waited until the drilling jumbo headed back toward the north bank, where it would draw the attention of the surveillance flight away from him. Then he sprinted back to the bend and jumped a meter-high weir into the irrigation canal.

No more than twenty meters wide, the canal was about five meters deeper than the riverbed, with high vertical walls coated in cloudy, silver-colored lechatelierite. As with the river channel behind him, the glass underfoot was pocked with impact divots and blast craters. Most of the damage was confined to the bottom of the canal and the lower few meters of the walls, so it seemed likely that the battle had started here with an air attack.

After a quarter kilometer, the canal's depth abruptly went from twenty meters to just four as it transitioned from storage reservoir to conveyance trench. The original dams and pumping equipment had been destroyed during the Covenant plasma bombardment, but a new draw pipe rose along the far wall to an overturned pump house—no doubt installed by rehab pioneers.

John climbed from the reservoir into the trench and found Fred and Kelly crouching along the canal's south side. Linda was higher, standing watch on a recessed platform that she had chopped into the lechatelierite about halfway up the wall. She had engaged her experimental GEN3 passive camouflage package, and her Mjolnir had assumed a fractal, ash-silver pattern that made her difficult to distinguish from the surrounding glass. It worked like a charm.

John checked the line of sight to the farmstead. Even when he jumped to get a better angle, he couldn't see any of the lookout towers ringing it—which meant that the Unggoy sentries couldn't see him either. That would change as they drew closer to the compound, but with the canal providing cover from any aerial surveillance that wasn't directly overhead, they would have at least three kilometers of easy movement. Maybe four.

"Blue Three, take point," John said over TEAMCOM. "Blue Two, you next—and keep that SPNKr handy."

"Count on it," Fred said.

Kelly set off at a fast run, and by the time Fred had taken the rocket launcher off its magmount, she was fifty meters up the canal. John pulled his assault rifle off its magmount and knelt to wait. The canal bed was oddly humped in the middle, sloping ever-so-gently down toward the outside edges, but the glass here was smooth and unblemished by combat damage.

"*Special* Leader," John asked, "what's your situation?"

"Slow," Van Houte replied. "The pioneers must have put up a hell of a fight here. The riverbed is really bad—and it's chewed up as far as I can see."

"It's taking a lot of time to avoid the hazards," Chapov added. "There are impact craters everywhere."

"You're in no hurry," John said. "Just sell it to those Seraphs. Don't make it obvious you're trying to be seen."

He started up the canal after Fred. When they'd traveled nearly three kilometers, Kelly's fist came up, signaling for a stop.

John assumed she'd spotted one of the lookout towers and was slowing down to engage her own camouflage. Like Linda, they all carried the experimental GEN3 passive packages on their Mjolnir armor, but the new technology still had a few bugs. For one thing, it didn't work well if you were running. The nanofilament adaptive coating adjusted continuously to the surrounding terrain, so the faster one moved, the greater the blurring effect. At a full sprint, the result could be more eye-catching than no camouflage at all.

But instead, Kelly tipped her chin back and spun in a slow circle, searching for something in the sky. John did the same and saw nothing but gray clouds.

"Blue Three," he said over TEAMCOM. "Report."

"I saw shadows on the glass." Kelly's helmet rocked forward again. "There must be something in the sky, but I don't see anything."

"Neither do I," John said. "Blue Four?"

"Nothing," Linda said. "And the sun is wrong anyway—unless Blue Three saw the shadows *behind* her?"

"Negative," Kelly said. "They were in front of me. Three dark shapes coming toward me."

"Shapes?" Fred asked. "What kind of shapes?"

"*Shapes,*" Kelly said. "Upright Ts, getting shorter as they approached. There was a round blob on top of each of the crossbars."

John had seen the shadows of enough passing aircraft to recognize the description. But there was usually *some* sort of sound accompanying a big craft passing overhead, and with Reach's sun hidden behind a thick mantle of clouds, shadows would be faint—not dark, as Kelly had described.

"No idea," John said. "Could have been some kind of surveillance bird dropping out of the clouds to light us up for images."

"Did *you* see any lights overhead?" Fred asked. "Bright enough to cast a shadow?"

"Negative," John said.

"Me neither," Fred said. "And I didn't see anything on the glass."

"I didn't imagine them," Kelly said.

"That's not what I meant," Fred said. "I was looking at the sky, so I *wouldn't* have seen them on the glass."

"Same here." John scanned the ground between them but saw no movement—only the same ash-colored glass he'd been walking on for the last three kilometers. It might have been a little lighter in the center of the canal, but it certainly didn't resemble anything Kelly had described. "And there's nothing like that now."

"Some kind of manifestation?" Fred asked. "That's the best I've got."

"How about unknown contact," John replied. "Let's drop the advance to a fast march. Blue Two, you're sky watch forward. I'll watch behind us. Blue Three, keep your eyes open for those lookout towers. Blue Four, keep us posted on that Seraph flight. If we're misreading the situation, they might be the first clue."

He did not call for engaging the experimental camouflage. If there *were* surveillance craft hiding in the clouds overhead, they would be using nonoptical sensor systems, and the passive camouflage packages were worse than ineffective. The adaptive coating increased the Mjolnir's thermal output a full 2 percent when it was active, and in certain configurations there could even be a spike in the suit's magnetic signature.

Everyone acknowledged their orders with green status flashes, and Kelly led the way up the canal again.

They'd traveled only half a kilometer when Major Van Houte spoke over TEAMCOM. "Blue Leader, we have a problem. We're stuck."

"How stuck?" John asked.

"We dropped the drilling jumbo's right side through the riverbed. It's resting on its chassis."

"The whole stretch is thin glass," Chapov added. "I was trying to squeeze between a crash crater and a pair of rocket holes. Then Chief Mukai dropped the LHD's rear wheels through a spall line trying to pull me out."

In other words, *not my fault.* The kid would be a decent operative if he weren't so damn insecure.

"Acknowledged," John said. "Take cover where you can keep an eye on the equipment. We'll extract it when we have our Phantom."

"Extracting it isn't the issue," Mukai said. "We can dig ourselves out with the plasma drill and the muck bucket. It won't be fast, but it's doable."

"Then what's the problem?"

"We've been in the Banished surveillance cone for ten minutes," Van Houte said. "And no Spartans have come to pull us out."

John understood at once. By now the Seraph pilots realized that their surveillance targets had stopped advancing. They might even guess that it was because the excavation machines were stuck. When the machines remained motionless, the pilots would start to wonder why the Spartans weren't pulling them out—and send someone to investigate.

"Blue Four, relocate to assist," John said. "I'll assume overwatch. Two and Three, continue toward the compound at normal march. I'll catch up when Blue Four resumes overwatch."

Three status LEDs winked green. John engaged his own passive camouflage package and used his gauntlets to smash a recessed observation platform into the canal wall. By the time he had finished and pulled himself into position, Fred and Kelly had traveled another six hundred meters up the canal.

From his new perspective, he could see their tiny figures—barely distinguishable to the unaided eye—continuing their advance. He could also see that there was a distinctly pale ribbon running up the canal for its entire length. At first he thought it was just the light reflecting off the little hump in the center of the canal bed. But when he polarized his faceplate, the difference remained. Whatever he was looking at, it was more than a reflection.

And those shadows Kelly had seen earlier—maybe they had been *under* the glass.

"Blue Two and Three, take a good look down through the lechatelierite." As John spoke, he was focusing his own attention southward again—as overwatch, it was his job to keep tabs on the surveillance flight. "See if there's something different about the center of the canal."

"Other than that little rise in the glass?" Fred asked.

"Affirmative," John said. "It looks paler from up here."

"You're wondering if those shadows I saw were under the glass?" Kelly asked.

"It's worth investigating," John said. "Cut a hole, if you have to."

Their status LEDs flashed green, leaving John to focus on the distant efflux points circling above the far horizon. He counted three of them, two traveling eastward and one westward. But he remembered five earlier—and his onboard computer brought up an image-capture that confirmed it.

John went to double magnification and swept the enhancement window back and forth across the sky, searching for the missing craft, and found nothing. It was possible that the two missing Seraphs had returned to their base for service, considering how long they'd been operating in atmosphere and a gravity well.

But it seemed far likelier they were trying to sneak in for a closer look.

"*Special* Crew," John said. "Incoming Seraphs probable. Blue Four, two of them, likely hugging terrain. Make it look like a trap."

Barely registering Linda's acknowledgment, he deactivated his magnification and began to sweep his gaze over the glass barrens across the river. Finally he saw a pair of round-topped specks zipping over the plain far toward his left, so low he could see the blue glow of their efflux tails reflecting off the lechatelierite.

"Blue Four, I have them swinging around to approach you from upriver. ETA canal entrance . . ." John paused, waiting for his onboard computer to measure vectors and distances. ". . . thirty-two seconds."

"Acknowledged," Linda said. "I have a good spot to set up."

"*Special* Crew—"

"We're on it," Chapov said. "We'll set up behind the LHD. They'll never know what hit them."

"Negative," John said. "Take a position *up* the river. We're trying to convince them this is a trap, remember?"

"On it, Blue Leader," Mukai said. "Move it, Lieutenant. I see a good spot."

John continued to watch as the approaching Seraphs grew from barely visible specks into minuscule twin-tailed disks and tightened their turn, lining up one behind the other for a pass along the river channel. He noted the ETA on his HUD over TEAMCOM.

"Twelve seconds."

When the Seraphs were directly over the channel, John took a second to make a quick all-around scan. The rest of the surveillance flight remained above the southern horizon, three tiny efflux points drifting back and forth in their prior holding pattern. He saw no other craft coming in from any direction, but that didn't mean there weren't any. An entire wing of Banished Seraphs could be approaching from beyond visual range, or a full squadron of Banshees skimming the glass just a few kilometers away, and without a friendly tactical satellite overhead, John would never know it.

Blue Team had intentionally inserted without a TacSat array in orbit. A bunch of new satellites broadcasting encrypted data across central Eposz would have been noticed by the rehab pioneers, who would probably have gone searching for answers they could not be permitted to have. Nobody had anticipated any trouble reaching Menachite Mountain, so John had decided to avoid the unnecessary risk and do without the satellite surveillance. Now that circumstances had changed, it was a decision he intended to reverse the next time the orbit of *Special Delivery*'s mothership *Bucephalus* brought it back through a comm window.

He saw the two Seraphs fly past the canal entrance, barely two meters above the riverbanks, showing their bellies as they followed the southward bend of the channel.

"Passing the irrigation canal now."

By the time John finished speaking, the craft were at the bottom of the bend and banking toward the west. The ETA in John's HUD counted down to 5 . . . 4 . . . then Linda's S5 sniper rifle boomed four times, and the lead Seraph pulled up and barrel-rolled away, its belly trailing long tails of flame.

The ETA reached 2 . . . and the rattle of distant small-arms fire rose from the river channel. The second Seraph went into a steep climb and banked away toward the south. John saw no sign it had suffered any damage, so it was hard to say whether it had seen the trapped excavation machines or if the *Special Delivery* crew had successfully convinced the enemy they were nothing but ambush bait. But another Seraph had been damaged, and that would buy everyone on the ground some reaction time.

"Well done," John said. "Blue Four, get those machines free and moving again. Blue Two and Three, move on the base *now*—but be ready for an overfly. The base commander is going to want to know what's happening at the river."

"On it," Fred answered. "And that pale stripe you wanted us to investigate?"

"Go ahead."

"We punched a hole through the glass. There's a tunnel running under the canal."

"How big?"

"Big. Maybe two meters in diameter. Looks like there was an underground water pipe before the canal got glassed. It's still there, except the top half melted away."

"Don't forget the tracks," Kelly said. "They seem important."

"Just getting to that," Fred said. "There are a lot of boot prints down there too."

"Human boot prints?" asked John.

"Affirmative," Fred replied. "Pointing in both directions."

"How recently?"

"Some are old, but a few sets look fresh. Someone's been traveling this thing pretty regularly."

"To do what?" John asked. "Hide?"

"Hiding would make sense," Kelly said. "But so would sappers."

She meant combat engineers who demolished fortifications, laid minefields, bridged rivers, and so on. The reference dated back to Earth's Middle Ages, when *sapeurs* breached castle walls by tunneling beneath them. John thought of the shadows Kelly had seen and realized the situation was about to get even more complicated.

He didn't like complicated. That got soldiers killed.

"Do we try to make contact?" Kelly asked. "If they're pioneers prepping an attack on the base, they might be of use."

"At the least, they could tell us what's going on around here," Fred said.

John scanned the sky, keeping an eye on the Seraphs to the south, but also alert for anything new—especially a scouting patrol from the base. It was clear that both Kelly and Fred wanted to contact the rehab pioneers—assuming they were the ones using the tunnel—and so did he. But John wasn't sure he trusted his team members' motivation. Or his own.

This was Reach, their home. It had been taken from them by the Covenant, and now the rehab pioneers were fighting to take it back. Everyone on Blue Team was going to sympathize with that and want to support them against the Banished. But helping the pioneers meant putting Blue Team's mission at risk, which meant jeopardizing humanity's fate, thanks to the machinations of Cortana. That wasn't something John was prepared to do—no matter how much he wanted to see Reach restored to what it once was.

"Negative on making contact," he finally said. "We stick to the original plan."

Three LEDs flashed green, and the mission continued. John watched in silence as the Seraph that Linda had damaged circled east. With the trail from its smoking engine it looked like an arrow, pointing straight toward the former site of the Szarvas Regeneration and Salvage Facility. No doubt some of the underground yards had survived the plasma bombardment, and now one of the Banished factions was using it as an operations base.

The second Seraph was on its way to rejoin the surveillance flight. So it looked like the formation was going to keep its distance, which suggested that neither of the pilots had gotten a good look at the stuck excavation machines. They were back to the status quo. But eventually, Blue Team needed to lose that tail.

"The spy birds are standing off again," John reported over TEAM-COM. "Status excavation machines?"

"The jumbo is free." Linda's voice sounded strained. "I'm working on the LHD now."

"Good," John said. "When you're finished, give me a GO flash and return to overwatch."

"Affirmative." Linda's status LED flashed green. "Moving into position now."

"And I thought Kelly was fast," John said. "*Special* Leader?"

"Go ahead."

"The next time you move out of the surveillance window, dig in and wait for us to capture transport." John hopped down from his watch platform. "I doubt those spy birds will be back for a second look anytime soon."

"I think not," Van Houte said. "Good hunting."

John disengaged his passive camouflage, then sprinted down the canal after Fred and Kelly. Barely visible, they were at least a kilometer ahead, with another kilometer to go before they reached the compound.

He glanced down. The lechatelierite underfoot was too ash-clouded to see down into the tunnel. But in the distance, he could easily identify the ribbon of pale glass that marked its location. It ran down the center of the canal, all the way to the red-glowing shield barrier the Banished had erected around the farmstead.

John increased magnification to 200 percent, and saw a swarm of cruciform specks rising from behind the shield barrier, swirling counterclockwise and forming squadrons.

.At least five squadrons, maybe more.

"We have a Banshee formation assembling over the base," John said over TEAMCOM. "Strength fifty, minimum."

"They're going after that surveillance flight that's been after us," Fred said. "Just as planned—excellent."

"They're early," Kelly said. "That wasn't supposed to happen until *after* we breached the shield barrier."

"This is better," Fred said. "Now they won't even know it's us attacking. They'll think it came from the bunch behind the surveillance flight."

"Then you will love this," Linda said. "We have Seraph squadrons inbound from three directions."

"You see?" Fred asked. "They never saw *us* coming."

"I hope you're right about that," Van Houte said. "We're just preparing to dig in. How long before you arrive with a Phantom?"

"The north tower's already in view," Fred said. "And nobody is looking our way. We'll be in SPNKr range in ten seconds."

John's HUD showed thirteen hundred meters to the shield barrier. He was still eight or nine hundred meters behind Fred and Kelly.

"Blue Two and Three, close to two hundred meters," John ordered. "Engage camouflage and hold for my command. I'm sixty seconds behind you."

Fred's and Kelly's status LEDs winked green. John checked his weapons as he ran, then looked for the two of them along the base of the canal's south wall, where they would have a good view of their target and be shielded from other lookouts. Once the rockets destroyed the north tower, the barrier shield would fall between it and the south tower, giving John a straight shot into the heart of the base. He had his onboard computer start a countdown.

Fifty-five seconds.

The Banshee swarm continued to swirl upward, growing larger and dividing itself into ten-member squadrons. So far, it looked like ten squadrons—a hundred craft in all—but he didn't see any more rising out of the base. They couldn't *all* be preparing to scout the river, but some of them would certainly be headed for it. One of the surveillance Seraphs had flown off with a smoking engine, and the base commander would need to find out why.

"Be ready, *Special* Crew," John said. "The Banshee wing is almost ready to leave, strength now one hundred."

"Confirm one *hundred*?" Chapov requested.

"Affirmative," John said. "I'd say you have half a minute to dig in."

"Not enough time," Chapov replied. "We're just starting to cut—"

"We'll handle it," Mukai said. "Just get us a Phantom, Master Chief. We'll take care of the rest."

"We will?" Chapov paused, then asked, "Where do you want me?"

Finally. The kid was learning.

John checked his HUD. Forty-five seconds. He would have Fred launch both SPNKr rockets at the fifteen-second mark, when John was still more than two hundred meters from the barrier. That way, he would be crossing the perimeter while the enemy was still reeling from the blast, with Fred and Kelly just a couple of seconds behind him. Together they would locate the Phantoms and commandeer one while the base defenders were still trying to figure out what hit them.

The first three squadrons of Banshees departed, the thrust pods beneath their stubby canards spewing white contrails as they swung westward to intercept one of the Seraph squadrons Linda had reported. The Banshees would be badly outmatched, even given the Seraphs' sluggish in-atmosphere performance, but their superior numbers and maneuverability would even the odds. John would not have cared to bet on the winner—even if he *had* understood why the two groups were fighting in the first place.

"Two squadrons coming your way, *Special*," John reported as the craft streamed over the barrier shield, heading south toward the river. "Probably headed for the surveillance flight."

No acknowledgment.

"*Special?*"

"I think they can't hear you," Linda said. "They went under the glass."

"What do you mean?"

"Under the riverbed," Linda said. "They drove out toward a rocket hole. When I looked back, there was an even bigger hole, and the LHD was disappearing under the glass."

"Under its own power?"

"It sure wasn't floating," Fred said. "Are we still doing this?"

Twenty-five seconds.

"Be patient," John said. "I have a plan."

Three more squadrons of Banshees crossed the shield barrier and headed east, one to either side of the irrigation canal—and one squadron flying straight over it.

John threw himself flat at the base of the south wall. "Take cover!"

"We're doing our best . . ." Kelly paused as the Banshees screamed overhead, then added, "But it's rather barren in here."

John rolled onto his back and looked down the canal, watching the Banshee squadrons continue eastward, passing over the river bend, then beginning to climb and meet a line of Seraphs coming down out of the Ujeger Highlands.

"I think we're okay," he said.

"Think again," Fred said. "Incoming!"

John rolled back toward the wall, coming up on his knees and facing the enemy base once more—where ten red-and-silver Banshees were streaming over the shield barrier and dropping into the irrigation canal, their plasma cannons already flashing.

Fred launched both SPNKr barrels, sending an M19 rocket into the nose of each of the two lead craft, filling the end of the canal with twin fireballs. Kelly threw herself into an evasive roll, tumbling across the glass and firing her MA40 as she went. Canards and cowlings rained down, twisted and trailing flame, and two more Banshees pulled up streaming smoke.

John opened fire, putting triple-taps straight through into the cockpits of two more Banshees and sending them crashing down on the glass.

But that left four intact, and they streaked down the canal toward the Spartans. Banshee plasma cannons were deadly, and there were four craft. Their bolts chewed the glass and filled the air with clouds of flying slivers.

Fred dropped the SPNKr and reached for his assault rifle, while Kelly ejected an empty magazine and grabbed another.

No time.

Fred's energy shield flickered and vanished as a flurry of bolts pinned him against the wall. Kelly's own shield went down as the cannons rolled her across the canal floor into the opposite wall. John emptied his magazine in response, sending two craft corkscrewing toward the canal walls behind him, then glimpsed the red streak of an approaching plasma bolt.

He twisted aside and heard a spray of glass shards clatter off his armor as the bolt impacted the wall next to him. He ejected the empty magazine from his MA40 and went for another one, automatically noting that the status LEDs in his HUD were flashing amber for both Kelly and Fred. Wounded, not dead—not yet.

John inserted the fresh magazine as the last two Banshees were on the deck coming straight at him, the one in front hugging the wall and just fifty meters away. The second was thirty meters behind it and staggered toward the center of the canal, ready to swing in behind the leader and finish the job.

John rolled toward the center of the canal, opening fire on the trailing Banshee as the leader flashed past to his left. He saw the second Banshee's cannons flash red and a crooked line of his own bullet holes punching through its cowling; then his energy shields flared and his Mjolnir armor knelled. Something punched through his left cuisse, and his quadriceps suddenly knotted into the worst charley horse of his life—a burning, aching, grating spasm that made him taste copper and want to vomit.

Stay focused.

The target Banshee dropped its nose and skidded toward John along the canal floor, its cannons now dark, its canards still spewing contrails, ribbons of under-hull peeling away.

John tried to jump up and nearly passed out as his leg erupted in pain, the ache traveling through his hip clear into his chest. The Banshee was almost on him, rocking on its belly, the nose dropping toward his helmet.

He rolled left, his entire leg burning as the Mjolnir's injectors pumped biofoam into the open wound. At the last possible moment, he let go of his rifle and delivered a powerful right hook that lifted the Banshee's front end and sent the craft spinning away across Reach's glass.

He then sat up and spun around to open fire on the lead craft, putting so many rounds into its left propulsion pod that the canard simply disintegrated. The Banshee flipped over and smashed down on its cowling, then spun across the canal bed until it crashed into the north wall, exploding and vanishing beneath a cascade of broken lechatelierite.

Fred's status LED now showed steady amber—wounded, but stable. Kelly's was still flashing.

"Blue Three, status?"

"Itooka boltinmy damn chest." Kelly's voice came thin and fast, a sign that her suit's emergency medical routine was using stimulants to keep her alert. "My HUDreadoutsays the right axillary vein is nicked. But myarmpit's packed full of biofoam and bleedinghasstopped. So . . . functional."

John spun onto his right knee, then got his foot under him and stood. His left leg exploded in pain as he put weight on it, but the onboard computer had already made an input adjustment, and the Mjolnir's force-multiplying circuits compensated flawlessly. He'd felt worse pain before, more times than he could count.

It still hurt like hell.

He spotted Fred and Kelly two hundred meters away. Kelly was sprawled in the center of the canal, not visibly moving. John went to four-times magnification and saw that her head was raised and her left hand was squeezing a plasma packet into her thoracic bioport. Fred was lying against the wall, half-buried beneath a mountainous heap of broken lechatelierite.

"Blue Two?"

"I was out for a while. My HUD says concussion." Fred paused, then added, "I'm seeing two readouts, so it might be right."

As Fred spoke, ten more Banshees started to stream over the shield barrier toward them.

"Heads up!" John said. "More Banshees!"

Fred began to push chunks of lechatelierite aside as Linda spoke over TEAMCOM: "On my way."

"Negative," John replied. Even if she managed to avoid being spotted, she would never arrive in time to do more than pick up the pieces. "Stay with *Special* Crew—and stay on mission. Blue Two and Three, I'll draw them off."

John began to dodge down the canal away from them. It felt like his Mjolnir was moving his leg, rather than vice versa, and every step was agony. But he was still able to run, and far faster than any normal man could. "Play dead and take them from behind."

"Permission to execute a better plan?" Kelly asked. Before John could reply, her shotgun began to boom. "Blue Two, I need SPNKr support *now*."

John swung around to find Kelly holding her shotgun in her left hand, firing strike rounds into the canal floor—directly above the tunnel.

"Permission granted," John said, as though he had a choice. He changed magazines and started toward her at a sprint, ignoring his screaming leg. He was still two hundred meters away. "Laying suppression fire overhead."

John raised his MA40 high and began to fire one-handed over

Kelly's head. Firing toward a team member was done only when the alternative was allowing the enemy to kill them; after the damage Blue Team had already taken, that seemed like a real possibility.

But the ten pilots lining up to attack now had just seen three Spartans take out an entire squadron with nothing more than a rocket launcher and a couple of assault rifles—and that *had* to be weighing on their minds. When they saw the muzzle flashes from John's weapon, they might not pull up and veer away—but he would make them flinch, and that might buy Kelly another second to open a hole.

John saw his rounds sparking off the lead Banshee's nose; then it wobbled and laid cannon fire to Kelly's right. Now only a hundred and fifty meters away, he dropped his aim, preparing to fire at the Banshee behind it—as a rocket streaked out of the glass heap where Fred had been buried.

The Banshee pulled up, and Fred's rocket hit the one behind it.

Fred fired again at the next craft in line, then switched the SPNKr for his MA40 and raced for Kelly's position. At the same time, the Banshee that had escaped his first rocket dropped its nose and barreled toward him.

John emptied his magazine into its port-side cowling and saw it corkscrew over Fred's head into the wall. Just a hundred meters from Kelly, he ejected the magazine and exchanged it for a fresh one.

"Fire in the hole!" Kelly warned.

She dropped a grenade into the basin she'd created with her shotgun, then stepped back. The next Banshee dropped to the deck, coming in behind her where it would be shielded from John's attack. The one following it stayed high, diving straight at her. Bolts flew from both craft, one passing over the spot where she'd just been standing, the other raising a wall of flying glass chips that was advancing directly toward her.

Fred took out the high one—a mistake that betrayed the severity of his concussion.

"Blue Three!" John yelled. "Down!"

He aimed for Kelly's helmet and opened fire on full auto the instant she started to move. By the time he actually had a clear view of his target, there was a void in the Banshee's cowling the size of his fist. It stopped firing and started to drop—then Kelly's grenade detonated beneath it, flipping it backward into the air.

John was fifty meters away, close enough to see the hole the blast had created. Another pair of Banshees was lining up for attack runs, this time side by side. It was a formation that left barely two meters between them and maybe a meter and a half between their outer canards and the canal walls.

Fred took a knee halfway to the hole and started to exchange his assault rifle for the SPNKr.

"Blue Two, negative!" John ordered. Fred was in bad shape if he was preparing to fire from a static position in the open. "Into the hole, *now*!"

Fred looked toward John. "But I have the—"

"That's an order, Spartan!"

The Banshees launched a devastating salvo, this time adding their fuel rod cannons to the attack. Calibrated for air-to-air combat rather than strafing, most of the rods overflew John's head. But the first two impacted a dozen meters from Fred and Kelly, raising fountains of chipped glass directly in line with them.

"You too, Kelly!" John shouted. "Go!"

Kelly was already scrambling toward the makeshift bunker, pushing with her feet and pulling with her good arm, so John fired on the Banshee behind Fred. It held its course, the next rod impacting so close to Fred that glass shards blasted his flank—and finally seemed to jar him back to his senses. He launched himself forward, flying five meters across the canal before he disappeared headfirst into the hole.

Kelly pulled herself in behind him, and then it was just John, still fifteen meters from safety and facing two Banshees.

They both veered toward him, one going low and the other high, green rods and red bolts flying from their cannons in unbroken streams.

John emptied his magazine at the lower one, pouring his rounds directly down the cannon muzzle until a blanket of fire mushroomed beneath it and sent the craft tumbling away. The second Banshee pulled up to avoid the collision—and John found himself suddenly facing three more craft, racing down the canal and stacked atop each other in staircase formation. Their cannons began to flash, and a curtain of flying glass advanced down the canal toward him.

"Heads up!"

John flung his MA40 forward and watched it spin across the glass into the pit. He didn't trust his wounded leg to launch him the last ten meters to safety, so he sprinted forward until his faceplate darkened against flashes of striking plasma bolts and the glass vanished beneath him and he dropped into the tunnel, his energy shield still sizzling from shrapnel impact.

His sabatons had barely touched sand before a pair of rifle butts hit him violently behind the knees, filling him with pain and dropping him to the ground. His faceplate returned to normal, and he saw Fred kneeling in the sand a few meters in front of him.

A gun muzzle clanked against the back of his helmet as a gruff human voice announced: "Hands still. One move, and we'll see how that helmet of yours stands up to a Desert Eagle."

"A Desert Eagle?" Fred asked. "Shouldn't that hand-cannon be in a museum somewhere?"

"It *was*," the voice said. A hammer cocked behind John's helmet. "But it still fires. Wanna see?"

"Why don't we just trust you on that?" John asked.

They were in the bottom of a tunnel two meters in diameter, directly beneath the hole Kelly had blasted to save them. The bottom half was an old water pipe, its bed filled with wet sand churned up by the passage of hundreds of boots. The top half resembled the vault of a lechatelierite cave, complete with glassy curtains and stalactites.

Kelly sat in the sand three meters away, leaning against the wall with a fist-sized puncture on the right side of her breastplate. Fred was kneeling in the middle of the tunnel in front of her, his fingers laced behind his helmet, wobbling ever so slightly.

They were surrounded by a dozen weary-looking humans, all armed with various models of MA5 assault rifles and wearing odd pieces of UNSC battle armor—likely salvaged from the subterranean remnants of a nearby armory. John's motion tracker showed another fifteen people packed into the tunnel behind him, no doubt equipped in a similar fashion and just as haggard-looking.

Reach's rehab pioneers, in the flesh.

The gruff-voiced man tapped John's helmet with the pistol barrel. "Hey. You've got some explaining to do, fella."

"You first."

This resulted in another barrel tap. "Try again, Tin Man. You bunch just blew an operation we've been setting up for weeks, so nobody's in the mood for no smart-mouthed cyborgs."

"Cyborgs?" Fred huffed. His voice came over TEAMCOM, soft enough that it would be audible to only John and Kelly inside their helmets. "How long do we have to put up with this? My head hurts, my knees are sore, and we need to get out of here before those Banshees land."

"Understood," John replied on TEAMCOM. "But let's give them a chance. The last thing we need is to make enemies of the Reach militia."

"How do you know they're militia?" Fred asked.

Clearly his concussion wasn't getting any better.

The barrel tapped John's helmet again. "Hello? I'm not asking a third time."

"Good," John said. "Because I can't answer. You don't have clearance."

"Clearance, huh." John watched in his motion tracker as the man stepped back, no doubt leveling his hand cannon at the back of John's helmet. "Okay, smart guy. If that's the way you want it."

"It isn't," John said. This fellow was on his last chance. "And you don't either. Really."

"Sure I do."

John spoke over TEAMCOM. "On my mark." He gathered himself to spring. "I'll take—"

"Hold on," Fred said. He seemed to be staring down the tunnel over John's shoulder, though it was hard to be sure behind the tinted faceplate. "Something's happening."

Any other time, John would have accepted Fred's recommendation without a second thought. But . . . *concussion.*

"You're sure?"

"It's okay," Kelly said, still over TEAMCOM. "Something *has* changed. Everyone is looking back down the tunnel."

"But where's his weapon pointed?" John asked.

"Well, still at your head," Kelly said. "But his finger is no longer on the trigger."

"Let me know if that changes."

Kelly and Fred flashed green status LEDs, and in John's motion tracker, he saw the crowd behind him parting to let someone come forward.

"Stand down." The voice came from within the tunnel behind John. It was brassy and female, and the militia members in front of him immediately stood a little taller when it spoke. "What's happening here, Major? I'm hearing reports of Banshees coming down in the canal."

John heard the hammer on the Desert Eagle click as it was returned to the uncocked position.

"That's right," the man—apparently the major—said. "And it's these cyborgs' doing."

"What are you talking about?" The woman stepped past the major, then placed herself between the three Spartans and carefully looked them all over. Long-faced and dark-haired, she appeared to be in her fifties, with baggy eyes and a face lined by worry. She wore a gray battle uniform with the name BOLDISAR above her breast pocket and Reavian eagles on her collar tabs. The rank of colonel. "Istvan, there's no such thing."

"Sure there is," Istvan said. "You're looking at three of them right now, ma'am."

The woman shook her head. "These aren't cyborgs. They're Spartans."

"*Spartans?!* Really?" Still holding the massive pistol in one hand, a burly, balding man with three days of gray beard stubble and the surname ERDEI above his breast pocket stepped around in front of John, then leaned in close to inspect John's faceplate. "Damn. You'd think they would be better at this."

# CHAPTER SIX

John wasn't limping—much—as he made his way down the old irrigation tunnel, but it was largely willpower and reactive circuits that kept him going. The biofoam wasn't performing as promised in terms of killing pain—in fact, some of it had coagulated into little lumps that were rolling around in the wound—and when he tried to lift his knee too high, his quadriceps just balled up in a quivering knot.

Nevertheless, he *was* moving—not quite running—on a leg that was still attached to his hip, and that was a pretty decent outcome after being blasted by a Banshee's plasma cannon. But he needed to get somewhere and apply a catalytic debrider soon. And Kelly too. Plasma bolts produced a lot of charred tissue in and around the wound, and if that matter wasn't dissolved and removed, it would become the ideal growth medium for antibiotic-immune bacteria and flesh-eating fungi from a hundred different worlds.

At least Fred didn't have to worry about infection. His helmet hadn't actually been breached by plasma bolts, and its titanium-alloy shell was more than enough to protect him from the flash heat of any strike short of a capital ship's plasma lance. Still, there was a big crease in the armor over his parietal skull area. So far he wasn't complaining of nausea or headaches or dizziness, and didn't appear to be staggering or drowsy—but there was no denying that Fred was making mistakes and seemed a bit reckless. John needed to keep an eye on him.

The three Spartans had positioned themselves at the back of the tunneling company in order to protect the column from any pursuit by the Banished. But the rehab pioneers understood how difficult it would be to survive an underglass firefight in such cramped confines, so they were jogging along through the pearly light at a swift clip—fast enough that John was in agony keeping up.

And they were doing it while a demolitions crew rigged traps every fifty to sixty meters, pushing cubes of C10 malleable blasting agent into pipe seams and glass crevices, then rigging the charges with various kinds of automatically triggered detonators—motion, heat, and photo-optic. On any other world, John would have wondered how a bunch of civilians had come into possession of so much military explosive. But this was Reach. Before it was glassed, there had been military facilities all over the continent, and in almost every one of those facilities there had been an underground bunker full of ordnance.

After four kilometers, the irrigation tunnel ended in a weir gate, half-melted and caked in glass that had flowed down from above. John expected the pioneers to produce a hidden ladder and climb out through a secret hatch in the lechatelierite ceiling. Instead, they pulled a section of curved pipe away from the wall, revealing a man-sized tunnel that descended into the damp bedrock at a ten-degree slope. The column bunched into a cluster as the pioneers began to enter the side tunnel. The passage was small enough that they had to travel in single file, and the sandstone floor was too uneven and slick to continue jogging.

John and the other Spartans were waiting at the back of the

bottleneck, keeping watch up the irrigation tunnel, when they saw the blue-orange flash of detonating C10. The rumble of the explosion arrived six counts later, indicating the blast had been about two kilometers distant.

The pioneers began to pack into the side tunnel, creating a snarl that only grew worse when someone near the front tried to run and slipped on the wet stone.

"Nothing to worry about!" called Erdei. "Everyone slow down. We have plenty of time."

A second explosion rolled down the main tunnel, just three seconds after the last one.

Fifty meters in three seconds was far too fast for any of the Banished species to be moving on foot.

John looked back over his shoulder. "They're on Choppers."

"How do you know?" It was Erdei's superior who asked this, the dark-haired Colonel Boldisar. "And are you sure?"

"I'm sure, Colonel."

"It's Sasa," she corrected. "And how do you know this?"

A third rumble came down the tunnel. "They're coming too fast to be on foot," John said. "And Choppers are the only vehicles narrow enough to fit down here."

"Choppers are no problem." Erdei's voice remained calm. He pulled a datapad from his cargo pocket and began to enter commands. "Slow and steady, people. I have something special planned for our friends."

A fourth C10 blast sounded, but the rehab pioneers had stopped pushing and were giving those at the front of the column time to regain their feet. Despite his brusque manner, Erdei obviously had the confidence of his company.

By the time the fifth blast came, half the column had entered the side tunnel. John did a quick calculation via his onboard computer and confirmed that Erdei was right. The last pioneers would be a few hundred meters down the passage before the first Choppers reached the entrance. And after dozens of blasts, the Banished riding them would not be eager to dismount and squeeze into a two-meter-by-two-meter corridor to continue their dangerous pursuit.

For the next minute, John watched the explosions grow a little brighter and larger as the enemy drew nearer. By the time he could actually discern the tiny bell of the first approaching Chopper, the last six militia members were lined up in front of the side tunnel.

And that's when Fred's faceplate fixed on Erdei.

"Wait, are you . . ." He stepped to the major's side and peered down at the datapad's screen. "Are you *linking* the rest of the charges?"

"You bet," Erdei said. "And setting them to remote-trigger. I want those damn bastards to think we botched the rest of our sets—then, *bam!* Take 'em all out at once."

"You can't do that," Fred said.

"Well, it seems to me I *am* doing it." Erdei tapped the power icon on his datapad. "It's worked before."

"Thirty C10 charges will have the brisance of a quarter tub of octa."

"The what of *what?*"

"Shattering power and octanitrocubane?" Fred sounded incredulous. Maybe his concussion was making it difficult to remember that not everyone learned to calculate destructive capacity when they were twelve years old. "Didn't they teach you anything at demolitions school?"

"Nope." Erdei slipped his datapad back into its cargo pocket, then followed the last member of his company into the side tunnel. "The only demolitions training I've had was right here on Reach. And Rendor didn't waste time on that fancy stuff."

"The blast is too big!" Fred called after him.

"Good!" someone else—not Erdei—shouted back. "We need to get something out of this mess!"

Fred continued to yell down the tunnel. "But we're in a confined space! The overpressure will be . . ." He paused, no doubt while his onboard computer did some calculations, then finished, ". . . almost twenty pascals!"

Boldisar looked to John. "Is that bad?"

"It will be if that tunnel is very long," John said. "Twenty pascals is enough to knock down a house."

"Then we'd better move it," Boldisar said. "I hope you Spartans can squeeze through. Istvan didn't drive this tunnel with someone your size in mind."

"We can duck our heads, ma'am," John said. "Or even crawl, if it gets that tight. We're pretty fast."

John waved her into the tunnel ahead of his team, but she motioned Fred and Kelly to enter.

"Guests first," she said.

Rather than waste time arguing, John flashed a green status LED to both Spartans. But when Boldisar gestured for John to go in ahead of her too, he stopped.

"I'll bring up the rear," he said. "This armor will stand up to the shockwave a lot better than you will."

Boldisar nodded and started down the tunnel at a fast walk. She managed to stay close behind Fred and Kelly even when the passage grew dark and she had to shine a handlamp on the floor to see her footing. John could tell by the amount of light spilling past Kelly that Fred was not far ahead, but was completely hidden by her hunched form. John stooped far enough to avoid scraping his helmet on the rocky ceiling and allowed Boldisar to walk a few meters ahead of him, in case the C10 charges detonated and he was pancaked by the shockwave.

They had traveled about fifty meters when a muffled rumble came down the passage behind them, drawing a collective gasp from the company.

"Nothing to worry about," Erdei called. "They tried to disarm a charge and set off the tamper switch."

John tried to judge how close the detonation had been by the sound volume, but between being in a side tunnel and the curvature of the tunnel itself, all his onboard computer could come up with was a range of somewhere between fifteen hundred meters and just three hundred. Not much help.

Another explosion, this time drawing only a few nervous chuckles. Whatever John thought of Erdei—and it wasn't much, after the way he'd dismissed Fred's concern over linking the C10 charges—the man clearly knew how to keep his people focused. After a third explosion that startled no one, the Banished pursuers evidently stopped trying to disarm the "botched" traps, and the pioneers continued their descent with calm efficiency.

Boldisar slowed her pace, allowing Fred and Kelly to move ahead while she fell back to an easy conversation distance with John.

"I'd keep some space between us, ma'am." John banged his helmet on the passage ceiling, then said, "When the overpressure hits, I might not be able to keep my feet."

"I appreciate your concern, Master Chief." She looked back over her shoulder, squinting against the glare of John's helmet lamps. "You *are* the Master Chief, right? Just wanted to confirm."

"Affirmative," John said. His GEN3 Mjolnir had a trimmer appearance than the GEN1 armor he had used during the war, but it still had his service number stamped on the breastplate. "117."

Boldisar gave a small smile and looked forward again. "I'm glad they sent the best."

"There's a difference between being the best and the best-known," John said. "All of us are pretty capable."

"From what I hear, that's the understatement of the decade." Boldisar paused, then said, "I want to apologize for your reception."

"Our reception was fine, ma'am. No one was hurt."

"I'm talking about your *continuing* reception—Istvan ignoring the warning about the overpressure, and his company's frustration with your unexpected arrival. We've been prepping this operation for a month—and tonight was the night we were going to execute."

"I'm sorry about our timing, ma'am." There were only twenty people in Erdei's tunneling company, so it was hard to imagine what they were planning that could justify a month's worth of work. "But whatever you're trying to capture, there must be an easier way."

"Capture?" Boldisar gave a dispirited chuckle. "We weren't trying to capture *anything*, Master Chief. It was more of a subterfuge."

"You spent a month driving a tunnel to set up a trick?"

"It's a hell of a trick." As Boldisar spoke, a pearly radiance began to fill the passage ahead, silhouetting Kelly's form. "You didn't see what we had to leave stowed at the far end of the irrigation tunnel."

Suddenly Kelly no longer seemed to fill the cramped space ahead, and John saw that she had stepped out onto an expanse of sandy ground. Her helmet vanished behind the tunnel ceiling as she straightened to her full height; then she moved out of view, revealing the narrow shore of a small underglass river. Over Boldisar's shoulder, John could see about half of Erdei's company standing directly in front of the tunnel. They were at the river's edge, checking weapons and shouldering rucksacks, their faces glowing in the soft light pouring through the lechatelierite overhead.

Boldisar stepped out of the passage, then moved to one side and faced John as he emerged behind her. "I'm not sure what the proper term is, but—"

John didn't hear the C10 charges explode. He simply felt the shockwave slap his backplate, and in the next instant he was lying faceplate-down in the sand. He plowed maybe a meter forward before he stopped, his leg wound throbbing. But that was the extent of it. No damage alerts, no new wounds, no ringing ears. His hydrostatic gel layer didn't even pressurize.

The tunneling company was not so lucky. When John lifted his head, it was to find nine of them lying flat in the sand or in the water, bleeding from their ears or noses. Most were gasping for breath and clutching their torsos, but some were yelling and rocking back and forth in pain.

Kelly's voice came over TEAMCOM. "Blue Leader, status?"

"No worse than before."

John rose and looked back toward the passage. He was relieved to see Boldisar standing with the other half of Erdei's company, whose location to one side of the tunnel's mouth had spared them being blasted by the shockwave. Their mouths were gaping and their eyes were round in amazement.

In their midst stood Kelly and Fred, helmets tipped back as they studied the glass overhead. John followed their gaze: less than a meter overhead, the lechatelierite ceiling was webbed with running cracks, creeping outward in all directions.

He raised his arm and pointed downriver. "Tunneling company, move out!" Over TEAMCOM, he added, "Blue Team, collect the casualties."

A pair of status LEDs flashed green. Kelly sprang past him; Fred followed a breath behind, stooping to scoop up a wide-eyed, bloody-nosed Erdei as his first passenger.

"Told ya," Fred remarked.

"Blue Two—" A chunk of lechatelierite clanged off John's shoulder and landed in the sand at his feet. "Not now. Focus."

Fred continued past. "I'd like to think I can gloat and rescue at the same time, Master Chief."

He bent to gather up a dazed woman, then threw her over his shoulder and dodged through a cascade of falling lechatelierite to pick up another man. Kelly already had two casualties, one over her shoulder and another cradled in her good arm. John scooped up the last four, positioning two of them over his shoulders like flour sacks, and limped after his fellow Spartans. It was impossible to protect his passengers from all of the dropping glass chunks, but they were still alive and groaning when he finally cleared the danger zone and joined the rest of the company.

Kelly already had her passengers seated in the sand, their backs resting against a section of vertical riverbank. With the help of the uninjured pioneers, Fred unloaded his casualties next to hers, and John did the same next to Fred's. Most of them appeared stunned rather than seriously injured, though it might be a while before the ones with bloody ears were able to hear again—the overpressure had probably ruptured their eardrums.

John broke out his medical kit and offered a roll of packing gauze to Erdei, whose nose was still bleeding as if a tap had been opened. But the commander shoved his hand away.

"Don't you think I've got my own damn kit?" He staggered to his feet and began to zigzag down the shore, one hand pinching the bridge of his nose and the other fishing through his cargo pockets. "We wouldn't be in this mess if you tin-can commandos had the sense to duck out of sight when there are Banshees overhead!"

The rest of the tunneling company bustled into action, using two-man carries to load the other casualties and start after Erdei. They all avoided looking toward John as they departed, but there were still three injured left behind when only Boldisar and the Spartans remained.

Boldisar motioned to the casualties. "Would you mind?" She turned to follow the rest of the company. "I'd better fix this situation before it gets out of control."

"Affirmative, ma'am."

John nodded to Fred and Kelly, and the three of them gathered up the last, somewhat reluctant pioneers, then started down the shore after the rest of Erdei's company.

The woman cradled in John's arms was groaning and coughing up small amounts of blood, the sign of a condition soldiers called blast lung—pulmonary contusion, with burst alveoli and blood vessels. Given that she wasn't coughing up a lot of blood, he thought she would probably survive, provided the pioneers had some kind of medical facility not too far away.

Boldisar hurried to the front of the company and slipped Erdei's arm over her shoulders, then began an animated discussion. John was glad to see that the colonel understood the urgency. Unit morale was one of the most decisive factors in combat survivability, and when the Banished recovered and renewed their pursuit, Erdei's company was going to need every joule of spirit it could summon.

As long as Blue Team stayed near the edge of the chortling water, there was enough space to stand upright without banging their helmets on the glassy ceiling. They were in the same section of river John had traveled along before parting ways with *Special* Crew, and it looked even more battle-pocked from below than it had from the surface.

He found it kind of beautiful, all things considered. There were circles of luminosity floating in the spall basins beneath the bullet strikes, and beams of radiance descending through the shell holes. Clusters of brass casings gleamed beneath the water or lay half-buried in the sand, while wrecked weapons and shredded armor—both human and Banished—decorated the ground wherever the lechatelierite had been breached.

The company had traveled about a hundred meters when a long crash sounded behind them. John looked back to see chunks of glass still dropping out of the twenty-meter web of cracks that the shockwave had created in the ceiling.

"At least we know where our next pursuers will pick up our trail," Kelly said over TEAMCOM. "I hope these people have a better plan than '*run*.'"

"They'd better," John said. "You two keep an eye out behind us. I'll see what they have in mind."

A pair of status LEDs flashed green. John stepped into the shallow water at the river's edge and began to advance past the rest of the column. As he moved, he tried to raise Linda and *Special* Crew on TEAMCOM, but received no response. It suggested they were no longer traveling along the river channel, since TEAMCOM utilized a multiband amalgam designed to maximize both line-of-sight and bounce propagation. To not be receiving under the current conditions, there had to be something literally blocking the signal—which didn't seem at all unlikely, given John's location.

As he drew closer to the front of the column, he began to hear Boldisar haranguing Erdei. "Nobody comes to Reach for R&R—not anymore."

"Look, three Spartans aren't enough to liberate the planet," Erdei said. Boldisar had him more or less trapped, with his arm wrapped around her shoulders and her own arm supporting him around the waist. "That's all I'm saying."

"How do you know there are only three?" Boldisar demanded. "That's the *Master Chief* back there. He wouldn't be here if the UNSC wasn't planning *something*."

This won a few approving murmurs from nearby pioneers, before one of them noticed John approaching and whispered a warning to Boldisar. As he stepped out of the water onto the shore next to her, it was clear from the now-friendly greetings and nods he received that she had convinced the company the Spartans were there to help in their struggle against the Banished.

It wasn't true, of course. But it would have been unthinkable to contradict a commanding officer in front of her subordinates—especially under the current circumstances, where she was attempting to keep morale up under such peril. John would have to give her the truth later in private, when she would have time to consider how best to explain the mistake—and when it wouldn't lead to a collapse of unit cohesion.

Boldisar saw John and smiled. "We were just talking about you, Master Chief."

"I heard." John used his free hand to tap the side of his helmet. "Enhanced audio."

"Why am I not surprised?" Boldisar asked. "Is there something you need?"

"I'm sorry to trouble you," John said. "But there's a twenty-meter hole in the ceiling behind us. That's going to make it pretty easy for another Banished force to catch up."

"How soon?"

"Uncertain," John said. "The size of the canal blast will disorient them for at least half an hour—"

"Half an hour is plenty of time," Erdei said. "We'll be long gone."

John ignored him and continued to look to Boldisar. "That hole is big enough for more than Choppers, ma'am. They won't have any trouble reaching us."

"Yes, they will," she said. "Because you're going to close the door on them."

Boldisar pointed forward, to where the river bent south and traveled two kilometers under the battle-pocked glass before vanishing from sight as it bent west again.

At first John didn't understand what Boldisar was indicating; all he saw was a sandstone slope ascending to the ash-clouded glass overhead. But as he scanned, he spotted the entrance to a passage similar to the one they had taken out of the irrigation tunnel.

"That corridor cuts out a seven-kilometer oxbow in the river," Boldisar said. She glanced over her shoulder, then pointed at a woman being carried in one of the collapsible litters. "Tundé over there is carrying a kilogram of C10. You'll have to ask around for a detonator, but there should be plenty."

"Yes, ma'am," John said. "Also, after we're out of immediate danger, maybe we can talk."

"I'd like that," Boldisar said. "I have a lot of questions."

"Of course, ma'am. I'll tell you whatever I can."

Setting down the casualty he was carrying, John collected the C10 package from Tundé, but didn't bother asking around for a detonator. Fred always carried an ample supply of M356 universal-application C-class detonators—and besides, John couldn't rely on the ones Boldisar's people had, which might have deteriorated in the damp conditions to be expected in underground bunkers with no working ventilation.

John rejoined Kelly and Fred, and by the time he had convinced Fred that he was in no condition to set explosives with a concussion, the rehab pioneers were already squeezing through the shortcut passage.

With so many casualties, progress was slow. The litters had no trouble at all, but the two-man carries were another matter. Either the bearers had to shuffle through the tunnel sideways, or the injured had to dismount and advance under their own power.

By the time everyone had made it through the six-hundred-meter passage, the half hour that John had estimated it would take the Banished to renew pursuit was already past. As he pushed the explosive into the cracks and crevices that seemed most likely to collapse the tunnel, he could not help pausing to peer back down the shoreline, looking for the bell-shaped silhouette of the first approaching Chopper.

But it never appeared, and by the time he'd finished, Fred had returned to fetch the casualty John had been carrying and disappeared down the tunnel again. John set the timer for five minutes and limped through the cramped passage, hunched over almost double, and emerged well downriver, on an empty shoreline under a ceiling of gray unbroken lechatelierite.

Alone.

The water was flowing less than a meter away, and the sandy riverbank to his left was churned up by the tires of two small, four-wheeled vehicles—presumably the excavation machines that Linda and *Special* Crew had taken underglass to avoid air attacks.

To John's right, the tire tracks had been destroyed by dozens of boot trails leading fifty meters north into a freshly cut tunnel entrance the size of a Mongoose ultralight all-terrain utility vehicle. There, the river veered west again, but the sand along its shore was smooth and unbroken. It didn't take a lot of imagination to guess that Linda and *Special* Crew had spotted one of the tunneling crew's passages and enlarged the portal enough for their excavation machines to pass through.

John activated TEAMCOM again. "Blue Four, status?"

Kelly appeared in the entrance to the passage. "We've already tried. No contact." She waved John forward. "Come along, will you? They're not waiting on anyone, and it would be easy to get lost in this place."

John hustled down the shore and stepped into a dimly lit warren of underglass passages, where Kelly was watching a pioneer demolitions technician pack C10 into sandstone wall crevices. There were no casualties anywhere and no sign of Fred or anyone else. But a trail of boot prints led fifteen meters up the main tunnel into a small, manmade side-passage.

Beyond there, the tire tracks grew apparent again, continuing up the main tunnel to a Y intersection barely visible in the dim light ahead. Kelly saw where John was looking and spoke over TEAMCOM to avoid being overheard by the demolitions tech.

"They claim the left branch ends in a sinkhole a kilometer away, and the right branch leads to a slew of dead ends, except for one connection that circles around to join the route we will be taking."

"Well done," he replied. "Did you mention the excavation machines?"

"Negative. I thought you might want to handle that yourself." She gestured toward the demolitions tech. "And I don't think they've guessed. That's why they're rigging this."

"Who do they *think* is making tire tracks?"

"They seem to be assuming that the Banished have recovered some of their vehicles," Kelly said. "They're terrified their underglass network has been exposed."

"Network?"

"That's what they say," Kelly said. "It sounds sizable."

Fred's voice chimed in over TEAMCOM. "And it might be safer to travel under the glass than on top of it at this point. Maybe we should conscript the demolitions tech to guide us. I can be back there in two—"

"Negative." A distant rumble sounded as John's charge sealed the shortcut passage that he had left a few minutes earlier. "Stand down and don't talk to anyone. Your judgment might not be the best right now."

"Acknowledged."

"That should be *affirmative*, Blue Two."

"What if they ask questions?"

"You might try saying you'll think about it," Kelly said. "They'll understand the delay."

"Just don't upset anyone," John said. "We need intelligence, and they have it."

"Understood," Fred said. "And . . . affirmative."

The demolitions technician finished her work, set a motion-sensitive trigger, and led the way into the side passage. The tech had done a decent enough job that there was a chance Linda and *Special Crew* would miss the trap if they came back this way, so John lingered at the entrance long enough to scuff a half-arrow onto the wall, pointing toward the traps. That way, Linda would know to look for trouble ahead.

After twenty meters, the side passage opened into a large irrigation tunnel, similar to the one in which they had met Erdei and his company. But the pipe that formed the tunnel bottom was even larger in diameter—big enough to hold what appeared to be a flatbed farm wagon. As John rose to his full height, he saw that the wagon was hitched to a hydrogen-powered field tractor—and that two similar rigs sat in line ahead of it.

The casualties had been loaded onto the first two wagons, and Fred was sitting on the third. Colonel Boldisar stood next to the driverless tractor, waiting for John and Kelly.

"No need to walk for a while." She motioned them aboard the wagon. "We can take the Juh Mező aqueduct most of the way to Base Gödöllő. The militia has a facility there where we can attend to your injuries."

"Thank you, ma'am," John said. "We'd appreciate anything you can do for us, and anything you can provide in the way of intelligence on the Banished dispositions."

"Of course, Master Chief," Boldisar said. "Whatever you need, we'll be happy to provide. We certainly don't expect the Spartans to do all the work on their own."

"Good thing," Fred said over TEAMCOM.

John flicked two fingers, ordering silence. "About that, ma'am." He took a quick glance around to make certain none of her people were within earshot, then said, "I need to tell you something. I'm afraid we're not here on the mission you assumed."

The color drained from Boldisar's face. She pulled her lips in, biting them, and looked away. "How do you know what I assume?"

"I heard what you told Major Erdei about me being here," John said. "About me *not* being here unless the UNSC was planning something. It's not what you may think."

"Of course not." Boldisar forced a smile. "What do I know about liberating a planet?"

"But, ma'am—"

"We'll have to talk about this at the debriefing," Boldisar said. "When I can give you that intelligence you need."

"Affirmative," John said. "As long as you understand—"

"I understand very well, Master Chief." Boldisar stepped away from the tractor and started toward the front of the column. "I will send your driver back shortly, but I'm afraid it may be some time before the corpsman can get to you."

"That's fine," John said. "We can look after ourselves. But if you have any spare debriding agent, we need to tidy up these wounds as soon as possible."

"I'll have the driver bring back whatever we can spare. Now, please excuse me. I have a great deal to attend to."

She strode off so fast that she nearly broke into a run. Fred turned his faceplate toward John, then held it there expectantly until John finally spoke over TEAMCOM.

"What?"

"That order about not upsetting anyone," Fred said. "Was that just for me?"

# CHAPTER SEVEN

1200 hours, October 8, 2559 (military calendar)
Dombräd Springs, Észac Plain
Continent Eposz, Planet Reach

A hundred and fifty paces across the glass, two Banished Phantoms sat in a rough triangle with Castor's own craft, their sterns facing inward toward a central point that denied the occupants a direct attack angle on the other vessels. Their loading ramps were nearly down, revealing darkened troop bays that were almost certainly packed with heavily armed escorts.

Once the ramps had settled onto the glass, Castor extended his hand for his *dokab*'s gravity hammer. Being one of the rare Jiralhanae who preferred the wisdom of killing his enemies from afar to the thrill of flattening them in melee, Castor rarely carried the weapon and had not even bothered naming it. But under the circumstances, the hammer was both a good choice and a ceremonial necessity. Without it, his fellow chieftains would view him as weak. And if that happened in any way, they would be unlikely to set aside their foolish power struggle long enough to help him figure out where the demons and their digging machines had gone.

Castor started toward the hatch—only to feel the hammer holding him back. He turned to look at the warrior still grasping the bottom of its handle, a stocky Jiralhanae in the blue-and-gold armor of the Keepers of the One Freedom.

"There is no need for worry, Feodruz," Castor said. "We come under a parley pact."

"There is always need for worry, Dokab," Feodruz said. As the commander of the Dokab's Escort, it was his duty to protect Castor—and it was his life that would be forfeit if he failed. "Especially with the Banished. They have broken parley pacts before."

"But they will not this time," Castor said. "*We* are Banished now, and due the same honor as any Banished clan."

"What honor?" Feodruz asked. "The Ravaged Tusks are smugglers and slavers, and the Legion of the Corpse-Moon are barely more than raiders. If either clan has any honor at all, it is only that of fearing Escharum."

"Under the circumstances, that is the only honor necessary," said Inslaan 'Gadogai. The Sangheili blademaster was standing at Castor's side, unarmored as usual, but wearing his plasma sword on the belt that cinched his tabard around his thin abdomen. "Fear is a more reliable guarantor than honor."

"Were that so," Feodruz said, "the Keepers would not be the only clan following Escharum's command to search for the Portal under the Mountain."

"There can be no arguing with that." 'Gadogai tilted his diamond-shaped head to the side, a peculiar gesture the Sangheili sometimes used to signal acquiescence. "As you wish, Commander. It is *your* life at risk."

"My fate is unimportant," Feodruz said. "I think only of the *dokab*'s life."

"As do we all," 'Gadogai said.

Castor looked down on the blademaster. "For as long as it serves Escharum."

"That need not be said." 'Gadogai clacked his mandibles in the Sangheili gesture of affirmation. "Does it?"

Castor grunted his annoyance, then nodded to Feodruz. "We will wait," he said. "It would not do to appear overeager."

Feodruz released the handle of the gravity hammer. "You are most wise, Dokab."

Castor lowered the hammer's head to the deck beside his foot; from the shadows at the back of the troop bay, he looked out over the helmets of twenty kneeling Keepers. There were ten Kig-Yar with pulse carbines and ten Jiralhanae with spike rifles, all gathered along both sides of the bay and ready to open fire at the first hint of trouble.

Though Castor could not see into the dim troop bays of the other two craft, he knew the situation in both would be much the same, with his two counterparts looking out over the heads of their own warriors. Even under the best of circumstances, Jiralhanae tempers and pride could turn prearranged parleys into bloodbaths, and knowing that a bevy of opposition longshooters were ready to open fire tended to have a calming effect.

After a few minutes, a towering Jiralhanae with a blocky head and massive shoulders filled the loading hatch of the Phantom on Castor's right. Though the distance was too great to make out facial features, Castor had met Deukalion before and could picture the chieftain's raw visage with its bony cheeks and sunken green-gold eyes the color of Soiraptian malachite. He remembered Deukalion's muzzle was almost cube-shaped, and his blunt tusks were covered in etchings that named all the condemned he had sent to die in the lung-liquefying atmosphere of the corpse-moon.

Deukalion spread his arms, holding his gravity hammer one-handed, and called out. Castor could not understand what he was saying, but after a breath, Krelis—whom Castor had brought along to serve as his adjutant—spoke from the information station in the corner of the bay.

"Dokab, he is saying that you are the one who begged for this parley." Krelis's tone was resentful. "He asks why you are afraid to show yourself."

"Make no reply," Castor said. "Have the sensor master listen to the sounds in his troop bay."

"You are *accepting* his insult?"

"I am considering my response," Castor said. He had hoped to repay his dead war-brother Orsun's loyal service by preparing Krelis for a higher station, but it was becoming apparent that his old friend's son may have too much pride and not enough wisdom to succeed. "What does the sensor master hear?"

"I will ask him."

"Do it quickly," Feodruz growled. "Your *dokab* needs your obedience, not your opinion."

Krelis spoke into the cockpit relay, then quickly replied, "The sensor master reports laughter and boasting. They are bragging that your head is Deukalion's for the taking."

"Let them brag." Castor lifted his gravity hammer. "If they are bragging, they are not preparing for battle."

He started forward, only to have Feodruz take his arm and stop him. "Ballas has yet to show himself."

"But he will," Castor said. "Only a fool lays a trap one-against-two, and Ballas is no fool."

As Castor spoke, the warrior in question appeared in the loading hatch of the Phantom on the left, dressed in his signature red armor. A short, stocky Jiralhanae almost as wide as he was tall, he filled the opening completely it would have been impossible for his long-shooters to fire past him. Like Deukalion, he stopped there and bellowed unintelligibly across the glass.

"Dokab, he assures you there is nothing to fear." Krelis's voice trembled with outrage. "And he commands that you show yourself."

Castor gnashed his tusks. It was merely a taunt, but one that gave him a choice between acting a coward or a thrall. The only reply that would not appear weak would be one that was equally insulting—and while that might prevent the other chieftains from escalating the situation, it wasn't likely to win their cooperation either.

Castor thought for a moment, then stepped into the loading hatch. "I fear only the gods and obey only my conscience!" he called. "But I have sworn service to Atriox, and it is in his name that I tell you to come forward and parley!"

"Excellent," 'Gadogai whispered. The blademaster stepped to Castor's side, then took the energy sword from his belt and passed it to Feodruz. "Now, leave the gravity hammer behind and start walking."

"What?" Feodruz accepted the sword, but shook his head at Castor. "Ignore this madness, Dokab. It will get you killed."

"Nonsense," 'Gadogai said. "I will be there as well."

"You are a single unarmored Sangheili," Feodruz said. "And now you do not even have a weapon."

'Gadogai dropped his head and swung his mandibles from side to side. "Ah, Feodruz. Always watching, never seeing."

The Sangheili started down the ramp, then seemed to notice that Castor wasn't following. He stopped and cocked his head so that one oval eye was looking back over his shoulder.

"What are you waiting for, Dokab?"

"You, to return to your senses," Castor said. "If I arrive without my hammer, they will think I come to them in weakness. They will refuse to join in the portal search."

"They will see no weakness if you show them strength." 'Gadogai began to descend the ramp again. "Trust me or not, Dokab. The choice is yours."

Castor passed the gravity hammer back to Feodruz and caught up to 'Gadogai in a single long stride. "You are certain this will make them listen?"

"I am certain it has a better chance than your gravity hammer."

"The gravity hammer is not for talking. It is for fighting."

"And which are we here to do?"

"To talk," Castor said. They reached the bottom of the loading ramp, and he forced himself to start across the glass unarmed. "But talking has a way of turning into fighting, and a good warrior is always prepared."

"Then be prepared."

"Without weapons?"

'Gadogai stopped and faced Castor, and Castor found himself halting as well. "Is it the warrior with the best weapon who wins the fight?" the Sangheili asked. "Or the warrior who *is* the weapon?"

"This is no time for your riddles." Castor started forward again. He had fought alongside several blades of the Silent Shadow, and there could be no denying their effectiveness. But he was affronted by the mysticism so many of them embraced. Instead of honoring the gods who bestowed their prowess, they claimed it to be the manifestation of some mysterious force that lived in their individual beings. "Next you will be suggesting that I give up my armor."

"Armor is an illusion."

"Remind me of that when there are twenty longshooters firing at us."

"One or twenty," 'Gadogai replied, "they will not strike me. But you—your armor will be the death of you."

"Because armor is an illusion?"

"Because the best armor is not needing armor," 'Gadogai said. "You will see, Dokab."

"Let us hope not," Castor said. "We are here to talk, remember?"

"Indeed. You are learning."

Castor snorted his disgust. "Enough learning for today. My ears hurt from so much sacrilege."

He shifted his attention to Deukalion and Ballas, who were about halfway to the center point of the meeting area. Like Castor, they had each been assigned a third of the world to search for the Portal under the Mountain, with all three sharing responsibility for searching the Eposz supercontinent—Ballas the southwest third, Deukalion the southeast third, while Castor took the north. But they had allowed themselves to become bogged down in a battle to subdue the human reclamation farmers who overlapped both their territories in the Arany Basin, then had foolishly begun to compete for the same bases and fallen into a fight against each other. Both were wearing full helmets and ornate suits of power armor, Deukalion in black trimmed with silver and Ballas in pure crimson, and both were holding their gravity hammers close beneath the heads. And, most notably, both were being careful to stay clear of the firing lanes from their Phantoms.

At thirty paces from the center point, the lechatelierite assumed a golden tint and began to bulge upward like an inverted bowl. A faint gurgling was audible beneath it, and Castor could not help looking down through the jaundiced glass.

Below he saw the same thing as the last time he was here—a curtain of yellow steam circulating over a pool of boiling water. During the cleansing of Reach, a plasma strike had fallen atop a hot sulfur spring and melted all but a thin layer of the stone above it. As the lechatelierite cooled, the sulfurous steam rising from the water was trapped beneath it, creating so much pressure that it collapsed the sandstone cap and forced the glass upward, creating the yellowish, semitranslucent dome upon which Castor and the others had agreed to hold their parley.

The thinking was that the meeting would be less likely to turn into a brawl since a single gravity-hammer blow would be enough to shatter the dome and drop them all into the boiling water below.

Except that Castor didn't have his gravity hammer.

He reached the top of the dome, where plumes of sulfurous steam rose from small vent holes in the center, then stood waiting as Deukalion and Ballas climbed the last few paces. The lips of Deukalion's blocky muzzle were pulled back in a sneer, revealing the white roots of his etched tusks, and Ballas seemed even more immense than he had three months earlier, when Escharum had first called them together to begin planning for their assignments.

Deukalion stopped and began to rest the head of his gravity hammer, Black Death, on the glass—then, scowling at a plume of steam rising between his boots, chose to cradle it in the crook of his arm instead. He studied Castor for a moment, then glared at 'Gadogai.

"What is the Four Jaws doing here?"

'Gadogai met Deukalion's stare in silence, and finally Deukalion grew uncomfortable and looked back to Castor.

"I await my answer."

"Is it not obvious?" Castor replied. "The blademaster is here because he wishes to be here."

"This parley is between clan chieftains only," Deukalion said.

Ballas finally arrived, positioning himself equidistant from Castor and Deukalion. "Yes. That is what we agreed."

"Think of me as an observer," 'Gadogai said. "On behalf of Escharum."

The four speakers were now arrayed in a diamond, standing about ten paces apart, with the blademaster at the bottom of the diamond, closest to Castor's Phantom. It did not escape Castor's notice that the Sangheili had managed to place himself so that he was shielded from rival longshooters by Castor on one side and Ballas on the other.

"If you do not want the blademaster observing," Castor remarked, "you are free to ask him to leave."

"Not that I expect anyone to do so," 'Gadogai said. "No one *here* has anything to hide from Escharum . . . do they?"

Deukalion's eyes flashed emerald, and Ballas merely grunted.

"I thought not," 'Gadogai said. He turned to Castor. "I am not here to participate, so perhaps you should offer the good news."

Ballas's eyes grew round, and Deukalion's jaw fell open.

"You have found it?" Ballas whispered.

"The portal?" Deukalion added.

It was not the way Castor had planned to open the parley, but he had to admit the gambit had a disarming effect.

"I have not been there yet," Castor said carefully. "But I do know where it is."

The faces of both chieftains tensed with alarm, and their hands tightly grasped the shafts of their gravity hammers. They shot each other wary looks, and Castor knew they were expecting someone to attempt a clan merging.

'Gadogai knew it as well. "Before either of you does something reckless," he said, "you should ask yourselves why we carry no weapons."

Deukalion thrust his lower tusks forward. "Because you are fools."

"Not at all." 'Gadogai looked to Ballas. "Why not venture a guess? You have always seemed like the more clever one."

Deukalion glowered and started forward—until Ballas warned him off by baring a chipped fang and glancing skyward. Deukalion stopped and looked up, searching for a strike craft that was not there.

'Gadogai rattled his mandibles in a Sangheili expression of mockery. "Do not concern yourself," he said. "I would never be that obvious."

"Obvious or not," Ballas said, "bringing extra guards breaks the parley pact."

"Does it now? I will be sure to mention that when Escharum asks what became of you." 'Gadogai faced Castor. "I must say, I do not think they want to help."

Castor stared at 'Gadogai for a moment, trying to decide what the blademaster was playing at. Was the Sangheili trying to extract them from a deteriorating situation, or hoping to bluff the two chieftains into submission? Finally he simply asked, "Why not?"

"I have no idea," 'Gadogai said. "It seems foolish, does it not?"

"I never said the Ravaged Tusks would refuse help." Ballas turned to Castor. "You have not yet explained why we are here."

"Yes, he did," 'Gadogai said. "He just told you—he found the Portal under the Mountain."

"I know where it is," Castor clarified. "But I need help—"

"He needs help securing it," 'Gadogai finished. His voice grew more menacing, and he stretched his neck toward Deukalion. "Or have you forgotten *that* is why Escharum sent the Legion of the Corpse-Moon to Reach in the first place?"

"I forget nothing, Four Jaws," Deukalion replied. "The Legion of the Corpse-Moon has been pacifying the humans, so the Banished will be able to hold the portal after we find it."

"My apologies, then," 'Gadogai said. "I fear my last report said the Legion of the Corpse-Moon and the Ravaged Tusks were fighting over human farmholds, while the Keepers searched for the portal . . . alone."

Deukalion's nostrils flared. "What report?"

"The one he sent to Escharum," Ballas said. "That is who he serves, remember?"

"In truth, I serve Atriox *through* Escharum." 'Gadogai paused to give a little head shudder, then added, "I can only imagine what Atriox's reaction will be."

"Atriox is *back*?" Deukalion asked.

"Fool," 'Gadogai said. "When Atriox finally loses patience with your contrivances, it will be you who goes to *him*."

Providing they could find the Portal under the Mountain and prepare it for activation, of course. But Castor was not about to explain *that* minor detail to the other clan leaders. The more accessible they thought Atriox was, the more likely they would be to help.

"That is why we must secure the portal at once," Castor said. "Before he loses patience with all of us."

"And you are willing to let us share in the honor?" Deukalion asked.

"I am," Castor said. "Provided you share in the effort."

"Why so generous?" Ballas tilted his round head sideways. "There is something you are not telling us."

"There are many things I am not telling you," Castor said. "And more things that I will not reveal until I have your agreement."

"Then you do not have it," Ballas said. "You cannot expect us—"

"He can, and you will," 'Gadogai said. "Do *not* make me threaten you with Escharum's retribution again. It is growing tiresome."

"For us all," Ballas said.

"And there is more than one way to stop it," Deukalion added.

'Gadogai's mandibles splayed at the threat. "You could try."

He started across the dome between Castor and Ballas, heading for Deukalion. Castor had no idea whether the blademaster was bluffing or truly meant to kill a fully armored chieftain with his bare hands—and neither did the chieftain. Deukalion's eyes bulged wide, and he watched in confusion and alarm as the Sangheili rapidly approached. But if 'Gadogai reached him, he *would* fight, and Castor had no doubt what would follow.

Rifle spikes and carbine bolts.

And, if they survived that, a final fate of falling through the lechatelierite to drown in a pool of hot sulfur water. Castor took a deep breath and stepped forward, talking as he moved.

"What I *can* tell you about the portal is this." He caught Ballas's eye and glanced at the glass, hoping to remind him of their danger. "It is in the Highland Mountains."

Castor used the human name. Rather than rename every location on Reach—or even Reach itself—it was more efficient to utilize the references that the Banished had learned from the maps and prisoners they had captured.

"In the Highlands? You are certain?" Instead of interposing himself between Deukalion and 'Gadogai as Castor had, Ballas was backing toward the edge of the dome. "How do you know this?"

"Because the Spartans know, and that is the direction they are headed," Castor said. He caught 'Gadogai by the shoulder and—hoping he wasn't taking his life in his hands by doing so—held the blademaster back. "We have been following them."

'Gadogai made a show of dropping his head in exasperation, but stopped three paces short of Deukalion and looked back at Castor. He could not read Sangheili expressions well enough to tell whether 'Gadogai was truly disappointed, but the blademaster did eventually allow himself to be drawn back toward their side of the dome.

The alarm began to drain from Deukalion's face, and he shifted his attention to Castor. "What do Spartans have to do with the portal?"

"They are here to destroy it."

"How do you know that?" Deukalion was careful to avoid looking in 'Gadogai's direction. "A communications interception? An interrogation?"

"My Seraphs forced down their dropship a day and a half ago," Castor said. "The Spartans escaped, but we found signs of excavation equipment near the crash site. We have been watching them ever since."

"Because they have excavation equipment . . ." Deukalion sounded doubtful. "That is all the intelligence you possess?"

"It is enough," Castor said. "They need it to reach the Portal under the Mountain."

"Or to attack *me*," Deukalion said. "You did not see the fight in the Kisköre Canal yesterday."

"How could I?" Castor replied. "Your base captain sent ten Banshee talons to chase us off. We lost sight of the Spartans."

"And *we* lost a talon and a half of Banshees," Deukalion shot back. "To the Spartans."

"In the canal?"

"Is that not what I just said?"

"But the Spartans were in the *river* channel," Castor said. "We followed them all morning, until they drew close to Kisköre Base and your captain messaged us to keep our distance."

"And you chose not to warn us?"

"So you could try to drive us away and follow them to the portal yourself?" Castor asked. "I am no saphead."

"You must be," Deukalion said. "For only a saphead would believe those tunneling machines are here to dig up the portal."

This was enough to draw 'Gadogai back into the conversation. "You have another explanation then, Legionmaster?"

Deukalion's tone grew instantly less contentious. "Yes. And a better one, I believe. The demons brought the machines here to prepare surprise attacks against us."

"Against the Legion of the Corpse-Moon?" 'Gadogai asked. "Or all of the Banished?"

Deukalion rocked his head from side to side. "That remains to be seen, Blademaster. All I know is they used a tunnel to attack the Kiskõre Base. That is how they came so close before our Banshees saw them."

"Your Banshees saw the Spartans in a tunnel?!" Castor asked, incredulous. "No Banshee I have seen carries ground-penetrating sensors."

"The demons were not in the tunnel when we saw them," Deukalion said. "They were already outside of it, preparing to attack our shield barrier."

"And *that* is when your sentries saw them?" 'Gadogai asked. "I admit I am growing confused."

"What does it matter when my sentries saw the Spartans?" Deukalion's tone had grown impatient—a sign he felt shamed by the poor performance of his sentries. "My Banshees drove them back into their tunnel before they could breach the perimeter."

"Their tunnel?" Castor asked. "A tunnel they finished digging less than a day after landing hundreds of kilometers away?"

"That would be some very fast digging indeed," 'Gadogai said. "What length is this tunnel?"

"The canal runs more than five kilometers from base to river," Deukalion said. "We think the tunnel ran beneath it the entire length."

"*Ran?*" Ballas had returned to his place in the diamond and was now standing opposite Castor. "Has it slithered away?"

"The enemy trapped it with explosives," Deukalion said. "Our trackers kept getting killed. And then the demons finally demolished the rest of the tunnel."

"And now you have no idea where the Spartans are—and no way to follow them." Castor could not quite keep the aggravation out of his voice—because *he* had no idea where they had gone either. It was as if they had simply vanished during the battle, excavation equipment and all. "Tell me I am wrong."

"I know where they are *not*." Deukalion's tone was growing sharp again. "They are not attacking my bases."

"They are not attacking any bases," Castor said. "Because they're on the way to destroy the portal, you muttle—"

"Dokab, I share your alarm," Ballas said, wisely interrupting before Castor could finish the insult. The last thing the parley needed was another confrontation. "But not your certainty. If the demons are here to destroy the portal, why did they attack Kisköre Base?"

"As a diversion," 'Gadogai said. "That is why *I* would have done it—so I could vanish."

"Of course you take the *dokab*'s side," Deukalion said. "You are practically his second."

"I am taking the side of reason, Chieftain," 'Gadogai said. "There is no possibility that four Spartans and a human crew could dig a five-kilometer tunnel within an hour or two—not with the two small machines they had."

"They escaped into a tunnel," Deukalion said. "I saw the hole they used with my own eyes."

"But how do you know the tunnel was not already there?" 'Gadogai asked. "Or that they did not have help?"

"You are thinking of the glass-breakers," Ballas suggested, using the mocking Banished nickname for the human settlers futilely attempting to reclaim the planet. "Perhaps the Spartans are here to help them."

Castor shook his head. "No. If they were here to help the glass-breakers, there would be more than four." He tried to keep his growing anger out of his voice; he would never intimidate Ballas and Deukalion into helping him find the Spartans. "There would be a hundred."

"How do you know they are not here already?" Deukalion's tone was agitated once more. "There could be three demons under every Banished base on this forsaken world, and we would never know it."

"And it still would not matter," Castor said. "We came to find the portal. It is time that you two ceased your petty skirmishing over farmland and helped me."

Ballas cocked his head. "I thought you already knew where the portal is."

"He knows it lies in the Highland Mountains," 'Gadogai said quickly. "And that the Spartans are on their way to destroy it."

"Maybe he does," Deukalion said. "Or maybe Ballas is right, and the demons are only here to help the glass-breakers defend their pitiful settlements."

"That is not a chance we can afford to take," Castor said. "If we lose a few bases, we can take them back later. But if we lose the portal . . . we lose everything."

"Including your heads," 'Gadogai added. "Escharum would be *very* unhappy, were the portal destroyed."

Ballas studied the blademaster, and Castor began to think 'Gadogai's direct threat might tip the balance in his favor.

Then Ballas said, "But there are thousands of separate mountains in the Highlands. Maybe tens of thousands."

"So you can see why we must find the Spartans," 'Gadogai said. "If we cannot follow them to the portal, we must kill them before they reach the mountains."

"We need to send everything we have," Castor said. "Right now."

Castor did not think that Deukalion's resentment would matter. Ballas was the key, and given his fear of Escharum's wrath, Castor was convinced Ballas would support him. Then Deukalion would be forced to go along, or stand as one against two until his clan finally grew so weak that the survivors joined the Ravaged Tusks.

But Deukalion's resistance was only increasing. "That is all you think of—the portal. And what happens if we open the portal, but cannot hold Reach?"

This thought had never occurred to Castor. The only concern was opening the portal so he could take his Keepers to the Ark and, if at all possible, begin the search for the blessed site that could activate the Sacred Rings. That was all that mattered to him. It had not even crossed his mind that once Atriox activated the portal, the Banished would need to hold it. Reach was a dead world with a handful of poorly equipped human settlers. He had simply assumed that the Banished *would* hold it.

But the presence of the Spartans changed everything.

"Yes, it leaves me speechless too," Ballas said after a moment. "Deukalion is actually right."

"No."

"Yes," Ballas said. "It would be worse to open the portal, then lose it to the demons, than to see them destroy it in the first place. The last thing we need is an army of Spartans portal-jumping into battle behind Atriox's back."

"It is only *four* demons," Castor said. "Not an 'army.'"

"Even *one* demon is too many," Ballas said. "You know very well of this. And you have seen only four—but who knows how many dropships you failed to intercept? There could be scores here right now, and we would be unaware of it. You cannot even locate the four you were tracking!"

"It matters not how many Spartans there are," Castor said. "To open the portal, they would need a shard of the Holy Light, and Atriox has all three shards with him on the Ark."

"All three *known* shards," Ballas replied. "Who is to say there are not four shards? Or ten? The humans could have found their own—or even had them all along. The only thing we know for certain is that the slipspace crystal was destroyed during the battle, and Tartarus recovered only three pieces of it afterward."

Castor had to admit that this had not occurred to him either, perhaps because he knew so little about the circumstances surrounding the Holy Light's theft and destruction. And, as valid as Ballas's argument might be, the Ravaged Tusks chieftain was hardly in a position to know more—he had not even been *in* the Covenant when the crystal was lost.

Castor turned to 'Gadogai. "Is this possible?"

'Gadogai spread his hands. "Anything is possible," he said. "I know only what I saw in the Sanctum of the Hierarchs. Who can say what happened before?"

Before Castor could reply, Ballas said, "The Ravaged Tusks' first priority is to secure our bases. Once we know the Spartan threat is neutralized, I will give you all the warriors you need to search the Highland Mountains."

"By then it will be too late," Castor replied. "The portal will be captured or destroyed."

"Not if you find the demons quickly," Deukalion said. "The Legion of the Corpse-Moon will join the Keepers in killing all the Spartans you can find. And once the enemy has been eliminated, we also will join you and the Ravaged Tusks in locating the portal."

Castor found his empty hands balling into fists and cursed the absence of his gravity hammer. He began to wonder if that had been the real reason 'Gadogai had encouraged him to leave it behind, because the blademaster had known all along that the parley would end badly.

"Escharum will take note of your devotion," Castor said. He doubted that either Deukalion or Ballas would be moved by the veiled threat, but his anger demanded some expression. "Will you at least allow us free movement near Kisköre Base? If we are to have any hope of finding the Spartans before they reach the portal, we must begin at the point where you lost them."

Deukalion's lips pulled back. "Had you warned us of their approach, the demons would already be dead. But I have no wish to interfere with your search. You may send ten Kig-Yar to track them across any of my territories."

"Ten Kig-Yar is nothing," Castor said. "The demons will slaughter them all without hesitation."

"Then you should remain in constant communication with them," Ballas said. "When the Kig-Yar fall silent, you will know where to find the demons."

"If you fail to find the Spartans the first time your Kig-Yar fall, you can send out another ten," Deukalion said. "I have no wish to be difficult."

"And yet, I will be forced to tell Escharum you have been *most* difficult," 'Gadogai said. "Both of you. Ten Kig-Yar is a farce."

Deukalion's eyes bulged, but before he could object, Ballas gestured for patience. "Let us hear the number the blademaster would find more reasonable, my brother."

"Ah. So now our two warring chieftains are *brothers?*" 'Gadogai tipped his head in Castor's direction. "Well done, Dokab. Escharum shall hear of your peacemaking talents."

"It was never a war—more of a disagreement," Ballas said. "What number, Blademaster?"

"They are not my Keepers," 'Gadogai said. "How many then, Dokab?"

"It will take more than warriors alone," Castor said. "They will need support."

"How much support?" Deukalion demanded. "I have no more trust for your Keeper zealots than I do for the Spartans."

"A hundred warriors of my choosing," Castor said. "And support in the form of . . ."

He started to calculate how many talons of Seraphs and Banshees he would need in the air, and the number of Prowlers and Choppers required on the surface, and the kind of equipment necessary to track the Spartans under the glass—and Castor realized the chieftains would never agree. They would interpret his requirements as a mere ruse to get his forces near enough to seize bases from them that he did not need or want.

And then Castor had an inspiration.

He did not need *any* troops to follow the Spartans across the basin.

Deukalion and Ballas were the ones with bases to protect, and they would take every precaution to defend them. To find the Spartans, all Castor need do was monitor the patrols that his counterparts sent out. He would know the demons had been found when Ravaged Tusks and Legion of the Corpse-Moon warriors started to die in droves.

Deukalion dragged him away from such thoughts. "In what form? Know that I will allow you one talon of Banshees and—"

"That will no longer be required," Castor said. "In fact, do not concern yourself. I have a new plan, one that does not need any support at all."

"Oh no?" 'Gadogai asked. "Are you certain?"

"I am," Castor said. "Because the Keepers will not be sending any warriors to hunt for the Spartans."

"I don't see how that would be wise," the Sangheili remarked.

"I do," Castor said. "That is all that matters."

'Gadogai's voice grew firm. "It matters that Escharum sees the wisdom too. Explain."

Castor thought about defying the blademaster as Deukalion and Ballas had been doing almost since the day they'd arrived, but 'Gadogai was Escharum's eyes and voice here on Reach, and the Keepers would still need Banished support even after they found the portal. Besides, 'Gadogai had treated Castor and the Keepers with nothing but honor, and he would not disgrace himself by behaving any less decently.

"If I am wrong," Castor began, "and the Spartans are here to help the reclamation settlers, we will know soon enough."

"When they attack the next base, you mean," 'Gadogai said.

"Exactly. It is a waste of the Keepers' time to follow them."

"That is fine for you to say," Deukalion said. "They are not *your* bases that will be destroyed."

"That is the *dokab*'s point," Ballas said. He looked to 'Gadogai. "But you can see how bad it would be for all of us, were Reach to fall. We must defend the planet to defend the portal."

"The portal we have not yet found?" 'Gadogai asked. "The portal that *you* have given up searching for?"

"I have not given up," Ballas said. "I have a hundred warriors scouting Szurdok Ridge right now."

"How impressive," 'Gadogai said. He looked back to Castor. "And if you are right? If the Spartans are here to destroy the portal?"

"Or claim it," Deukalion added. "As is more likely."

"If you say so," 'Gadogai said. "Dokab? What if the Spartans are here for such a purpose?"

"They have been traveling west across the Arany Basin toward the Highland Mountains," Castor said. "All the Keepers need do is be there when they arrive."

"True enough," 'Gadogai said. "But the Highland Mountains is a large range, many hundreds of kilometers long. How can you be certain you'll see them when they arrive?"

"That will not be a problem."

Castor wasn't foolish enough to reveal that he would be using his Seraphs and Banshees to follow the trail of dead Ravaged Tusk and Legion of the Corpse-Moon warriors the Spartans left in their wake as they crossed the basin. The last thing he wanted was for Deukalion and Ballas to grow cautious and hold their patrols close to home.

"The Keepers will continue searching for the portal in the mountains," Castor continued. "But I have no expectations of finding it before the Spartans arrive. We will have our best rangers hiding in the foothills, watching for them along the entire range. By the time the demons leave the glass barrens, we will have a good idea of where they might be going."

"And if not?" 'Gadogai asked.

"Then we kill them anyway," Castor said. "One should never take chances with Spartans."

# CHAPTER EIGHT

The doctor held the necrometer so John could see the status bar, which was hovering inside the yellow area. Apparently John had not reached all of the dead tissue when he squeezed the debriding agent onto his wound through the burn-hole in his armor's damaged cuisse.

He was standing in a subterranean medical bay, being examined by a middle-aged militia member who had introduced herself as Dr. Somogy. The room was lit by the diffuse silver glow coming down through its lechatelierite ceiling, and three of the walls were made of ash-infused glass blocks. The fourth was a canvas privacy curtain, drawn across a three-meter opening. Although the glass-block examination table behind him might actually have supported his weight, John had not wanted to test its strength and had chosen to remain standing for the entire procedure.

"Are you experiencing any nausea or chills?"

Dr. Somogy did not look up as she asked the question. Seated on a folding chair in front of his left thigh, she was small and a little younger than John, with strands of flaxen hair hanging loose from an unruly bun. She had glass-gray eyes framed by deep laugh lines, and a broad mouth with upturned corners. A holographic locket around her neck displayed the images of two preteen boys who had her gray eyes and thin nose. The locket made John wonder. Reach had been glassed just seven years earlier, and now it had been invaded by the Banished. He wanted to ask whether the boys were still alive, but the question kept sticking in his throat.

Forty-seven years old, and he still didn't know how to ask a personal question.

"Master Chief?"

"Sorry, ma'am." He smiled—not that she could see it through his mirrored faceplate. "Negative on the nausea and chills."

"How about headache or heart palpitations?"

"Negative on the headache." John checked his bio readouts on his HUD. "Negative on the palpitations."

"Your temperature is normal, and I don't see any signs of cognitive impairment." She stood. Instead of a lab coat with a proper name tape, Dr. Somogy wore a white chef's apron over a tunic and canvas pants. John only knew she was a doctor rather than a medic because of how she had introduced herself. "So I don't think you're suffering any sepsis yet. Remove the damaged plate, reapply the debriding agent—*thoroughly* this time—and you'll recover."

"Will do, as soon as we return to—" John caught himself about to say the *Infinity*, and wondered if she was totally correct about the cognitive impairment. "Our vessel."

Somogy frowned. "Now would be better. Sepsis can set in quickly with plasma burns, and our antibiotics don't always work on alien—"

"I understand, ma'am. I've taken plasma hits before."

"And you're still on active duty?" She shook her head, then slipped the necrometer into an apron pocket. "How bad is the wound beneath?"

"Better," John said. "I can run on it without much pain."

"From what I heard, you were running on it while molten armor was still dripping down your leg."

"Affirmative. But it hurt."

"You should let me do an NPI," Somogy said, referring to a nanoparticle image, used in combat hospitals to examine soft tissue damage. "We should confirm that all your muscles are still properly attached."

"Can you do it through five centimeters of titanium alloy?"

"Uh . . . no."

"Then that's a negative. Mjolnir armor isn't designed to be removed casually."

"Treating an injury is hardly casual."

"Still not going to happen," John said. "How about a medical readout?"

Somogy rolled her eyes. "Sure. I'll take what I can get."

John had his onboard computer isolate the data relevant to his wound, then transfer it to the palm-sized medical pad inside her apron pocket. When the device chimed, she lifted her brow and pulled it out.

She blinked at the display a few times, issuing ocular commands, then studied the screen for a few moments. "It says you were wounded a day ago. Is that right?"

The precise date and time of the injury appeared on John's HUD. "Just over, ma'am."

Her eyebrows rose. "Then you have remarkable healing powers." She slipped the medical pad back into her apron pocket. "It appears a large chunk of your quadriceps was burned away when the plasma bolt impacted, but your functionality records and metabolic panels are already at the levels I'd expect to see after ten days of bed rest. Is that due to your augmentations?"

"I couldn't say," John replied, silently adding: *Because it's still classified.* For much of its existence, the SPARTAN-II program had been a secret so tightly held that even most UNSC personnel weren't aware of its existence. That had changed late in the Covenant War, when someone far above John's pay grade realized people needed a reason to believe that humanity could prevail against the implacable aliens. But the specifics of the Spartans' training, equipment, and especially their biological augmentations remained highly restricted. "What augmentations would those be?"

"The ones that prevented your femur from breaking when you had that hole blown in your armor," Somogy replied. "I've treated a lot of combat injuries since the Banished arrived, so I know what happens to a human body when it takes a bolt from a Banshee's plasma cannon."

"It's great armor, ma'am." John tapped his right thigh. "Titanium shell. Energy shield."

"Sure—it's the armor. Look . . . just stay off the leg for a couple of days and remove that thigh plate—"

"Cuisse."

"Whatever," Somogy said. "Just take it easy for a couple of days, and you'll be fine."

"Define *easy*."

"No running, no jumping. No forced marches. No combat. You know—rest."

"Thanks for the suggestion."

"You're not going to take it, are you?"

"I can't," John said. "We have a mission."

"Then why bother me? I have patients who actually need my services, you know."

"Colonel Boldisar insisted," John said, "and it seemed easier not to argue. I know rear admirals who aren't that stubborn."

"I'm not surprised," Somogy said. "Sasa Boldisar is the founding director of the Eposz Reclamation Collective."

This revelation wasn't wholly unexpected. After loading the three Spartans onto the wagon in the Juh Mező Aqueduct, the colonel had sent Istvan Erdei to tell John that he would receive the debriefing he'd requested when they reached Logistics Base Gödöllő. When John asked how long the trip would take, Erdei had simply responded that it didn't matter, because Sasa wanted him there. Had John realized the journey would be a twenty-five-hour wagon-ride through an abandoned aqueduct, he might have resisted the invitation.

Which would have been a mistake. The long ride had rendered his Mjolnir's inertial navigation nearly useless. But he had paid careful attention to the light glowing through the lechatelierite overhead and determined that they were traveling generally westward, toward the Highland Mountains—and their mission objective in CASTLE Base.

And they were doing it all underglass and unobserved.

John had lost contact with Linda and *Special* Crew, and he hadn't wanted to compromise their security by asking the militia about them. He could only hope they had stumbled onto the underglass network of passages themselves when they took cover under the riverbed, and were even now using it to continue moving the excavation machines toward CASTLE Base as ordered.

When John remained silent, Dr. Somogy continued her explanation. "That also makes her the commander in chief of the Viery Militia."

"So, what Sasa wants . . ."

"Yes . . . Sasa gets." Somogy flashed a commiserative smile, then added, "But I wouldn't want to seem ungrateful. Sasa has more at stake here than any of us."

"And that qualifies her to be commander in chief?" John asked.

"That, and her organizational skills," Somogy said. "Don't you know who Sasa Boldisar *is*?"

John queried his onboard computer and got nothing. "No idea."

"She's the founder of Kerepes Agricultural. Her great-great-grandfather was Ferenc Kisvárda."

John didn't need his computer to identify either of *those* names. Before the fall of Reach, Kerepes Agricultural had grown into a major food supplier to the UNSC—he had seen their crossed wheat-stalks logo on thousands of supply crates and self-cooking meal canisters. And while Kisvárda Metals had started on Reach mining titanium and rhodium, it had grown into one of the largest mining and metals production conglomerates in the Inner Colonies.

"Okay, she has resources and knows how to get a job done," John said. "But why *this* job? She could live on any planet she wants."

Somogy shrugged. "It's a matter of gratitude. Reach has blessed her family with so much, she says she couldn't live with herself if she didn't restore it."

"You buy that?"

"I don't *not* buy it," Somogy said. "We all have our own reasons for returning to Reach. Istvan Erdei says it's the one place in the colonies where a man doesn't need a piece of paper to prove he's useful. Rendor Borbély claims it's because he and his family won't join their ancestors in the afterlife if they're buried on a different world. I'm here because these are *my* people, and there weren't a lot of doctors volunteering to come back with them. I doubt any of us really understand why the others are here—and I don't see that it matters. We're here now, and there is no leaving . . . at least not until you've driven these aliens away."

John couldn't tell her the truth, and he didn't want to lie. So he said nothing.

But Somogy wasn't about to let him off that easy. "That *is* why you're here?" she asked. "Is it not?"

John tipped his faceplate down, so she would know he was looking her in the eye. "Sorry, ma'am, I can't tell you that. Our mission is classified."

Somogy's expression floated for a moment between disappointed and confused, then she finally gave her head a little shake and said, "Well, as I say, we all have our own reasons for being here. It only matters that you *are*." She tapped his damaged cuisse. "You have my recommendation, Master Chief. If you don't follow it, there will be problems with scar tissue."

"Scar tissue, I know about."

"I imagine you do." She folded her arms. "So . . . is there anything I can actually *do* for you here?"

John glanced at the holographic locket hanging from her neck, but couldn't bring himself to ask—even when she seemed to sense where his gaze was directed, despite the mirrored faceplate, and unconsciously put a finger to the images.

"Yes, ma'am. First, can you tell me the status of Spartan-087 and -104?"

Somogy hesitated, no doubt weighing medical privacy concerns, which simply did not exist for Spartans.

"Normally I'd just tap into their BIOS," John said. "But the datalink is blocked."

Somogy nodded. She drew the medical pad from her pocket again and flicked her eyes at the screen.

"Um, Frederic-104 was willing to remove his helmet, so they're giving him a handheld CT to confirm the absence of intracranial hemorrhaging. But I wouldn't expect any. His TBI is rated at mild." She paused to look up at John, then added, "That's rather remarkable, given the dent in his helmet."

"Fred has a hard head. It's one of his best assets."

"Apparently so." Somogy returned to the screen. "Kelly-087's axillary vein was obstructed by the emergency biofoam repair. She wouldn't remove her armor either, so Dr. Kelemen used a vascular scope to go through the breach and do a revision. I'd say she'll be fine in a week, but—"

"We don't have a week," John said. "What's realistic?"

Somogy considered, then said, "If she heals as fast as you do, the risk of a catastrophic bleed should be minimal by tomorrow."

"I'll keep that in mind, ma'am. Thanks for being clear."

"My pleasure," she said. "And?"

"Ma'am?"

"You said *first*. That implies you wanted something else."

"Right." John took a deep breath, then pointed at her locket. "Your two boys, are they . . . ?"

The smile that spread across her face told him the boys were alive. "Laszlo and Vidor." She indicated first a blade-nosed youth who looked a little older, then his slim-faced brother. "They're in the Drifts with their father."

"The Drifts?"

"The Gönc Drifts—a network of old mining tunnels in the Lébény district," Somogy said. "They'll be thrilled to hear that I consulted for the Master Chief."

"It might be better if you didn't mention it, ma'am. Our presence on Reach is classified."

Somogy laughed. "Well, good luck with that. You've been the talk of the base since Istvan had to call off his operation."

"We have?"

"Yes, you have," Somogy said. "People are pretty excited."

John didn't bother asking why. He could guess.

Instead he asked, "The Lébény district—isn't that in the Highland Mountains?"

"It is," Somogy said. "Do you know where the Scheelite Workings are?"

John didn't, but he knew that scheelite was an important tungsten ore, and there had once been a lot of tungsten mines near CASTLE Base, to the north of the Military Wilderness Training Preserve.

"Somewhere near Gönc, I assume."

"That's right. Above the old town, in Gönc Canyon. We're using the old mines as a training reservation."

"How so?"

Somogy frowned. "Well, we'd have been pretty foolish to wait for the UNSC to show up to help us out right now, wouldn't we?"

"Yes, ma'am," John said. "So your sons and their father are in the militia too?"

"This is Reach, Master Chief. *Everyone* is in the militia. My husband commands Training Battalion Ács." She touched the locket. "Laszlo is in Bicske Battalion. Vidor is in Érd Battalion."

John studied the holographic locket. Laszlo, the older boy, looked to be about twelve. His brother, Vidor, was ten, if that. It seemed the days of shaping children into soldiers had not yet passed on Reach. Maybe they never would.

John had long ago come to terms with his own childhood conscription and was even proud—enormously proud—of what it had made of him. That didn't make it something he wished on today's children, though—not *one* of them.

Finally Somogy covered the locket with her hand. "It's a relief to know that they won't have to fight now."

John didn't know how to respond, so he didn't.

"They're so young," Somogy continued. "They wouldn't survive a day in a battle against the Brutes and Jackals. Probably not even against Grunts."

"I'm afraid not, ma'am." She was using war-era nicknames: *Brutes* for Jiralhanae, *Jackals* for the most common subspecies of Kig-Yar, *Grunts* for Unggoy. "And I'm sorry to report that Reach isn't out of danger yet. It would be helpful if we could get some intelligence on enemy dispositions."

"You don't have a surveillance net up?"

"We didn't want to alert the enemy prematurely," John replied. His answers were less than forthright, but he knew the value—and the art—of protecting classified information, even from friendly forces. "It's always smart to assess the situation on the ground before revealing your presence."

"I can see *that* went well." Somogy drew the canvas privacy curtain aside. "As it happens, they're waiting for you now."

"Who's 'they'?"

"The commanders." She waved him toward a circular waiting room with a glass-block nurses' station ringing a central support pillar. "Thank you for coming to Reach's aid."

"Don't thank me, ma'am. Not yet."

He stepped into the waiting room, where instead of the commanders he had been promised, he saw a slender woman with blond hair cut blunt at the jawline. She wore black-dyed coveralls with a length of gray cloth sewn onto the collar tabs—apparently a makeshift lieutenant's bar.

Next to the lieutenant stood Kelly, her right arm armor-locked into the sling position. She had not yet repaired the breach in her breastplate, and John could see the singed edges of the grenade-sized ruptures that had been burned through the underlayers. As bad as the damage looked, however, it would have even less effect on the Mjolnir's functionality than Kelly's wound would have on her. Every layer was equipped with self-directing autorepair, as well as a bypass system that would keep each element operating at the highest possible efficiency.

The lieutenant stepped forward and snapped off a crisp salute. "Master Chief, I've been assigned to escort your team to the map house."

John returned the salute. It wasn't worth the trouble to explain that as enlisted personnel, he should be the one who saluted first.

"Thank you, Lieutenant . . ." He looked for a name tape that wasn't there, then turned to Kelly. "Where's Blue Two?"

Kelly pointed to the only closed curtain in the circle of exam alcoves. "Still under treatment, I'm afraid."

"I'm fine!" Fred called. His helmet was clearly off, as his voice came through the curtain clear and unmodulated. "Just a little hungover."

"You don't drink." John thought Fred was probably joking, but it was hard to be sure under the circumstances. "And even if you did, we're on a mission."

"Then why am I hungover?"

"It's not a hangover," John said. "Report to me when the doc says you can put your helmet on."

"Affirmative," Fred said. "When will that be?"

Instead of answering, John turned to the militia lieutenant.

"They'll send word as soon as he's cleared to leave." She eyed the curtain, then lowered her voice. "Given what I've heard so far, I doubt they'll keep him any longer than absolutely necessary."

"Understandable," Kelly said.

The lieutenant led them out the exit into an underglass cavity that looked to be no more than fifty meters wide, but at least five kilometers long and perhaps a hundred meters deep. John already knew from the inquiries he'd made during the wagon ride that it had been formed when the Covenant plasma bombardment ignited a subterranean coal seam. The rehab pioneers had been in the process of converting it into an underglass reservoir when the Banished arrived two months ago, but had quickly decided to convert it into a secret logistics base that they would use to support their resistance.

Now it looked like an underglass village, with rows of glass-block buildings sitting on shale and sandstone terraces. The infirmary was located near the top of the cavity, so as soon as the group drew near the terrace edge, John could see that the entire base was bustling, with thousands of men and women loading weapons and ammunition into vehicles and tractor-pulled wagons nearly everywhere he looked. There were even a few hundred surplus Warthogs serving as mobile platforms for rocket launchers, gauss cannons, and three different types of heavy machine guns.

John followed the lieutenant to an M12 Warthog and climbed into the passenger seat, leaving the rear compartment for Kelly.

Once the lieutenant had settled into the driver's seat and started the hydrogen-injected engine, he remarked, "Looks like you're getting ready for a battle."

"No choice." She put the Warthog into gear and started toward a ramp that led to the terrace below. "Someone blew our cover. You'll see."

"Oh, *this* is going to be a lovely chat," Kelly said over TEAMCOM.

"Not if you're talking to me," Fred said, also over TEAMCOM.

His voice was barely audible, no doubt because his helmet was still sitting on the examination table rather than on his head. "They won't let me put my helmet on yet, so I'm having a little trouble hearing you. So are the doctor and his assistants."

"Acknowledged," John said. Fred wasn't entirely befuddled, if it had occurred to him to let them know that their TEAMCOM conversation was less than private. "How's the head, Blue Two?"

"The doc hasn't found any brains yet. At least, that's what he keeps saying."

"Brain *bleeds*," chimed in a tiny male voice. "Your friend has a very droll sense of humor, Master Chief. Is that normal for him?"

Before John could answer, the number-four status LED flickered yellow . . . then went dark again.

Number four was Linda.

"Master Chief?" The tiny voice sounded annoyed. "That's a serious question. A change of personality can be an indication of—"

"Actually, Fred has a *very* droll sense of humor," Kelly said, stepping in. She would have seen the flicker too, and would know that John needed to figure out what it meant. "I seldom find him funny at all, but he keeps trying."

"So, this is normal." The voice sounded less concerned. "Then I haven't found anything to be worried about yet. I'll have him out of here within the hour."

"*Hour?*" Fred asked.

"You can't put your helmet back on before I reduce that hematoma," the doctor said. "If you try, you'll most likely pass out from the pain."

"No, I won't."

"Fred, there's no need to find out." As John spoke, he transmitted two amber status flashes, then a single green one—a sequence that he knew would be appearing on the internal displays of all of Blue Team's helmets. "Take the time necessary, Doc. We'll need him with his helmet on."

Inside John's own helmet, Linda's status LED remained dark.

The doctor's faint voice asked, "Fred, did your helmet just flash at you?"

"I'm not sure what you mean," Fred said. "Helmets don't flash."

"I mean those little lights inside."

"Doc, maybe you should run that CT over your own head," Fred said. "You're seeing things."

Denying the obvious was not a deft way to avoid discussing classified technology, but even without a concussion, Fred was not a deft conversationalist. None of them were. Making small talk was pretty low on the list of desirable Spartan skill sets.

The Warthog reached the ramp, and the lieutenant steered down it at a speed that had John reaching for the front roll bar. It wasn't that he minded traveling fast on narrow roads with steep drop-offs—he just preferred to have a Spartan behind the wheel when he did.

John flashed his status LED again, in case the amber flicker had meant Linda was passing somewhere near the base during their conversation about Fred and his helmet—which wasn't as unlikely as it sounded.

After ducking under the lechatelierite back at the Lapos River, Linda and *Special* Crew had clearly elected to enter the militia's labyrinth of underglass passageways. If they were following orders—and with Linda, that was unquestionable—they would still be trying to reach CASTLE Base, and might well have decided that the safest way to proceed was to stay underglass and travel through the militia's labyrinth for as long as possible.

But Linda would still be eager to determine Blue Team's status, and if she'd been close enough to overhear the TEAMCOM transmission, she wouldn't hesitate to leave *Special* Crew somewhere safe for a few hours to investigate. As the Warthog descended the ramp, John scanned the perimeter of the base, looking for likely observation posts that might also block a TEAMCOM signal. There were plenty of empty buildings, idle equipment yards, and untended materiel stacks where she could be hiding.

But there were only five openings by which Linda could have arrived, all vehicle-sized passages located on the upper terrace. Each was guarded by a five-member sentry detail, and they looked attentive enough that it would have been difficult for even a Spartan sniper to slip past without disabling someone. And since John saw no sign of a search, Linda was probably not inside the base.

The Warthog reached the next terrace, and the lieutenant whipped it into a tight hairpin turn that had the rear end skidding toward the edge. John glanced over the drop-off and, on the terrace below, saw a company of M274-M Gungooses forming up in a long double column.

Apparently interpreting his glance as a comment on her driving, the lieutenant slowed down and said, "I'm sorry, sir. I forget that not everyone knows who I am."

"And who would that be?" John asked.

"Bella Disztl," she said.

John had never heard of her. He glanced back at Kelly, who gave a quick helmet shake.

Disztl sighed. "Don't they have DuroCam on Spartan bases?" she asked. "Five-time winner of the Tantalus Ten Thousand?"

John queried *Tantalus 10,000* on his onboard computer and saw that it was a five-day cross-continent open-buggy endurance race on the planet Tantalus. Bella Disztl had won it outright four times and been awarded a judge's victory once—when the two drivers who finished ahead of her tested positive for stim-pack enhancement.

"Oh," John said. "Sorry. Reach is just the last place I expected to meet a famous buggy driver. It's an honor to have you behind the wheel, Lieutenant."

Disztl snorted a laugh. "If you say so, sir."

It was the second time she had called him "sir," and John didn't think she was trying to be inappropriate.

"I'm not really a 'sir,' ma'am," he said. "Master chief is a senior enlisted rank, not a commission."

"In the Viery Militia, we measure soldiers by their capabilities. So you're a 'sir' to *me* . . . sir."

Once they were past the column of Gungooses, she took another ramp, and they dropped to the next terrace. When John looked over the edge this time, it was down forty meters of smooth shale into a long pool of stagnant water. In several places, he could see bubbles rising from the murky depths with a clockwork cadence.

At the far end, four kilometers away, a barely discernible fan sat in a tunnel mouth, surrounded by a glass-block collar. To be visible at such a distance, the fan had to be at least twenty meters in diameter, and it was drawing so much air across the water that the pond rippled in the breeze.

"Why is that fan there?" John asked, pointing.

"Smoke and firedamp," Disztl explained. "The coal seam is still smoldering down there. The fans pull the gases out before they rise into the base."

She floored the accelerator, and the Warthog shot down the terrace, horn blasting as it squeezed between the glass-block buildings on her side and the forty-meter drop on John's. He held on to the roll bar, reminding himself, probably not for the last time, that he was riding with a five-time Tantalus 10,000 winner.

# CHAPTER NINE

During her three decades of interstellar war, Linda-058 had traveled countless kilometers of empty trail on more dead planets than she could name. No path had ever seemed quite so desolate to her as the abandoned aqueduct through which she was running now, no journey half so bleak. There were no gossamer-winged cherots flitting through the underglass gloom, no gupers fleeing the droning excavation machines behind her, no kropeys slithering away from her pounding boots. There was not a strand of moss dangling from the cracked lechatelierite overhead, no mildew staining the damp walls . . . nothing.

And she hated the Covenant for it.

Before they came, Reach had been a bustling world of verdant beauty and quiet joy. It was here Linda had been taught to fight and think, been molded into a super-soldier who could stand against any enemy. Here, she had come to trust the only friends she had ever known, and learned to embrace what the Office of Naval Intelligence had made from a confused six-year-old girl.

Now Reach was a barren sweep of glass. All of it gone.

The Covenant had stolen her past. She wanted to put a 114mm HEAP round through the head of every alien she saw (yes, even the ones who were supposedly allies now, she realized with a sharp pang of guilt), to burn their homes and raze their cities and wipe even the memory of their malevolent empire from the galactic record.

And she despised herself for being so weak. Because hate was surrender.

Hate gave control of one's thoughts and feelings to the enemy. It made a soldier predictable, and when a Spartan became predictable, the next thing she became was dead.

So a Spartan could not hate.

Linda allowed her dark thoughts to wash over her, observing her anger and despair without bringing it into her heart, letting it all pass through and be gone. The last order John had given her was to carry on with the mission, so she began to focus her attention on *that*—on trying to lead *Special* Crew westward without exposing the excavation machines to attack, on the tire tracks in the bottom of the aqueduct. She wondered where they might lead, and whether John and the rest of Blue Team could be in the vehicles that had made those tracks . . . but none of that was her reason for following them.

Yesterday Linda and *Special* Crew had spent five hours in an under-glass labyrinth of erosion channels, drilling and digging their way through sand-clogged passages and man-made connector passages, trying to move toward CASTLE Base while remaining protected from the Banished air attacks. They had finally given up after making only two kilometers of westward progress, then returned to the point where they had left the river—and found a half-arrow scratched on the wall, indicating an explosive trap placed ahead.

It was a common warning sign used by UNSC special forces, so it had seemed reasonable to hope it had been made by someone on Blue Team. Their hope had been reinforced by a few large boot prints among dozens of smaller ones in a sandy, churned-up trail that led into the aqueduct—where *all* of the boot prints had been replaced by the tire tracks that Linda and *Special* Crew were now following.

Because the aqueduct was large enough to drive through, and ran northwest away from the Banished base, Linda had made the decision to continue along. *Special* Crew had enlarged a short section of passage so the excavation machines could pass through, then traveled after the tire tracks up the aqueduct.

Maybe they were behind the rest of Blue Team. Or a party of starving scavengers—or even a pack of Banished. There was no way to tell. Linda's efforts to clarify the situation by raising someone on TEAMCOM had failed—which meant nothing. With a multi-hour head start, whoever they were following could now be hundreds of kilometers ahead. TEAMCOM simply did not have that kind of range—not without signal boosters and repeater stations.

The feeling of hate that had consumed Linda earlier was gone. But now her thoughts were racing wild—and, once again, her attention was wandering. She took a breath, then returned to the present, to the simple task of pursuing the tire tracks, noting the sensation of her heel coming down in the wet sand and her foot rolling forward until she sprang off her toes. She studied the gray light that filled the circular passage ahead, filtering down through the roof where the molten ground had burned through the titacrete and left behind a ribbon of ash-impregnated lechatelierite.

As her stomach unclenched and her mind cleared, Linda grew more aware of the steady thrum of the excavation machines behind her, and of her own breath pushing through her helmet air exchanger, and of a steady hissing, like a tire losing pressure. But the sound was coming from alongside her, not from behind, and it seemed to be growing louder as she advanced. She stopped and raised a clenched fist, signaling the excavation machines to wait, then listened more carefully.

The sound behind her gentled to a whisper, and the hissing

became more of a whooshing. There was a barely perceptible rise and fall of volume, and it seemed to be coming through the west wall of the aqueduct. She turned to the excavation machines—the drilling jumbo was in front—and drew her finger across her throat.

It took a solid moment for the machines to shut down. As Linda waited for quiet, she pressed her palm to the aqueduct's titacrete wall . . . and felt no vibration. But the *whoosh* grew more discernible as the machines behind her fell completely silent. And when Linda held her helmet close to the curved wall, the sound blossomed into something closer to a roar.

"What's that rushing noise?" Chapov called. "Some sort of fan?"

Linda looked up to see Lieutenant Chapov leading Major Van Houte and Chief Mukai down the aqueduct toward her. They were all carrying their weapons, a precaution that, after a dozen reminders, she was glad to see had finally been ingrained in them.

"I think not." Linda stepped back and motioned Chapov toward the wall. "Listen and tell me what you hear."

She could have increased the sensitivity of her helmet's auditory sensors, but that was no substitute for putting an ear directly to the wall and listening to the sound waves reverberate through the titacrete.

Chapov removed his helmet and pressed the side of his head to the wall, and his brow rose. "It's a waterfall."

"It is?" Linda waved her arm along a five-meter section of wall. "Where is it loudest?"

Chapov moved back and forth, selecting three separate places along the wall, then finally stepped back and pointed to the rightmost spot.

"There."

Linda banged the titacrete with her gauntlet and heard an echo from the other side. "Hollow," she said. "Step back."

Chapov scrambled out of the way, but as she drew her arm back, he said, "Wouldn't it be safer to use the drilling jumbo?"

"How?" Mukai asked. "There's barely room to drive it straight down this pipe, and the drilling heads only articulate thirty degrees."

"Trust me. This is safe," Linda said.

She stepped forward and drove her titanium gauntlet through the titacrete, creating a hole a little larger than her fist. The roaring grew instantly more distinct and identifiable as the sound of a small waterfall. She punched four more times, enlarging the opening to about twice the size of her helmet.

Beyond it lay a deep sinkhole, with a bottom of jumbled sandstone blocks half-buried in mud. It was easily forty meters long and fifteen wide, and lit by a lozenge-shaped "skylight" of gray lechatelierite. The waterfall she'd heard was at the far end, pouring out of an underglass erosion channel that looked double the size of the aqueduct.

It reminded her of the waterfall at the head of Black Iron Gorge, which she had descended during a training mission with John, Fred, Kelly . . . and Sam-034, who had been the first of too many Spartans lost to an alien attack. She had not thought of that event in years, but the sight of the waterfall brought back their wild ride through the gorge, on rafts of lashed logs. Sam had been a natural riverman, and had nearly gotten them through the worst of the rapids in one piece.

*Nearly.*

Chapov shoved his head into the hole next to Linda's. "*There's* our route west."

Linda glanced up at the cavity ceiling and saw a rosy blush at the far end. Between the heavy overcast and the ash-impregnated lechatelierite, a diffuse glow was the closest thing to a setting sun they could expect to see from under the glass. And it was brightest directly over the erosion channel behind the waterfall.

"Maybe," Linda said. "But how do we get there?"

"Get where?" Van Houte asked.

Linda backed out of the hole so he could take a look.

"Very pretty," Van Houte said. "But if that's the way out, and even if we *can* get there, how do we know it'll take us west? The last thing I want is to spend another day wandering through this underglass maze."

"The mountains are to the west," Chapov said. "And streams generally flow straighter than rivers. They don't drop as much sediment, so they don't form as many oxbows. Trust me, that stream will take us into the mountains."

"Eventually," Van Houte said. "*If* the erosion channel stays deep enough, and *if* it doesn't come up out of the ground the way it's disappearing into it here."

"Maybe that'll happen. If it does, we wait until dark and break out onto the surface, then make a dash for the mountains." Chapov pulled his head out of the hole, then pointed up the aqueduct they'd been following. "But our current route is carrying us northwest, when we need to go southwest. For every kilometer the aqueduct takes us in the right direction, we're also traveling half a kilometer in the wrong direction."

Van Houte stepped away from the hole. "I know how to navigate, Lieutenant." He faced Linda. "But he does have a point. The longer we take to reach CASTLE Base, the greater our chances of being discovered and attacked again."

"All other things being *equal*," Linda said. "But traveling on the surface under a hostile air umbrella is not equal to concealed movement under the glass."

"We're only concealed until the hostiles figure out where we went and follow us under the glass," Chapov said. "Then we're rats in a maze full of cats."

"And our excavation machines are no match for Choppers," Mukai said. She took her turn looking through the hole. "But we'd have to get our equipment across that sinkhole first, and it doesn't look very stable."

"Our excavation machines are no match for Banshees or Seraphs either," Van Houte pointed out. "What happens when the erosion channel closes, and we're forced to travel over the glass? It won't even be a contest."

"It doesn't matter." Mukai backed out of the hole. "Because you're not taking my machines across that sinkhole."

"We don't have to," Chapov said. "We just cut a new road around the edge. That won't be much harder than some of the excavation we've done already."

Mukai put her head back through the hole, then fell silent as she studied the possibilities. Van Houte cradled his MA2B in his arm and backed away. "I don't know about this," he remarked.

"You don't like this idea?" Linda asked.

"Not much," he replied. "What about the rest of Blue Team?"

"Our orders are to continue the mission," Linda said. "We proceed to CASTLE Base. If Blue Team is still capable, they'll find *us*."

"I know how it works," Van Houte said. "But I don't see how we *can* continue the mission without them. Especially not with thousands of Banished on our tail. They're going to find us sooner or later, and I hate to break it to you, but you're the only Spartan here."

"But she *is* a Spartan," Chapov said. "And we can run the equipment. We've already proven that."

Mukai stepped away from the hole, then stared at the ground and shook her head. "We can probably cut a road," she said. "But that's a sinkhole for a reason. If we touch off another collapse, we could lose the machines."

"And if we lose the machines," Van Houte said, "the mission fails."

"Look, there are a lot of ways the mission could fail right now," Chapov said. "We're in dire straits, which means we need to change our situation again. And that's worth taking a few risks."

"There's no arguing with that," Linda said. "But we also need to maximize our chance of success."

She tried TEAMCOM again.

The only reply she received was *Special* Crew touching their fingers to their headsets, straining to hear a response that didn't come.

"We have to do it," Chapov said. "It's our best chance."

"Maybe you're right," Linda said. She paused for a moment, searching for the calm inside herself—and wondering whether what she heard it telling her came from her head or her heart. "But if Dr. Halsey had believed that one Spartan could do this job, she would not have sent four. We stay in the aqueduct and follow these tire tracks until we know what happened to the rest of Blue Team."

# CHAPTER TEN

John glanced over as Lieutenant Disztl pulled the Warthog into the crowded parking area and was relieved to see the speedometer dropping below thirty kilometers an hour. But instead of swinging into an empty spot, she continued past a long line of more Warthogs and Mongoose ultralight ATVs, then swung to a sideways stop in front of a glass-block building large enough to quarter an entire mechanized platoon with their vehicles.

A pair of sentries in gray combat utilities with no insignia stood in front of the open entrance. The man was armed with an MA37 assault rifle and the woman with an MA5B, both likely salvaged—like everything in the Viery Militia—from the underground storage bunkers of an old UNSC facility. As John and Kelly dismounted the Warthog, the woman leaned through the door.

"They're here."

John expected to be challenged at the entrance, or at least told they would have to check their weapons. But the man simply waved them through.

"Straight ahead, Spartans. They're expecting you." He pointed at the door lintel. "Mind your heads. One bump, and you could bring this place crashing down."

"And thanks for coming," the woman said. "You're the last thing we were expecting."

"That's how we prefer it," Kelly said. "The element of surprise and all that."

"*Surprise* being the operative word," John said. He had not yet had the debriefing Colonel Boldisar had promised, so this would be his first opportunity to disabuse her of the notion that Blue Team was on Reach to support her rehab pioneers. "For everyone."

They ducked through the door into the foyer area of a large square chamber covered by a white nyonlin canopy supported by rods of bowed fiberglass. The perimeter was filled with dozens of support personnel in uniforms repurposed from random services, most bustling back and forth between two-meter display modules, updating unit-readiness reports, and reconciling intelligence dispatches. A few paused to gape at John and Kelly, but nobody stepped over to escort them—and none so much as blinked at the small armory attached to their Mjolnir's magnetic mounts.

"Not much in the way of headquarters security, is there?" Kelly said through her external voicemitter.

"No, not much," John said. "I wonder if any of them have actually ever been in the military?"

He started toward the center of the room, where Colonel Sasa Boldisar stood on a ring-shaped platform with nine of her commanders. They were staring down at a holographic display in the center of the ring, scowling and gesturing and snapping at one another with an alarming lack of discipline. When Boldisar saw them coming, she stepped away from the scrum to meet them.

John and Kelly stopped at the edge of the platform and came to attention. John brought his hand up in salute, but with Kelly's right arm locked in a sling position, she simply remained at attention.

"Spartans-117 and -087 reporting as requested," John said.

Boldisar's brow shot up. "That's not necessary, Master Chief." She waved the gesture off with a flip of her hand. "We seldom stand on ceremony around here."

"I can see that, ma'am." John held his salute. "But a salute is a sign of trust and respect—for both parties."

"Oh. In that case, thank you." Boldisar touched her fingers to her temple in an awkward salute toward John, then glanced at Kelly with a look of uncertainty.

Kelly used her left hand to tap the vambrace of her sling-locked armor. "My arm is impaired, and I'm afraid a left-handed salute is considered offensive in some services."

"Forgive me." She saluted Kelly. "I can see I have a lot to learn about commanding Spartans."

John and Kelly turned their faceplates toward each other; then John said, "Ma'am, we're not under your command. The UNSC doesn't detach Spartans."

"Detach?"

"Assign to another authority," Kelly explained. "One doesn't trust assets like us to someone else's control."

Boldisar's expression changed from disappointed to determined. "I see." She pointed toward a set of stairs that provided access to the meter-high platform. "In that case, please join us. There's something I'd like to ask of you."

She started back toward the knot of her commanders.

Rather than bothering with the stairs, John and Kelly clambered onto the platform and followed Boldisar. Also made of glass block—as most man-made structures were in the reclamation zone—it was a little wider than a Warthog and strewn with upright touch displays and holoprojection equipment, where technicians and aides were hard at work monitoring systems and correlating data.

In the interior of the ring floated a holographic map of the Eposz Reclamation Project. Easily ten meters across, the image depicted the heart of the Arany Basin on three different levels—surface, underglass, and subterranean. The upper layer portrayed the landscape that John had seen from the mouth of Tárnoc Falls, with a vast sweep of glass barrens broken by hundreds of swaths of open ground. The map was incredibly detailed, with tiny likenesses of the local buildings and red cubes or orange rings representing Banished facilities and perimeter defenses. Waterways—including the irrigation canal where John and his companions had been strafed by the Banshees, and the Lapos River where Linda had gone underglass with *Special* Crew— were shown in shimmering blue.

The middle layer of the holomap was a web of purple veins, depicting a vast network of hollow areas that lay hidden beneath the lechatelierite. Most of the passages appeared natural, being serpentine lines that lay beneath water features such as rivers and streams. These were often dotted or broken, probably indicating areas that were difficult to transit due to wet conditions or underglass flooding. Occasionally a tunnel simply ended at a lake or pond marked on the surface map.

Scattered randomly around the middle layer were other, larger features: long narrow openings that resembled the burn cavity in which the logistics base was located, big irregular depressions that might have been sinkholes, and several gently weaving lines that John could not even guess at. These all entered from the west edge of the map and often extended for great distances eastward without connecting to the network at all.

The lowest level of the holomap showed the deep caves and underground mines in the area. There were only a few dozen, and most were not connected to the rest of the underglass network. But a purple line running up to the surface indicated where each mine or cave could be accessed, and whether it was via vertical shaft or decline tunnel.

By the time John and Kelly reached the huddle of commanders, John had oriented himself well enough to identify the location of the farmstead where they'd first met Boldisar and Erdei—on the eastern edge of the reclamation zone—and Logistics Base Gödöllő—where they were now—a hundred kilometers outside the zone, directly to the west.

He also now had a detailed copy of the entire map stored in his Mjolnir's onboard memory. If the Viery Militia was going to treat its battlefield intelligence so casually, he saw nothing dishonorable in helping himself to it.

Boldisar had to push into the middle of the huddle before the commanders stopped arguing. Most of them wore either a hand-sewn mael leaf or a cedar bough on their collar tabs—no doubt the Viery Militia's equivalent of the gold or silver oak leaves worn by majors and lieutenant colonels in the UNSC marines. Other than Sasa Boldisar herself, the only officer John recognized was the bald and burly major, Istvan Erdei.

Once her commanders had fallen quiet, Boldisar ran through a quick round of introductions—which John relied on his onboard computer to record—then gestured to John and Kelly.

"I'm sure you've heard that the Master Chief and his team of Spartans will be joining us," she said. "Maybe *they* can take control of the situation."

Before John could object to being volunteered for a mission on behalf of an army he didn't even belong to, Boldisar turned to him, then pointed toward the holographic map, indicating a knot of darkened passages just to the east of Logistics Base Gödöllő.

"There's an enemy scouting patrol out there watching us," she explained. "And it's too good for our people to handle."

"That's premature, Sasa," protested a raw-featured lieutenant colonel. John's HUD identified him as Rendor Borbély. "My rangers were dispatched less than an hour ago."

"How long would it have taken those Brutes to see our preparations?" Boldisar demanded. "Then send someone back to report?"

"Not as long as it took them to follow *you* and Istvan all the way back from Kisköre," Borbély retorted.

John began to have a sneaking feeling that maybe the scouts

weren't Brutes at all. He and Kelly and Fred had arrived with Erdei's company only an hour ago . . . which made the timing about right, given that if Linda *had* been following them, she would have lagged behind and reconnoitered the area before approaching the base.

"*Nobody* followed us." Erdei sounded weary and angry, as though he had said the same thing many times already. "I *told* you, we had a rotating rear guard the entire way."

Linda would have expected a rear guard. She would have slipped past it as easily as most people opened a closed door, then spent her time traveling in the one place her surveillance targets wouldn't be looking for her—in the pocket between the main body and the rear guard.

"The last squad just came in five minutes ago," Erdei continued. "*After* the perimeter cams went out."

"And how do we even know we're looking for Brutes?" asked a slender major—Darda Tabori, according to the name on John's HUD. She wore her blond hair pulled back in a waist-length ponytail, but otherwise carried herself with a military bearing. "The perimeter cams didn't see anything before they went out, and we haven't found any tracks."

"Jackals, then," Boldisar said. "Or hinge-heads or Grunts, for all it matters. If Rendor can't track them down, we are lost."

"Give me time," Borbély said.

"Time is the *last* thing we have." Boldisar looked to John. "Will you explain that to them, Master Chief?"

"Certainly, ma'am," John said, ignoring for the moment that Boldisar probably had a lot more time than she thought. "Once I've been briefed on the situation."

"Isn't it obvious?" Boldisar gestured at the knot of darkened passages in the holographic map. "The enemy has taken out our perimeter cameras."

"How much of the network do you have under surveillance?" John asked. "It can't be everything we're looking at."

"Of course not," Boldisar said. "Just the approaches to our bases. The entire network would be almost a hundred kilometers. We don't have that many signal relays."

John studied the map, then pointed to the three intersections just beyond the darkened tangle. "But you blocked the egress routes, right?"

"The minute the first camera went down," Borbély said. "I'm not an idiot."

"I never said that you were," John said. That was the issue with an undisciplined army—when the pressure was on, its personnel started to focus on themselves instead of the problem. He faced Boldisar. "I'm sorry, ma'am, but I can't honor your request."

"What request would that be?"

"That I confirm you're running out of time. As long as you keep those intersections blocked, that scouting patrol isn't going anywhere."

"How would you know that?" Boldisar seemed more suspicious than she did relieved—and John didn't blame her. "How do we know they haven't slipped away already?"

"The way I've been *telling* you," Borbély said. "Some of the cameras went down *after* we blocked the intersection."

"Then why haven't you found the patrol?" Boldisar insisted. "That's less than two kilometers of passage, and you've had a hundred men searching in there for an hour."

John studied the knot of darkened tunnel. There was nothing in it that looked even remotely man-made, so it was probably some combination of erosion channels, burn cavities, and subsidence hollows. A Banished patrol might not be able to hide from a hundred men in there, but Linda certainly could.

"Ma'am, the colonel is right," John said. "The situation is under control."

"I wish I could be certain of that," she replied. "Our entire attack depends on the element of surprise."

"Attack?" John had hoped that the battle preparations he was seeing were for a defensive fight, because the pioneers might actually have a chance of surviving that. "How many soldiers do you have?"

"Doesn't matter," Erdei said. "*Someone* forced our hand when they busted into our tunnel at Kisköre. Now those alien devils know our plan, and we've got to move before they start closing up our tunnels."

"How many soldiers do you have?" John repeated. This was getting them nowhere.

"Five thousand," Boldisar said. "Give or take."

"What about the other bases?"

"That includes the other bases," Boldisar said. "Three thousand here, another two thousand spread between seven smaller bases."

"Including the Drifts?"

Borbély scowled. "How do you know about the Drifts?"

"Your security is rather poor," Kelly said. She looked to Boldisar. "And please tell me that strength figure doesn't include the Gönc Drifts, because half-trained children will not do anything in a battle but die."

"No, it doesn't," Boldisar said. "What kind of monsters do you think we are?"

"No kind at all," John said. Boldisar couldn't have known that John and Kelly had started their Spartan training at age six, as that information was still highly classified. "But no one trains soldiers they don't expect to need."

"We were preparing for a long war," Tabori said. "The last thing we expected was for the UNSC to come to our rescue."

John forced himself not to glance in Kelly's direction. It was hard to read much through a mirrored faceplate, but he suspected just about anyone present would have been able to read *that*.

"Understandable," John said. He began to study the holographic map in more detail, noting how a man-made passage departed the network near each Banished base and extended toward it. In three cases, it even reached beneath the base. "You were going to attack from underneath?"

"We were," Boldisar said. "But it's taken two months to get *this* far, and it would take another three to finish the tunnels."

"And the Banished will destroy it all in three weeks," Borbély said. "If it takes them that long."

"So we have no choice," Boldisar said. "We have to take them out now—before we lose the only advantage we have."

"Attacking over the glass?" John asked.

"Except where we have other access, yes," Boldisar said. "We'll approach as close as we can underglass, then break out onto the surface and attack."

"No good." John spoke only over TEAMCOM, not caring that he might be overheard by the personnel tending to Fred in the infirmary. "It's a desperation move."

"They'll be slaughtered," Kelly replied on TEAMCOM. "They have no air support, and from what we've seen so far, they are poorly—"

"*Still* can't put my helmet on," Fred interrupted. "And I've got two nurses right here next to me, working on that hematoma."

"Affirmative," John said. The TEAMCOM signal was a good reflector that bounced off almost any nonabsorbent surface, so he was not surprised that Fred was still receiving despite a line of sight blocked by forty meters of sandstone slope. And since Fred's helmet would serve as a signal repeater, he was hoping that if Linda was somewhere nearby, she would be able to receive too. "Just stay where you are and await orders. Leave the equipment alone."

"I'm sorry?" Fred asked.

"You heard me—the equipment. We don't need you causing any more trouble than you have," John said. "Confirm, Blue Four."

"Blue . . . *Four*?" Fred hesitated, then seemed to realize that John's message wasn't intended for him at all. Maybe his concussion was getting better. "Fine, I'll confirm."

At the same time, Linda's LED flashed green inside John's helmet. It wasn't as good as a verbal confirmation, but John would take it. If

Linda hadn't been the one disabling the perimeter cameras, she would have flashed red or yellow.

"Master Chief?" Boldisar asked. "Did you have some thoughts you'd like to share?"

Boldisar and her commanders were watching John intently, the ones with eager eyes no doubt waiting for him to pronounce their plan sound, the ones with furrowed brows probably hoping he would tell everyone else how crazy it was.

But John had his own mission to think about, and that meant gathering intelligence wherever he could.

He walked along the platform until he was above one of the gently weaving lines that entered from the western edge of the map. There were several breaks in the line—presumably the impassable sections— but the route was one of the few that linked to the militia's tunnel network, joining it via a cave some distance west of Base Gödöllő.

"What's this passage?" he asked.

"We call it a tubeway," Tabori said. She'd been among the brow-furrowing contingent when Boldisar asked for John's thoughts. "You see how steeply downward it slopes?"

"Now I do," John said. "This is where the Arany Basin starts to rise toward the Highland Mountains?"

"Exactly," Tabori said. "The lechatelierite cooled more slowly next to the ground than on the surface. The tubeways formed wherever the slope was steep enough for the molten glass to flow away before it solidified, and where there was a place for it to drain. The lechatelierite filling the bottom of that cave is a hundred meters thick. The crust is still hot to the touch."

"And that is how you travel back and forth to the Gönc Drifts, is it?" Kelly asked. Sometimes it seemed like the members of Blue Team had worked together so long that they could read each other's minds. "Through the tubeways?"

"Not unless we want to crawl," said Borbély. "Most of those tubes are only half a meter high."

"Then how *do* you move back and forth to the Drifts?" John asked. "You can't travel overglass—not with the kind of Banished air presence we've seen."

Tabori started to point, but Boldisar pushed her arm down before John could determine what the major had intended to indicate.

"Why are you so interested in how we access the Gönc Drifts?" Boldisar asked.

"I should think that is obvious, ma'am," Kelly said. "Your survivors will need a ready route of retreat."

Boldisar's face grew stormy. "*Retreat?*"

"Yes, ma'am," John said. "I count nineteen Banished bases in your reclamation zone alone. At five hundred warriors per base, that's over nine thousand Banished. Minimum."

"And the figure is closer to a thousand per," Tabori said. "We're estimating twenty thousand."

"And that's just in the zone," Borbély added. "There's another group that's been reconnoitering sites all over Eposz. It's harder to estimate their strength, but it has to be in the thousands."

John had to force himself not to look at Kelly. For the second time. "What are they looking for?"

Borbély shrugged. "All I can tell you is they seem *really* interested in mountains. Especially the unusual ones."

"Unusual how?" John asked.

"The highest, the biggest, the sheerest," Borbély said. "Standing alone, odd shapes—you know, special."

"Why, Master Chief?" Boldisar glanced from him to Kelly, then asked, "Is there something we should know about Reach's mountains?"

"No, ma'am," John said. "Not that I'm aware of. But if you understood what the Banished are doing here on Reach, it might help you get rid of them."

"*Us.*"

"Ma'am?"

"It might help *us* get rid of them," Boldisar said. "Isn't that what you meant to say?"

"Nobody likes seeing the Banished on Reach," John said. *Especially Blue Team*, he added to himself. "But launching a suicide attack is no way to rid yourselves of them."

"And that's what you think this is?" Tabori asked. "A suicide attack?"

John looked to Kelly and nodded.

Kelly repeated the gesture right back, then asked Tabori, "Don't *you*? You're outnumbered at least four to one. The Banished will be fighting from defensive positions, *with* air superiority. They are better equipped and better trained. You won't even reach their shield barriers, much less breach them."

"But we'll have the element of surprise," Boldisar said.

"No, you won't," John said.

"We'll attack at night," she said. "We'll take them in their sleep."

"They won't *be* asleep," John said. "By the time you crawl out of your tunnels and form up, they'll be awake and dropping mortar rounds on your heads. By the time you start your advance, they'll be spraying your line with ballistic spikes. By the time you close to fifty meters, your survivors will realize there aren't enough of them left to take down the lookout towers, so the advance will stall while they try to figure out what to do next. Then the Banshees will start strafing, and they'll retreat in disorder. It will be a massacre."

"*Maybe* ten percent of your original force will make it back underglass, and half of them will be wounded." Kelly studied the commanders. "Didn't any of you serve in the military?"

"There aren't a lot of Reavian soldiers left here after 2552," Erdei said. "The ones who survived the Covenant invasion were generally in the UNSC on assignment somewhere else, and most of them have remained in service."

Tabori raised a finger. "I was a logistics specialist in the 717th Xeno-Materials Exploitation Battalion."

"You were on Gao?" Kelly asked.

Tabori nodded. "Stationed at the Vitality Center. But I was at Wendosa."

"Forget Wendosa," Kelly said. "This will be a thousand times worse. Most of you will die, and those who don't will wish they had."

"We'll concentrate our attacks," Boldisar said. "We'll take the three bases we're under now—and make them attack *us*."

"Then you'll die later," John said.

Boldisar frowned. "So what *do* you suggest we do, Master Chief?"

"Evacuate to the Gönc Drifts. Wait for the enemy to leave."

"Run and hide?" asked Erdei. "*That's* your strategy, Mr. Spartan?"

"Only if you want to live," John said. "The Banished aren't here to stay. Whatever they're looking for, they'll leave as soon as they've found it. We can arrange a supply drop to help you survive until then."

"Supply . . . drop?" Erdei craned his thick neck toward Boldisar. "You—you said they were here to liberate us."

"They are. They just want us out of harm's way." She gave John a hard stare. "Isn't that right, Master Chief?"

"No, ma'am, it's not," John said. "Seriously, you should go to the Gönc Drifts and wait it out."

Before Boldisar could reply, Borbély asked, "For how long?"

"However long it takes the Banished to find what they're looking for and leave," John said. "I thought I made that clear."

"Not entirely," Borbély said. "If you're so confident the Banished will leave, then you must also know what they're looking for."

"Not with certainty," John admitted. "But we have our suspicions."

"Which are?" Borbély asked.

"Classified," John said. "But everything I know points to the Drifts as your best option."

Erdei turned to Borbély. "How long do we have?" he asked. "The Tin Man is dodging us, and we can't hold out another two months."

Borbély sighed. "Not even another month," he said. "We don't have the reserves."

"You *did* hear him say we can arrange a supply drop?" Kelly said. "It will be a lot of paste rations, but it should keep everyone from starving to death."

"It's more than just food," Boldisar said. "We're trying to rebuild a world here. The microbes and humus have been burned out of the soil, and now it's just dirt."

"Microbes?" John asked. "You're going to war with the Banished over . . . microbes?"

"And humus," Borbély said. "The microbes need organic matter to survive. If we don't reclaim our land and start working it in the next few weeks, everything will start dying again. And all of the work we've put in over the last two years? We'll have to write it all off."

"A few hundred farms are too big to write off?" Kelly asked. "Truly?"

"Didn't anyone brief you?" Boldisar asked. "The farms are just the first stage—the breadbasket that will support everything else."

"It's the mines that are the thing," Erdei said. "Reach has the richest titanium, gallium, and osmium reserves in the Colonies. That didn't go away just because it got glassed."

"We want our world back," Boldisar said. "And we need an economic base to support it. That isn't going to happen if we don't remove the Banished soon."

Borbély stepped to within a meter of John and looked up into his faceplate. "So we need a straight answer, Master Chief. How soon will the Banished find what they're looking for here—and leave?"

Kelly's voice came over TEAMCOM. "We have to be honest with them, Leader. They're gambling their future on what we tell them."

"Affirmative," John replied over TEAMCOM.

The trouble was, he didn't have an answer the pioneers could rely on. If Blue Team and *Special* Crew were successful in their bid to slip away, they might recover the assets from CASTLE Base and extract without the Banished ever realizing their mission had become unviable. He switched back to his external voicemitter. "It could be as soon as a few days, but—"

"*Could* be?" Erdei shook his head in disgust. "He's dodging again."

"Agreed." Boldisar turned to the other commanders. "Look . . . if we delay the attack, we're done on Reach. Dead, probably."

"We're not dead if we leave," Tabori said. "Maybe it's time we think about cutting *our* losses. We could use the last of our funds to hire an evacuation ship."

"No, we couldn't," said Borbély. "There's not a commercial transport line in the Colonies that would enter orbit as long as the Banished are here." He looked to John. "The Banished destroyed our ship, so we'd have to rely on the UNSC."

*And that would be a mistake,* John thought. Even if Captain Lasky were willing to engage the Banished and ultimately risk drawing Cortana's attention, the *Infinity* was a warship under the AI's sustained pursuit. The rehab pioneers would have a better survival chance hiding out in the Gönc Drifts—especially if one of Cortana's Guardians ever caught up to the supercarrier.

"I doubt the UNSC is an evacuation option right now," John said.

"You doubt?" Tabori asked. "Or you know?"

"I could make an inquiry—in . . ."

John activated his HUD chronometer to check the time until twilight, when the *Bucephalus* would be passing directly overhead and open to point-to-point transmissions—then realized that, after a day of meandering underglass travel, his onboard computer was unable to determine his exact coordinates to calculate the answer.

"At dusk," he finished. "But I would have to be on the surface."

Boldisar checked the commpad on her wrist. "Dusk was thirty minutes ago."

"At dawn, then," John said. "But we wouldn't receive a reply until dusk tomorrow."

"We could be under attack by then," Erdei said. "And those

Banished bastards will *definitely* be deep into our underglass network at that point."

"It's the best we can do," John said. "And, honestly, I don't think the answer would be worth waiting for."

"Because you already told us what the answer will be?" Tabori asked.

"Yes, ma'am. I'm certain the task force commander would come to the same conclusion I have." It was a bit of a stretch to call a single supercarrier a task force—even if it packed the power of one—but the last thing John wanted to reveal right now was just how desperate and shorthanded the UNSC really was since Cortana had unleashed the Guardians. "You'd be better off hiding in the Drifts."

"The Drifts are not an option." Colonel Boldisar pointed a long finger at John's chest. "I won't ask our members to starve in the dark for who knows how long just because you refuse to do what you were sent here to do. You can put that idea out of your mind right now, Spartan."

Tabori's face sank, and Borbély actually retreated a step. They, at least, understood the situation—and recognized what would become of them if the rehab pioneers pressed ahead with Boldisar's plan.

"Ma'am, with all due respect, you don't know what my orders are because I haven't told you," John said. "But I promise you, they do not involve taking part in your suicide attack."

"What if it didn't need to be a suicide attack?" Erdei asked.

"If you lot attack," Kelly said, "it's *going* to be suicide."

"But what if it wasn't?" Erdei insisted. "What if we could get them to attack *us* at a disadvantage?"

Boldisar gave him a look. "Go on."

Erdei crooked a finger and started walking, leading the group halfway around the platform to the southwest side of the holomap. He gestured toward a massive Banished base on what looked like the site of a collective village.

"What if we took something they *had* to take back?" he said. "Like the armory at New Mohács?"

Over TEAMCOM, Kelly said, "Permission to remove helmet? This foolery is making me feel sick."

"Permission denied," John said. "We can offer advice, but we can't make them take it. Let's stay focused on the objective."

"Affirmative." Kelly switched to her voicemitter, then said, "That is a big base. Once you've captured it, you would need to bring in reinforcements from the Drifts. How would you get them there?"

Instead of answering, Erdei asked, "So you think we can capture it, then?"

"Would you attack from underneath?"

"The hardest part would be punching through the last thirty meters of ground without giving ourselves away," Erdei said. "But this is New Mohács, built on the site of old Mohács. It's all packed dirt under there, and once we broke into the old sewer system, we could pop up all over the base."

"Then you could capture it. It's *holding* it that would be your problem." Kelly looked toward the western edge of the holomap. "How would you get your reinforcements down from the Drifts without being interdicted?"

Tabori looked toward the middle of the holograph's left edge, where several tubeways snaked downward, ending at caverns, lakes, and something that looked like an old quarry. None of these tubeways seemed to connect to the pioneers' underglass tunnel network, at least not from what John could see. But Tabori extended a finger—and Boldisar stepped in front of her.

"Again, all these questions about reaching the Drifts," Boldisar said. "I am beginning to think you Spartans are more interested in *them* than us."

"Even attacking from underneath, you'd lose a lot of fighters," John said. "You would find yourselves fighting building to building, and that would cost lives."

"You should count on losing a third of your force, at the minimum," Kelly said. "And the survivors would be exhausted and in shock. You would need to reinforce them before the counterattack came, because you would still be outnumbered—and those shield barriers belong to the Banished. If they can't turn them off from a distance, they would know how best to take them out."

"So how would you bring your reinforcements in from the Drifts?" John asked. "There's no use taking the armory if the enemy is only going to overrun you when they counterattack."

Boldisar and the other commanders' only reply was to stare at John with raised brows and slack jaws.

It was Tabori who finally recovered enough to answer John's question. "We don't *have* reinforcements," she said. "I thought you understood. There is no one in the Drifts but children."

"No one?" John asked.

"Except for a few hundred trainers," Tabori said. "And most of them were too old to fight when Reach was first glassed."

"Then you cannot even *consider* this attack," Kelly said. "After the first battle, you might still have three thousand half-trained soldiers without mechanized armor—"

"We'd have mechanized armor after the attack," Erdei said. "We're taking an armory. Full of Wraiths and Marauders."

"A *Banished* armory," John said. "It's filled with alien vehicles you've never trained with, and some you've never even seen. You'd suffer two or three percent casualties learning to use them. Best case, you'd end up a poorly trained, well-equipped force. That's not much better than half-trained and poorly equipped."

"And you would be outnumbered six or seven to one," Kelly added. "At those odds, your defensive advantage wouldn't much matter."

"So we shouldn't even try?" Boldisar asked. "We should go hide in the Drifts just so *you* can find out how we travel back and forth into the mountains?"

"She didn't say that," John said.

"She didn't need to," Borbély retorted.

"It couldn't be any more obvious if you painted it on your helmets,"

Erdei added. He glanced toward Boldisar. "I don't think they're here to liberate Reach."

"It's beginning to look that way," Boldisar said.

"I told you—from the start—that isn't our mission," John said.

Boldisar's tone grew sharp. "You didn't tell me much of anything, Spartan. You let me assume you were an advance unit."

John hadn't let her assume anything, but he hadn't led the Spartans for three decades without learning a few things about political infighting. She was trying to shift the blame onto him to protect her own position. And if she was willing to make that kind of gamble against someone as publicly revered as the Master Chief, her position couldn't be as strong as she tried to make it appear.

That left John with two options. He could try to undermine her, and hope that whoever emerged as the new militia leader would be more willing to help Blue Team reach the Highland Mountains undetected. Or he could do the unexpected and try to make an ally of her—and it was usually the unexpected tactic that worked best.

Politics was a lot like combat that way.

Maybe the Diplomatic Corps was worth a shot someday.

"It wasn't my intent to mislead you, Founding Director," John said. "I'm sorry if I did."

Boldisar's jaw dropped, further elongating her narrow face. "You . . . uh, very well . . . apology accepted."

"Thank you, ma'am," John said. "But no matter our reason for being on Reach, we are not your enemy. Spartan-087's advice is sound. You wouldn't be able to hold the armory when you're outnumbered so badly—especially not against an enemy with mechanized armor. You wouldn't even inflict many casualties before you died."

"What if we weren't outnumbered six to one?" Erdei asked. "What if it was more like three to one?"

"Then you might have a chance, *if* the Banished can't deactivate their shield barrier remotely." John paused, trying to guess how Erdei hoped to reduce the enemy's strength by half. "But if you have no reinforcements, I don't see where you would find the strength to launch a convincing diversion."

"I think Istvan is hoping we wouldn't need to," said Boldisar. "We've been stirring up trouble between the Red Armors and the Moon Helmets for weeks."

John had not yet seen any of the Banished up close, but he assumed that the nicknames reflected the appearance of the two factions he'd seen fighting from the mouth of Tárnoc Gorge.

"*You're* responsible for that?" he asked. "All the internal fighting?"

Boldisar offered a coy smile. "Let's just say we've been quietly encouraging their natural tendencies."

"What we've been doing is trying to get them angry and suspicious enough to wipe each other out," Erdei said. "That would only leave us with the Keepers of the One Freedom, and we could probably put up with them until they left of their own accord."

"The *Keepers*?" John asked. Maybe his initial assessment of the Seraphs that had taken down their Owl hadn't been a mistake after all. "They're working with the Banished now?"

"They are if they wear blue armor with gold trim," Erdei said. "More Grunts than the other two tribes, lots of Kig-Yar, not many hinge-heads?"

"That certainly sounds like the Keepers of the One Freedom," Kelly said. "Though why they're consorting with the likes of the Banished, I can't imagine. They're supposed to be more ideological."

"It's the Keepers for sure," Tabori said. "I recognized the armor from Gao—that's how we identified them. They're the ones who've been doing most of the sniffing around the mountains too."

"The Keepers have been on Reach the whole time?" John asked. "For two months?"

Tabori nodded. "That's right. They were the first to land."

Kelly tipped her helmet to one side, a *something doesn't make sense here* signal. And John was thinking the same thing.

The timing was all wrong. The decision to retrieve the assets from

Dr. Halsey's lab had been made only three weeks before Blue Team inserted. And it hadn't even occurred to Dr. Halsey that Blue Team would need to spoof the vault's biological safeguards until John had asked about the security systems.

"They couldn't have been waiting on us," Kelly finally said over TEAMCOM. "Even *she* couldn't have planned that far ahead."

John had quickly discounted Lieutenant Chapov's suggestion that Dr. Halsey might have set them up so the Banished could capture the spoofers. But her history of collaborating with the enemy, and implementing long-term schemes for her own purposes, had made it impossible to disregard that theory entirely.

But now he could. The timing issues alone were enough to disprove the theory—and even more conclusive, had Halsey been working with the Banished, the Keepers would not have been conducting a blind search of the mountains. They would have already known where to find CASTLE Base.

"Agreed," John said over TEAMCOM. He was mindful that there might be medical personnel within earshot of Fred's helmet, so he was careful about what he said next. "But they've still been following us, and it's not because they like our shiny armor."

"*Hello?*" Boldisar said. "If you two know something about the Keepers that would affect the armory assault, we need to hear it. Now."

"I'm sorry, ma'am," John said. "It appears your intelligence is better than ours. We've been making some faulty assumptions about the Banished's goals."

"Which are?" Borbély asked.

"In light of the information Major Tabori just provided," John said, "we're going to have to reappraise that."

Boldisar smirked. "Then I guess we can rule out hiding in the Gönc Drifts until they decide to leave." She ran her gaze around the group of her commanders, pausing to make eye contact with each one, then asked, "Are we all agreed?"

They mumbled their assent or gave curt nods, and once she had their commitment, she faced Erdei.

"Let's put together a plan to take the New Mohács armory." She glanced up at John and Kelly, then closed her eyes for a moment and seemed to come to a decision. "But I'm concerned about the advice our Spartan friends are giving us, and I have a feeling our attack will bring the Banished together in a manner we won't like."

"It might," Erdei said.

"It *will*," Kelly said. "You have them squabbling among themselves now, but you're prey to them. When they realize you bite back, they'll come together to put an end to you."

Finally Kelly seemed to be getting through to the woman. Boldisar nodded. "I agree." She looked back to her commanders and held their gazes. "In fact, I'm *counting* on it."

Over TEAMCOM, Kelly said, "This can't be good."

John dropped his chin to indicate agreement, then watched as Boldisar continued to speak.

"So let's think of the armory as the bait—not the trap."

Erdei appeared confused, but Tabori's face paled, while Borbély's eyes grew round.

"You want to use a Havok?" Borbély asked.

"Draw them in, blow them up," replied Boldisar.

"Wait." John was aghast. "You have a Havok?"

"We have several nuclear devices," Borbély said. "But so far I've only been able to bypass the lockout circuits on the BB 2550s."

"*Bloody hell*," Kelly said over TEAMCOM. "They're serious."

John didn't reply. He studied Borbély's sharp features and weather-beaten face more carefully, seeking some hint of the technical skill it would take to bypass a nuclear device's safety lockout system.

Borbély flashed a sheepish smile. "I was a systems engineer at Rajtom."

"That answers one question." Rajtom had been a Misriah Armory R&D facility located outside the Reach city of Erőd. John had no idea how many weapons systems had been created there, but the Havok *was* a Misriah Armory design. "And I assume that's where your devices came from?"

Borbély nodded. "We had an assortment in the storage bunker for research purposes."

"How lucky," Kelly said. "Did you recover any other surprises you haven't mentioned?"

"Why should we tell you?" Boldisar asked. "The Master Chief has made it clear that you're not here to liberate Reach."

"No, ma'am," John said. "But we might be able to advise you on how to use your forces and weapons most effectively."

"I like the plan we're developing now," Erdei said.

"You *would*," Kelly said. "You haven't had time to think through the problems yet."

"Such as?" Boldisar asked.

"To begin with, you'll have to be there," Kelly said. "You can't just leave the device in the village square and be on your merry way. Your enemies will grow suspicious and send someone to investigate while the rest of them stand off."

"I'll lead the volunteers," Erdei said. "There'll be no shortage of them, if our efforts will rid us of the Banished."

"You might succeed in eliminating most of them," John said. The instant-death blast radius of a thirty-megaton Havok was nearly seven kilometers. The heat flash would inflict third-degree burns on clothed flesh out to forty-four kilometers. So any Banished taking part in the assault on the New Mohács armory would be neutralized. "But you'll never get them all. There will be plenty of survivors outside the kill zone."

"True," Boldisar said. "But you're underestimating how the thermonuclear annihilation of their friends will affect their morale. I think the survivors will abandon Reach before we do it to them again."

"That's one possibility," John said. "The other possibility is that the Banished have their own nukes."

The flash in Boldisar's eyes suggested she had not considered that. But Erdei said, "Good point. You Spartans think of everything—especially when it comes to avoiding a fight."

"That might have something to do with how many we've been in," Kelly said. "We know the cost—and how to weigh it."

Erdei ignored her and addressed his fellow commanders. "So you disperse after we take the armory. What could they nuke that they haven't destroyed already?"

Boldisar thought for a moment, then said, "We'd need to disperse the training battalions too. But I like this idea." She stepped to the edge of the holograph and called, "Enlarge New Mohács. Let's see what we can do about planning our evacuation routes."

As the commanders gathered around her, Kelly's voice came over TEAMCOM. "I don't think we're going to talk them out of it."

"Yes, we are," John said, also over TEAMCOM. They were cornered, and he knew it. Even if they left the rehab pioneers to their own devices, Colonel Boldisar would use the Havok—and that could not be permitted. "There are still thousands of utility satellites in the Epsilon Eridani system. If a thirty-megaton nuke detonates on Reach, one of them is going to notice it—and feed an alert into Waypoint."

"Oh, that would be bad." Fred's voice no longer sounded tinny and distant—a sign, John hoped, that the hematoma on his head had finally diminished enough for him to put his helmet back on. "Cortana would pick up on that for sure."

John felt Kelly tense without even looking in her direction. "Let's avoid using her name in comms."

"Sorry," Fred said. "I have a concussion."

"At least you have an excuse," Kelly said. "This time."

"Is this channel secure now?" John asked.

"My helmet's back on, if that's what you mean."

"It is," John said. "Stand by for orders. Blue Four, status?"

Linda's status LED flashed green, an indication that the rangers searching for her were so close she could not risk speaking, even inside her armor. John flashed green on his own status to acknowledge that he understood, then pushed his way into the line of Boldisar's commanders.

"This plan would interfere with my mission," he said through his voicemitter. "I can't let you execute it."

Erdei whirled on him with fire in his eyes. "Try to stop us."

"If it comes to that, Blue Team *will* stop you." John turned to Boldisar. "But I'd rather strike a deal."

"Okay, talk," she said. "What kind of deal?"

"There's a risk that it would draw one of her Guardians." John pointed upward, indicating Cortana, the unseen *her* who had the potential to tap into any data feed in the system. "Then again, so would detonating a Havok—just faster."

"Guardians we can live with," Boldisar said. "In fact, given our trouble with the Banished, it might be nice to have one around."

"It won't be," Kelly said. "I'm willing to give you my word about that."

"Still, we'd have a chance with the Guardian," Borbély said. He looked to John. "What are you proposing?"

"An alliance," John said. "We help you rid yourselves of the Banished. In return, you forget the nukes, and help us get where we need to go in the Highland Mountains."

"Where do you need to go?" Boldisar asked. "And what exactly are you doing there?"

"I'll answer the first question when it's necessary for you to know," John said. "And I'll forget you ever asked the second one."

Boldisar gave him a hard look, then said, "No deal. I'm not agreeing to something like that blind."

"And surely not for three Spartans," Erdei said. "So far all you've done is talk about avoiding fights—and exposed our tunneling operations to the enemy. I don't see you three turning the tide against twenty thousand Banished."

John stepped toward the major, causing the man to stagger back ever so slightly. "Two things: first, it's *four* of us." He glanced over at Borbély. "Are you in contact with your rangers?"

"I can be."

"Do it," John said. He switched to TEAMCOM. "Blue Four, reveal yourself to the search party. Try to avoid harming anyone, but defend yourself if required."

"It's not," Linda replied. "They're surrendering now."

"Acknowledged," John said. "Call *Special* Crew forward and stand by for orders."

"Affirmative," Linda said. "It'll take a while for *Special* Crew to arrive. They're resting in a hide five kilometers back."

"That will be fine," John said. He looked toward Borbély, who was now holding a headset to one ear and staring at the platform with a gaping mouth, then spoke through his voicemitter. "What are you hearing, Colonel?"

Borbély looked up. "It was a Spartan? *You* were the ones who took out our perimeter cameras?"

Kelly used her left hand to pat him on the shoulder. "Don't be offended. We weren't allies at the time." She looked over at Boldisar. "We *are* allies now, are we not?"

Boldisar swallowed. "We're getting close. But I'm not making any deals for *four* Spartans, either. You may be good, but you're not worth a Havok."

"Which brings me to the second thing." John looked back to Erdei, then said, "Four Spartans are just the beginning."

# CHAPTER ELEVEN

**0234 hours, October 11, 2559 (military calendar)**
**Underglass Approach, Banished Armory, New Mohács**
**Arany Basin, Continent Eposz, Planet Reach**

The load-haul-dump machine went into reverse with a loud whine, then raced past the alcove where John waited with the rest of Blue Team and twenty Reavian rangers. Stella Mukai was driving, her swiveling control seat facing aft so she could run the vehicle backward as easily as she did forward. The only light came from the green dimdots glowing almost imperceptibly along the edges of the passage, but her helmet's flip-down night-vision visor utilized light-gathering technology that allowed her to see clearly even in such dark conditions.

The underglass pond where Mukai had to empty the bucket was seventy meters back, so John took the opportunity to step into the tunnel. It felt like he had a permanent charley horse in his quadriceps, but in the two and a third days since his visit to Dr. Somogy in the Gödöllő Infirmary, the wound had already healed to the point that he wasn't limping as he walked forward.

The faint light from the dimdots was more than adequate for his Mjolnir's fused-mode night-vision system to provide a crisp picture of the ground through which they were excavating the passage. Unlike the sandy soil prevalent in most of the Arany Basin, the dirt around New Mohács was dense clay, so compacted it broke away from the working face in helmet-sized chunks.

John came to the demarcation line between the sandy ground where the Viery Militia had stopped digging and the clay soil where Mukai had started work with the LHD. He didn't know why the ground changed so abruptly there, but the militia's engineering battalion had already driven the tunnel almost a kilometer, branching off an underglass erosion channel, and there was no possibility of rerouting it now.

The tunnel's working face was ten meters ahead, which meant Mukai still had roughly twenty meters to dig before passing beneath the shield barrier that surrounded the Banished armory. After that, it would be another ten meters to the storm sewers that had served old Mohács, which Blue Team would then enter and chart, doing their best to relate the passages to a map of New Mohács that the pioneers had drawn from memory. With any luck, their guesses about which buildings served as the Banished barracks, hangars, and weapons vaults would prove reasonably accurate, and John would be able to select attack points under the most important facilities.

Then came the hard part: moving five hundred nervous militia soldiers out of the underglass tunnel network into the old sewer system and guiding them to their jump-off points. It would have to be done in near-darkness, with only a handful of soldiers wearing night-vision equipment, and it would have to be done quietly, with no yelling or shouting or accidental weapon discharges.

And it all had to be done in less than an hour, because at oh-three-twenty, four thousand militia members would be launching an overglass mechanized assault on the base. The lookout towers and shield barriers had to be down by then, or the surface attack would not even reach the base perimeter. The rehab pioneers would simply be cut down out on the barrens, and then the thousands of UNSC troops that Blue Team had requested from the *Infinity* would be inserting without a secure landing zone.

So John had bigger things to worry about than what kind of dirt Mukai was excavating.

He glanced at the lechatelierite overhead. Through his NVS, it looked as bright as a cloud full of ball lightning. But from above, particularly from the lookout towers surrounding the armory, he knew the glass would appear to be as dark as ink—until someone inadvertently shined a handlamp up from below. Even a single LED cluster would light up the surface like a ribbon of moonlit sea. How the Viery Militia was going to move five hundred inexperienced soldiers into position as quickly as it needed to, without alerting the enemy, he had no idea. But over the last two days of planning, preparation, and movement, Borbély and Boldisar had assured him numerous times they *would*, and the entire assault depended on the militia's ability to keep that promise.

He wished it didn't. As a Spartan, John was not accustomed to relying on citizen-soldiers to execute an assault. But there were at least a thousand Banished inside New Mohács, and those odds were a little steep—even for Blue Team.

He heard the LHD crunching up the passage behind him and retreated to the alcove, rejoining the rest of Blue Team and the Reavian rangers. None of the "rangers" had actually served in a military unit before joining the militia, but they had all been in at least one firefight with a Banished patrol, as that was the recruitment criterion.

The platoon selected to join the Spartans in spearheading the attack had been avid hunters before the fall of Reach. According to Borbély, they could all move silently, conceal themselves, and fire their weapons accurately. Fred had also given them a crash course in combat demolitions, so "blasting stuff to hell" could be added to their skill set. That hardly made them Orbital Drop Shock Troopers, but it *did* make them willing, courageous, and, under the circumstances, better than nothing.

A muffled *crump* sounded over the noise of the LHD, and John peered out of the alcove to see the squat machine pushing its bucket through the compacted dirt at the head of the passage.

The LHD lurched forward into a blackness so dark that not even his dual-mode night-vision system could penetrate it. The front tires sank, as though dropping off a ledge, and the rear wheels stopped spinning. The machine quieted to a ready thrum, and then sat motionless, with Mukai leaning forward over the controls, evidently peering into the blackness ahead.

"*Special* Three?" John asked over TEAMCOM. "Report."

No response. He waited a moment for the LHD to reverse; when that didn't happen, he stepped into the passage and started forward. He caught a whiff of dampness through the Mjolnir's ventilation system; then an alarm pinged inside his helmet, and his system switched to purified air.

A message appeared on his HUD: $CO_2$ 12% $CH_4$ 3%

Carbon dioxide and methane. Neither was breathable, and methane's explosive properties could make it instantly fatal.

"No sparks," John ordered, both over TEAMCOM and through his voicemitter. "I'm detecting high levels of methane."

The percentages climbed rapidly as he continued forward, the carbon dioxide now at 17 percent and the methane at 7 percent. At least he understood why they hadn't blown up yet. There wasn't enough oxygen in the air to support an explosion.

But methane could still burn at those levels.

John reached the LHD and slipped alongside it, then pulled Mukai's unconscious form back in her seat and killed the engine. The carbon dioxide levels had topped out at 21 percent, but the methane was at 12 percent and still climbing.

"Evacuate down the—"

"Too late," Fred said. "The rangers are down."

"Might I inquire as to what the hell happened?" Kelly asked.

"Bad air." John pressed the pad of his left ring finger to Mukai's throat. The sensor activated, and her pulse rate appeared on his HUD—a frantic 120 beats a minute. "We need ventilation. Now."

John pulled the MA40 off its magmount and fitted the sound suppressor onto the barrel, then began to fire—quietly—at the ceiling, his rounds chipping away at the meter-thick lechatelierite. Even with so much carbon dioxide in the air, there was still a slim chance that a gunshot would ignite the methane and cause a flash fire. But for Mukai and the rangers to pass out so quickly, the oxygen levels had to be almost nothing, and methane couldn't burn without it.

And if he was wrong—well . . . Mukai and the rangers wouldn't be any more dead than if he'd let the bad air asphyxiate them.

He continued to fire—it took a *lot* of kinetic energy to punch through a meter of ash-impregnated lechatelierite—creating a half-meter circle of weakened glass directly over the rear engine compartment of the little LHD. Down the passage, he glimpsed Kelly firing her own sound-suppressed MA40 into the ceiling. Once he had emptied the magazine, he climbed onto the back of the machine and rolled onto his back, then began to punch.

It took three blows to create a hole to the surface, and the carbon dioxide and methane readings in his HUD began to fall immediately. He unbuckled the safety harness holding Mukai on the operator's seat, raised her night-vision visor and pulled the helmet off her head, then pushed her up into the hole, just high enough that her head would not protrude above the surface.

As he waited for her to recover, he looked back to find Fred and Linda starting down the passage with two Reavians slung over each shoulder. They were dragging four more by the wrists, but they would never be able to get everyone out of the bad air in time. John could see at least fifty rangers lying in front of alcoves down the way, and more people were dropping as the foul air moved down the tunnel.

Kelly was using the butt of her assault rifle to punch through a circle of lechatelierite she had weakened. Her hole and John's would help reduce the methane levels, since it was lighter than oxygen. But carbon dioxide was heavier, so the makeshift ventilation would only dilute the bad air. Elevated levels were going to continue being a problem as long as there was gas coming out of the pocket ahead.

Mukai returned to consciousness with a startled gasp. She began to mutter and babble, trying to make sense of her sudden detour into oblivion.

"Whatever you do," John said, "don't scream."

"I wasn't planning on it," Mukai muttered. "Am I going to want to?"

"Not sure yet," John replied. "You hit a pocket of bad air. I haven't had time to assess."

Mukai got her legs under her, placing her boots on John's chest, then looked down with a blank stare and whispered into the darkness, "Am I standing on *you*?"

"For now," John said. "We're on the LHD's engine compartment. When you're feeling steady enough, I'll slip out from beneath you."

"I'm okay," Mukai said, still whispering. She picked up one foot and began to feel for the engine hood. "But I can't see a damn thing down there."

"Sorry about that," John said. "I need you to watch the base. We've fired a lot of ammunition down here, and that glass over our heads isn't so thick that an enemy lookout couldn't have noticed something."

"I can do that," Mukai said. "But my natural night vision isn't something I've ever bragged about."

"I'll pass your helmet and visor up to you," John said. "Just be careful not to stick the helmet too far above the surface."

"You think?" Mukai said. "I can see the top of the shield barrier from in here. It's right there. I mean, in grenade range—for *me*."

"Understood."

John guided her boot onto the hood next to him. He waited until she had shifted her weight to it, then slid out from beneath her other foot and swung himself back onto the tunnel floor. Mukai gave another startled gasp as the LHD springs decompressed and lifted her twenty centimeters higher into the hole.

John grabbed the helmet from the operator's seat and passed it up, then changed the MA40's magazine and returned it to its magmount. He slipped forward alongside the LHD and peered through the hole it had punched through the working face of the tunnel.

Now that he was closer, his night-vision system was no longer being compromised by the heat of the LHD engine, and the dimdots were visible along the edges of the passage. He could see the faint red glow of the Banished shield barrier overhead, shining down through a circle of lechatelierite thirty meters in diameter. A three-meter band of crimson cracks ran down the center, where something heavy had driven across it and nearly collapsed the entire span of glass.

The gas readings on John's HUD shot up to 27 percent for the carbon dioxide and 14 percent for the methane. He had his onboard computer check the oxygen level, which was only 5 percent—less than a third of normal. At those levels, he wasn't sure whether methane could burn.

The answer appeared on his HUD, informing him that it could not. So at least they had *that* going for them.

When John tried to scan the rest of the chamber, it took a moment for his night vision to adjust—and when it did, he found himself looking across a shallow basin filled with hundreds of rotted trees. The trunks lay next to and atop each other, all running parallel as though they had been blown over by the same powerful wind. Everything was blanketed in mold, sometimes so thickly the trees seemed to have all dissolved into a single amorphous mass, and there was so much humidity in the air that it quickly formed droplets and ran down his faceplate.

He grabbed a chunk of lechatelierite from the passage floor and tossed it into the basin. The mass didn't ripple—it was more of a shudder—but at least he knew where the bad air was coming from. Bogs produced a lot of carbon dioxide and methane, and it had all been trapped underglass until Mukai opened the pocket.

Over TEAMCOM, John said, "We've hit an obstacle."

"I'd say it's more like a titanium wall," Fred said. "The bad air is moving faster than we are. The tunnel back here is paved with unconscious soldiers."

"Understood," John said. "Lieutenant Chapov, are you and Major Van Houte still with us?"

"Affirmative." Chapov was with the drilling jumbo back at the erosion channel, almost a kilometer distant. "Should we start the drills and cut away the ceiling?"

"Negative. Use your head." John spoke more harshly than was really necessary, but he was not accustomed to having to tell mission personnel what *not* to do. "What are you thinking?"

"That you need fresh air in that tunnel—and fast."

"Not if it means flashing a big blue HERE WE ARE sign along the attack route," Fred said. "This fight is going to be tough enough already."

"You're still planning to attack?" Chapov asked. "Without the rangers?"

"Withdrawing isn't an option, Lieutenant," John said. "For anyone."

The Banished had entered the militia's underglass tunnel network two days ago, and they were not being subtle about taking control of it. Whenever they ran into a pocket of resistance, they simply brought in a Griever fighter-bomber to turn the pocket into a crater. So if the rehab pioneers wanted to survive until the *Infinity*'s marine complement arrived to relieve them, they needed to capture the New Mohács armory and establish some anti-aircraft emplacements on the surface.

Chapov didn't answer for a few heartbeats, perhaps chastened by John's sharpness, then said, "Sorry for not seeing that, Master Chief." The hum of a transmission engaging sounded in the background. "Carbon dioxide needs a place to sink. I'll look for some big bedrock fractures in the floor and open them up. Maybe we'll even get lucky and hit a cavity."

"Good plan," John said. "But stay back from the contact zone. You're not going to save anybody by going down yourself."

"Affirmative." It was Van Houte who said this. "No need to worry about us, Master Chief. I'm enough of a coward for both of us."

"Glad to hear it, Major." John could not help smiling inside his helmet—Van Houte was anything but. "Blue Team, you're with me, and bring all the rangers you can carry. We're crossing the—"

"Check that," Mukai said. She dropped her head out of the ventilation hole, her head and eyes still obscured by her helmet and night-vision visor. "We have a sentry squad . . ."

She started to wobble, then tumbled off the LHD into the wet sand. John grabbed his MA40 off its magmount, stepped over her, and squatted on the back of the LHD with the barrel pointed into the ventilation hole.

He could hear Kig-Yar approaching, chattering to one another in barely lowered voices. It sounded like there were five of them, which was going to be a problem. The hole was only large enough for two of them to look into at once—which meant he could only shoot two at a time. He laid the MA40 on the LHD hood so both hands would be free.

A moment later, the blue glow of a personal lamp began to travel back and forth through the lechatelierite, then slid into the ventilation hole and stopped. A Kig-Yar chortled in excitement, and the beam began to descend the wall of the opening.

John waited until two beaked heads appeared above him, one peering over each side, then reached up with both hands and grabbed their necks. He pulled the one holding the lamp into the hole first, allowing it to drop squealing to the passage floor, then jerked the other one down after its companion.

The other three squawked in surprise, but John already had his sound-suppressed MA40 in hand and was pushing it up out of the ventilation hole. He turned the barrel toward the most distinct voice and fired a short burst. It sounded like someone coughing. As he continued to rise, he swept the barrel in the opposite direction, toward the other voices, and fired a longer burst.

When he stuck his head out of the hole, three Kig-Yar were lying motionless on the glass, their pooling blood glowing white in the infrared mode of his night-vision system. He took a moment to scan the surrounding area, searching for more sentries or some sign that these five had been under observation, but saw only the radiance of the shield barrier looming twenty meters away. A lookout tower stood fifty meters away in either direction, but the Unggoy sentries seemed to be watching the horizon rather than the perimeter patrol—a common mistake that hinted at complacency. Had the Banished been expecting an attack, one of the tower sentries would have been watching to see if the Kig-Yar patrol ran into trouble.

Not that it mattered. When the patrol didn't report, a larger one would be sent to check on it, and the base would go on alert. Blue Team and the rangers had maybe ten minutes before that happened.

John pulled the three bodies down through the hole, then looked down to find Kelly checking to make sure they were really dead. She had already put a round through the heads of the first two—special forces units rarely took prisoners, and they never left a live enemy behind themselves.

Linda and Fred stood behind Kelly, each carrying one ranger over each shoulder and another in their arms. John motioned to the LHD bucket.

"Load up. We're going now." He adjusted the LHD's seat all the way back, then squeezed into the operator's compartment. Backing the machine up a couple of meters, he dumped the bucket's contents at the edge of the bog. "And don't forget Chief Mukai."

Kelly slipped alongside the LHD to the front, then began to take unconscious rangers from Fred and Linda and load them into the bucket, laying them on top of each other. John wondered how long had passed since Mukai had opened the pocket of bad air. A counter appeared on his HUD and began to run upward.

3:41 . . . 3:42 . . . 3:43 . . .

Brain cells died at just one minute without oxygen. After three minutes, permanent damage could occur. After five minutes of no oxygen, there was no coming back—and the survivors wouldn't be in any shape to fight.

Kelly stepped into the bog basin and moved away from the LHD, testing her footing before each step. Moss and wet sand squished up around her boots, but she didn't sink more than a few centimeters. Maybe the LHD wouldn't mire after all. John depressed the forward pedal, and the machine lurched out of the passage into the bog.

He felt the LHD settle and slow as the tires began to tear through rotten logs and fling sand.

3:55 . . . 3:56 . . . 3:57 . . .

The LHD reached the middle of the basin and started to sink faster—then suddenly slid forward. He checked his motion sensor and saw the rest of Blue Team lined up behind the cargo platform in back, pushing against the haulage buckets and other equipment. He let off the pedal a bit so the tires would stop digging, but still kept them turning, and the LHD went the last dozen meters to the far side of the bog, where the basin dead-ended in a dirt slope similar to its counterpart on the other side.

John dumped Mukai and the rangers onto the slope where they would be out of the way, then backed up, moved over a few meters, and drove the bucket a meter and a half into the dirt.

4:20 . . .

The air was still 5 percent oxygen, even in the bog pocket. That wasn't much—humans normally breathed air that was 19 to 22 percent oxygen—but maybe it was enough to slow the brain damage Mukai and the pioneers had to be taking.

John backed up the LHD, emptied the bucket, then raced forward again, pushing it another meter and a half into the slope. He thought he should be beyond the shield barrier by now, which meant there would be no glass overhead. The rehab pioneers who'd built New Mohács had spent several months stripping all the lechatelierite from the ground inside the perimeter and using it in their buildings and pavement.

John glanced up as he reversed to empty the bucket—and saw a red glow in the dirt overhead. He was directly under the shield barrier now.

4:26 . . . 4:27 . . . 4:28 . . .

He emptied the bucket again and advanced under the glowing barrier, pushed another meter and a half into the dirt. The plan had been to carefully dig ten meters past the shield barrier and open the wall of an old concrete storm sewer that had served old Mohács, then crawl through the sewer system and attack all corners of the armory at once.

4:34 . . .

No time for that now. As John backed out of the short passage he had dug, he glanced over at Mukai and the six unconscious rangers. They still had their weapons and packs full of C10 cubes. They would be shell-shocked when they regained consciousness, but that was the normal condition of any soldier who had ever survived an artillery barrage.

John spoke over TEAMCOM. "Make ready." He emptied the bucket. "Blue Three, you're point—secure the breach point. Blue Two, find the Banished birds and break their wings. Blue Four, take out the tower guards, then drop the shield barrier. I'll handle the armor."

Militia recon scouts had started watching New Mohács long before Blue Team had inserted on Reach, so they had a pretty good idea of what they would find inside the base.

John started back into the passage.

Chapov's voice sounded over TEAMCOM. "Wait, you're attacking now?"

"Never say *wait* unless you mean it," John said.

4:43 . . . 4:44 . . .

"Do you mean it, Lieutenant?"

"No—uh, sorry," Chapov said. "I mean *negative*. Just surprised."

"Don't let it happen again." John raised the bucket as high as it would go. "What's the situation back there?"

"I found a cavity," Chapov said. "Carbon dioxide levels must be dropping, because people aren't passing out anymore."

"Anyone waking up yet?"

"Negative." It was Van Houte who said this. "I think we have at least three hundred incapacitated."

*Three hundred.* Sixty percent out of the fight for now, and the enemy hadn't fired a single plasma bolt yet.

"Everyone else is ready to resume the advance." Chapov lowered his voice. "They're not going to wait much longer. I'm telling you, these people are crazy."

"Acknowledged. Shut down your plasma drills." John depressed the forward pedal as far as it would go, and the LHD rocked back on its rear wheels as the bucket punched through the roof of the passage. "You're about to get some fresh air, but the rise in oxygen levels may turn the methane combustible again."

John lowered the bucket, bringing a cascade of dirt and glass block down with it, then slammed his heel down on the reverse pedal. The LHD shot backward into the bog. The rest of Blue Team slipped into the passage ahead of the machine, everyone holding silenced MA40s, and Fred carrying three packs filled with C10 charges over each shoulder. The trio disappeared briefly behind the bucket, then came back into view as they jumped up through the opening and into the base.

John heard the chuff of silenced weapons as they took out a few nearby aliens. He killed the LHD's engine and climbed out of the operator's compartment, then took a couple of seconds to strip the remaining demolition packs from the unconscious rangers and drag them and Chief Mukai under the opening. He wasn't sure if the fresh air would do them any good, but the sooner it reached them, the better their chances of recovery.

By the time John had pulled his sound-suppressed MA40 off its magmount, Mukai was already struggling to sit up.

He pointed to the dark opening overhead. "Send up anyone who can hold a weapon," he said. "We're going to need all the support we can get."

Still wearing her helmet with the night-vision visor down, Mukai slowly tipped her head back and looked up through the hole. "Wow," she said. "Pretty clouds."

"*Breathe*, Stella." John had learned to use first names with casualties, both for its calming effect and as a way of keeping them focused on what he was saying. "*Deep* breaths."

"Cool," Mukai said. "Does that mean I can call you John?"

"You can call me anything." John looked up through the breach. "I'm going to go blow up some tanks now. What are you going to do?"

"Send up anyone who can hold a weapon. Hey, *I* can hold a weapon."

"Not you. You have a job to do. Remember?"

"Right. Send 'em up. You're going to need all the support you can get."

# CHAPTER TWELVE

0244 hours, October 11, 2559 (military calendar)
Banished Armory, New Mohács
Arany Basin, Continent Eposz, Planet Reach

John sprang through the opening into New Mohács, jumping more off his good leg than the wounded one because he knew the damaged muscle could take only so much exertion before it began to fail him. He landed two meters inside the shield barrier, on a broad perimeter road that the Banished had constructed around the entire base. His motion tracker showed no one nearby, though he knew that at least one Spartan—Kelly—would be hiding somewhere in the dark, ready to take out any hostiles unfortunate enough to stumble onto the security breach. There were no dead enemies visible—their bodies would have been dragged out of sight before Kelly concealed herself. He checked the adjacent lookout towers and found the sentry platforms unoccupied—at least by living guards. Linda had been busy.

John called up the map of New Mohács and oriented it to a large glass-block building identified as REPAIR GARAGE. A smaller building stood just across an alley from it, labeled HARDWARE HOUSE. He flashed status green to let his team members know he was inside the base and moving on to his assignment; he received three green flashes in reply. So far, so good.

John turned left and started down the perimeter road counter-clockwise. During the planning phase, they had identified a large fabrication plant near the center of town as the only building large enough to serve as a fighter-craft hangar. So that's where Fred would be heading, with Linda leading the way. She had to take out all of the sentries in the lookout towers before deactivating the shield barrier. Otherwise the remaining sentries would sound the alarm and send someone to reactivate the sectors she had taken down.

John intended to follow Fred and Linda's route for as long as possible, then cut across the town to a complex of old sports fields that were the only open space expansive enough to be an armored vehicle depot. He passed a couple of ruined buildings that had been half-razed to make room for the perimeter road, and pools of blood showed up in his NVS regularly—an indication that Linda or Fred had eliminated a hostile target, then stashed the body somewhere. Such measures could not hide Blue Team's infiltration indefinitely, but they would delay the inevitable moment of discovery for minutes, and every second that passed before the Spartans were detected increased their chance of success.

John passed the alley that led to the fabrication plant. He glimpsed a pair of blood smears high on a wall where Fred had killed two Jiralhanae, then saw a live one strolling through an intersection at the opposite end. He continued on, relying on speed, darkness, and the sound-dampening soles of his sabatons to conceal him as he passed the alley mouth—and aware that Fred would be taking out the Brute in a few moments anyway.

He heard the cough of Linda's suppressed MA40 up ahead, then a soft *thud-thud* as a dead sentry tumbled from a lookout tower. The sound was followed by the scuff of big feet coming down the alley he had just passed, so he stopped and peered back around the corner. Now there were two Jiralhanae, lumbering toward him from the direction of the intersection. One was drawing a mangler from the weapon's hip mount, and the other held a spike rifle at chest level. John dropped to a knee and brought up his weapon—then heard two soft huffs as Fred opened fire with his suppressed MA40.

The heads of both Jiralhanae rocked backward, a single round taking each of them through an eye, and they toppled over backward. Fred remained hidden for a moment in case there were more Banished coming around the corner, then emerged from a derelict building to stash the bodies. John flashed a green status LED to let him know he was covered, then waited until Fred had carried both Brutes through the darkened doorway from which he'd emerged. The utilitarian design of New Mohács's glass-block apartment buildings and square-grid street plan seemed a poor replacement for the arched windows and domed towers that had distinguished the architecture of traditional Reavian towns, but it still angered John to see how much of the pioneers' hard work had been destroyed by the Banished occupiers. It would have been too much to say that he was going to enjoy making the aliens pay for what they had done to the village—but he certainly wasn't going to regret it.

Fred flashed status green and came back out with his demolition packs over his shoulders, and John continued along the perimeter road. In the distance behind him, he heard a muted squealing—maybe a plasma rifle, or an overhead door rising on an unlubricated track—then muffled voices. He couldn't tell what species. Then silence again.

Normally he would never have sent his entire team out solo. Even for a Spartan, it was too easy to find oneself cornered and outnumbered. But in a situation like this, where surprise was everything and there were more targets than operatives by several orders of magnitude, it was a risk he had to take. And New Mohács was only a couple of kilometers across. If someone got into trouble, support was likely less than sixty seconds away.

That was a lifetime in a firefight, but if anyone could last a lifetime in a firefight, it was a Spartan.

As John approached the turn to the armor depot, his motion tracker lit up, showing ten figures coming down the avenue. He could slip into the shadows and hit them as they entered the intersection, but the attack would not be neat or pretty. There were simply too many of them to kill before the others reacted, and it would only take a couple of shouts or plasma bolts to alert the entire base as to what was happening.

He would have to hide and hope they didn't see him as they passed.

John stopped and looked around. There wasn't much cover, just a solid glass-block wall on one side and the shield barrier on the other. No place to conceal himself along either. He could race back to the last alley and hope to clear fifty meters faster than they could walk five, or he could ambush them as they rounded the corner and almost certainly alert the base.

John slipped the demolition packs off his shoulders—if he took a plasma bolt in a detonator, there wouldn't be enough left of his Mjolnir armor to tell he was a Spartan—then switched the MA40 to full auto.

Linda's voice came over TEAMCOM. "Blue Leader, let them into the perimeter road. You draw their attention, I'll finish them off."

John didn't bother asking where Linda was. To see him and the patrol both, she had to be on the roof of a nearby building. He hoped it was on the far corner, since that would give her a clear shot at the backs of their heads when they faced him. But no matter where she was, she would dispatch them.

He flashed status green, then moved into the middle of the street and took a knee. He was only ten meters from the demolition packs—not nearly far enough—but it was all he had time for.

John shouldered his MA40 and waited.

A gang of Unggoy in full armor walked into the perimeter road and split into two groups, turning in opposite directions. They were probably guards on their way to relieve the previous watch, and the last thing they were expecting to see was the shadowy figure kneeling in the dark in front of them. The ones moving in his direction stopped and squealed with surprise.

There were only eight in the street, and still ten on John's motion tracker. But waiting for the last two was out of the question. He opened fire, his assault rifle huffing steadily as it spat rounds into their heads. Four of them immediately went down, then the other four as Linda opened fire from somewhere above him.

They were still falling as John sprang up and raced forward, his rifle already aimed down the avenue as the last two Unggoy came into view. They had their plasma pistols in hand, but were not yet ready to fire.

John shot them both in the head.

Linda stuck her helmet over the edge of the roof opposite. "Toss the bodies up here. I think we're still undetected."

"Seems too good to be true," John replied.

They were attacking a complacent enemy at the hour when their troops were most likely to be asleep or inattentive, but . . . still. It had been more than five minutes since John breached their defenses with the LHD. Even for Spartans firing sound-suppressed weapons, that was a long time to remain undetected inside a densely occupied base.

John put a fresh magazine in his assault rifle, then returned it to his magmount so he could toss the ten dead Unggoy onto the roof. That took another forty seconds, and retrieving the demolition packs took another ten. Linda had to keep watch for him the whole time. They were no longer following an attack plan, but if they had been, that would have been fifty seconds they couldn't spare.

John checked the map on his HUD. He was six hundred meters from the mechanized armor depot, six-fifty if he went down the next alley instead of the avenue the Unggoy had used. Fred should be approaching the hangar by now. John continued down the perimeter road toward the next alley.

"Blue Three, sitrep breach?"

"All quiet for now," Kelly reported. "I eliminated a Kig-Yar patrol hustling toward the gate. There was some noise, but nothing seems to have come of it."

"Acknowledged." The Kig-Yar had probably been on their way to check on the first patrol—the one John had killed outside the shield barrier, then pulled down into the underglass passage. "We're running out of time. Blue Four, how far along are you?"

"The south side is complete," Linda said. That was good, because the militia's mechanized assault would be coming from that area. "But that's only sixteen towers."

Sixteen towers was bad. In total, there were sixty-four towers guarding the circumference of the base. And Blue Team needed to take them *all* out. The Banished would reoccupy any surviving towers and use them as firing platforms once the battle moved into the town proper.

"But charges set?" John asked. "Detonators remote?"

"Affirmative to both," Linda replied. "Frequency tango-alpha-ten."

"Good."

Under normal conditions, Blue Team would not have talked this much during an attack. Encryption and frequency-hopping made it almost impossible to intercept and decipher TEAMCOM messages, but the transmissions themselves could still be detected by any decent signals intelligence unit, and that alone was usually enough to put an enemy on high alert. In this case, however, pre-attack reconnaissance had revealed no antennas or dishes to suggest that this base even had a SIGINT unit—and if it did, the unit would assume that any transmissions originating inside the shield barrier were from their own forces.

"Anything we can do to move faster?" John asked.

"Negative," Linda said. "The work is slow. Sometimes there are two sentries, sometimes three or four."

"Understood," John said. Before killing any of the sentries in a lookout tower, Linda had to wait for an opportunity to take out all of them in less than two seconds. Otherwise one of the targets would have just enough time to sound the alert. "We may have to do this the hard way."

"I fear so," Linda said.

"Then occupy a tower and be prepared to take down the shield barrier along the south side. Wait until the shooting starts, then eliminate the rest of the sentries at long range."

"Understood." So far, Linda had been using her sound-suppressed MA40 because the rounds of her SRS99-S5 AM sniper rifle traveled at supersonic speeds, creating a sonic crack that could never be silenced. "I'm sorry I couldn't be faster."

"Not your fault," John said. "Blue Three?"

Kelly flashed green to show she was listening.

"Vacate breach guard," John said. "As Blue Four clears each tower, you set the charges."

"Understood," Kelly said. "Blue Four, counterclockwise?"

"Affirmative."

"Any questions, anyone?" When no one spoke up, John said, "Carry on."

A gold arrow appeared on John's HUD map, pointing into the second alley down from the avenue the squad of Unggoy had used.

"Follow this route," Linda said. "I'll provide overwatch as long as possible."

It would add another fifty meters to John's trip, but it would be worth it. A vacant lookout tower stood across the street from the alley mouth; once Linda occupied it, she would be able to cover him all the way to the armor depot.

"Affirmative."

Linda dropped off the rooftop onto the street and climbed into the lookout tower a few seconds before John reached the designated alley. He traveled down it and stayed close to the buildings, but otherwise did not worry much about concealment. Now that a second Kig-Yar patrol had been dispatched, speed was a more important element than stealth in maintaining surprise.

Fred would be inside the hangar by now, taking out the roving guards so he could proceed to planting C10 cubes on each of the fighter craft sheltered there. The militia had estimated that there were fifty

Banshees and twenty Seraphs operating out of New Mohács, which sounded about right. Fifty Banshees would be five squadrons, or a whole wing, and twenty Seraphs would be two squadrons. To support more fighter craft than that, the base would have to be twice as large as it was. Once Fred had eliminated the guards, it would take him about six minutes to attach the charges and evacuate to a safe distance.

John didn't think they actually had six minutes, but maybe fate had different plans.

The number of armored vehicles was less certain. Militia recon patrols had seen squads of three to five Marauders, and up to ten Wraiths, accompanied by lighter armor such as Ghosts and Choppers. They had also reported seeing almost every kind of armored vehicle being transported into the base for repair. A smart armor commander tried not to send more than a quarter of his available force out on patrol at once, so that meant John could expect to find at least twenty functional Marauders and forty Wraiths at the depot.

But probably more.

Armor was always a high-maintenance asset. In the UNSC, 10 percent of any armored force could be expected to be out of service even at its home base, and that figure doubled when it was on the move, and doubled again once it entered combat. Among the Banished, where the supply lines would be less certain and the repair personnel less well-trained, John suspected he could double those figures yet again. So there were going to be a *lot* of armored vehicles at the depot, easily more than a hundred large pieces, in various stages of repair.

As a result, John was going to need perhaps twice as long as Fred to plant his charges, and he wasn't going to get it. The most he could hope for was to create enough confusion to keep the armor from deploying until reinforcements arrived to capture it.

If there were going to be any reinforcements.

A trio of armored Jiralhanae stepped out of a doorway ten meters ahead. He shouldered his MA40 and continued toward them, aiming at the one in the middle because he knew Linda would take the third figure in line, being closest to the door and therefore most likely to escape into cover. John took two more steps before the shimmer of an energy field enveloped the third figure's form, and he realized Linda had opened fire.

"Shields," he warned, firing on the middle figure.

He put a long burst into the Jiralhanae's head, overwhelming the shields and punching through the helmet on the eighth or ninth round. He swept his fire toward the door, where the third figure was already escaping back into the building, and saw three holes open in the flank armor before his target vanished into the room beyond.

"Go," Linda said over TEAMCOM.

John raced forward, noting as he ran that the first Jiralhanae in line was going down on his back, a line of bullet holes running up his chest. A puncture appeared in the warrior's helmet just before it hit the glass, but by then his arms were already limp and his legs akimbo.

John arrived at the doorway through which the surviving Jiralhanae had disappeared and reached around the jamb, holding his MA40 one-handed as he put three more rounds into the Brute's back. When no return fire came through the opening, he changed magazines, took a grenade off his load-carrying harness, and tossed it into the room without activating the fuse.

He heard the *thunk* as it hit the floor, then gravelly voices crying out in alarm. He stepped through the door and, seeing five unarmored Jiralhanae diving for cover, started around the room counterclockwise, putting two rounds into each of their heads, then reversed direction and put two more rounds through each of their torsos.

He remained in the room long enough to confirm that there were eight sleeping pallets and five remaining sets of empty armor carefully stowed next to the empty couches. An alarmed voice was coming from the comm devices inside the helmets, no doubt demanding a situation report.

John retrieved his undetonated grenade and started up the alley again, speaking over TEAMCOM as he ran.

"They're onto us. Blue Four and I just took out an inspection team with active shields." Meaning the Jiralhanae had taken the time to power up before leaving their sleeping quarters, so they had probably been warned to be wary of infiltrators. "And there was a commander on their comm net demanding an update. Time to go to plan B."

"I thought this *was* plan B," Fred said.

"Right," John said. "Plan C, then."

"There's a plan C?" Kelly asked.

"There is now," John replied. "Blue Four, patch me through to Colonel Boldisar."

Linda's status flashed green, and a moment later Boldisar demanded, "Who's on this channel?"

"Sierra-117," John said. "We need you to start the mechanized assault now."

"Twenty minutes early?!" Boldisar exclaimed. "Are you even in position?"

"As much as we're going to be," John said. "We need a diversion, so make it loud. Make it bright."

Boldisar hesitated only a moment, then said, "We can do a diversion. Just tell me—are we going to make it into the base?"

"At least some of you will," John said. "We're doing what we can to improve on that."

"I understand," Boldisar said. "Should we bring a Havok?"

"*Negative!*" The entire reason John had agreed to call for UNSC support in the first place was to keep the pioneer militia from using a nuke. "You have the Havok with you?"

"Two of them," Boldisar said. "Just in case."

"You won't need them. I already told you that."

"Then how come we're attacking early?" Boldisar asked. "We're bringing them."

Five Jiralhanae came around the corner, leaving John no time to argue. The Brutes were in full armor and moving fast. Three wielded mangler revolvers, while the other two carried skewer antitank weapons with rocket-sized projectiles sticking out of the barrels and sword-length bayonets mounted beneath. They were vicious weapons designed for an anti-armor role, but gleefully used by Banished Jiralhanae against enemy infantry.

John's only advantage was that they were not wearing night-vision equipment, while he was sticking to the shadows along the walls where they would have difficulty spotting him.

At least until he opened fire.

He stopped and knelt, then aimed at one of the warriors carrying a skewer. "Right-hand skewer," he said over TEAMCOM.

"Left-hand skewer," Linda replied. Now five hundred meters behind John, she was well out of range of the manglers, so she asked, "Me first?"

"Affirmative," John said. They were taking out the skewers because those big tank-busting spikes in the barrels could bring down the shields and punch through the titanium shell of even GEN3 Mjolnir. "When you're—"

A supersonic crack echoed through the alley, and the left-hand skewer-bearer's head erupted into a white spray in John's NVS. He fired a seven-shot burst, and his target's jowly face turned into a bloody mess before the knees started to buckle.

Linda fired again, and the head of a third Jiralhanae exploded into mist. The last two warriors attacked blindly, spraying spikes into the glass walls at the height of their own chests. John ran a line of bullets across their faces, and they dropped in the middle of the lane.

He slipped a fresh magazine into the MA40, then glanced up at the wall above his head and found the glass pocked by spike divots. Half a meter lower, and it would have been him lying in the street.

Or billowing skyward, had they hit one of his demolition packs.

The shrill whistle of a battle alert rose over the base, then Fred's voice came over TEAMCOM.

"Permission to blow stuff up?" he asked. "A *lot* of stuff?"

"Permission granted." John rose and raced down the alley toward the armor depot. "Blue Four, release overwatch. Take out the sentries."

Linda's status LED flashed green in John's HUD, and her sniper rifle began to boom again. John's leg wound was starting to throb, but he was still three hundred meters from his objective, and he needed to be waiting in the dark when the enemy crews headed for their vehicles. He willed himself to sprint faster and heard his breath rushing inside his helmet.

He was two hundred meters from his objective when the first crews began to pour into the alley and race toward the depot. They were primarily two Kig-Yar Marauder groups led by Sangheili squadron commanders, and single Jiralhanae Wraith drivers, all lightly armored and carrying only compact weapons such as plasma pistols and needlers. But John didn't open fire. He couldn't afford to get bogged down in a firefight. There would be dozens of other crews pouring into the depot from other routes, and if he wanted to keep the Banished armor from turning the militia's mechanized assault into a bloodbath, he had to stop all of them.

A long chain of muffled explosions sounded from the hangars, shaking the entire base and filling the sky with an orange glow. The armor crews stopped in their tracks and looked up, the Kig-Yar chittering and squawking, their Sangheili commanders simply staring with mandibles splayed wide.

John kicked in the door of one of the glass buildings, then stepped inside. It was a sleeping quarters, lined with nests so recently vacated that the heat of the occupants' bodies still showed in the infrared mode of his night-vision system. He opened one of the demolition packs and set the delay on ten detonators to two seconds, then stepped back through the door and saw that the armor crews were once again headed toward their vehicles.

John activated the first detonator and threw the C10 cube down the alley as far as he could, then reached for the next one.

The first cube exploded with a deafening rumble, blasting through walls and filling the alley with a fireball. He raced thirty meters forward before he finally emerged from the smoke to find a group of armor crews cowering in the darkness next to the buildings, their heads turned skyward, probably looking for the nonexistent bomber that had just attacked them.

He activated the next detonator and threw the C10 cube into their midst, then did it twice more before he finally reached the end of the alley and could see the depot yard off to his left.

Too late.

The yard was swarming with armor crews, the closest already climbing into the open hatches of their vehicles.

His earlier estimate of their numbers had been low. There were at least forty Marauders and sixty or seventy Wraiths—and judging by where the crews were going, most of them seemed functional.

The depot exit was directly opposite John, on the west side of the yard where nothing but the shield barrier separated the vehicles from the glass barrens outside New Mohács. Whatever he did next, it had to happen before someone lowered that barrier and the armor streamed out to meet the militia's mechanized assault. The Banished would be badly outnumbered, but it would be tanks against Warthogs. The rehab pioneers might still win—but at a price so steep they'd wish they hadn't.

John retreated into the alley, then kicked in the rear door of a large building that overlooked the depot yard. His plan was to climb up through the interior to access the roof. But he found himself looking into a large office filled with bustling Sangheili and bellowing Jiralhanae—probably the armor unit's headquarters. He activated a detonator and tossed a C10 cube into the center of the suite, then stepped back through the doorway and crouched behind the wall of the adjacent building.

The C10 charge detonated, blowing the walls out of the headquarters building next to him. At least the Banished armor would now lack central control.

"Blue Leader is late to the party," John said over TEAMCOM. "Blue Two, can you back me up?"

"Affirmative," Fred said. "Thirty seconds out, but only nineteen cubes left. Plus six rockets."

"Acknowledged," John said. "Come in on the north corner of the yard and work your way westward toward the exit. I'll do the same on the south side."

Fred flashed green.

John continued issuing orders. "Blue Three, occupy the lookout towers flanking the depot exit. Keep the exit barrier raised as long as possible. Maybe we can bottle them up for a while."

Kelly's status LED flashed green; then Lieutenant Chapov came on. "Blue Leader . . . enemy armor . . . depart New Mohács at . . . yard?"

"Confirmed," John said. The signal was cutting out, probably because Chapov was still underglass, transmitting up through a ventilation hole. "Why?"

No reply. John repeated his response, both the confirmation and the question.

When there was still nothing, he stopped trying and glanced up along the wall he was next to. The building was three stories tall—just inside the range of the grappleshot on his left forearm. John raised his arm and fired the hook at the overhanging eave. Once it had caught, he checked to see if it was secure, then jumped hard and retracted the cable at the same time.

The grappleshot pulled him up to the eave, where he smashed his free hand through the nitralume roof and used the resulting hole as a handhold to pull himself completely onto the steep pitch. After a quick check to make sure nobody was watching from a nearby roof or window, he fired the grappleshot at the ridgeline, then secured the hook and pulled himself to the top.

The view to the south was obscured by dozens of other roofs, most just as high and some even higher. But in the distance, just four kilometers out, he could see a long line of Warthog silhouettes racing across the gray glass toward New Mohács. They were not traveling with their lights on—that would have made them easy targets and suggested that they were actually trying to draw attention. But spotlights and handlamps were flickering on and off irregularly, a nice touch that would make sure the Banished focused on the assault headed their way.

Down in the depot yard, the demolition of the headquarters building was not creating as much chaos as John had hoped for. A couple of enemy crews near the explosion were incapacitated or dealing with casualties, and a handful of Wraith drivers were cowering behind their vehicles searching for the source of the attack. But by far the majority were climbing into their rides and buttoning up.

John had three full demolition packs left, each containing ten C10 cubes with detonators already inserted but not set. His fourth pack was half-empty, leaving him a total of thirty-five cubes. Fred had just twenty-five charges, including the M19 rounds for the rocket launcher. Even if they hit with everything—and they wouldn't—that was less than half of the Banished's armored vehicles.

Better than nothing.

John straddled the roof ridge and lined up the C10 cubes from the half-used pack. He reset the detonator delays, starting at fifteen seconds and working his way down to eleven, then lobbed each cube out into the depot yard, trying to scatter them over a fifty-meter circle. Even with his night-vision system, it was too dark to see how many actually landed on a vehicle and adhered to it—if *any* did—but that was okay. The purpose of the first volley was to create confusion about the source of the attack and give him time to be more accurate with the rest of his throws.

Leaving the empty pack behind, he slid off the roof—

—and dropped into a street filled with Jiralhanae drivers on the way to their Wraiths. Firing the MA40 one-handed, he managed to shoot three in the head before the other twelve recovered from their initial shock and charged him.

John raced out of the alley to the edge of the depot yard—where the first C10 cube erupted just thirty meters away, creating a fireball ten meters high and flinging shards of armored vehicle in every direction. Then the second cube detonated—and the third, fourth, and fifth. The shockwaves hurled John through a glass-block wall, his armor pinging with the sound of striking shrapnel, and he felt the heat of the explosions through his faceplate and hoped the detonators in his remaining demolition packs wouldn't malfunction and go off at that moment.

They were military grade, so the chances weren't high—but it was hard to forget they had been sitting on a shelf in a damp bunker under a meter of lechatelierite for the last seven years.

John was back on his feet while the blast-white was still fading from his NVS. He checked to make sure he had all of his weapons and equipment, then went to the street-side wall of the building into which he had just been hurled and kicked an exit hole.

Through the glass blocks, with his wounded leg.

Even Spartans made dumb mistakes in the heat of battle. His thigh instantly knotted up the way it had when the plasma bolt first burned through his armor, and he found himself imagining Dr. Somogy admonishing him, *Idiot, I said to rest.*

He kept going, limping and once again relying on his armor's reactive circuits. *Everyone* made mistakes. The important thing was to recover fast and keep moving.

John peered through the hole he'd made and found a street full of open-beaked Kig-Yar being herded through the darkness by their Sangheili squadron commander. He set a detonator for two seconds, then activated it and tossed it down the street.

The explosion collapsed the wall he was using as cover, and he bolted out of the building just in time to avoid being buried beneath three stories of glass block. Some semblance of order was beginning to return to the depot yard, with crews climbing into their vehicles and the first Marauders and Wraiths rising on their antigravity pads.

John ran westward along the edge of the yard, reaching into the open demolition pack slung over his weapon arm and randomly setting a detonator delay. He did his best to pick battle-ready targets that were already on the move and under power, with a strong preference for the Marauders, since their direct-fire missiles would prove even more devastating to the militia's Warthogs than the heavy plasma mortars mounted on the Wraiths.

Every twenty steps or so, he crossed paths with an enemy who seemed to realize he was an infiltrator and reacted to stop him. Mostly he took them out with two head shots or a burst to the torso, but on occasion the contact was so unexpected that he simply ran them over or broke his foe's neck with a quick hammerfist—sometimes while still holding a cube of C10.

But for the most part, the darkness and the chaos in the depot yard served him well. He scored hits with most of the C10 cubes he threw, and by the time he drew near the exit, he was down to a single half-empty demolition pack. He was also out of MA40 ammo, and had only one magazine for his M7 submachine gun.

Not wanting to silhouette himself against the shield barrier's red glow, he went down an alley and crossed to the perimeter road, where he was surprised to see that Linda had already blown the lookout towers and taken out the shield barrier along the entire south side of town. That meant the militia was less than two minutes out, since bringing the barrier down any earlier would have given the enemy time to react to the breach and prepare a defense.

To the north, the shield barrier remained up and glowing, so from the vantage of the depot yard, it would appear that the entire town was still protected. Once a squadron commander crossed the perimeter road and saw the truth, he would rush south to intercept the Warthogs as they entered town. Whatever else John did, he needed to stop that from happening. It would mean the difference between a hard-fought victory and a devastating defeat.

He went to the edge of the yard and took a position in a half-razed building on the corner of the perimeter road. Between his remaining C10 cubes, eight grenades, and his single M7 magazine, he had enough ordnance to fight for maybe sixty seconds. After that, he would have to draw his M6 and hop onto a Wraith, then pry open the hatch and capture it for use against the enemy.

It would be tough, but he'd done it many times before.

He set two of the timers on his last five detonators to seven seconds, and the rest to three seconds.

"Blue Two, status?"

"Northwest corner of the depot yard," Fred reported. "No cubes, bingo MA40 ammunition, still six M19s."

"Save the M19s," John said. "The column will try to turn south on the perimeter road. We have to bottle that up. Blue Three?"

"No explosives," Kelly said. "Plenty of MA40 ammunition. You want me to toss down a few magazines?"

Before John could answer, a deafening thrum filled the depot yard, and the surviving armor began to move forward, pushing disabled craft out of the way and scattering anyone still on foot. Clearly they had heard about the approaching Warthogs and were moving to intercept.

"Negative," John said. "Vacate the towers and stay out of sight."

Kelly flashed green; then the first Marauders were moving past his hiding place into the perimeter road—no doubt expecting the shield barrier to drop so they could exit the yard.

John rose and threw his first two C10 cubes at the Marauders leading the way across the perimeter road. To stop the rest of the armor from plowing through his area to bypass the coming wreckage, he hurled the last three cubes at a trio of Wraiths passing close by, then fled the building and began racing down the perimeter road.

Three steps later, the first shockwave hit, taking him square in the back and carrying him a good fifteen meters before dropping him facedown on the glass paving. He slid another ten meters on his chest plate, then managed to get an arm under himself and spin around.

"Uh, Blue Leader," Fred said over TEAMCOM. "I don't think they're going to—"

John's faceplate flashed white as a Marauder missile streaked away from the column and destroyed the closest lookout tower. He rolled to one side of the street and came up on his knees, the butt of his M7 pressed to his shoulder. With his NVS still blast-blinded, he couldn't actually see the column flowing out through the now-opened shield barrier, but he could hear them—and the rising deep hum of their boosted antigravity propulsion drives, swiftly building to battle speed.

John opened the Viery Militia command channel. "Sierra-117 reporting armor breakout west side New Mohács," he commed. "Repeat: armor breakout west side—"

"No worries," Chapov interrupted. "We have you covered."

"*No worries?!*" John realized he was starting to yell and ordered himself to calm down. It didn't work. "Explain yourself, Lieutenant."

"Give me a minute," Chapov said. "Kinda tied up right now."

Before John could object, a series of earsplitting bangs sounded out on the glass barrens. His NVS had cleared the blast-white from his faceplate, but when he turned toward the sound, he found himself looking at the only section of shield barrier still standing within half a kilometer.

Another series of seismic bangs sounded out on the glass, and John began to hear cheering voices over the militia's command channel. He pounded south along the perimeter road and, three hundred meters away, saw lines of militia Warthogs rolling into town, rocket launchers shrieking and Vulcan machine guns chugging as they mowed down Banished defenders.

A third round of explosions sounded out on the barrens as John reached the lookout tower at the south end of the shield barrier. Conscious that he had nothing with which to defend himself but a submachine gun and a pistol, he stepped into the tower base and allowed the gravity lift to carry him up to the watch platform. He took a moment to verify that the three Unggoy lying on the platform floor were actually dead, then peered through one of the gun ports designed to protect the sentries during a battle.

Out on the glass, he saw a heavily cratered trench that had been cut into the lechatelierite perpendicular to the village boundary—not parallel to it, as would be normal. It was anchored at the shield barrier just south of the depot yard, and extended eight hundred meters west, so the Banished armor could not intercept the stream of arriving Warthogs without crossing it.

And the Banished *had* crossed it. A line of armored vehicles lay broken and smoking inside the trench, and a hundred meters south of it lay a second trench and a second line of destruction, and beyond that lay a third trench and a third line of demolished armor. A fourth line—perhaps half the column's total strength—was pursuing some seventy militia rangers south across the barrens . . . toward a *fourth* trench.

The rangers were taking tremendous casualties. In the time it took John to estimate their number, another seven fell to plasma cannons or rockets. No sooner had the survivors reached the next trench than the Banished armor was upon them, the Marauders and Wraiths spinning in place to fire plasma mortars down its length, the Ghosts and Choppers racing along, spraying plasma bolts and cannon rounds.

No more than forty rangers remained to climb out, pausing to lob grenades and fire rockets at the vehicles behind them.

Kelly's voice sounded over TEAMCOM: "They're quite mad. Imagine what they could do with proper training."

"I'm not sure I want to," John said. "At least not until we get the nukes out of their hands."

As soon as the surviving rangers were ten paces out of the trench, a series of C10 charges detonated behind them, hurling Ghosts and Choppers skyward, splitting Marauders down the center, and blowing pillars of flame through Wraiths. A quarter of the vehicles failed to emerge on the other side, leaving eight Marauders and fifteen Wraiths to continue the pursuit, and not even fifty pieces of smaller armor.

John estimated thirty rangers—the only ones left alive—running across the glass, headed for a fifth trench about a hundred meters away. The Banished armor lingered behind, lobbing fire after them, but clearly evaluating the wisdom of keeping up. A hundred meters beyond that fifth trench, *Special* Crew was using the drilling jumbo and LHD to finish a sixth trench. John opened a magnification window and saw that Van Houte and Chapov were together on the jumbo, one driving while the other handled the drills. Mukai was on the LHD.

And three hundred meters beyond the sixth trench, a long column of Viery Militia Warthogs and Gungooses was continuing to stream into New Mohács, taking almost no fire from Banished defenders and no casualties that John could see. This town might not be liberated *yet*—but it would be by dawn.

Lieutenant Chapov's voice sounded over TEAMCOM. "I apologize for cutting you off, Master Chief," he said. "I needed to finish that trench."

"That's understandable," John said. "I'm glad you did."

"You are?" Chapov seemed rather stunned. "Uh, I know I shouldn't have risked the excavation equipment without talking to you, but TEAMCOM—"

"No need to explain. Well done, Lieutenant."

Chapov fell silent for a moment, perhaps because he was watching the last of the Banished armor flee across the glass. Finally he said, *"Really?"*

"I wouldn't make him say it twice," Fred said, breaking into the conversation. "He *hates* that."

# CHAPTER THIRTEEN

**0504 hours, October 12, 2559 (military calendar)**
**UNSC flagship *Infinity***
**Orbital Approach, Planet Reach, Epsilon Eridani System**

atherine Halsey stepped onto the bridge of the UNSC *Infinity* and found herself looking down the length of a bustling command aisle toward a large, multi-pane viewport. Beyond it hung a pale orb about the size of a mass spectrometer, its albedo so high even its night side shone like alabaster in the light of its two moons. It pained Halsey to see Reach so barren and lifeless. It had been her home since she was eighteen, so it was only natural to be troubled by the tragedy that had befallen it. But her disquiet ran deeper than that, perhaps because the desolation reflected her own misgivings about some of the work she had done there.

Not *all* of it, but enough that she had to practice lucid dreaming if she hoped to get any sleep at all. It had been on Reach that Halsey had conscripted seventy-five six-year-old children into her clandestine SPARTAN-II program. She and her staff had molded them into the finest warriors humanity had ever produced, bioengineered super-soldiers who could be deployed in small numbers to leverage the outcomes of major battles and put down the Insurrection that had threatened to tear apart humanity's nascent interstellar civilization. But the cost had been terrible. Thirty recruits had perished during the physical augmentation procedures that she herself had designed and performed. Another dozen had been crippled. She had been able to rehabilitate a number of them, but not all. The loss still weighed heavily on her.

That had been forty years ago, when Halsey had been one of the youngest and most trusted scientists working for the Office of Naval Intelligence. At the time, she had told herself she was sacrificing the few to save the many—and, of course, her superiors had agreed. But even then, such platitudes had done little to soothe a conscience burdened by the knowledge of what she had stolen from those children.

Reach was also where Halsey had created Cortana, one of the most unique AIs who had ever existed, and who had helped John-117 win countless battles before losing her way in rampancy and becoming perhaps the greatest tyrant in human history.

At least Halsey had no misgivings about *that* part of her work.

Had Cortana never been created, humanity would simply no longer exist. Without Cortana, John would never have been warned about the true nature of Halo, and the Forerunner monitor 343 Guilty Spark would have convinced him to activate the Halo ring designated Installation 04—and destroy all sentient life within a radius of twenty-five thousand light-years. Had Cortana not outwitted the monstrous Gravemind a few months later, the parasitic Flood would have spread throughout the galaxy and turned humanity into a collective of mindless ghouls. If Cortana had not been there to infiltrate the *Mantle's Approach*, the ancient Forerunner known as the Didact would have composed the entire population of Earth, destroying their bodies and trapping their digital essences forever. Before going rampant, Cortana had saved humanity *many* times over.

So, if it had now fallen to Halsey and Blue Team to liberate humanity from Cortana's despotism, she saw no reason to feel guilty. When it came down to it, the human race still existed to be liberated.

But there wasn't much time now. The *Infinity* needed to keep to its schedule.

Captain Thomas Lasky was not at the holographic situation display near the back of the command aisle, so Halsey started forward. Her gaze remained on Reach, where the splinter-sized silhouette of an *Anlace*-class electronic warfare frigate floated above either pole, with a third over the equator, cones of almost-imperceptible radiance shimmering from their bellies as they wrapped the world in a full-spectrum jamming blanket. The blue specks of a hundred efflux tails were sweeping across the planet's pale disk, Longswords systematically searching out and destroying thousands of old satellites still in orbit around the planet. Most of the satellites were probably nonfunctional or incapable of contacting a Waypoint station nearly a trillion kilometers away, but even a single escaped transmission might be enough to alert Cortana and bring a Guardian through slipspace to investigate.

As Halsey continued walking, it became obvious that the apparent size of the planet was growing no larger—which meant the *Infinity*'s orbital approach had stalled. She passed a doorway leading to a bustling combat information center where two dozen operators and compilers sat at an oval console bank, analyzing input streams and evaluating messages before feeding the data into the tactical holograph that floated in the center of the array.

Halsey paused only long enough to confirm that Lasky wasn't peering over the shoulder of some plotting director or sensor supervisor, then continued toward the front of the command aisle. The *Infinity* was thirty-three minutes behind schedule and there was no indication that anyone aboard was trying to make up time. According to Halsey's calculations, the ship had to enter orbit in the next twenty minutes. A minute more, and there wouldn't be time to insert the assault force before dawn reached New Mohács. If that happened, the troop drop would be delayed until nightfall, and the Viery Militia would be forced to hold the village for another twelve hours.

And Blue Team would be forced to help them, because right now they were stranded behind enemy lines with no means of transport. Orbital communications were being jammed, so they wouldn't know the *Infinity*'s situation. They would, of course, take matters into their own hands and steal something from the Banished, then try to cross a thousand kilometers of glass barrens under hostile air superiority.

They wouldn't make it. Halsey knew this, because she had run the simulations a thousand times. And they *never* made it.

Not once.

Halsey came to the bridge's holographic situation display at the center of the command aisle. Flanking it along the perimeter of the compartment were easily over a dozen operators, monitoring ten different kinds of sensors pointed in twenty different directions, plotting trajectories, listening for enemy transmissions, coordinating screening patrols, evaluating contacts, and performing all the myriad tasks necessary to safeguard a five-and-a-half-kilometer supercarrier in hostile space.

She spotted Sarah Palmer first, a giant brunette woman in Mjolnir armor towering over a cluster of senior officers gathered around a bank of sensor consoles at the fore of the deck. This wasn't a good sign. A Spartan-IV, Palmer hadn't even been born when Halsey dispatched John-117 and her Spartan-IIs on their first missions. Now Palmer was the commanding officer of the *Infinity*'s complement of Spartan-IIIs and -IVs—and she was supposed to be in the launch bays, preparing to insert with her troops in the first wave of drop pods.

The *Infinity*'s commander, Captain Lasky, stood on Palmer's far side, completely hidden save for a gesturing hand and forearm with his captain's stripes on the sleeve cuff.

Halsey reached the forward end of the holographic situation display and cut across the deck toward the sensor station. She had barely taken two steps before her escort said, "Ma'am, you can't go any farther."

She ignored the woman and continued toward the sensor station.

Ensign Teslenko, one of several young officers who rotated escort duty whenever Halsey left the Science Decks, had no doubt been ordered to keep tabs on Halsey and make sure she didn't attempt to depart the *Infinity*. But that wasn't how the arrangement had been presented to Halsey. Lasky had claimed the escorts were there to serve as aides and liaisons, and that was how Halsey treated them—as her assistants, not her keepers.

When she continued across the deck, Teslenko took her by the arm—by the *left* arm, meaning the ensign was holding on to a robotic prosthetic. Halsey's natural limb had been amputated a year and a half earlier, after she was wounded during an ONI assassination attempt ordered after Halsey dared to think for herself one time too many. She tried not to take the maiming personally. Over the decades, her relationship with ONI *had* grown rather complicated.

The prosthetic, which had been installed courtesy of the UNSC after she returned to warn them of the Cortana situation, utilized the latest military-grade robotic technology. In many ways, it was superior to the arm it had replaced—but it had no feeling, so Halsey didn't realize her escort had grabbed it until forward momentum was converted to angular, and she found herself whirling around to come nose-to-nose with the scowling ensign.

"Ma'am," Teslenko said, "you're not even authorized to be on the bridge during a combat action."

"Are you authorized to stop me?" Halsey asked. When Teslenko lowered her carefully plucked brows in uncertainty, Halsey twisted her arm free of the ensign's grasp. "I didn't think so."

Halsey stepped backward and spun around, then began weaving her way toward Sarah Palmer's looming figure. Teslenko followed a second behind her, calling out, but it was too late. Halsey was already carving a path through the huddle of officers toward Captain Lasky. A tall man with short-cropped brown hair, Lasky had square shoulders and a similarly shaped face that seemed utterly appropriate to his strong moral compass.

Palmer saw Halsey first and rolled her eyes in exasperation. Halsey smiled and raised her prosthetic arm in greeting. It had been Palmer—acting on orders from ONI's commander-in-chief—who had made the shot during the unsuccessful assassination attempt. Halsey delighted in every available opportunity to remind the Spartan-IV of her failure.

Palmer's expression returned to neutral, and she spoke to Lasky so quietly that Halsey had to resort to reading lips.

"Incoming," Palmer remarked. "Halsey."

Lasky's chin dropped, but before he could reply, Ensign Teslenko's voice sounded from somewhere behind Palmer.

"My apologies, Captain. I told Dr. Halsey she wasn't allowed on the bridge during a combat action."

"Not quite." Halsey came to a stop directly behind Lasky, looking past Palmer's back toward Teslenko. "You said I wasn't *authorized*. There's a difference, Ensign."

Lasky nodded to the young officer. "It's okay, Ensign. You're dismissed."

"Very good, Captain," Teslenko said. She shot Halsey a dark look, then departed.

Before Lasky could completely face her, Halsey edged toward the bank of sensor consoles, squeezing between the captain and a balding, jowly lieutenant commander wearing a sensor-systems badge on his breast pocket. She didn't know the lieutenant commander by sight, but his name tape read MEOQUANEE. This must be Tag Meoquanee, then—*Infinity*'s sensor supervisor.

As Lasky adjusted to her new location, Halsey took the opportunity to peer over an operator's shoulder at the sensor console Lasky and the others had been studying. The two-dimensional display showed an image of Reach's dual moons hanging above the right side of the world, ringed Csodaszarvas trailing a little behind its knobby counterpart Turul and just crossing the edge of the disk. To the left of the two moons, there were five sets of data lines that Halsey recognized as mass, temperature, and magnetometer readings. They were leading vector arrows down toward the planet, and each vector arrow represented a moving object—no doubt a hostile ship.

Halsey did not bother to ask how five hostile ships had gone undetected until now. It was fairly easy to spot a spacecraft with an active propulsion tail, especially if it was also emitting a lot of electromagnetic radiation. Usually, it was even possible to detect a vessel drifting quietly hundreds of thousands of kilometers away, with all nonessential systems powered down. But when a ship was hiding inside an atmosphere as thick as Csodaszarvas's, or remaining concealed under the rim of a deep crater like those found on Turul, discovering it was a matter of luck more than skill.

"*That*'s why we're behind schedule?" she asked. "A few Banished corvettes?"

"Destroyers," Palmer said. "Three of them are heavy destroyers. And one of them is a karve."

"I don't care if they're heavy cruisers," Halsey said. The karve was a Banished vessel designed explicitly for siege and invasion operations, so the Banished were clearly determined to recapture New Mohács. "We can't allow them to delay the insertion. If you don't relieve New Mohács, Blue Team is stuck. And if Blue Team doesn't reach CASTLE Base—"

"I know how important it is for Blue Team to reach CASTLE Base," Lasky interrupted. "What I *don't* know is whether those vessels have supraluminal comm capability—or the ability to activate a relay satellite that does."

"And you're waiting to find out?" Halsey asked. "That's hardly wise."

"We're waiting until we know we've spotted all of them," Lasky replied. "If we miss one and it transmits a supraluminal message, we'd have to leave before Blue Team has time to achieve their objective."

"Whatever that may be," Palmer added icily, looking over Lasky.

There was a lot of negativity in Palmer's voice, and no wonder. She hadn't been informed of Blue Team's mission on Reach, and probably resented having to make a full-scale hot drop just to free them up to continue it. But Halsey had no intention of trying to win Palmer's support. The Spartan-IV was a by-the-book soldier who had proven several times over that she would rather obey every rule in the Uniform Code of Military Justice than stray even a little to save humanity.

Had Palmer known the contents of the cryobins Blue Team was tasked with recovering, she would have arrested Halsey on the spot.

In fact, Halsey had only hinted at the nature of the contents to the captain—though he undoubtedly had his suspicions. When committing gross violations of Unified Interstellar Law, she had always found it wise to involve others to the minimum extent possible. There was a tendency to lose fewer friends that way.

A sixth vector line appeared on the console, emerging from Csodaszarvas's atmosphere and passing beneath its rings. It took a moment for the data lines to appear in front of it, and then the operator craned his neck to look over his shoulder at Lasky.

"That one looks like a cruiser, sir."

"Any indication we've been spotted yet?" asked Tag Meoquanee.

The operator dragged a finger over his tracking pad, bringing up a bar graph of frequencies and message traffic along one side of his display.

"Their comm traffic looks moderate," he replied. "About what I'd expect for launching an operation. There certainly isn't a message flurry yet."

"We'll stay quiet a little longer," Lasky said. "If there are three factions, I'd expect three cruisers."

"Perhaps," Halsey said. "But John's situation report indicated there had been some trouble between the factions on the ground. Why assume all three of their fleets are hiding in the same place?"

"Because it's the only place they *could* be hiding," Meoquanee said. "Our EW frigates have been actively scanning since they set up the jamming blanket. If there was anything larger than a Warthog within ten light-minutes of Reach, they would have found it by now."

"Then I suggest we activate the *Infinity*'s jammers and move to attack," Halsey said. "If we fall any further behind schedule—"

"Commander Meoquanee knows what he's doing," Lasky said. "There's a hole in the jamming blanket behind Turul. Any vessel hiding on its far side would be able to transmit away from us."

"Toward the star," Halsey said. "That would be a very small transmission window. Especially for a supraluminal signal."

"But that little window happens to include Libration Point Five," Meoquanee said. "Right now, at least fifty relay satellites in various standby modes are parked there—and *their* transmission windows are wide open. At least a quarter of them could probably relay a supraluminal signal."

"And if that happens, I *will* leave Blue Team behind," the captain said. He didn't need to explain why. A supraluminal signal originating from Reach was likely to draw one of Cortana's Guardians. "I'm sorry, Doctor. I won't sacrifice the *Infinity*."

"Leaving so abruptly would be rather overcautious, you think?" Halsey knew better than to hope Lasky was bluffing—the man only bluffed his enemies. But he was susceptible to reason. If she reminded him of the stakes, he would have to see how insignificant the risk to the *Infinity* was in comparison to what she was trying to do. "If we don't recover those assets, I won't be able to stop Cortana. If I don't stop her, the destruction of the *Infinity* is only a matter of time. You can't hide from her forever—not in a vessel like this."

Lasky stared out the viewport. "I understand that. But if it comes to it, I'm willing to take the chance. Even small odds are better than certain destruction."

Halsey decided it would be wiser to argue the point later. Lasky would have her removed from the command bridge before he allowed her to debate him in front of his subordinates. Besides, he probably believed that if worse came to worst, she could create another set of assets—and it would require far more time than they had available to explain why that wasn't possible.

A spray of vector arrows appeared beneath each of the Banished vessels on the console. The operator cursed under his breath and leaned forward, dragging a finger across his tracking pad to enlarge the plethora of data lines that appeared in front of each one.

"It's not missiles," the operator said. "Too slow."

There was a moment of silence before Meoquanee asked, "Drop-ships?"

"That would be an awfully long drop," Lasky said. "They haven't even left high orbit."

"But I think that's what it is," the operator said. "I'm reading Phantoms and a couple of Spirits."

"What the heck are they up to?" Lasky was not one for cursing, but his frustration was evident in his tone. "They'll be dropping through our fighter envelope. Most of those—"

He broke off and keyed his throat mic. "XO, engage engage engage!" he ordered. "Initiate frigate defense, then commence *Infinity* jamming operations—and destroy that cruiser and those destroyers *ASAP!*"

Lasky was wearing a comm bud in his ear, and Quinby Okpara was at her post on the other end of the command aisle, so Halsey did not hear the executive officer acknowledge the order. But in the next instant, she felt her stomach flutter as the *Infinity*'s artificial gravity went into compensation mode to prevent any damage or injuries from the vessel's sudden acceleration. Outside the viewport, Reach's disk began to swell rapidly.

The Banished ships scattered from their formation, one heading for each of the *Infinity*'s EW frigates. The Longsword satellite-cleaners broke their sweep formation and rushed off to defend the frigates—and Halsey finally saw what Lasky had recognized the moment the dropships appeared.

"You can't let them draw off our fighter envelope," she said.

"I can't let them take out the frigates either," Lasky replied. "This is erupting into a major fight, Doctor. The minute that jamming blanket goes down, automatic satellite alerts are going to start flying. If just one of them triggers a supraluminal relay, the *Infinity* will have to withdraw."

As he spoke, half a dozen flights of missiles appeared in the forward viewport and streaked toward the planet, the white circles of their thrust nozzles curling in six different directions as they turned after their individual targets. They didn't have much chance of actually causing damage, but they *would* limit the Banished captains' ability to maneuver—and force them to divide their countermeasures between the missiles behind them and the *Anlace* frigates and Longswords in front of them.

"I understand your concern," Halsey said. "But allowing those dropships to reach the ground is far worse. If New Mohács falls, the pioneers *will* use their Havoks."

Palmer glared over Lasky's head at Halsey. "You can't expect us to believe that, Dr. Halsey. They're bluffing—or the Master Chief is."

Impossible. In John's transmission requesting support, he had outlined for those present the Viery Militia's original plan to draw the Banished forces into New Mohács and detonate a Havok. He'd gone on to say that he believed the rehab pioneers had, in fact, recovered an ample supply of Havoks, and that their militia would use them to drive the Banished off Reach—unless the UNSC did it first.

"John doesn't bluff," Halsey said.

"John does what he needs to do," Palmer replied. "If he was willing to go AWOL for Cortana—and take Blue Team with him—who knows how far he would go to save an entire rehab colony?"

"*I* do," Halsey said. Now Palmer was getting on her nerves. "John understands the importance of his mission."

"Good for him. But you understand why I can't take your assurances on faith."

"There's no need to, if you trouble yourself to think it through," Halsey said. "Nobody is bluffing, because the rehab pioneers *can't* bluff. They've sacrificed everything to return to Reach, and now the

Banished have destroyed their transports. Even if they wanted to give up, they couldn't."

Palmer's expression grew thoughtful, and her gaze drifted forward, where Reach had grown so large that its disk filled the entire viewport and the enemy vessels had swollen to the size of teardrops. Csodaszarvas and Turul were hanging in the right corner, with a broad wedge of star-speckled space between them and the planet. Halsey was relieved to see that there were no other Banished vessels present, which meant the *Infinity*'s jamming blanket was still covering all known Banished ships.

Sensing that she might actually be winning Palmer over, Halsey continued, "If the pioneers think we've abandoned them, their best option will literally be to use the Havoks to drive the Banished off the planet, then hope they have enough survivors among them to put the pieces together."

"And I wouldn't blame them," Captain Lasky said. "But that doesn't change our situation up here. Our first priority is keeping a blanket on the satellite network, and that means defending our frigates. We'll just have to trust that the Master Chief can keep the pioneers from using a Havok until we can get there."

"Then we'd better let them know help is on the way," Halsey said. "Because when those pioneers see a wave of Banished dropships descending ahead of ours, they're going to lose hope—and if they set off a thirty-megaton nuclear device, even a surface blast *will* be detectable from Reach's libration points."

"How detectable?" Lasky asked.

"There isn't time to calculate a precise answer," Halsey replied. "But the gamma-ray burst would be strong enough to awaken any close-emergence slipspace monitoring stations that survived the fall of Reach. And the EMP effects would linger in the planet's ionosphere long enough to confirm a nuclear detonation."

Lasky's face paled. "And *that* would trigger an automatic Waypoint emergency transmission."

"No. I'm not buying it," Palmer said. "*If* any of those monitoring stations are still functional, they would have activated when the *Infinity* entered the system. Or the Banished."

Lasky shook his head. "Why do you think we left slipspace in the heliopause?"

Halsey doubted that Palmer knew the *Infinity* had entered the system in the heliopause—the boundary at the outer edge of the star system, where the outbound stellar wind met the interstellar medium and no longer had enough pressure to push forward—because *Halsey* hadn't. She had been vaguely aware that the sublight transit had taken a day longer than expected, but she hadn't given it much thought beyond that.

"Dr. Halsey is right," Lasky continued. "Either we make sure those pioneers know we're coming—and soon—or we pack up the *Infinity* and hightail it out of here."

"And leave Blue Team behind?" Palmer asked. She actually sounded unhappy about it. "Are you sure?"

"We're not leaving Blue Team behind," Lasky said. "Not if we can avoid it, anyway. Put a hundred and twenty Spartans in the HEV pods. We'll launch them as soon as we know the enemy line ships can't break off to come after you."

"You want to high-drop a hundred and twenty Spartans?" Palmer's voice was on the verge of shrill. "Into enemy air superiority? In *daylight?*"

"Commander, do I look like I'm crazy?" Lasky then spoke into his throat mic: "XO, have the Commander Air Group ready all Broadsword squadrons. I want ten squadrons to lead the first wave of drop pods, and the rest to lead the second wave."

There was a pause while he listened to Okpara's reply in his earbud.

"Tell the CAG she'd *better* have our Longswords back by then," Lasky said. "Listen, Quinby, I wasn't planning to liberate Reach either. Heck, I didn't even know it *needed* liberating. But we're here now, and the situation demands it. So stop telling me what you can't do and start figuring out how to get it done."

Another pause.

"I appreciate that." Lasky caught Palmer's eye, but continued to speak into his throat mic. "Commander Palmer will coordinate with General Doi before the first wave drops, but I want ODSTs behind the Spartans in the SOEIVs, and in the first run of Albatrosses and Pelicans."

Lasky listened for another moment, then said, "Very well. Get to it."

As soon as he signed off, Palmer asked, "You're anticipating that I'll drop with the Spartans in the HEVs?"

"It's your option. I assumed you would take it."

Palmer smiled—sort of. "You know me better than I thought, Captain."

"I do my best, Sarah." Lasky pursed his lips, then said, "You'll have air superiority on the first wave, and probably for the second. But once you're on the ground, you won't have anything until the hangar crews can refuel and re-arm the surviving Broadswords, and that will take a few hours. So plan accordingly."

"I always do."

"I know," Lasky said. "There's one more thing."

Palmer cocked her head and said nothing.

"Take Fireteams Intrepid and Taurus with you. I want the militia's nukes secured asap—all of them. That's the price of our help."

"Understood." Palmer then said to Halsey: "It seems Blue Team's mission is more important than I realized. Maybe it's time to read me in."

"You don't want to know," Halsey said.

Palmer exhaled sharply and looked to Lasky.

"You don't," Lasky concurred. "You really don't. I only *suspect* what they're trying to recover, and I wish I didn't."

"But if something happens to Blue Team—"

"You can't *let* it," Lasky said. "If I could just send in another team, do you think I'd be committing the *Infinity* to liberate a glassed planet, especially *this* one? It *has* to be Blue Team."

Palmer swallowed hard and inclined her head. "Understood."

A chain of orange flashes blossomed against Reach's alabaster disk as the first missile volley caught their targets and started to erupt. The shields of one of the smaller destroyers went down, and the *Infinity* was close enough that Halsey could actually see the column of vapor and flotsam venting from its breached hull.

A squadron of UNSC Longswords was quick to take advantage, swooping in to launch their ASGM-10s before the Banished repair crews could bring the shields back up. Half the Longswords were cut open by the destroyer's pulse lasers, but their missiles struck home, and the enemy vessel's bulky bow disintegrated into a spray of bodies and metal.

The Banished dropships continued their approach, skipping across the outer layers of Reach's atmosphere, heading for the terminator line to begin their descent.

"It looks like I'd better get to the drop bay," Palmer said. She came to attention and locked her gaze on Lasky. "With your permission, sir."

Lasky nodded, but didn't dismiss her. "We won't be in direct communication because of the jamming envelope," he said. "We'll have to pass messages via the Broadsword pilots."

"I'll be sure to monitor their channels."

"And I'll tell the CAG to pass your messages along as soon as she receives them," Lasky replied. "Good luck, Commander. The Reavians couldn't be in better hands."

"Thank you, sir. We won't let them down."

As Palmer departed, the *Infinity* turned toward the distant silhouette of the Banished cruiser, Reach sliding across the forward viewport. The last of the *Infinity*'s escort complement—five *Strident*-class frigates—swept out in front of the supercarrier. They quickly moved into screening position, forming a ring that would keep the enemy cruiser trapped inside the *Infinity*'s kill-cone.

Then the Banished cruiser's weapons turrets came to life, flinging balls of plasma at two of the UNSC vessels approaching from behind her port side. Even Halsey could see that the enemy cruiser was trying to open up some maneuvering room away from the planet—a doomed effort. The two vessels took the initial strikes on their shields and returned fire with their MAC systems; then the entire ring of frigates simply rotated, bringing two fresh ships into position on the cruiser's port side.

A steady stream of missile volleys began to pour from the *Infinity*'s launchers, harrying the Banished cruiser and giving the enemy point-defense weapons something to worry about while the supercarrier brought its forward magnetic accelerator cannons to bear. But the Banished captain was no fool. He rolled his cruiser in the same direction and continued to erupt plasma fire into the two vessels he had hit earlier.

They held their positions and launched another pair of MAC rounds to prevent the Banished cruiser from escaping by dropping parallel to Reach. Their shields went down, and the enemy plasma began to sink into their bow armor, launching white sprays of molten titanium into space.

The bridge lights flickered as the *Infinity* fired its first MAC, launching a three-thousand-ton slug toward the Banished cruiser at a quarter the speed of light. Halsey didn't even see the round strike. In one instant the cruiser was still there, a dark mass of nanolaminate hull being pushed along by the blue ovals of its repulsor engine drives, and the next it was a ball of white glitter, expanding across the entire viewport.

Then the white ball began to disperse and slide across the viewport as the *Infinity* began the pursuit of its next kill.

Lasky turned to Halsey. "Your plan *is* going to work, right?" he asked. "I'm not risking the *Infinity* on a long shot, am I, Dr. Halsey?"

"Whether it's a long shot or not is irrelevant, Captain Lasky. It's our *only* shot."

Halsey watched in silence as the distant teardrop of a Banished heavy destroyer slid inexorably toward the center of the viewport. Then, finally, the bridge lights flickered again, and the destroyer blossomed into a blinding spray of flotsam.

"But if you find it reassuring," she added, "we have a far better chance than those Banished destroyers do right now."

# CHAPTER FOURTEEN

0540 hours, October 12, 2559 (military calendar)
Glass Barrens outside New Mohács
Arany Basin, Continent Eposz, Planet Reach

How many times John and Blue Team had lain belly-down on some battlefield listening to the rain drum on their Mjolnir armor, he did not know. Probably a thousand times on a hundred different worlds, united through training and comms even when they were hundreds of meters apart. It was in those moments, before battle came, that he felt most connected to his team, sometimes to the point it seemed he knew their states of mind as well as his own: Fred utterly focused and aware, but chafing at the wait . . . Kelly ticking off the minutes by reciting the chorus of that old song about a killer queen over and over . . . Linda so calm she was barely *there*.

Thirty years of war had molded four childhood friends into far more than brothers- and sisters-at-arms. They were extensions of one another, certain enough of their teammates that at times it felt like they were all limbs on the same body. So, lying there on the wet glass waiting, John knew that the rest of Blue Team was as angry as he was about what had befallen Reach—that they all held the rehab pioneers in the same high regard, and while everyone recognized that recovering Halsey's assets had to come first, they were all quietly relieved that their mission had become so entwined with the campaign to drive the Banished off Reach.

A campaign that should be starting any moment now.

After liberating New Mohács from the Banished, the Viery Militia had spent the next twenty-six hours preparing to hold what they had captured, calling on Blue Team's expertise and *Special* Crew's excavation equipment to erect a ring of fortifications around the village.

To no one's surprise, the Banished had spent their own time bringing in forces to counterattack, and now New Mohács was surrounded by enemy formations. The gentle ridge where John was hiding along with Fred and Kelly was about fourteen hundred meters south of the village, above a swale where two thousand Banished infantry stood waiting in the rain. They were gathered behind a long line of mechanized armor, twenty Wraiths interspersed among fifty Marauders, arrayed along the ridge ahead.

The Wraiths were already attacking, lobbing rounds of crackling plasma across a kilometer of glass barrens in long blue arcs that frequently overshot the ring of freshly raised breastworks surrounding New Mohács. In John's night-vision system, their oval-domed hulls and overlapping armor plates made them look vaguely like giant floating tortoises.

But it was the Marauders he was most worried about. Wide in front and narrow in back, they were longer but slimmer than the Wraiths, with smaller reservoirs of carrier gas for their plasma cannons. Unfortunately, they were also nimble and quick, and in the narrow alleys and streets of New Mohács, their top-mounted gunners' turrets would make them far more effective than Wraiths. So they were the vehicles Blue Team would be concentrating fire on first.

Besides, the three Spartans had already arranged a little surprise for the Wraiths.

Similar forces of Banished had assembled on the other three sides of New Mohács, ready to advance as soon as dawn came and they could see what they were shooting at. Blue Team couldn't stop them all, of course. But John hoped that by disrupting the group on the south side of the village, the Spartans would cause enough confusion to delay the assault until support arrived from the *Infinity*.

Assuming there was going to be any support, which was beginning to look doubtful. The gray light of false dawn was already spreading along the eastern horizon, and it would be morning in less than thirty minutes. General Doi would not insert the first wave of drop-troops after daylight—not when John's request had included a warning to expect large enemy forces and hostile air superiority. The UNSC's ubiquitous night-vision technology was about the only advantage the initial drop-troops would have, and Doi would not surrender it lightly.

John backed a meter down the slope so his helmet wouldn't be silhouetted against a brightening horizon, then flashed status green three times—*make ready*. He checked the silenced MA40 assault rifle lying at his side, clearing the suppressor and muzzle of mud, making sure the firing selector moved freely through all positions. Next he inspected the dust seals on the M41 rocket launcher on loan from the Viery Militia. Finally he examined the reload tubes on his mag-mounts, then switched his status to steady green.

Kelly and Fred went green immediately after he did, and only then did Linda's LED turn green as well. She was seventeen hundred meters away, lying atop a four-story building inside New Mohács. She was well beyond the barrage zone, but the steadily falling curtain of blinding plasma would prevent her from providing overwatch until the artillery was silenced—which John expected to be very soon.

Over TEAMCOM, he said, "Ready Volley One."

"Volley One ready," Fred replied.

John shouldered the M41 and linked the sight to the night-vision reticle in his HUD, then returned to the ridge crest. The twenty Wraiths were the only armor actually firing on the Viery Militia right now, but not for much longer.

An hour earlier, he and his two companions had infiltrated the enemy lines, then lurked in the darkness, quietly tossing cubes of C10 wrapped in adhesive sleeves at passing Wraiths as the Banished artillery glided into barrage formation. They hadn't hit all of their targets, but they had managed to stick a cube near the mortar mounts of most of the Wraiths—and behind the turrets of fifteen Marauders as well.

John targeted a Marauder near the middle of the line. Even with his helmet's optical systems maximized, there was no way through the rain and darkness to tell whether it was one of the vehicles that had been tagged with a C10 cube. But the odds were good that it wasn't— and that was what he was hoping for.

He flashed his status LED to indicate he was ready to fire. Once Fred and Kelly had done likewise, John spoke over TEAMCOM again. "Execute."

The first fifteen cubes detonated in a simultaneous volley, sending pillars of white flame shooting skyward.

John fired the M41 at his targeted Marauder. At such long range, it would take the rocket a few seconds to arrive, and it was hard to be sure the attack would disable the Marauder. Rather than waiting to see, John swung his reticle to the next Marauder and fired again.

The first rocket was still in the air as he detached the empty firing tubes, grabbed his assault rifle, and speed-crawled backward. The exhaust flash could easily give away his firing position, so a failure to relocate was a good way to get killed.

Once he'd traveled five meters down the slope, John deactivated his status indicator so Kelly and Fred would know he was moving to his second firing position, a similar spot about two hundred meters away. He could hear the Reavers, the Banished's anti-aircraft walkers, on the other side of the ridge stomping through the darkness in search of aerial attack-craft. To the enemy, it would seem like the C10 blasts were the result of bombs dropped from above.

As John ran across the wet glass, his thigh wound began nagging him again. He'd have to keep the injury in mind and avoid sprinting or jumping if he could. His performance metrics already had his functionality down to 96 percent. If he tore any more of the half-healed muscle, that would drop even further, and this was not the sort of battle where a Spartan could limp along at 85 percent without endangering his team.

When he reached the second position, John attached the new tubes to the M41 rocket launcher, then crawled back to the ridge crest and switched his status back to green so the rest of the team would know he was ready. Kelly's and Fred's lights were already green. They were about a hundred and fifty meters to either side of him, well beyond motion-tracker range and far enough apart so they couldn't all be eliminated by a single plasma round—but close enough to concentrate firepower if necessary.

The enemy still seemed to have no idea where the initial attack had come from. The mechanized armor was moving into staggered formation to avoid making themselves easy targets for an aerial bombing run. The infantry was scattering, trying to avoid bunching up or being run over. John magnified the image and, through his helmet's night vision, saw that most of their faces were still looking skyward, searching for nonexistent bomber craft. But a handful of grizzled Jiralhanae and sly-looking Kig-Yar were scanning the area of the ridge where John and the others had just been. Even if none of them had actually *seen* the rocket flashes behind them, they were certainly smart enough to realize that a rear attack was possible.

Five Banished Reavers were walking back and forth along the bottom of the swale that separated the two ridges, their sensor dishes and shoulder-like missile pods tipped toward the sky. Before John could begin the sequence for firing the second C10 volley, Fred's voice came over TEAMCOM.

"Maybe we should target those Reavers instead of the Marauders. Five of them could take out a bunch of Pelicans."

"If there were Pelicans coming, I would think we'd be seeing insertion trails by now," Kelly said.

John glanced eastward, where the silver light of false dawn was rapidly turning into the red glow of true dawn. Then he looked overhead, searching the black sky for the tiniest streak of crimson that would suggest the fiery trail of a Pelican dropping out of orbit, and saw only the darkness of night clouds.

"Good thought, Two," John finally said. "But let's stick with the Marauders. It's beginning to look like we'll need to improvise our own extraction from this mess."

John didn't need to add that improvising their own extraction would mean returning to New Mohács to regroup with Linda and *Special* Crew—and *that* meant doing their best to minimize the number of Marauders screaming through the streets, blasting everything in sight.

"Can't blame a guy for thinking positive," Fred said. "Give the word."

"Ready Volley Two," John said.

"Volley Two ready."

John set his assault rifle on the glass beside him and shouldered the M41. "Execute."

Another round of detonations sent pillars of white flame shooting skyward. The Reavers immediately began to spray suppression fire into the air, filling the brightening sky with missile trails and tracer spikes. John fired on a Marauder sitting behind two Wraiths, then shifted to the next one—and found it already backing out of formation. He launched his second rocket at it, but it had barely left the tube before the Marauder spun toward him.

"Stay sharp!" John grabbed his assault rifle and began to back down the slope. "We've been spotted!"

The Marauder's gunner followed the rocket's propulsion tail back to John and sent a pair of plasma mortar rounds flying in his direction.

Rockets were slower than plasma, so both of John's attacks were still in flight as the plasma rounds shot past wide to either side. He saw his first rocket strike his originally targeted Marauder, sending a

Jiralhanae gunner flying and a geyser of carrier gas shooting skyward as the pressurized turret feed emptied the tank; then he was too far below the crest to see whether his second rocket struck home.

He heard it detonate too far away, just before another pair of plasma trails stretched past overhead and confirmed his miss. He lay flat on the wet glass, about forty meters below the ridge crest. The Marauder was coming up the other side, so its gunner would not be able to depress his plasma cannons far enough to hit John until the vehicle crossed over and started downhill.

John checked his HUD. Neither Kelly nor Fred was in motion-tracker range, but both had switched to green status, which meant they were on their way to their third designated positions. Being careful to keep his helmet pressed to the glass and his hand low enough to avoid the stream of plasma rounds sizzling overhead, he pulled his last set of rocket tubes off his magmounts and reloaded the M41.

As he worked, he said, "Blue Leader pinned down at position two. Blue Three, call the next volley while I take care of this."

Kelly's status light flashed in acknowledgment. John heard her begin the sequence, then saw the Marauder's two intake pods rising over the ridge crest. They were spread wide like a scorpion's claws, and in his NVS, their mouths were glowing red with the heat of the engines they were feeding. He centered the M41's sight midway between the intake pods and forced himself to wait until the front edge of the hull appeared, the antigravity field beneath it bright white in his NVS. He waited two more breaths . . . until he had a clear view of the forward projection pads.

He fired.

At such a short range, the rocket struck in less than a second, punching through the vehicle's unarmored underside and detonating within the hull. Both Jiralhanae flew from their cockpits on towers of flame, and the hull dropped to the glass and began to bleed fire and carrier gas into the darkness.

Normally John would have checked for escorts before moving. But the booming of the third C10 volley was rolling over the ridge crest, providing the perfect diversion. Carrying his MA40 in his left hand and the M41 in his right, he leaped to his feet and raced away—his left leg heavy as lead for two steps, his boot slipping on the wet glass until his thigh muscle loosened under the influence of the Mjolnir's reactive circuits.

He traveled ten steps before a stream of plasma bolts lit the sky over his head. He turned to see a third Marauder cresting the ridge, its cannons depressed as far as they would go and the gunner leaning forward in the turret, trying to get the vehicle to rock downward so he could hit his target.

John raised his assault rifle and put a pair of three-shot bursts into the gunner's faceplate. A cascade of blood, red and bright in John's night vision, poured from beneath the helmet's jaw-guards, and the Brute slumped forward over the plasma cannons.

The driver swung the Marauder in John's direction and accelerated, trying to run him down. John brought the M41 SPNKr up, stopped, and fired one-handed.

The rocket entered the right intake pod and detonated, blowing it apart and flipping the Marauder onto its cannon turret just a few meters away. As it skidded past, John put a couple of rifle bursts into the forward cockpit for good measure. Once he was sure the driver wouldn't be able to scramble free and come after him, he detached the SPNKr's tubes and slapped the empty launcher onto a magmount.

Kelly's voice came over TEAMCOM. "Shall we fall back now?" She was a hundred meters away, holding her MA40 and kneeling in the bottom of the shallow swale at the base of the ridge. Fred knelt a hundred meters east of her, both of them silhouetted against a silver band of dawn light pushing through the rain clouds. "Or were you thinking of destroying the enemy out here in the barrens?"

The question was tongue-in-cheek, of course. Even Blue Team couldn't fight off a squadron of Marauders and two thousand infantry out in the open. They weren't carrying enough ammunition.

TROY DENNING

"No need to do it the hard way." John started toward her at a fast run, holding back just shy of a sprint. He didn't want to hold up the team by aggravating his thigh wound, and if he got sloppy and pushed too hard, the Mjolnir's reactive circuits wouldn't be able to compensate. "Let's fall back."

The trio performed a rapid combat withdrawal, one member covering while the other two moved. It was standard procedure under the conditions, but the destruction of so much artillery had left the Banished too disorganized to pursue—or even identify the attack source. Fred had to empty most of a magazine taking out two sets of gunners and drivers when a pair of Marauders suddenly appeared over the ridge. Other than that, the three Spartans were able to skirt the enemy's flank unchallenged, then move north toward New Mohács.

The original plan had called for them to remain outside the village until the *Infinity* drop began, then link up with the first wave of troops to coordinate a counterattack. Absent the drop, the best defense would be to hide in the barrens and launch a high-intensity guerrilla campaign that would keep the enemy's attention focused on them rather than New Mohács. But that would leave Blue Team separated from *Special Crew* and the excavation machines, and—as much as it pained John to admit it—their primary mission on Reach was to recover the assets Dr. Halsey needed to stop Cortana, not to support the Viery Militia.

Blue Team dropped into an old streambed that cut across the barrens in front of the Banished artillery, angling toward the fortifications on the west side of the village. The entire channel was strewn with Lotus antitank mines, but Fred was the one who had put them there, and the sensors were not engaged.

The stream bottom was slick with mud and knee-deep in flowing water, so it was slow going—and painful. They were traveling against the current, and every step tightened the knot in John's thigh. It didn't help that the lechatelierite-covered banks were only shoulder height. To keep their helmets below the rim, they ran hunched over for more than a kilometer.

They were almost to the crossover point when the crack of an SRS99-S5 sniper rifle punched through the general roar and rumble of the plasma barrage surrounding New Mohács. A second crack sounded.

Linda's voice came over TEAMCOM. "Run faster." Another crack. "You've been spotted."

*Crack.*

Kelly slowed her pace, moving back toward John's left side, and Fred appeared on John's motion tracker, coming up from behind. John's performance metrics had only fallen to 94 percent, but even a 6 percent drop-off was noticeable to a pair of soldiers who had been fighting at his side since they were fifteen.

"Don't even *think* about bunching up," John ordered. "Blue Three, move out. I want you on a Vulcan when those Marauders open fire. Blue Two—"

"I know, I know," Fred said. He had already dropped out of motion-detector range again. "The rear guard stays in the back."

"Actually," John replied, "I was going to tell you to keep up."

He picked up the pace and, ignoring the stab of pain that shot down his leg with each step, began to cross back and forth across the streambed, trying to stay in the shallow water, which didn't put as much drag on his shins. John had intended to have Fred take the middle position, but Fred had clearly guessed that and taken action to make the switch impractical. It was okay; had it been Fred—or any other Spartan—contending with the effects of a wound, John would have done the same thing.

Linda's sniper rifle cracked again. John raised his helmet just high enough to see over the bank and found the glass barrens already shining with the light of a gray dawn. A half kilometer out, a ragged line of fifteen Marauders was coming fast and converging on his position. Another half kilometer behind them, only two Wraiths—all that remained after Blue Team's C10 detonations—were still lobbing plasma toward the militia fortifications outside New Mohács.

*Crack.* One of the Marauders went into a wild spin as the slain driver's hands slipped from its controls.

John hunched back down and continued to run. A tremendous rattle arose as someone behind the fortifications opened up with a pair of Vulcan light anti-aircraft guns. The attack was answered an instant later by streams of plasma bolts. John didn't dare raise his head to look again, but he knew the LAAG fire would be dealing some serious damage to the oncoming Marauders. For Vulcans, designed as close-in air defense weapons, five hundred meters was medium range, and they fired five hundred armor-piercing rounds per minute that were just as devastating to ground vehicles as they were to Banshees.

By the time John reached the crossover point to the militia fortifications, the plasma fire had dwindled to half its original ferocity. He opened the militia's South Quarter comm channel and heard a panicked garble as dozens of inexperienced soldiers choked the frequency with pointless chatter. No use trying to offer the pass phrase. Even had the sentries been able to pick it out of the stream of babble, they were probably too busy shooting at Marauders to respond with an *advance* command. John would just have to hope they weren't so excited that they mistook him for a Jiralhanae in power armor—and that they hadn't mistaken Kelly for one, either.

John switched back to TEAMCOM. "Blue Three, Blue Leader beginning the crawl."

To his surprise, it was Lieutenant Chapov who answered. "Come ahead, Blue Leader. The sentries are expecting you."

"Great," John said. "But what's one of my equipment operators doing on the front lines? You're mission-critical."

"It was my call," Linda said. "When I saw you were changing the plan, I decided it would be wise to have a cool head at the sentry post when you returned."

John was not used to thinking of Chapov in those terms, but Linda was right. It had been the lieutenant's quick thinking that prevented the Banished armor from interrupting the militia's assault on

New Mohács. And Chapov's composure during the insertion run had allowed him to safely land a crippled Owl, just seconds after awakening from a high-g blackout. Despite John's misgivings and the kid's bumpy start, the lieutenant had proved himself worth having along twice already—whether he realized it or not.

"Makes sense," John said. "Coming across."

John poked the top part of his faceplate above the rim of the streambank and saw a line of tracer rounds sailing a couple of meters over his head. Thirty meters away, at the origin point of the tracer stream, he spotted a Vulcan LAAG firing over the top of the breastworks, with Kelly's dome-faced helmet peering through the aiming slot in its gun shield.

Confident she wouldn't allow a round to drop, he glanced back to check on the enemy and found a trio of Marauders only two hundred meters away. They were weaving wildly in an effort to avoid Kelly's fire, pouring plasma bolts back in her direction and clearly trying to converge on the crossover point. As soon as they saw John crawling the twenty meters to the militia fortifications, they would almost certainly switch their fire to him. There was only one reason for the Marauders to make such a foolish charge—and that was to kill the Spartans who had savaged their artillery line.

A burst of LAAG fire hit the middle vehicle, punching a row of holes straight up the center, through the driver and then the gunner. The Marauder dropped an intake pod into the glass and launched itself in a series of cartwheels, sending weapons and pieces of vehicle flying in all directions. Linda's sniper rifle cracked twice, and another Banished driver and gunner slumped in their cockpits and veered toward the edge of the battlefield.

John pulled himself over the bank and began a high crawl toward the militia breastworks, head raised and assault rifle cradled in his elbows. A kilometer to his left, the Banished artillery was lined up along the edge of a farm field, lobbing so much plasma toward New Mohács that the fiery arcs reminded him of a cathedral interior. Their hulls were only partially defiladed by the drop-off where the rehab pioneers had cut the lechatelierite away—an indication of just how badly the enemy was underestimating the Viery Militia.

The fortifications were mostly for show, occupied by a force just large enough to suggest the rehab pioneers planned to make their stand *outside* New Mohács. The real defenses—the bunkers and the tank traps and the minefields—were hidden just inside the village. Earlier, Blue Team had worked with the militia commanders to set up a series of collapse pockets that would funnel the enemy into kill zones flanked by emplaced gauss cannons and man-portable rocket launchers.

The preparations were going to be a deathtrap for attackers, but they weren't going to save the village. Without UNSC reinforcements, New Mohács would surely fall when the Banished air support arrived. The only thing the militia could do about that was make them pay a heavy price.

John reached the breastworks and slipped through a dogleg entry passage into a sandy trench beyond. Wide enough for a Warthog to navigate easily, it was the source of the glass block that had been used to construct the breastworks ringing New Mohács. It was now strewn with Lotus antitank mines, which wouldn't be activated until the token force of defenders withdrew from the fortifications.

Because the Viery Militia was located on Reach, and Reach had been the UNSC's primary depot world before being obliterated by the Covenant, it was the best-equipped force of irregular troops that John had ever seen. They had made good use of the assets still functioning, placing an untended assault rifle or light machine gun every two meters along the breastworks. A handful of volunteers were running back and forth along the firing platform, selecting weapons at random and pausing just long enough to take potshots at whatever they saw moving out on the barrens.

The deception seemed to be working pretty well. The Banished artillery lines had spent half the night trying to soften up the ring of empty fortifications. They had dropped so much plasma into and behind the trench that the ground had become a virtual moonscape, with one rain-filled crater overlapping the next. There were a few dozen half-charred bodies and a handful of burned-out Warthogs scattered around the devastation—but the losses were almost nothing compared to what they would have been had the breastworks actually been manned.

John found Kelly standing in a Warthog thirty meters to his left. She was no longer firing the Vulcan because she had taken out the last Marauder, but she continued to keep watch as Fred made the cross-over crawl. In the Warthog's driver's seat was a slender lieutenant with blond hair cut blunt at the jawline.

She smiled and saluted. "Master Chief."

"Lieutenant Disztl." John returned the salute and called, "You're here to collect us?"

She raised her chin toward the firing platform that overlooked the entry passage. "As soon as Spartan-104 arrives. They want to consult."

John did not bother asking who "they" were, or what they wanted to consult about. He had told Colonel Boldisar and her commanders that the UNSC drop would happen by sunrise, or not until the following sunset. Now the Viery Militia was wondering how to hold on until nightfall. He wished he knew what to tell them.

Fred emerged from the entry passage, and John pointed him toward the Warthog. Then he waved Chapov down from the firing platform that overlooked it.

"You too, Lieutenant," he said over TEAMCOM. "We need to do some planning."

Chapov hopped down. He was still dressed in his flight suit and wearing his pilot's helmet with the night-vision equipment, but he had traded his MA5B bullpup for an BR75 service rifle. The kid understood the principle of the right tool for the right job. The MA5B bullpup was a good weapon for close-quarters fighting in buildings and village streets, but the BR75 was long-range, ideal for laying cover fire across a kilometer of glass barrens.

As they followed Fred toward the Warthog, Chapov asked, "Planning for what?"

"For how to get out of *here*," Fred replied, "and on with our mission."

"What about the militia?" Chapov asked. "Are we going to just abandon them?"

"It's either that, or stay here and die at their side," Kelly said, also over TEAMCOM. "And to blazes with retrieving those assets for Dr. Halsey."

"That's right," Fred said. "Who needs to worry about mission priorities?"

Chapov's chin dropped, and John realized the young lieutenant did not recognize the banter for what it was—an indication that Fred and Kelly viewed him as an equal member of the team, someone they trusted to look past the barb and see the point.

John wasn't sure how to communicate that. Developing young special-forces officers had never been part of his brief. But Chapov's relentless efforts to impress him had helped John recognize that being considered by the broader UNSC as *the* Master Chief, some of his informal responsibilities were just as important as the ones spelled out in writing. Youthful soldiers idolized him in a way he had not given much thought to until now, and how he responded to that adulation would shape the kind of soldiers they went on to become.

After all, John wasn't going to be around *forever*. Beyond his enhancements and experience, luck had been on his side for years now. But sooner or later, he was going to take a plasma strike in the chest . . . or fall into a star . . . or maybe even just get too old and slow to lead the fight.

And it wasn't the next generation of Spartans he was thinking about. The UNSC had that eventuality well in hand with the SPARTAN-IV program. Dr. Halsey might look down her nose at them because they didn't have the same kind of physical strength and durability as her Spartan-IIs, but John had been training with some of the IIIs and IVs aboard the *Infinity*. What they lacked in brute force, they made up for in grit and resourcefulness—and in sheer numbers. He still found it hard to imagine *hundreds* of Spartans.

Mostly John was thinking about all the nonaugmented men and women he had fought with—the Halima Ascots and the Avery Johnsons and the Miranda Keyeses who had dedicated their lives to defending humanity. Soldiers like that didn't make themselves. They were developed by older, wiser leaders who recognized in them the same kind of potential that Marmon Crowther had seen in John all those years ago . . . that day on the edge of Covenant space, when Crowther had affixed the insignia of the master chief petty officer to John's armor. Now, as hard as it was to accept sometimes, it was *John* who was the "wise old leader." And with that reality came a duty he had never been trained for—and one for which it was probably impossible to be trained.

But it was a duty nonetheless.

As they arrived at the Warthog, John gestured Lieutenant Chapov toward the front passenger's seat.

Chapov shook his head. "I can squeeze into the back."

John continued to hold his hand out. "You'll never hold on," he said. "You haven't seen the way Lieutenant Disztl drives."

Chapov looked more surprised than confused, and made no move to climb in.

"Go on. You deserve it." John gently shoved Chapov into the front seat, next to Disztl's compact frame. "Lieutenant Maks Chapov, meet Lieutenant Bella Disztl, five-time—"

"Winner of the Tantalus Ten Thousand—I *know*." He extended a hand toward her. "Wow. What are *you* doing here?"

"Taking my world back." Disztl studied Chapov's hand without taking it. "So, you're a buggy fan?"

"I drive a little too," Chapov said. "But I followed all five of your wins on DuroCam. I knew those two clowns in forty-nine were on stim-packs."

Disztl flashed him a wide smile. "A pleasure to meet you, Maks Chapov." She finally reached across and gave him a long handshake. "Any friend of the Master Chief's is a friend of mine."

"Oh," Chapov said. "The Master Chief and I aren't exactly—"

"Sure we are." John lightly slapped Chapov on the shoulder, then hopped into the back of the Warthog. "Go with it, Lieutenant."

The bed was filled by the LAAG, its mount, and standing room for the gunner—in this case, Kelly—so there were no seats. John sat on top of the side panel behind Chapov, then wrapped an arm around the roll bar. Fred was sitting opposite him, simply grasping the top of the panel with both hands.

John pointed to the roll bar. "You'll need to hang on."

Fred's faceplate turned toward the bar. With their augmented strength and balance, Spartans did not generally have a hard time staying inside any moving vehicle.

"Seriously?" he asked.

"Oh, seriously." Kelly swung the LAAG around so the barrels were pointed rearward and her back was braced against the roll bar. "If you haven't ridden with her—"

Disztl floored the accelerator and the Warthog shot down the trench, tires rubbing against one wall and then the other, dodging twisted equipment and chunks of glass block and the remnants of other vehicles. Banished plasma bolts continued to rain down, the frequency no greater than before, but occasionally landing close enough to spray the Warthog with shards of shattered breastworks or beads of fused sand. Once Disztl even bounced a wheel off an overturned Mongoose to avoid dropping the passenger side into a still-fiery crater.

John peered past Kelly's legs and found Fred's arm curled tight around the roll bar. "Now do you believe me?"

# CHAPTER FIFTEEN

As John expected, it was a wild ride back into New Mohács. After five armor-clanging minutes in the trench, Disztl put the Warthog into a side-skid and made a fishtail turn onto a ramp John had not even seen until they were on it, then took them on a serpentine run across a hundred meters of barrens, banking off crater walls and bouncing rim to rim as they dodged through the plasma barrage into New Mohács and shot down a dogleg alley lined by LAAG bunkers, decelerating hard as they entered an even shorter dogleg alley lined by firing ports with rocket launchers and gauss cannons. At last they came to the checkpoint and Disztl stood on the brakes, bringing the Warthog to an abrupt stop that rocked them forward so hard John felt a jolt as the rear wheels dropped back to the ground.

A pale militiaman stepped out of the guardhouse to greet them. Uniformed in a dark farmer's shirt with a corporal's double chevrons sewn onto the sleeve, he carried an M6E Magnum sidearm in a secured holster, with one hand on the flap. A little behind him, off to one side where he would have a clear firing lane at Disztl, stood a

— 273 —

private holding an MA5B assault rifle at port-arms. In the street between them lay two Lotus antitank mines. The status LEDs on top were dark, indicating that the sensors were not activated. John knew there would be a third guard, concealed nearby, ready to activate the mines.

Good. Their commander hadn't forgotten the fifteen-minute lecture on checkpoint security that Fred had presented two days earlier.

The corporal stopped a meter from the driver's side of the Warthog.

"Hello, Bella—um, Lieutenant Disztl." He eyed Chapov for a moment, then said, "Identify your passengers."

"Really?" Disztl wiped the rain from her brow and flicked it vaguely in his direction. "They're *Spartans*."

"I can see that," the corporal said. "But it was the *Spartans* who said we had to identify everyone."

"By everyone, he means me," Chapov said. He turned so his face would be visible through the opening left by the flight helmet's retracted face shield. "Lieutenant Maks Chapov, UNSC special forces. That's Master Chief John-117 behind me, Kelly-087 on the gun, and Fred-104 on your side."

"You can let us through now," Fred said to the guard. "Apparently we're late for a meeting."

"Yes, sir." The corporal checked to confirm that the Lotus mines were still inactive, then nodded to his rifleman and saluted Disztl. "You're free to pass, Lieutenant. Watch the mines."

Disztl rolled her eyes. "Yeah, you think?"

She advanced cautiously for once, weaving the Warthog from one side of the road to the other to avoid the mines, then turned down a cross street onto the main boulevard. Here she actually had to drive even slower, as the puddle-dotted street was filled with tank traps and barricades designed to convert it into a killing field once the Banished armor entered the village. Still, New Mohács was only two kilometers across, and the militia headquarters came into view a couple of minutes later. A three-story glass-block building that had once served as the village school, it had been chosen not because of its size or central location, but because it had a subterranean storm shelter large enough to house the tactical planning suite.

Disztl stopped in front of the building's fortifications and dismounted so she could identify her passengers to the sentries stationed at the entrance. But only Chapov went with her. Kelly remained standing behind the LAAG with her helmet tipped back, looking into the sky, and John and Fred weren't going anywhere until they knew what she was staring at.

"Trouble?" John asked.

"Maybe." She pointed northwest, where a faint cluster of tiny orange trails was beginning to glow through the clouds, slowly growing larger and brighter as they came closer. "Maybe not."

John swung out of the Warthog, then motioned to the sentries. "Get Colonel Boldisar and her commanders out here," he said. "Do it *now*."

The post sergeant scowled, but looked skyward—and immediately nodded to a female sentry whose braided black hair was so long it covered the rank insignia on her shoulders.

"Do as he says, Földi," the sergeant said. "Tell them to hurry."

John turned to Disztl. "I want you back in the driver's seat. Chapov, get over to *Special* Crew. Make sure those excavation machines are ready to move—and make sure Major Van Houte puts someone on the roof, where TEAMCOM won't be blocked."

"On it," Chapov said. He circled the Warthog, timing it so that he was passing the driver's seat as Disztl climbed in. He flashed her a big grin. "Nice to meet you, Bella."

"You, too, Maks." She winked, then said, "Look me up when this is over. Maybe we can go for a buggy ride."

Chapov shot a guilty look toward John.

"Move it, hotshot." John pointed across the street. "Tell Major Van Houte to keep me posted on *Special* Crew's readiness."

He returned his gaze to the sky, where the cluster of flame trails had grown long and bright enough to confirm that an insertion was definitely inbound. The flame heads were already showing their oval shape, even through the clouds and the rain, so it was clearly a flight of dropships rather than a fall of Single Occupant Exoatmospheric Insertion Vehicles.

Colonel Sasa Boldisar came rushing down the steps, Istvan Erdei, Rendor Borbély, and several more of her subordinates close on her heels.

"They're inserting in daylight?" Boldisar asked. "I thought they wouldn't do that?"

"I said in my request that supporting your militia is mission-critical," John said. "I guess they took me at my word."

"Perhaps." Kelly spoke over TEAMCOM to avoid being overheard. "But don't you think something is missing?"

John scowled inside his helmet, then increased his image magnification until the spray of glow trails filled his faceplate. He still couldn't see much through the clouds and rain, though the glow trails were a bit longer and more distinct, and the flame heads more clearly drop-shaped. He asked his onboard computer for a count. A number ticker appeared in the corner of his HUD and began to go up as infrared sensors identified a growing number of distinct entry trails.

83 . . . 87 . . . 92 . . .

"Nothing missing I can see from down here," John replied over TEAMCOM. "It looks like a hot drop to me. Probably forty or fifty Pelicans, escorted by five squadrons of Broadswords."

"Then where are the interceptors?" Linda asked. She was still at her overwatch post on a village roof, where she would have a clear view of the surrounding horizon. "The Banished can see the drop coming, the same as we can."

John disengaged his image magnification and looked lower in the sky, then understood why Kelly and Linda were concerned. There should have been whole wings of Seraphs and Banshees rising to engage the insertion craft. Instead, the only thing he saw between the rooftops and the clouds was rain. Meanwhile the Wraiths continued their barrage, and the cluster of glow trails was growing larger without spreading out or growing longer.

"That drop is coming straight at New Moháchs," John said over his voicemitter. "Colonel Boldisar, I suggest you activate Air Defense Alpha, Phase One."

"We can't do that, Master Chief." It was Rendor Borbély, the former Misriah Armory systems designer, who said this. "To those Scythes, a Pelican is just another target."

"I understand how automated targeting systems work, Colonel." John looked back to Boldisar. "You should still activate the Scythes, ma'am. Hold the Lances and Anacondas for Phases Two and Three."

Boldisar looked toward the approaching glow trails, and her face paled. "That isn't the UNSC?"

John flashed status green to Kelly, and she told Boldisar, "Most likely not. If that drop was *ours*, the Banished would be putting everything they have up against it."

"The easiest place to end an insertion is in the air," Fred added. "Once boots are on the ground, it stops being target practice and turns into a fight."

As Kelly and Fred explained the situation to Boldisar, John was on his comm unit, trying every possible channel to raise any UNSC vessels that happened to be overhead—and getting nothing. The Pelicans, if there were actually any coming, might still be in insertion blackout. But if there *was* a UNSC drop going on, there would be UNSC vessels overhead.

And since he couldn't make contact . . . it wouldn't be smart to conclude anything. There might not be any UNSC vessels up there at all. Or they might have wrapped a jamming blanket around the entire planet to delay a response from Cortana. Or they might be on the wrong side of orbit at the moment.

The only thing John could be sure of was that the enemy didn't seem at all concerned about the inbound drop. And that meant *he* should be.

"The Spartans were playing us all along," Istvan Erdei said. He pushed forward next to Boldisar. "There was *never* going to be a UNSC drop."

"We don't play," John said. He looked at Boldisar over Erdei's balding head. "You should have the deception teams fall back so you can activate the tank traps in the outer fortifications."

As he spoke, the first dropship broke through the cloud ceiling and continued through the rain, its flame trail a foreshortened orange arrow, coming straight toward New Mohács.

"Do it now," John said.

Boldisar nodded to Borbély, who immediately raced back into headquarters to obey, and to Erdei, who ignored her and remained where he was.

"There's no shame in giving them a chance *once*," Erdei said. "But you can't keep trusting them—not when they didn't deliver the first time."

Another dozen dropships broke through the clouds and continued toward New Mohács. The cluster remained tight, the oval flame heads slowly growing larger as they approached.

Over TEAMCOM, Linda said, "At that speed, the angle of descent is too steep for Pelicans. They wouldn't be able to pull up in time."

"So they're Phantoms or Spirits," John concluded. "On approach to New Mohács?"

"They're two thousand kilometers away," Linda said, "so they still have time to change course. But I think they *are* coming to us. ETA . . . fifteen minutes, at the most."

Which was about the same time it would take the Banished infantry to cross a kilometer of glass barrens and attack New Mohács. John had his onboard computer begin a fifteen-minute countdown, then studied the officers standing behind Boldisar. He fixed his gaze on a slender major with a blond, waist-length ponytail—Darda Tabori, who had actually served in the UNSC and probably understood the concept of an order.

"Major, you have about one minute before the enemy armor starts its advance." He looked toward the western side of the village. "Ten minutes after that happens, the Banished air squadrons are going to hit your anti-aircraft weapons with every strike craft they have. Then the Griever fighter-bombers will come in and level the place."

Tabori's eyes grew wide. "Why are you telling *me*, Master Chief?"

"Because it would be wise for *someone* to obey Colonel Boldisar," John said. "You need to order the deception teams to fall back so you can activate the tank traps in the outer fortification ring."

"I understand."

Tabori didn't even bother glancing in Boldisar's direction. She simply sprinted into the headquarters to act on John's "suggestions."

He looked back to Boldisar, who was still being lectured by Erdei about the folly of trusting the Spartans. He clasped Erdei's shoulder.

"I'm going to interrupt now." He squeezed until Erdei stopped talking. It didn't take long. "In about fourteen minutes, the Banished infantry will be crossing your tank trench to launch an attack behind their surviving Marauders."

Erdei tried to say something.

"I'm not done yet, Major." John squeezed harder and continued looking at Boldisar. "Don't fall for it, ma'am. They're trying to draw you away from the armor yard so their dropships can land unopposed."

"They're going to drop *in* New Mohács?" she asked. "Is that what you're telling me?"

"Yes, ma'am," John said. "They're going to hit you everywhere at once."

Boldisar's eyes widened. "How do we stop them?"

"We can't," John said. He could see already that she wouldn't take the truth well, but he had to be straight with her. "Not without air superiority. Now that the Banished realize you need to be taken seriously, they'll be a ferocious war machine that doesn't make many mistakes. All you can do is make them pay."

"So much for all that help you promised," Erdei said.

John didn't reply. He wanted to assure them that the UNSC drop *would* be coming, that *Infinity* wouldn't be jamming orbital communications if it wasn't launching an operation—but he had no way of knowing whether communications were actually being jammed, or whether the *Infinity* had simply departed because it expected one of Cortana's Guardians to arrive at any moment. And even if an insertion was coming, it seemed unlikely that General Doi would launch before nightfall, when he could at least give his troops the advantage of their night-vision equipment.

And New Mohács wasn't going to last until nightfall. The Banished were too powerful . . . and too damn smart.

John released Erdei's shoulder, but continued to look at Boldisar. The counter in his HUD had dropped to thirteen minutes.

"Ma'am," he said. "If I were you, I'd give serious thought to preparing a breakout to the south."

Boldisar seemed confused, perhaps even in shock. "You mean run?"

"I mean fight your way out," John clarified. The tunnel they had used to sneak into New Mohács had been destroyed to prevent the enemy from using the same tactic. So now the only way for the militia to leave the village was by shooting. "Blue Team neutralized most of the artillery on the south side of New Mohács. Once the enemy commits to an encircling attack, you should hit their south line with heavy machine guns. It'll be primarily infantry there, so you may be able to punch through with a staggered column of Warthogs."

"What about strafing?" Erdei asked. "We can't punch through if we're being chased down by Banshees and Seraphs."

"There won't be much strafing," John said. "The Banished air support will be over the armor yard, trying to protect their drop. If you can break through, you'll be clear to withdraw."

"And by that, you mean run," Boldisar said.

"I mean live to win tomorrow," John said. "If you die now, it doesn't matter whether a drop is coming later. Your first step is to survive."

"And to make them pay," Boldisar said. "As you said."

"Always make them pay." Silently, John added, *Especially on Reach*. Even almost lifeless and blanketed in lechatelierite, this world was still *his* ground. "Always."

Boldisar considered his reply for a moment, then nodded. "I'm glad we agree." She nodded to Erdei. "You know what to do."

John's stomach sank, and Erdei's round head tipped to one side. "You're sure?" Erdei asked.

"There's no other choice," Boldisar replied. "You heard the Master Chief."

"Ma'am, a Havok is hardly what I'm suggesting." John had hoped Boldisar wouldn't leap straight to what was quite literally the nuclear option, but of course she had—because she didn't understand how inappropriate it was to their situation. "A thirty-megaton device is the wrong tactic—"

"We lured the enemy to New Mohács to destroy them," she said. "Is your breakout operation going to accomplish that?"

"Of course not, but—"

"Then there's nothing to debate here." Boldisar dipped her chin to Erdei. "You have your orders, Major."

Erdei snapped off a salute and headed toward the rear of the headquarters building.

Over TEAMCOM, John said, "Blue Two, you're with him."

Fred started after Erdei. "Orders?"

"Keep us informed," John said, still over TEAMCOM, audible only to Blue Team and *Special* Crew. "Don't let him arm the device until I give the okay."

By the time Fred flashed green, Boldisar was glaring at his back. "Where does he think *he's* going?"

"To assist," John said. The counter on his HUD had dropped to eleven minutes. The Banished infantry had already begun its advance. In five or six minutes, the first Banshees would attack the anti-aircraft emplacements—at least the obvious ones. "On my orders."

"As long as it's only to—"

"Ma'am, it's nonnegotiable. If you intend to use a Havok, I need to protect my people and my mission. That means supervising its deployment."

"Supervising? Not stopping?"

"You have more than one device, and there's no time to go looking for the others," John said. "It seems more efficient to come to an arrangement."

"I'm listening."

"You need to be," John said. "If the breakout goes well, forty to fifty percent of your force will survive. Even if the UNSC *doesn't* insert later, you'll have over two thousand combat-blooded veterans who can continue the fight. They'll be worth twice what your entire militia was before the battle. And with Blue Team to advise you, that might be enough to harass the Banished into leaving Reach."

"Wait," Boldisar said. "You're staying to fight?"

"If there's no drop, it's because the fleet is gone. What else would we do?"

Boldisar's expression grew thoughtful. "So what do you want in return?"

"To advise you." John's onboard computer began to project facts and figures onto his HUD. "In a thirty-megaton surface detonation, the crater will be twelve hundred meters across and two hundred ninety meters deep. The fireball will have a radius of five kilometers. The shockwave will kill most people within fifteen kilometers, and cause major injuries to a distance of thirty-five."

"You're not going to talk me out of using it," Boldisar said. "We won't get another chance to hit them this hard again."

"I'm trying to make sure there will be enough of your people left alive to fight the Banished you *don't* kill," John said. "The heat flash will inflict third-degree burns on a hundred percent of those exposed out to forty-four kilometers. A Warthog's top combat speed is around a hundred kilometers an hour, and there's going to be some time lost in fighting. I'd recommend giving the breakout column at least thirty-five minutes to get clear. Your rear guard should be able to hold the enemy that long. Ask for volunteers. Soldiers ordered to go on suicide missions don't usually perform well."

Alert sirens began to wail across New Mohács, confirming that the Banished assault was under way and militia members should take their fighting positions.

"Is thirty-five minutes enough time?"

"It's all you'll have," John said. "The Banished will take the village in thirty minutes. After that, your survivors will just be trying to hold their attention. Five minutes is all you can count on before they're wiped out."

"I notice you keep saying *you*."

"That's right. As I said, I need to protect my people and my mission." John activated TEAMCOM so that Blue Team and *Special* Crew would hear what he said next. "Blue Team and *Special* Crew will handle drop-zone defense and secure transport for ourselves and our equipment. Once we have what we need, Blue Two will arm the Havok and enable Major Erdei to initiate a thirty-five-minute countdown. Colonel Boldisar will notify the major when the breakout column punches through. Then Major Erdei will initiate. Everyone clear?"

Three status LEDs flashed green in John's HUD, and Van Houte acknowledged for *Special* Crew. John continued to look at Boldisar.

"Do I have a choice?" she asked.

"I asked if you understood, ma'am, not whether you agreed," John said. He motioned Kelly into the passenger's seat of Bella Disztl's Warthog, then climbed into the gun well behind her. "Lieutenant Disztl, how would you feel about serving as my driver on mobile defense?"

She glanced back, her mouth hanging agape. "Are you *kidding*?"

"I'll take that as an affirmative," John said. "Move out."

# CHAPTER SIXTEEN

With the Banished shield barrier destroyed, John could look across New Mohács's wreck-strewn armor yard and see well into the rain-swept barrens. A line of speeding Marauders was inbound across the lechatelierite, swerving around downed Banshees and lobbing their first plasma rounds at the fortifications ringing the town. A dozen kilometers beyond, a dark cloud of Banshees swarmed just above the horizon. It was impossible to get an accurate count through the rainfall, but the number had to be in the hundreds.

Most were holding there, well beyond the range of the antiaircraft guns. But every few seconds, two squadrons of Banshees would break free of the swarm and sweep toward New Mohács. The militia's automatically targeting M71 Scythes would open fire at two thousand meters, filling the air with clouds of high-explosive incendiary/armor-piercing shells.

What happened next had become a pattern. Three or four Banshees disintegrated before the rest reached firing range and their noses began to flash white with cannon fire. A few more Banshees went down, sometimes crashing into the infantry formations behind the Marauders. Then the surviving Banshees pulled up, revealing the ungainly Seraph they had been screening from the Scythe.

The Scythe switched targets, and the Seraph opened fire with everything it had. Plasma bolts and explosive fuel rods began to stream in one direction, and HEIAP shells back in the other.

John had watched the matchup thirty or forty times already. Sometimes the Seraph won, and the anti-aircraft emplacement erupted in pillars of flame and shrapnel, its hundred-thousand-round drum of ammunition cooking off in a terrifying display of pyrotechnics. Sometimes the Scythe won, overwhelming the Seraph's energy shield and punching holes through its nanolaminate hull armor, sending the craft spinning away into the glass barrens.

More often, both lost, filling the air with smoke and debris and flame, destroying each other in a flash of combat that lasted a few seconds.

Now New Mohács was down to its last Scythe emplacement. The cloud of Banshees on the horizon had thinned to a haze, but the Viery Militia was losing the war of attrition. And the Banished commanders were damn well smart enough to know it.

When the next two squadrons of Banshees swept toward New Mohács, five enormous, tri-hulled silhouettes dropped out of the clouds and started across the barrens behind them.

Kelly looked up over her shoulder. "You *do* see those Grievers, correct?"

"Sure do," John answered. "All five."

They were still in Disztl's Warthog. John was standing in back, behind the M41 Vulcan light anti-aircraft gun in the gun well. Kelly was wedged in on top of the passenger's seat, with her boots braced against the dashboard and her back against the roll bar. She was holding an M41 SPNKr rocket launcher, with an ample supply of M19 reload tubes strapped into the seat and stuffed into the foot well below her. Disztl was leaning over the steering wheel a little too eagerly as she watched the air battle from their hiding place in the alley mouth.

After a moment, Kelly asked, "Have you thought of a solution yet?"

Disztl finally moved away from the steering wheel. "What do you mean?"

"To the Grievers," John said. "Five fighter-bombers, four Anaconda batteries."

"Oh. That seems bad."

"It could be, if we fail to adjust," Kelly said.

The trouble with "failing to adjust" was that Grievers were heavy bombers, capable of spreading enough plasma to melt half of New Mohács back to glass. They were also heavily armored, so it took a lot of punch to knock one down.

"Those pilots don't know how many Anaconda batteries we have," Disztl said. "Maybe the fifth will turn back when the last pilot sees the other four go down."

"Possibly," Kelly said. "Were the pilots likely to be Kig-Yar."

Disztl was silent for a moment, then asked, "But they're not. Right?"

"I'm afraid the Banished don't place much value on caution," Kelly said. "The pilots will be Jiralhanae or Sangheili."

"Oh," Disztl said again.

"No worries, we'll adjust." John activated TEAMCOM. "Blue Two, Blue Four, take control of the forward Lance batteries. You'll have to hold your missiles until the Anacondas fire, then coordinate your attack."

Linda acknowledged with a green status flash.

Fred asked, "What about Erdei and the Havok?"

"Erdei can stay where he's at or follow you to the M79 station," John said. "But whatever happens, you're taking the Havok along."

There was a short pause; then Fred said, "He wants to stay with me and the Havok."

"Fine. Don't let him slow you down."

Fred's status light flashed green, and then the last Scythe opened fire on the approaching Banshees. The first two craft went down over the barrens, before their squadrons opened fire. But there was only one Scythe firing and eighteen Banshees shooting back. The emplacement took out two more before the enemy's fuel rod cannons found the apartment building where the Scythe was hidden and began to chew through the walls. The Scythe dropped through the floor, still firing, and the rest of the edifice disintegrated around it.

The Banshees immediately began to swirl over the village, looking for targets of opportunity, and the Seraph streaked past, pouring fire at anything below it.

Darda Tabori's voice came over the militia's command channel. "Shall I have the reserve LAAGs—"

"Negative," John interrupted. He had asked Colonel Boldisar to place Tabori in command of the militia anti-aircraft batteries because she'd been in the 717th at Gao and had at least a little combat experience. "Stand down all air defenses."

"Confirm *stand down*?"

"Confirm. If we give the trap away before the Grievers go down, we're dead. Every one of us. Make sure your people understand that."

"Acknowledged," Tabori said. "Stand down."

John gave her thirty seconds to pass along the order, grinding his teeth as he watched the Grievers swoop in for their attack run. The things seemed even more enormous than he remembered, with cannon mounts large enough to see from two kilometers away.

The Banished insertion was coming in thirty kilometers behind the Griever flight, a mass of drop-shaped silhouettes discernible from the rain only because they were growing larger and coming closer rather than falling toward the glass. There were easily a hundred craft, already traveling at subsonic speed and descending on a gentle glide path. Judging by their relative sizes, they were primarily Phantoms, but there were about twenty Lich transports rising from the surface to join them—craft so large they could carry an entire Phantom slung underneath them.

And above the Phantoms and Liches, the clouds were already flashing with the glow trails of a second wave. Whatever the Banished were looking for on Reach, they were determined to have it.

Maybe Boldisar had been right all along. Maybe using the Havoks was the only way to stop them from finding it.

The Griever cannons began to flash, hurling vehicle-sized bolts of plasma over the Banished lines into the village. The corners of buildings melted into glowing loafs of glass, and ponds of molten lechatelierite formed in the streets. John waited until the huge bombers were less than a kilometer from New Mohács, about to overfly the advancing Marauders, then spoke over the militia command channel.

"Fire Anacondas, Major Tabori. Anacondas *now*."

Two seconds later, stripes of white fire began to flash from the missile bunkers at the edge of the village. The Grievers did not have time to evade or deploy countermeasures. Their energy shields simply began to flicker under the impact of two Anacondas per second, and by the third volley, the missiles were punching through their fuselages and engine nacelles.

The first Griever simply disintegrated, pouring shrapnel and hot plasma down on a pair of Marauders. The next three broke apart more gradually, shedding nacelles and going into flat spins, one simply flipping over and landing on the glass like a dropped plate. Another five Marauders and a couple of hundred Banished infantry troops perished in the sudden debris and flame.

But the advance continued. The last Griever crossed over the armor line, dropping flares and chaff, its dispersal nozzles already swinging down to begin spreading plasma.

The trouble with countermeasures was that the only thing they prevented was target-lock, and most missiles—even relatively small ordnance like the M95 Lances that Fred and Linda would be using—required a kilometer or so to achieve it. So when the two Spartans fired their batteries, they were simply aiming the missiles along an interception vector calculated by their onboard computers.

John doubted that the last Griever pilot ever knew what hit him. One instant, he was likely ordering his bombardier to flood the dispersal nozzles. The next, he was on the inside of a plasma ball, gone so fast his nervous system wouldn't have even registered his fiery death.

"Well done, Major," John said.

He checked the dropships and saw they had closed to ten kilometers. They were decelerating hard, but still on approach for a hot landing. Of course they were. The Banished were fierce warriors who understood the ebb and flow of battle as well as John did. They were not going to abandon their attack. He doubted they would need to.

"Release Vulcans to fire at will," he continued. "Hold M79s and man-portable systems in their bunkers."

Tabori confirmed the order, and a moment later, Warthog LRVs began to burst from their hiding places all over New Mohács, and the M41 LAAGs in their gun wells began to spray rounds into the air. Seven Banshees went down before the enemy had even begun to evade, and the survivors dropped to roof level, trading a bird's-eye view for the shelter of adjacent buildings.

John didn't need to look to know that the last of the Banshees were sweeping in from their holding area. The Banished would be throwing everything they had into the battle, trying to overwhelm the New Mohács defenders as the drop hit—and they were going to succeed, especially with a second wave coming.

But the Viery Militia wasn't going to make it easy for them.

John waited until the enemy drop was five kilometers out—less than a minute—then spoke over the militia command channel again.

"Move the M79s and man-portable systems into attack position. M95 Lance batteries to target largest craft only."

Tabori confirmed the order, and Warthog M12s equipped with the M79 Multiple Launch Rocket Systems emerged from garages and warehouses all over the village and sped into preassigned positions that offered clear fields of aerial fire. Thirty of those vehicles, half of the total, stationed themselves in the alley mouths surrounding the armor yard.

At the same time, fifty soldiers carrying M41 rocket launchers climbed onto rooftops ringing the armor yard. Unlike Kelly, who had an ample supply of reload tubes strapped into the passenger's seat beneath her, most of the militia members had only one standard M19 reload tube. Only about half of them would survive long enough to take a second shot—and none would last for a third—so asking them to carry additional ammunition would only unnecessarily encumber them.

By the time Tabori reported that everyone was in position, the first Banished craft were coming in over the barrens, a kilometer away and no more than seven hundred meters off the ground. The big Liches were in the center of the formation, screened by a shell of Phantoms, and they had timed their arrival perfectly. On the ground, the Marauders had just reached the ring of empty fortifications. They were laying fire into New Mohács itself, suppressing—and in some cases eliminating—the anti-aircraft weapons defending the village.

An unintelligible message chortled over the UNSC combat information band—the first communication John had had from the *Infinity* all day—probably someone trying to explain what had happened to the support John had requested. He didn't waste time asking for a repeat. Every second would mean another lost battery.

"Release all weapon systems." John was still on the militia command channel. "Fire at will, Major Tabori."

Tabori did not even acknowledge the order. Sheets of missile fire erupted from New Mohács, burning through the still-falling rain, turning the air into clouds of smoke and mist.

A few Phantoms leading the drop erupted into flames. Others simply dived or slipped from the sky, smoking and trailing fire, and crashed into the no-man's-land between the fortification ring and the New Mohács perimeter.

The Liches and remaining Phantoms returned fire, their plasma cannons sweeping village rooftops and probing alleys, punching through walls and collapsing buildings. Columns of flame started to rise just outside New Mohács as Marauders and Wraiths broke through the breastworks and tried to cross the Lotus-packed tank trenches. Only a handful would make it, John knew, but behind them followed thousands of Banished infantry—Jiralhanae and Sangheili and Kig-Yar who would pick their way through the wreckage and slay every human on sight.

With the lead Phantoms out of the way, the M95 Lance batteries made their presence felt, flinging shafts of white fire through the battle smoke into the noses of the approaching Liches. Flight deck after flight deck was immediately demolished, and sixteen of the big transport craft fell from the sky, crashing to the ground at the village edge, crushing buildings and weapons emplacements and soldiers beneath their bulk, bodies and equipment and flame spilling from their cracked hulls.

But four of the Liches reached New Mohács and began to descend into the armor yard, their cannons hurling plasma into the surrounding alleys and buildings. Behind them followed ten Phantoms, all that remained of the original insertion force—and more than enough to take the village.

Over the militia command network, John said, "Colonel Boldisar, that breakout column better be ready."

"Almost!" The voice was not Boldisar's—and it sounded scared. "We need five minutes."

"Ask the Banished," John said. "I can't give it to you."

Another garbled message sounded over the UNSC combat information band.

"Repeat." Without awaiting a response, he slapped the roll bar and ordered, "Go go go!"

He was yelling into three comm channels at once, but it hardly mattered because the command applied to everyone—even the mysterious transmitter on the combat information band. If any responses came, they weren't clear enough to discern over the battle roar. It seemed the entire village had detonated into flames and shrapnel, and the conflagration was only growing.

The lead Lich took a missile volley from each side, then dropped the last fifty meters to the ground, belching still more flames from three hull breaches and its bay mouth. A Phantom in the back of the formation disintegrated in midair, while two more dropped into the tank trench and were torn apart by Lotus detonations.

The Warthog shot from the alley mouth and dodged past a spray of molten glass, Disztl asking, "Where to?!"

"Liches first," John said. Disztl was linked into TEAMCOM through her helmet comms, and he had already explained the principles of infiltration combat. He opened fire and continued in a calm voice, "Remember, keep our passenger side toward the enemy—"

"So the aliens shoot you instead of me," Disztl finished. "Like I could forget."

She swung in beside the burning Lich, positioning the Warthog so other nearby craft could not fire on it without also hitting the Lich, and John immediately cut down twenty Jiralhanae and Sangheili trying to leap out of the bay. It was probably overkill—they were all engulfed in flames—but better safe than sorry.

Besides, this was Reach, and they were trying to take it. Again.

Kelly's voice came over TEAMCOM. "Firing."

Disztl immediately straightened out the Warthog so Kelly could aim without being jostled; Kelly put two M19 rockets into the belly of a Lich seventy meters away. A ball of fire billowed out beside it, leaving no doubt about the fate of the warriors in the troop bay, and it swung its nose around, trying to bring its plasma cannon to bear.

Disztl put the Warthog into a side skid, then accelerated hard, taking them past the flaming troop bay—and straight toward the emitter nozzle of a third Lich, sitting on its struts less than fifty meters away.

"Whoa—sorry!"

She started to turn, but Kelly said, "No, steady on."

*"Really?"*

Despite the quaver in her voice, Disztl held course toward the now-glowing emitter nozzle. Kelly already had a fresh set of tubes on the SPNKr and put both rounds straight up the cannon mouth.

"Now you can—"

Disztl downshifted and cranked the wheel hard to the left. The Warthog went into another skid and spun around in the opposite direction, its rear end bucking hard when Kelly's rockets disrupted the cannon's plasma-focusing cycle and blew the Lich apart from the inside.

Disztl floored the accelerator and allowed the front wheels to pull them back toward their previous target. This Lich was still in the air with the flames boiling from its troop bay, trying to spin around so it could train its nose cannon on them.

"Duck!" Disztl shouted.

Kelly flattened herself atop the rollbar. John squatted down so his helmet was even with her and held the Vulcan so its barrels were level as the Warthog shot under the chin of the Lich—then emerged safely on the other side. Disztl began weaving and juking down the opposite side of the craft toward the last intact Lich.

This one was a hundred meters away, sitting on the ground so its Jiralhanae passengers could ride their Ghosts out of the troop bay. John opened fire, the LAAG cutting down five of them before the line stopped coming. The Lich rose off the ground again, turning around so it could fire on the Warthog.

"Same trick?" Disztl asked.

"You're a mind reader," Kelly said.

Kelly waited as the emitter nozzle swung toward them. Another broken transmission sounded over the UNSC combat information band, just as garbled but a little longer this time.

"Repeat transmission." John continued to pour Vulcan fire at the Lich's troop bay. "Cannot copy. Repeat transmission."

The combat information band returned to silence. If John couldn't copy them, the same was likely true on the other end.

It wasn't like he had time to talk anyway. Kelly pointed the barrel of the rocket launcher over the Warthog windshield.

"Steady."

The emitter nozzle was already glowing, but Disztl straightened the wheel in the same instant it lined up on them. Kelly fired both tubes.

The plasma bolt met the rockets ten meters in front of the Lich, then burst into a formless white cloud that left burn spatters in the transport craft's nose.

John opened fire with the Vulcan, putting fifty rounds up the emitter nozzle, and something inside made a loud zapping noise complete with a display of sparks.

Disztl began to weave and juke again, heading for the troop bay on its starboard side.

"No, break off." John had already stopped a squad of mechanized infantry from dismounting—which meant they were still inside, gathering themselves up to leave en masse. "Swing around the other side. We'll take them from behind. Kelly, is that Lich behind us still—"

"On it." She twisted around, placing one foot on the console next to the driver's seat. "But on second thought, no need."

A chain of detonations sounded in back of them. She quickly spun forward again, aiming her rocket launcher at the last Lich, and Fred's voice came over TEAMCOM. "You're welcome. But you'd better hurry, if you want one of those Phantoms for us. They're almost gone."

"Affirmative." John didn't bother to look at what had become of the burning Lich—Fred would have warned him if it were still a danger. "If you have a shot at—"

"Affirmative," Linda said.

A triple volley of M95 Lance missiles came streaking out of the rubble on the south side of the armor yard. The first two hit the Lich's hull at an angle and deflected before they exploded. But the last four punched through and filled the troop bay with a boiling cloud of shrapnel and fire.

"Thanks," John said. "Collect *Special* Crew and meet us at the capture."

It was Major Van Houte who replied. "We're with Blue Four now." Given the devastation the Banished had already laid on the village, John was relieved to hear his voice. "Bear to your left, and you'll see a Phantom just starting its approach. That one should land close to us and the excavation equipment."

"Then that's the one we'll capture," John said. He glanced down at Disztl's helmet. "You heard the man, Lieutenant."

"I did. Hold on."

She swung the Warthog past the demolished Lich and started across the armor yard, angling left. Between the rain and the battle smoke, visibility at ground level was barely a hundred meters, and even looking into the sky, it was less than five hundred meters. Still, Disztl drove like she was racing across the Tantalusian wasteland on a clear day, bouncing through craters and brake-bounding over debris heaps, swerving past living pillars of flame and clusters of gray shapes dodging half-seen through the smoke.

With the Warthog in good hands, John took the opportunity to feed a fresh belt of ammunition into the Vulcan, then made sure his grenades and M7 submachine gun were in good order. Kelly placed a new reload tube onto her SPNKr, then checked her own grenades and shotgun. They would use the anti-aircraft gun and rocket launcher only if necessary to extract themselves—the heavier weapons, and their MA40 assault rifles, had too much penetration power and could end up disabling the very craft they were trying to capture.

It was less than a minute before Disztl swung the Warthog sharply to the right and said, "There she is."

The Phantom was still higher in the air than John had expected, the last of three craft coming in fast, plasma cannons firing blindly down into the battle smoke. As Van Houte had promised, the one at the end *did* seem to be going for the south side of the armor yard—and it was descending at a steep angle, suggesting it intended to land toward the perimeter of the village. Clearly the Banished pilots had taken notice of the devastation that had met the rest of their drop.

But the battle was about to change tide. Above and behind the Phantom, the clouds were already aflame with the entry trails of the next wave. And the second drop was even larger than the first, approaching across a front that could end up being ten kilometers.

If Blue Team and *Special* Crew didn't get out of New Mohács right now, they might never leave.

John opened the militia command channel. "Major Tabori, silence all anti-aircraft attacks." There weren't any antiaircraft batteries actually launching, but John couldn't risk being unable to continue their mission. "Blue Team will handle the last three Phantoms."

No response.

"Acknowledge."

The only reply was unintelligible crackle over the combat information band. *Another* one.

"Repeat transmission."

More crackling. Whoever was up there, their orbit was carrying them into comm range. By the time the battle was lost, they might even be able to understand each other.

"Lieutenant, swing us around to the edge of the yard," John said. "When that Phantom lowers its boarding ramp, drive straight inside, then drop into the foot well."

Disztl cranked the wheel, picking a route through the yard that kept them concealed among the wrecks of all the other dropships and disabled armor.

"What if they *don't* land?" she asked. "Our intelligence reports say Phantoms have gravity lifts."

"They do," Kelly said. "But how eager would *you* be to hover over the battlefield, waiting for a missile strike while we pick off the troops you're lowering one at a time in your gravity lift?"

"Good point."

Disztl dropped the Warthog into a crater sheltered by a wrecked Marauder on one side and a still-smoking Phantom on the other. It had an unobstructed view of their target's expected landing zone, though the smoke was so thick that if it landed very far away, they would have to track it down by its drive glow.

"Will this do?"

Before John could reply, the Phantom answered for him, coming in fifty meters overhead and landing about the same distance away. The stern of the craft was canted at a slight angle to them, but making that turn would be child's play for Disztl.

As John waited for the first crack to appear at the top of the boarding ramp, he tried the militia command channel again.

"Colonel Boldisar? Anyone?" He waited a moment for a reply, then said, "If that breakout column hasn't left yet, now is—"

"Soon, Master Chief." The voice belonged to Rendor Borbély, and John could hear yelling and shrieking in the background. "We had to load some casualties."

John could think of only one casualty worth delaying the breakout attempt. "Boldisar?"

"Among others," Borbély said. "She may survive."

"Damn. I hope so." The Phantom's boarding ramp began to swing down. "Get out of here now, Colonel. You're out of time."

Another crackle, this time longer and louder, sounded over the UNSC combat information band. John was beginning to think he had a bad relay somewhere in his helmet.

He reached down and tapped Disztl on the shoulder. "*Now*, Lieutenant."

Disztl punched the accelerator, and the Warthog climbed out of the crater and raced through the smoke toward the Phantom. The ramp was only halfway down when she swung in behind it, accelerating anyway. It was only three-quarters of the way down, with over a meter between the lip and the ground, when the Warthog reached it. Disztl slammed on the brakes, dropping the front of the vehicle so hard that John was thrown into the Vulcan's handgrips.

Thinking Disztl might have lost her courage, he slapped his submachine gun onto a thigh magmount and reached for the Vulcan triggers. Then she punched the accelerator again, releasing the Warthog's compressed suspension so suddenly that the front end bounced upward, allowing the tires to grab the ramp edge and pull them the rest of the way up.

The Warthog began to shudder and jerk as it plowed into the packed troop bay, knocking aside Jiralhanae and crushing Sangheili, hurling them into the bulkheads and one another. Kelly's shotgun began to boom and John's submachine gun to chatter, and bellows of confusion and rage filled their ears. And still Disztl kept the accelerator pinned to the floor, spinning the tires until they smoked, pushing alien bodies forward, packing them so tight their armor began to split and pop like smashed cans.

Out of nowhere, a voice sounded over the UNSC combat information band. *"Inbound ten squadrons Broadsword ground support mission. Target Banished armor and dropships, New Mohács village. Missiles away. ETA ten seconds. Over."*

Disztl gasped into her comm unit, then turned toward Kelly with a look on her face that was equal parts confusion and terror. John didn't blame her. With the missiles on the way, calling off the strike was not an option. He stopped firing and lunged over the roll bar, reaching for the Warthog's gearshift.

"Retreat, Lieutenant! Retreat now!"

Kelly already had one hand on the lever and was sliding the Warthog into reverse, her shotgun tucked between her knees and her left hand reaching for the steering wheel.

"Pedal to the floor, Lieutenant! Get us out of—"

John was still stretched over the roll bar when Disztl floored the accelerator and the Warthog leaped out of the troop bay backward, the rear wheels high off the deck, John banging his helmet off the upper hatch jamb.

They slammed down at the bottom of the ramp and raced backward across the armor yard until Disztl spun the wheel and brought them around a hundred and eighty degrees, then hit the accelerator, with John nearly thrown clear as he reached for the Vulcan.

Spikes and plasma bolts began to arrive seconds later, burning through his energy shields in a breath, ricocheting off his Mjolnir armor and burning dimples into the titanium shell. He swung the Vulcan around and opened fire on a gang of Jiralhanae clustered in the hatchway.

They were still falling when a white streak lanced out of the sky and touched the Phantom, and then the dropship was a thousand pieces of twisted alloy spraying from a ball of white fire.

The spikes and plasma continued to come, now from both sides and in front of the Warthog. John saw a curtain of smoke in every direction, bolts streaking out of the dark fumes on three sides, a wall of flame glowing through the smoke, rising in pillars out where the Banished armor had been trying to push through the fortifications and tank traps into New Mohács.

*Special* Crew's status still showed green in his HUD, so John put them and the excavation equipment out of his mind for the moment and fired blindly into the smoke, doing his best to follow the Banished salvo back to its source but not really seeing his targets, only the nebulous gray forms of the wreckage they were using for cover, or the pearly smoothness of the crater they were firing from.

"*Broadsword run successful—heavy damage Banished armor and dropships. Will circle area for further support requests. Estimated twelve minutes bingo fuel and ammo. Be advised HEV insertion New Mohács landing zone one hundred Spartan-IVs, followed by additional heavy insertions. Over.*"

John didn't have time to be impressed, but he was. He'd

expected maybe three thousand ODSTs supported by a few teams of Spartan-IVs and some air. But John had classified his support request as mission-critical, and apparently Captain Lasky had taken him at his word. Or maybe he just hated the idea of the Banished on Reach as much as John did.

He continued to fire, at the same time speaking into TEAMCOM.

"*Special* Crew, withdraw to safety. Blue Team, fall back one fifty meters and set LZ perimeter."

All status LEDs flashed green.

"Lieutenant Disztl, fall back and find us some cover."

"Yes, sir." Disztl dropped the Warthog into a crater and banked a power-slide turn off the far wall, then rocketed out in the opposite direction. "A hundred Spartans? In the first wave?"

She'd heard the same UNSC combat information transmissions as everyone else hooked into TEAMCOM.

"Affirmative." John was continuing to aim at plasma bolts coming out of the smoke, and Kelly was doing the same with her MA40. "Reach belongs to you again. The Banished can leave or die."

"Damn straight," Disztl said. "Thanks for—"

A volley of spikes hit them from the left side, punching through the Warthog's skin with a dull, cracked-bell clanging. John spun the Vulcan toward the crushed-dome shape of a downed Phantom and loosed hellfire into the smoke, probably not hitting anything, but at least suppressing the Banished attacks.

He didn't realize they were decelerating at first, just noticed that the wreckage wasn't drifting past quite as fast as before. Thinking one of the spikes had damaged the Warthog's engine, John continued to lay fire on the downed Phantom.

"How bad, Lieutenant?" he asked. "Can you get us going again?"

It was Kelly who answered. "It's not the Warthog, John."

John glanced at the driver's seat and saw Disztl slumped against the steering wheel, her arms hanging limp. Blood was running down the side of her helmet, spilling out through a large split over her ear.

"Oh . . . hell no."

The cracked-bell clanging resumed, and John saw the shield-level indicator in his HUD fall as he started to take hits. He stretched an arm toward Kelly.

"SPNKr."

She slapped the rocket launcher into his hand. He put it on his shoulder, arming and HUD-linking it as he moved, and fired the first rocket into the smoke. It struck the downed Phantom roughly in the center of its silhouette, spreading an angry crimson blush across its shadowy hull.

A trio of Sangheili forms leaped up to flee, their legs and backs flickering with flames. John fired the second rocket at the ground two steps in front of them, and the blast sent them flying back through the smoke in flaming parts.

By then, Kelly had settled Disztl's body in the passenger's seat and taken control of the wheel. She flashed a yellow status LED to warn John they were about to move, then hit the accelerator and began to look for a firing position. With her training and Spartan reflexes, she was almost as good a driver as Disztl. Almost.

John stayed behind the Vulcan, firing at shapes in the smoke and cutting them down in a cold fury. He had seen too many soldiers fall to feel broken or drained by Disztl's loss, and he knew she had died for something she held dear. It still seemed like such a damned waste. The Banished should *never* have set foot on Reach—and Reach should never have been glassed in the first place. He had met, and even fought beside, too many noble aliens to believe they were all responsible for this entire mess. But those who were here—those he was happy to deal with.

The first wave of HEV drop pods were already plunging out of the clouds when Kelly slipped the Warthog in behind an overturned Marauder. John was too busy picking off Jiralhanae and Sangheili to spare more than a quick glance skyward, but the cloud ceiling was low enough that the UNSC had emerged from it with their drag panels deployed, in a tight group and on course for an on-target landing.

After a few seconds of firing, he glimpsed a squad of slender shapes moving through the smoke to his left, dashing or crawling from one piece of wreckage to another. That was what happened when you attacked from one spot too long—someone tried to flank and kill you. He had Kelly drive around to the other side of the blasted-out Wraith the squad seemed to be heading toward.

There were six of them, all Kig-Yar, still moving into position as the Warthog rounded the corner. These were Skirmishers, an aggressive subspecies of Kig-Yar that had once belonged to the Covenant. Unlike Jackals, who were consummate opportunists on the battlefield, Skirmishers were far less cautious than the rest of their kind. John opened fire, cutting four of them in half before they had even raised their weapons. Then he felt a pair of heavy thumps as Kelly promptly ran over the other two.

Expecting her to keep going, John started to swivel the Vulcan around to finish off the two they had just run down—then Kelly threw the Warthog into reverse and thumped over both bodies again. She continued backward until both Skirmishers lay visible, one helmet crushed flat and a tire-sized depression running across the torso of the other.

"I must say," Kelly said, "that was satisfying."

John understood completely. "Yeah."

The roar of the Vulcan must have covered the thunder of the drop pods' braking jets, because suddenly there were Spartans in GEN3 Mjolnir everywhere. They raced past the Warthog on both sides, covering one another and firing at alien shapes as they advanced into the smoke.

Nobody was shooting at the Warthog any longer, so John and Kelly remained behind the Wraith. John took a moment to do a health check on his team and found all lights green, except for Disztl's, then opened the militia command channel.

"Colonel Borbély," he said. "Blue Leader."

"Rendor is dead," answered a female voice. "This is Captain Eötvös. Go ahead."

"Sorry to hear that, Captain." John was starting to wonder just what the breakout column had run into—and whether any of its senior officers had survived. "What about Colonel Boldisar?"

"Badly wounded," Eötvös said. "I'm in command for now."

"Understood," John said. "I wanted to advise you that the UNSC drop is under way."

"Yes, we had noticed," Eötvös said. "Blue Team and the UNSC have our thanks. Truly." She didn't sound like Blue Team had their thanks, but she probably had about a hundred other things on her mind right now—all of them unfamiliar and enormously stressful. "Is there anything else, Blue Leader?"

"Only the breakout column," John said. "The situation has changed. It's no longer—"

"Necessary." Eötvös chuckled. "We are not *that* inexperienced. It has already been recalled."

"Good," John said. "I'll tell our officers to coordinate with you at HQ."

"I'll look forward to it," Eötvös said. "I hope you'll be with them."

"Sorry, ma'am." As John spoke, a squad of Spartans showed up on his motion tracker, approaching from behind the Warthog. "I still have my own mission to wrap up."

He quickly signed off and turned to see Sarah Palmer leading two teams of her Spartan-IVs toward the Warthog. She was wearing her standard GEN3 kit, and there was no mistaking her for someone else. The red emblems stamped into her torso and forearm shells gave it away—as did the paired M6H Magnums she wore on her thigh mounts.

Over TEAMCOM, which—in theory, at least—Palmer wouldn't be able to hear, Fred said, "Uh-oh. Looks like she's on the warpath. Should I prep a getaway vehicle?"

"Fred . . ." John said, slightly exasperated.

After John had taken Blue Team AWOL to search for Cortana, he and Palmer were hardly on good terms—especially given that she was the one who had sent Fireteam Osiris to attempt their capture. But she actually seemed to bear a certain respect for John, and she was the straightest of straight arrows. She wasn't going to interfere with a legitimate mission—assuming, of course, that the mission Dr. Halsey had sent Blue Team on *was* legitimate.

"She probably just wants a sitrep," John finished.

"Sure," Fred said. "That's why she brought two teams of S-IVs to back her up."

John didn't have a chance to reply, because by then Palmer was standing at the back of the Warthog looking up at him.

"Commander Palmer." John did not salute. They were on an active battlefield, and he didn't want her to think he was trying to get her killed. "Thanks for coming."

"You can thank Halsey and Lasky," Palmer replied. She shot a quick glance at Kelly and Disztl's limp body, then looked back to him. "How's your team, Master Chief?"

"A hundred percent," John said. Not quite true, but he wasn't going to give her any reason to question Blue Team's fitness to continue. "Lieutenant Disztl was on loan from the militia. A fine soldier."

Palmer dropped her chin. "Aren't they all?" She nodded sincerely, then looked around the armor yard, taking in the dense-packed wreckage, and finally looked back to John. "Whatever Halsey has you doing down here, it must be big. Lasky sent everything."

"Right now we're liberating Reach," he said. If Lasky and Halsey hadn't briefed Palmer on Blue Team's mission, it would be a security violation for *him* to do it. "It means a lot to me. And to the entire UNSC."

"Enough to risk a Guardian showing up?" Palmer asked. "While most of *Infinity*'s fighting force is off-ship mopping up *pirates*?"

"Let's hope that doesn't happen," John said. He didn't blame her for being concerned about the risk—if a Guardian arrived now,

*Infinity*'s survival probability rating would plummet to single digits. The situation would become virtually intractable. What Palmer couldn't possibly have known, however, was that given the objective of Blue Team's mission, such a risk was entirely worth it. Even so, John was curious about the number of Spartans he saw. Standard infantry and armor made perfect sense in order to engage the Banished forces, but risking this many S-IVs on the ground meant there were other factors in play. "Why did he send so many Spartans?"

"The Havoks. *Infinity*'s jamming blanket can't hide a detonation that big," Palmer said. "After the Banished beat us to the drop, Halsey convinced him the pioneers would use a nuke if we didn't come running."

"Dr. Halsey was right," John said, "so you have our gratitude. And Reach's."

"I'm sure that we do," she said, scanning the billowing smoke in the direction of the Banished lines. "I've been ordered to give you whatever you need to continue your mission." She paused, then laid her hand over the back rail of the gun well. "And don't tell me you're here to liberate Reach, because mopping up these Banished pirates is *my* mission now. How exactly can we get your team back on task?"

"We need something that can fly and carry cargo," John said.

"Will a Pelican do?"

"You read my mind."

"I doubt that. I have Pelicans coming with the third wave. You can take your pick. Will you need a crew?"

"We have our own," John said. "But thanks."

"Don't thank me yet." She spun half away from John, giving him a clear view of the Spartans behind her. "There's something we need first."

John studied the Spartans a little more closely now, taking in the names fed to his heads-up display: GRIFFIN, VETTEL, DIMKA, OSHIRO . . . all on Fireteam Taurus. The others were from a similar outfit, Fireteam Intrepid. Two of the best crews *Infinity* had when it came to

Spartan-IVs, trained explicitly for high-risk operations well behind enemy lines. John had seen them in action on several occasions. If Lasky had sent these two fireteams, it was clear that he was just as serious about neutralizing the threat the Havoks posed as he was about Halsey's mission.

"Understood, Commander." John switched to TEAMCOM. "Blue Two, escort Major Erdei and his Havok down here. Someone needs to have a word with him."

# CHAPTER SEVENTEEN

0905 hours, October 12, 2559 (military calendar)
Landing Zone Bella, New Mohács
Arany Basin, Continent Eposz, Planet Reach

The rain had stopped hours before all the fires were out, so a steady pall of smoke continued to blow over the small courtyard where Blue Team had established Landing Zone Bella. John and the rest of the Spartans were standing behind the D77H-TCI Pelican that would soon carry them to CASTLE Base. *Special* Crew had already pulled the rearmost seats out of the troop bay and made some other modifications to accommodate the excavation equipment and other cargo. Now, under Crew Chief Mukai's watchful eye, they were finally securing the drilling jumbo and LHD in place at the back of the deck. John was eager to get moving, but didn't dare set foot on the loading ramp until he received Mukai's permission to board.

A Portable Spartan Support Module had landed with the fourth drop, so he and Kelly had spent some of their downtime having the damage to their armor repaired. They had even had their half-healed wounds cleaned and field-mended. John's quadriceps hurt worse than ever, but the vat-grown myosin mesh that had been grafted onto the damaged muscle would prevent the injury from degrading his fighting performance any more than it already had.

Kelly meanwhile was no longer at any risk of reopening her axillary vein, and seemed more irritated by the fresh sutures itching under her armor than by the wound itself. Fred would simply have to live with his dented helmet for now. With their integrated communications, HUDs, and neural interfaces, Mjolnir helmets were too complicated to risk repairing in the field, except under the direst of circumstances.

Mukai poked her head out between the LHD and the drilling jumbo. "Ready in ten, Master Chief," she said. "Palmer find any Keepers yet?"

"Not that I've heard about."

After the Banished had been pushed back out of New Mohács, John had noticed that all the enemy armor was either crimson or black trimmed in silver. He had not seen a single attacker wearing the colors of the Keepers of the One Freedom—blue and gold. And that had given him real pause. The Keepers had started this war by downing Blue Team's Owl, then tracked them halfway across the Arany Basin—only to disappear when the real fighting started? Something didn't make sense, so he had asked Palmer to send out an intelligence team to look for the Keeper colors. She'd acted on his request almost two hours ago, and there had not been a single report so far.

"We could be in for another bumpy ride," John added. "Better double-secure that equipment."

Major Van Houte peered over the top of the drilling jumbo. "This is why it's taking so long to prep," he said. "Chief Mukai is making us triple-secure everything already. To do better, we'd have to weld it to the deck."

"Don't give her any ideas," Lieutenant Chapov called out. He was somewhere behind the LHD, clattering away ferociously as he tensioned a tie-down chain. He had been working a little *too* hard since learning of Bella Disztl's death, and it was he who had suggested naming the landing zone in her honor. "Chief Mukai thinks it's *her* fault D rings can't take ten-g decelerations."

"I should have upgraded to titanium," Mukai said. "You can have them custom—"

A raid alert sounded over their helmet comms, echoed by a whooping siren that rang out over the entire village.

Nobody scrambled for cover. The Banished had been probing New Mohács's air defenses regularly for the last two hours, trying to draw out the small deterrent force of Broadswords that had been left to protect the village while the rest of the wing returned to the *Infinity* to re-arm and refill propellant tanks. But so far, no attack had come. The probes were pure harassment, designed to lull the defenders into a false sense of security and make the UNSC waste propellant and ordnance.

The enemy tactic was doomed to fail. Palmer was too disciplined a commander to allow her Spartan-IVs—or the ODSTs—to let down their guard, and the main body of the Broadsword wing would soon be escorting eight big D96-TCE Albatrosses filled with deuterium propellant and plenty of ordnance into New Mohács.

But this time, it wasn't a squadron of Banshees or Seraphs that had triggered the alarm. A Banished intrusion corvette was dropping into view, its jagged bow still glowing with entry heat and trailing plumes of steam, its down-hooked stern slicing through the dark clouds, almost seeming to drag the sky behind it.

The corvette was probably three hundred kilometers to the south of the bombed-out village, and it was traveling east to west, parallel to New Mohács rather than toward it. But John knew better than to take comfort in that—the old Jiralhanae intrusion corvettes were nimble vessels that could pivot their heading on a pinpoint.

"Major Van Houte, you and Lieutenant Chapov should prep for takeoff—*now*," John said. "Blue Team can help Chief Mukai finish securing the load."

"No, you can't." Mukai's head popped out from under the LHD. "You won't fit under the equipment."

"We'll find a way."

"That sounds urgent." Van Houte slipped between the drilling jumbo and the bulkhead, then started aft toward the open hatchway. "Are they coming for real this time?"

"They're doing *something*." John continued to watch the intrusion corvette, still waiting for it to turn toward New Mohács. "I just don't know what."

Three squadrons of Broadswords, the entire deterrent force left to defend New Mohács, rose into the sky over the old armor yard. After the battle earlier that morning, the strike fighters were hardly prepared for a skirmish with a ship of the line—even a small one. They were short on missiles and cannon ammunition, and they lacked enough deuterium propellant to reach orbit unassisted. But two of the squadrons shot off to meet the corvette as far south of the village as possible, while one remained on-station to defend against a second attack coming from another direction.

The corvette continued westward, descending on a gentle glide path. Van Houte stopped at the bottom of the boarding ramp and followed John's gaze, looking out over the jagged ruins toward the gray southern horizon.

"We'll never beat them, you know." Van Houte's eyes were fixed on the enemy craft. "They're still at Mach six or better. By the time we launch, they'll *be* there."

"Be where?"

John didn't wait for an answer, because no sooner had he asked the question than he understood what Van Houte had seen—what any pilot would see. The corvette was traveling too fast to change course.

It wasn't on approach to attack New Mohács.

It was descending into the Highland Mountains.

Sarah Palmer's voice came over the insertion comms channel. "Blue Leader, Liberation Command. I've been asked to relay an urgent message from Orbit Actual."

That would be Captain Lasky, and the message was being relayed because Reach was still wrapped inside the *Infinity*'s jamming blanket.

"I bet I can guess," John said. "They think a Banished stealth corvette slipped through the orbital picket."

"Close," Palmer said. "They *know* a stealth corvette launched from a Banished supercarrier. They didn't challenge it because they were afraid of drawing Cortana's attention."

Kelly huffed into her comm set, and John answered by making a twirling gesture with his index finger. *Load up.*

"Acknowledged," John said. "I'm going to need two Broadsword squadrons."

"*What?*"

"Sorry," John said. "I'd like to *request* two Broadsword squadrons immediately. Don't even let them land."

"Don't bother with the sweet talk, John," Palmer said. "You're no good at it."

"Thanks for the advice, Commander. Does that mean I have my Broadsword squadrons?"

"It might, if I had some idea what you intend to do with them."

"Complete my mission. That intrusion corvette is landing in the Highland Mountains."

"So?"

"My bet is it's on the way to meet the Keepers of the One Freedom. And they've been waiting for us."

**0920 hours, October 12, 2559 (military calendar)**
**Figyelő Point, Bíbor Cliffs**
**Highland Mountains, Continent Eposz, Planet Reach**

How Castor could have been so wrong, he did not understand. For three of Reach's day-night cycles, he had paced the crimson cliffs of the human-designated Figyelő Point, waiting for the demon Spartans to lead him to the Portal under the Mountain. It seemed inconceivable that they had inserted on Reach to deliver digging equipment to a group of farmers fighting to retake their meager holds. Yet for *three days* the sensor dishes arrayed along the cliff rims had failed to detect any sign of the Spartans, and for three days his air patrols had returned with not a single sighting.

Instead, the night before, Castor had watched the pinpoint flashes of battle somewhere far out in the Arany Basin. Then, earlier this morning, the rain clouds had been striped by the flame trails of one insertion drop after another. He had finally broken his self-imposed comm silence and contacted Ballas, chieftain of the Ravaged Tusks, and learned of the human surprise attack on New Mohács. Worse, Ballas had told him of the orbital jamming glove the UNSC had wrapped around Reach—and delivered a message from Escharum requiring a report on the search for the portal.

And now an intrusion corvette was dropping out of the clouds, its bow-shields still glowing red with entry heat. Castor did not even entertain the possibility that the vessel would divert and swing around to attack the humans at New Mohács. It was coming straight at Figyelő Point.

Castor stopped pacing and spun toward the broken line of sandstone blocks they were using to camouflage the command post, then stepped over to the block he had come to think of as 'Gadogai's Throne. As he had been for much of the last three days, the blademaster was kneeling atop the stone, his hands resting in his lap, his eyes closed, and his mandibles splaying ever so slightly each time he exhaled.

Castor grabbed the block by the sides and spun it toward the cliff. 'Gadogai rode atop it, eyes still closed. Then, an instant before Castor launched the stone off the precipice, the blademaster simply stepped off and stood next to him, peering over the edge as the block plunged two hundred meters and began to cut a swath through the carpet of saplings that covered the slope below. The tumbling block continued down the steep slope, encountering nothing sturdy enough to stop it and flattening the saplings until it finally bounced into a ravine and vanished.

'Gadogai said, "A splendid toss. I doubt Escharum could do better."

Castor spun to face the Sangheili. Despite the chill wind and recent rain, the blademaster wore only his usual tabard and energy sword.

"You told Escharum where to find us."

"We weren't hiding from *him*."

"And now we are not hiding from *anyone*," Castor said. "Every human in the basin will see where he lands."

'Gadogai spread his palms. "He is starting to doubt that the Spartans are looking for the portal at all. When they retook their city of New Mohács, there were reports of excavation equipment on the battlefield."

"How would you know *that*?" Castor demanded. "I banned communications."

"And Escharum commanded me to keep him informed. A pity your plan to follow the Spartans to the portal failed. He thought it cunning."

"Then he should have given it more time to work."

"He gave it more than three day-night cycles," 'Gadogai replied. "And now the Banished are on the verge of losing Reach."

"Reach only matters if we find the portal," Castor said. The corvette had slowed to landing velocity and was beginning to descend toward Figyelő Point, so he turned to the small shelter that the sensor operators had erected to protect their monitoring equipment. "Send the humans to the caves. At once."

A moment later, four of the Keepers' human acolytes emerged and looked in his direction. There were two males and two females, all of them with their heads shaved on the sides and narrow falls of hair hanging between their shoulder blades. All wore Keeper colors, with blue torso armor over gold shirts and trousers, and all carried human sidearms on their hips. Castor was no judge of their species' appearance, but the smallest and oldest of the group, a female with black hair and brown eyes, seemed to be their leader. The others protected her as though she were a *dokab* and sometimes called her "Mom," a human bloodline colloquialism, even if they did not look young enough to be her offspring.

But what did Castor know? When it came to humans, it was all he could do to tell the males from the females.

When they stood staring at Escharum's incoming corvette a little too long, he waved them away. "Go! I have enough to explain without reminding Escharum that I abide humans in my clan."

They placed their palms together and bowed, then fled toward the hangar caves in the valley behind the cliffs.

"Why *do* you abide them?" 'Gadogai asked. "Humans are such faithless creatures."

"Not those four," Castor replied. "They are a gift of the Oracle."

"The Oracle you have not heard from for a year?" 'Gadogai's voice was mocking. "*That* Oracle?"

"The Oracle that was sent to show me the True Path." Castor knew it was impossible to unnerve the blademaster, but he allowed a little menace to seep into his voice. Most Banished believed the Oracle to be a Forerunner ancilla who had been captured by the infidel UNSC and turned to their purposes. But Castor knew better. She was more powerful than either the Banished or the UNSC realized, for the Oracle had spoken to him many times since her supposed "capture." "Beware how you speak of her. I can stomach only so much blasphemy—even from you."

'Gadogai clacked his mandibles, as he sometimes did when he was amused. "Then we must do what we can to settle your stomach. Escharum would be disappointed to find you already gone when he arrives."

Escharum's corvette was just gliding past a few hundred meters south of Figyelő Point, so Castor chose to pretend he had not heard the blademaster's threat. He watched as the vessel swung toward a relatively flat area between the rim of the cliff and the valley behind it. Once he was sure that was where the pilots intended to land, he summoned his warriors and went to receive the Banished's second-in-command.

Castor had only two hundred warriors atop the cliff to line up behind him, but it would be enough. Unlike Sangheili, who positioned their warriors to honor arriving dignitaries, Jiralhanae reception formations were meant to intimidate—or at least to show that one was unintimidated by the person arriving. Castor arranged his host in a battle wedge, with himself at the tip and Feodruz and Krelis behind him, to his right and left. As a presumed neutral, 'Gadogai stood a few paces off to his side, still within sword's reach, but too far away for Castor to reach with a gauntlet smash.

The corvette settled onto its struts just fifty meters from Castor, so close that a wave of nausea and pain ran through him as his body reacted to gravity tides generated by its repulsor drives. The energy field in its hangar mouth sizzled out; then a column of Jiralhanae in dark-gray power armor poured out in triple file and formed a three-rank crescent so wide its horns extended past the base of Castor's own wedge formation. There were three hundred of them, all easily as large as Orsun had been. They held shock rifles at port-arms and wore short-handled gravity maces on their belts.

Castor gnashed his tusks and made a show of signaling Feodruz to stand fast. 'Gadogai shuffled his feet and looked at the sky, but Castor ignored him. It wasn't the Sangheili he was trying to beard.

The two hosts of warriors stood staring at each other for a full five minutes. Finally the two center rows of the crescent formation neatly pivoted to face each other, creating a three-meter-wide aisle. A grizzled Jiralhanae in rugged gray armor with scarlet trim appeared at the far end and started forward, holding a huge gravity axe in one hand. Though not quite as tall as the giant warriors flanking him, he was broader in the shoulders than any—so large that, as he passed, his shoulders seemed to brush the torso armor of the escorts to both sides.

Reaching the end of the aisle, he paused and seemed to stare across the intervening distance at Castor. It was an unusual thing to do, and Castor did not know what to make of it.

"Spread your hands to show they are empty," 'Gadogai said quietly. "Otherwise he will bring his weapon with the singular intent to use it. The war chief is as old as I am, and he is not one for petty games of intimidation."

Castor had no idea how old 'Gadogai was, but Sangheili lived far longer than Jiralhanae. That could make Escharum eighty or ninety years old—a remarkable age for such a legendary figure.

Castor spread his hands.

Escharum dipped his head, perhaps in thanks, then passed his gravity axe to the warrior on his right and started across the space between them. Castor went forward to meet him, 'Gadogai falling in at his side. The blademaster's energy sword still hung on his belt, but Escharum's escorts seemed to take no notice of it—perhaps because they knew that it made no difference whether 'Gadogai was armed. The Sangheili was either of no concern to Escharum because of their alliance, or just as deadly without need of a weapon.

Escharum crossed fully half the distance between him and Castor, a gracious gesture no doubt meant to put Castor at ease. Castor began to watch 'Gadogai more closely, and when they reached Escharum, he stood at an angle so he could see them both.

Castor touched his fist to his breast.

"You honor the Keepers with your presence," he said. "Had I known you were coming, I would have brought some prisoners for the proper welcoming games."

Escharum brushed his fingers against his own breast, acknowledging Castor's salute without returning its honor. He had a weathered face with flaring nostrils, a heavy jaw, and a long gray beard hanging from his chin. His right eye was cloudy and white, the result of an injury that had left a deep scar descending from his right brow to his hollow cheek. His left eye was as red as human blood.

"Had we been in contact," Escharum said at last, "you would have *known* I was coming."

"You had no trouble finding us." Castor shot a glance in 'Gadogai's direction. "I understand the blademaster has kept you informed of our efforts."

"And of your lack of results," Escharum said. "It may be time to give up waiting and return to more conventional methods, Dokab Castor."

"We are already employing conventional methods, War Chief," Castor replied. "We have two thousand Keepers and three hundred craft searching every hole under every mountain in the entire chain. We have aerial images of the mountain range as well. It is one of the largest on Reach. If the portal truly is hidden under a mountain on this world, it would be here."

"Yet you have found nothing."

Castor could not tell if Escharum said this out of frustration with the Keepers, or with the situation in general. The war chief's intimidating visage, so weathered by decades of battle, made him nearly impossible to read.

"That is not entirely true, Great One," 'Gadogai said, much to Castor's surprise. He had not expected the cynical blademaster to speak in his defense—or to address Escharum with such a fawning honorific. "We found elderly humans and children hiding in some mining tunnels to the north. *Thousands* of them."

"Elderly humans and children?" Escharum looked to Castor, who was just as mystified. "I fail to understand the significance."

"As do I," Castor said, looking to 'Gadogai. "We found them, but they have nothing to do with the portal."

'Gadogai spread his hands. "I did not say they did. Only that we found them."

"And what did you do with them?" Escharum asked.

"Nothing," Castor said. "Slaying them would have meant pulling hundreds of Keepers off the search, and guarding them would require even more."

"So you just left them where they were?"

"We destroyed their communications devices first," Castor said. "Of course, we also searched their tunnels, to make sure the portal was not there."

"And we took some of their males to use as guides," 'Gadogai added. "But they have not been much use. Most do not know the mountains any better than we do, and they are so old that they tend to collapse as soon as we make them start climbing."

Escharum glared at 'Gadogai. "What difference does this make, Blademaster? Explain yourself."

"Certainly, War Chief," 'Gadogai said, as though his statement should have been plain to all. "It is quite simple. These humans belong to the same tribe as the ones who have been harassing the Legion of the Corpse-Moon and the Ravaged Tusks. The *dokab*'s thinking was that if the demon Spartans failed to lead him to the portal, he would take this group of frail humans captive and use them as hostages to force the rest to leave this world. Then Deukalion and Ballas would no longer be compelled to devote their efforts to securing Reach, and they would be free to join Castor in the search for the portal."

Castor was stunned. Not only had 'Gadogai posed a logical rationale for the Keepers' reluctance to slaughter the helpless humans, he had also provided a fallback plan that was strategically brilliant and accurately pointed out the failure of the other chieftains to participate in the search for the portal. And the Sangheili had done this at the risk of his own favor in the eyes of Escharum and the Banished—and *that* was the most surprising thing of all to Castor.

Escharum looked back to Castor. "Very well. We have run out of time, Dokab." He raised his hand eastward. "I will summon the others. Lead us to these humans and we shall end this now. Atriox has waited far too long to return."

"To return?" Castor asked. "I thought we were going to *him*. On the Ark."

"You doubt *me*, Dokab?" Escharum demanded. "Did I not say that Atriox would come to *us* and provide transport to his location . . ." He let his sentence trail off, then raised his hand and pointed eastward. "What *is* that?"

Castor turned to look and saw the tiny dart shapes of well over twenty UNSC fighter craft, racing in from the direction of New Mohács. They were not approaching Figyelő Point directly, but angling across Arany Basin toward the southwest portion of the Highland Mountains.

"That, War Chief, is what we have been waiting for," Castor said. "The enemy is heading into the mountains."

Without bothering to excuse himself or explain further, Castor raced to the sensor shelter. Inside the dimly lit room, he found a trio of Kig-Yar operators squawking at their Sangheili supervisor, all pointing at the holographic display in the center of the room.

The supervisor turned toward Castor. "There is no need for concern, Dokab," he said. "They are not coming toward—"

"I could see that from outside." Castor pushed him aside, then stepped up to the holograph. Roughly a meter in length, it showed an image of almost the entire Highland Mountain range. He saw twenty-four identical arrow symbols swarming around a single box symbol, their pace increasing as they moved toward the mountains. "What am I looking at?"

"Two talons of human utility fighters," a Kig-Yar operator answered. "Escorting one of their . . ."

Heavy footfalls sounded at the door behind Castor, and the Kig-Yar fell silent as 'Gadogai and Escharum entered. No doubt, they did not expect to see the Banished war chief himself in their monitoring shelter.

"One of their *what*?" Castor demanded.

The Kig-Yar looked back to his screen. "Apologies, Dokab. One of their dropships."

"And this dropship?" Escharum asked. "It is large enough to carry digging machines?"

"Small ones, yes."

Castor was already running his eyes along the flight's course. "Show me the terrain along the projected flight path," he said. "From the time it crosses over the mountains until it leaves."

The Kig-Yar ran his fingers through a few light bars and pressed a couple of pressure pads on the emitter base. An image of a dotted line crossing over some very rugged mountain terrain appeared in the projection, and Castor knew as soon as he saw it where the dropship was headed. He faced the Sangheili post commander.

"Send everything we have after that human vessel. Shoot it down *now*!"

"*What?*" the post commander gasped. "Is this not what you have been waiting for, Dokab? For the demons to lead us to the portal?"

"They just did," Castor said. He pointed to where the projected flight path crossed a flat circle surrounded by a ring of high craggy peaks. "We need no further confirmation. The reason we have not found it until now is clear. The portal was not *under* a mountain. Not at all."

"What do you mean by this, Dokab?" Escharum's tone had grown less menacing—perhaps even respectful. "Show me."

"What I mean, War Chief, is that the portal is there." Castor pushed his finger into the holograph, placing it atop the flat circle. "Under the *Missing* Mountain."

# CHAPTER EIGHTEEN

Six days into Operation: WOLFE and Blue Team was right back where it had started, strapped into a dropship troop bay on the way to CASTLE Base, crossing Arany Basin with a horde of enemy fighters vectoring in to kill them. John was monitoring the tactical situation in his HUD, while Linda floated in inner stillness and Kelly rocked her helmet to some ancient classic music about biting dust.

They even had Stella Mukai in the jump seat again, warily eyeing Fred as he polished a nick out of his combat knife. But she hadn't told him to put it away, apparently deciding his quick reflexes were reason enough to ignore the prohibition against unsecured equipment inside the bay. At least *that* was different, Mukai playing nice.

She had to be pretty worried.

Van Houte's voice sounded over TEAMCOM. "Visual or tactical situation monitor?"

Van Houte was riding in the gunner's chair today so his hotshot lieutenant could do the flying. Chapov clearly had the skills, and now that he had settled into his place on the team, everyone trusted him to listen to Van Houte's experience.

"Visual," John said. "Thanks."

A tactical display would present only the air battle, which wouldn't do Blue Team much good, as they were just along for the ride. But a visual image would show the terrain ahead, and that would prove *very* useful if they were forced down.

A moment later, the view from the nose camera appeared on the situation monitor above Mukai's head. There were twenty-four Broadswords scattered across the screen, all brightly marked by paired circles of blue propellant pouring from the nozzles of their main engines. Beyond the strike fighters rose the brown wall of the Highland Mountains' highest peaks, their jagged summits hidden within a charcoal pall of rain clouds.

The Highland Mountains were one of the few areas on Reach to escape the Covenant plasma bombardment. But it would have been wrong to say the range had been spared. A firestorm of apocalyptic proportions had swept up from the molten plains, consuming everything combustible . . . and melting so much that wasn't. The verdant slopes had been reduced to banks of seared dirt and charred stone, the once-lush meadows blanketed in cinders and ash. In the months-long deluge of black rain that had followed, the mountainsides had been washed bare, and landslides the size of cities had tumbled into the valleys below. Now there were naked scarps of bright stone where there had been forests, and kilometer-deep bogs of mud and ash filling the dales. The only hints of recovery to be found were on the lower slopes, where a few streaks of barely noticeable green had begun to emerge between slide-scars.

The team's destination was just visible in the middle of the situation monitor, a tangle of craggy ridges and plunging valleys that had formerly been the location of many of the UNSC's sprawling military facilities on Reach, including the Reach Military Complex and the Military Wilderness Training Preserve. There the Spartan-IIs had learned not only to fight, survive, and thrive, but to nurture the bonds of loyalty and fellowship that had allowed them to endure so many decades of hardship and loss. John had returned here a handful of times since that devastating day seven years ago, but none of that seemed to blunt the anger he still felt for what had happened to this place, and to the ones who had lost their lives defending it.

Now, robbed of its forests—and even the soil those forests had grown in—the terrain looked more rugged and forbidding than when John and the rest of Blue Team had trained there. At its heart lay their current objective, a jagged ring of distant peaks with a tiny gap in the center—a gap that had been created during the war, when the Covenant literally removed the mountain over CASTLE Base.

The aliens had been trying to reach an ancient Forerunner installation that happened to be located deep under the base, but the UNSC had not realized that until Dr. Halsey was forced to take refuge there with Fred, Kelly, and several other Spartans. While they were searching for a way out, Halsey had discovered the item the Covenant was seeking—a slipspace-altering crystal that had some *very* strange effects on gravity, time, and space.

Shortly after Halsey's find, John had led a rescue mission that almost literally plucked her and the others out of the Covenant's hands. The enemy's hunt for the crystal had quickly become an interstellar chase as they pursued the humans who now possessed it, but it had ended shortly afterward when the crystal was destroyed in an accidental explosion. As far as John knew, even Dr. Halsey had never figured out why the Covenant had been so desperate to have it.

But the war with the Covenant was long over, and Blue Team's mission to recover the assets in CASTLE Base had nothing to do with the Forerunner installation—or the mysterious artifact Halsey had found inside it.

Tiny splinters of blue light began to spill out of the Highlands and out over the rolling glasslands at the base of the mountains, vectoring toward a convergence point directly ahead of the Pelican. John checked the synced information displays in his HUD and confirmed his suspicions. Banshees and Seraphs, ninety of them, with more entering detection range every second. About the only good thing he noticed was that the craft seemed to be arriving from every part of the range, rushing in from distant patrol circuits. Their pilots would be tired and slow.

"That doesn't look like an ambush." Fred looked toward John, his faceplate barely showing above the big stack of ordnance and recovery equipment secured to the deck between them. "Weren't we expecting an ambush?"

"Maybe they're going to try to force us down instead," John said.

"Maybe." Fred's tone was doubtful. "But then they'd be trying to draw off our escort and get around behind us. *That* looks like a denial operation."

Fred was right. The random vectors, the harried rush to converge on their position; none of that spoke of a planned ambush.

"Acknowledged," John said. "Interesting."

"Interesting *how*, precisely?" Kelly asked. "As in *maybe the Keepers are willing to shoot us down in flames after all*—that kind of interesting?"

"No, not that kind," John replied. "They can't risk destroying the bio-spoofers if we crash."

"Not if we're wrong in assuming they actually need the spoofers," Kelly said. "What if they *don't*?"

"They would *need* the spoofers if they're after the assets," John said. Without the biometric gloves and contact lenses Dr. Halsey had prepared for them, it would be impossible to bypass the vault's security system. "They can't get into the vault without them."

"Oh, they can get in," Fred said. "You can get into *anything* with enough blamex."

"I meant without blowing it," John said. Manufactured from the same Subanese blamite crystals used in needler ammunition, blamex was one of the favorite high-explosives used by ex-Covenant and

Banished forces. "Don't forget about the self-destruct mechanism. We open the vault without the spoofers, and everything goes up. Us included."

"What if *that* is the point of their operation?" Kelly asked.

John couldn't quite see what she was driving at—but it was still troubling. "Go on."

"The only thing we knew for sure was that the Keepers, one *part* of the Banished forces, were following us. We assumed the rest— that our mission was compromised, and that they are trying to reach CASTLE Base to recover the same assets we are. Given our lack of intel on them, it was the most prudent course of action."

"It's still the most prudent course," John said. "Whether they're after the assets or something else, we need to assume their priority *is* the assets. Given everything we don't know about their objective here on Reach, it would jeopardize the mission to assume anything else."

Linda emerged from her meditation, raising her helmet to look across the stack of cargo at John.

"This is true, as far as it goes," she said. Then she pointed a finger at the situation monitor. "Until your prudent assumption leads to an imprudent expectation."

John saw the implication. "If they aren't trying to recover the assets, they don't need our spoofers."

"And if they don't need our spoofers," Fred said, "they don't need us in one piece."

"That *is* what I've begun to think," Kelly said.

"Only one problem," Fred said. "Why care about the assets at all, if they're not trying to recover them?"

"You've read the same intelligence reports I have on the Keepers," Kelly said. While John was stranded in space with Cortana, missing in action for nearly five years, the rest of Blue Team had joined up with a hotshot Ferret team to tangle with the Keepers across several missions. "You know how their *dokab* worshipped Intrepid Eye. She's a Forerunner AI, so maybe he's expanded his pantheon. Maybe he's trying to stop us because now he venerates . . . you know."

She pointed skyward, to indicate Cortana.

"Seems unlikely," John said. "If that was the case, this mission would have been over the millisecond we touched the ground, because there would have been a Guardian here waiting for us. And if we're going to question assumptions, let's question them all. There's no solid evidence that our mission was compromised by a security leak. Take that away, and what makes us think the Keepers even *know* about the assets?"

"Uh, the fact that they were following us," Fred said. "We didn't assume that."

"Very true," Kelly said. "But perhaps it was just surveillance. Maybe they were just trying to determine why we're on Reach."

"And now they're in the Highland Mountains," Fred said, "mounting a major operation to stop us from reaching CASTLE Base. That's no coincidence."

"Maybe they're not interested in CASTLE Base at all," John said as the situation's list of unknowns entered a dark territory in his mind. "Maybe they're interested in what's *underneath* CASTLE Base."

"Oh boy." Kelly sighed, then looked to John. "What could possibly still be under there?"

"If anything could survive a Covenant planetary bombardment, it'd be something Forerunner," Fred said. "And they *are* Keepers. Forerunner stuff is definitely high on their 'I want' list."

"Whatever they may be after down there, it's outside our mission parameters," John said. "The assets are our priority. We need to get to CASTLE and secure them before that ceases to be possible. Getting down there in one piece is the only thing that matters right now."

As the Spartans talked, Banshees and Seraphs continued to stream toward the convergence point. Their propellant trails had grown so numerous that the situation monitor looked like it was filled with blue static-dashes. The band of glasslands at the bottom of the monitor had narrowed to half its former width, a sign that the Pelican and its escorts would soon be flying into the Highland Mountains proper—if they weren't shot down first.

Chapov's voice sounded over TEAMCOM. "Master Chief, are you seeing this? It might be smarter to wait until that support you requested is available."

Shortly after leaving New Mohács, John had contacted Sarah Palmer again, requesting that eight squadrons of Broadswords and two marine battalions with full armor support be readied for deployment to the Highland Mountains. Palmer had promised to pass his request to General Doi on the next messenger relay. But John knew the support would not arrive anytime soon. The main body of the *Infinity*'s Broadsword wing was still being re-armed and refueled, and it took time to arrange an infantry deployment that size. The *Infinity* was at full battle alert, so the delay would be a matter of hours instead of days—but there wasn't much anyone could do to speed the process beyond that.

"Master Chief?" Chapov asked.

"That's going to be a long wait," John said. He paused, trying to figure out why the Keepers were willing to risk a major air battle to keep Blue Team away from CASTLE Base . . . trying to figure out whether the two enemies could be after different things . . . trying to weigh uncertainties against uncertainties. Finally, he realized his lack of intel made an informed decision impossible. The Keepers might not be interested in CASTLE Base at all, but they were clearly interested in stopping Blue Team—and *that* meant nothing had really changed. John still needed to assume the worst, and Blue Team still needed to reach CASTLE Base as soon as it possibly could.

After a moment, John said, "You're the pilot, Lieutenant Chapov. You're the only one who knows whether you can get us there."

Chapov hesitated for a second, then said, "Let me talk to the major."

The channel fell silent, and John continued to watch the situation monitor. As the mountains loomed larger, the band of rolling glass-lands at the bottom shrank, and the enemy fighters grew more distinct. The tiny slivers of propellant trails elongated into needles, pushing along the cruciform specks of Banshees and the teardrop dots of Seraphs.

Chapov came back on the channel. "It's going to be a rough ride, but we'll get you there. Chief Mukai, set the LAAG sling and weapon. We could need a tail gunner."

"Permission to add some missile capability to that station?" John asked.

"It couldn't hurt," Chapov said. "But be sure you're braced. We're going to encounter some turbulence."

Mukai's eyes went wide, but she quickly unbuckled from her crash harness. She removed the mounting sling from the forward storage locker, then paused to raise a brow at the combat knife in Fred's hand. After he secured it in the shoulder sheath under his pauldron, she made her way aft, slipping between the two excavation machines to rig the sling to its support assembly in the overhead.

Once she'd returned to her jump seat, John and Kelly freed the M41 light anti-aircraft gun from the cargo stack and went aft themselves. There was only half a meter of space between the two excavation machines—not enough for a Spartan in Mjolnir armor to squeeze through. John climbed onto the engine compartments, scraping his back-mounted fusion reactor against the overhead as he crawled forward.

When he reached the LHD's driver's seat, Kelly passed him the LAAG so he could secure it into its sling assembly. By the time he was done, his HUD showed that their Broadsword escorts had assumed a loose cone-formation, with the Pelican protected in the center. The cone was three kilometers long and five kilometers wide at its base, but in the tactical display, it looked almost solid.

He felt the Pelican accelerate and watched in his HUD as its velocity climbed past supersonic. Fred and Kelly had each grabbed an M57

Pilum from the cargo stack and were working their way aft. There was more room alongside the excavation machines than between them, so they were shuffling along the bulkheads sideways, Fred on the LHD side and Kelly on the side with the drilling jumbo. Linda was holding two Pilums, one in each hand. She had stopped behind the excavation machines and had two cases of high-explosive multipurpose missiles wedged between the two vehicles at chest height. There wouldn't be room for her to fire a Pilum past John and the LAAG—and the backflash would have ignited the ordnance behind her anyway—so she would be handling reloads for Fred and Kelly.

Meanwhile Mukai was struggling to keep her feet against the Pelican's acceleration—it was already at Mach 2—as she checked the tie-downs on the cargo stack, making sure everything had been properly secured after the weapons were removed. In the situation monitor behind her, the swarm of bright-blue propellant discs had doubled from almost fifty to just under a hundred as the Broadswords called on their auxiliary engines to continue accelerating. A steady stream of smaller disks was pulling away out in front of them, ST/MMP air-to-air missiles streaking ahead to thin the cloud of whirling Banshees.

Beyond the Banshees, John could see the drop-shaped hulls of probably thirty Seraphs, circling in front of the familiar peaks and cliffs of the Military Training Wilderness Preserve. The Seraphs would prove far more difficult to handle than the Banshees. Their lack of agility wouldn't matter because their shields would simply deflect the Broadswords' missiles, so it would come down to nose-to-nose dogfighting—the Keepers' heavy plasma cannons against the Broadswords' asynchronous linear-induction 35mm ASW/AC autocannons.

John watched Mukai as she struggled back to her seat and buckled in for a rough ride. The velocity readout in his HUD showed the Pelican climbing past Mach 3, and then they were in the Banshee swarm.

The little fighters rained down in flames as the ST/MMP missiles struck home, and dozens simply disintegrated beneath the Broadswords' autocannons. But a handful slipped through the cone formation to make an attack run, their plasma bolts zinging and sizzling off the Pelican's armor.

Moments later, the dropship was through the Banshees, and the troop bay fell quiet again.

John checked his HUD and saw dozens of Banshee survivors, all circling around to pursue. But at the speed the Pelican and its escorts were traveling, the little fighters were already twenty kilometers behind the battle—and falling another kilometer behind with every passing second.

The Seraphs came in firing, approaching in a dangerous head-on attack, hammering away with their plasma cannons, a few swinging out to risk fuel rod shots at the Pelican.

Bad mistake.

Knowing their smaller missiles would be useless against the Seraphs—if they had had any left—the Broadsword pilots had already switched to their ALI-35 autocannons. Accelerated to a tenth the speed of light by magnetic coilgun technology, the heavy rounds could deplete Seraph shields with a single hit and punch through nanolaminate hull armor as though it were rolled steel.

Half a dozen Seraphs spiraled to the ground before the two formations even met.

John ached to join the fray, but for now all Blue Team could do was watch as Lieutenant Chapov flew the Pelican through the heart of a firestorm. Explosions everywhere. Broadswords bursting into kilometer-long flame plumes, plasma bolts burning down the length of their fuselages. Seraphs dissolving into shard clouds under the hail of ASW/AC rounds. Keeper attackers and UNSC escorts going head-to-head, then blossoming into fireballs as they turned in the same direction and touched noses.

A heartbeat later, the Seraphs and the Broadswords were past each other—fourteen Broadswords pulling up hard to shed velocity and claim the high ground; fifteen Seraphs converging on the Pelican, their plasma cannons starting to flash three kilometers away.

"Everybody hold on!" Chapov said. "Things are about to get wild!"

Fred glanced across the LHD at John, but said nothing. The joke that could relieve *this* tension simply didn't exist. John braced himself between the overhead and the LHD seat and watched the situation monitor.

Which suddenly grew blurry.

John didn't notice the Pelican had dropped into a dive—at Mach 3—until he felt his stomach rising into his throat, then his back pressing into the LHD seat as they went into a spin—at Mach 3. He had no idea how far it was to the ground, but he was pretty sure it wouldn't be far enough.

He checked Linda and found her wedged between the excavation machines under the two crates of missile reloads, then located Kelly peering over the top of the drilling jumbo. He couldn't see her expression, but he could imagine her humming one of her old songs. Chief Mukai, eyes shut, had both arms crossed over her chest, clenching the straps of her crash harness, pressing her helmet against the bulkhead as if that might keep the mounting bolts from failing.

John was afraid to check the tactical situation on his HUD, but did it anyway.

The Pelican was spiraling toward a long, deep canyon that descended out of the heart of the mountains, fifteen Seraphs on its tail and all still blazing plasma fire at it. But the Keepers were two kilometers away and falling farther behind as the ground approached— and, unlike Chapov, they were decelerating hard.

Two kilometers above *them*, the remaining Broadswords were wheeling out of their climb and starting the long dive back into battle.

A pair of thumps rumbled up from the deck, and John's throat clenched. Then he felt himself floating above his seat as the Pelican exited its roll and pulled up. The situation monitor on the forward bulkhead unblurred itself—and blossomed into a flashing ball of orange that instantly filled the screen and seemed to swallow the entire craft. The hull crackled and popped with heat expansion, and John felt himself being thrown forward as the Pelican decelerated. *Hard.*

It wasn't a crash. At the velocity they were traveling, he wouldn't have felt *anything*—just blossomed into a spray of atoms dispersing into the atmosphere.

John checked the tactical display in his HUD. Again. The Pelican had dropped into the gash of a canyon he'd glimpsed earlier and fired a couple of missiles into the walls, filling the air with sensor-blinding debris that forced its pursuers to pull up. Now it was flying through the same narrow canyon nose-up . . . yet continuing to travel parallel to the ground as Chapov used the belly shield and vector pylons to decelerate. Incredible piloting skills. That was something John had never seen before—and something he hoped to *never* see again.

Assuming he survived this time.

Then the Pelican's nose dropped to level, and the g-forces began to push John around as the dropship banked and slipped from side to side, following the canyon's sinuous channel upriver, deeper into the heart of the mountains. The Pelican's own sensors were blocked by the walls looming to either side, but its onboard computer was being fed data from its Broadsword escorts. So the tactical display showed the complete battle, and it seemed apparent that the Seraphs weren't going to be a problem for much longer. The Broadswords had fallen in behind them, now in textbook attack position.

The smart choice for the Seraphs would have been to cut and run. They were too ungainly in Reach's atmosphere to switch positions and turn on the nimble Broadswords, which meant they were just flying targets. And if they tried to drop down on the Pelican from above, they wouldn't last long enough to open fire.

Instead of doing the smart thing, the Seraphs did both dumb things. The first group, seven craft, pursued the Pelican. The second group fell back on Jiralhanae pack-hunting tactics, dividing into two elements of four. The elements turned in opposite directions, then circled back toward each other, trying to lure their pursuers into a suicidal head-on double pass.

But the Jiralhanae weren't the only ones who understood team flying. The Broadswords sent just four craft after the pursuit group—and began to down all seven Seraphs, one by one.

The rest of the Broadswords climbed into a loop, then went into a tight line formation as they began their descent and arrived on the enemy's flank—just as the two elements were crossing. They unleashed a wall of cannon fire that demolished all eight Seraphs in little more than a breath.

By then the Pelican's velocity had dropped to subsonic. Which meant the Banshees were a problem again. The swarm Lieutenant Chapov had outrun earlier was coming up fast, arranging itself into a long, narrow file so it could drop in behind the Pelican and open fire. There were still more than fifty Banshees, and while they were slower than Broadswords, they were also more agile. John couldn't think of a better craft to pursue a Pelican through a mountain canyon—which made him wonder why Chapov wasn't climbing up where the Broadswords would be better able to protect them.

Looking forward again, John switched his attention from his HUD to the situation monitor above Chief Mukai's head. It took a moment for his mind to resolve the reddish-black blur into canyon walls, flashing by so fast that it was difficult to make out the familiar jags and curves—but when he did, he realized that the Pelican was exactly where Chapov and Van Houte had planned to be all along: running up the Black Iron Gorge, straight into the heart of the Reach Military Complex hidden in the Highland Mountains.

The gorge ended at the very location where John and the other Spartans had lived for years. Nestled among the hills and heavily wooded terrain was the compound that had housed them, the academy where they had learned combat tactics, and a vast network of obstacle courses and training facilities where they had become what they now were—Spartans. It had been home to Blue Team—but it was also the perfect staging area for a covert approach. The site lay only a few kilometers from the entrance to CASTLE Base. Even better, the two locations were connected by a series of ravines that would provide ample cover for sneaking into position unseen.

Assuming they hadn't been filled by mudslides, of course.

And as fate would have it, the Complex was not far from Military Reservation 01478-B, known as "Painland" by those intimately familiar with it—home to the very same obstacle course where John and Cortana had worked together for the first time, long before she had gone rampant. It had been seven long years since, but he remembered that initial run with her like it was yesterday.

It had been described to him as a live-fire test to familiarize them with each other's capabilities. But one of Dr. Halsey's rivals had rigged it to undermine the entire SPARTAN-II program. That John had survived and passed was largely due to Cortana's ingenuity and situational awareness. It pained him that the place where it had all begun might now play a part in putting an end to her.

Van Houte's voice sounded over TEAMCOM. "Secure troop bay for slipstream exposure."

Mukai did a quick visual check of the bay, lingering on the cargo stack between her and the excavation vehicles, then shifted her gaze to the Spartans.

"Passengers, report status."

John slipped out of his seat and positioned himself between the LHD bucket and the drilling jumbo's boom assembly. He grabbed the LAAG handle with one hand, ready to spin it around and open fire the instant the loading ramp opened.

"Blue Leader ready."

As the rest of the team reported, he checked the tactical display in his HUD. The Banshees had closed to firing range and were dropping into the gorge to begin their attack. The Pelican was flying thirty meters above the river, with nearly sixty kilometers of twisting gorge ahead.

This would be a long ride.

Once everyone had reported ready, Mukai extended her arm and gave a thumbs-up sign. "Troop bay secure."

"Lower loading ramp to control-neutral position," Van Houte said. "All weapons, fire at will."

Mukai acknowledged the order, then pulled a control relay from her thigh pocket, tapped a three-key sequence, and held her thumb on a toggle control. A ferocious howl filled the troop bay as the ramp dropped to a horizontal position, and the Pelican's tail slued side to side as the slipstream began to suck at the open bay.

John swung the LAAG around and waited for the first targets to drop into his firing window; he knew that Fred and Kelly would be doing the same with their Pilum rocket launchers. Their field of fire upward was blocked by the tail assembly and downward by the open loading ramp. Normally that would have left the Pelican vulnerable to attack from both above and below. But in the narrow, twisting confines of the Black Iron Gorge, any craft trying to dive down from above would hit nothing but a canyon wall, and the Pelican was flying so close to the river surface that it would be impossible for a Banshee to come up under it.

The only attack possible was from the rear.

The entire file of Banshees dropped in behind the Pelican almost at once. Although they boasted the crimson-and-gray armor of Banished designs, no matter what the arrangement had been, John knew that inside these craft were Keeper pilots, just as devoted and zealous as the Covenant had ever been. They were almost as crazy as Chapov, flying through the narrow gorge two abreast and stacked two high, forming four-craft elements that would be able to unleash a hellish storm of concentrated fire. The lead element's plasma cannons were already flashing, the Pelican's armor pinging and sizzling as their fire hit home. A couple of bolts flashed through the hatch into the LHD bucket. John was already squeezing the LAAG triggers, not even thinking about it, just reacting on instinct and pouring rounds back toward the fiery muzzles of the enemy.

The rounded noses of the two lower Banshees collapsed inward under his attack. Both craft dropped into the river and tumbled along its surface. A pair of HEMP missiles hit the upper two Banshees, and a curtain of fire stretched across the canyon.

Fred and Kelly, of course.

John was already letting loose on the bottom two craft in the next element, swinging back and forth between them, punching holes in their canopies as they began to return fire. Then everything went sideways and he felt himself being pressed toward the deck as the Pelican banked hard around a sharp bend in the canyon. His targets didn't make the turn and slammed into the cliffs on the outer wall of the curve.

Another pair of missiles flashed from the Pelican's hatch and took out the two Banshees in the top of the element as they rounded the bend, eliminating the enemy threats before they had a chance to bring their cannons to bear.

"Reload!"

Fred and Kelly called the word simultaneously, throwing their empty Pilums back toward Linda and catching the ones she had already tossed toward them. With no enemy craft in view, John simply filled the canyon behind them with LAAG rounds, and when the third element of Banshees came around the bend, they ran into a wall of armor-penetrating rounds and disintegrated in midair.

By then Fred and Kelly had their Pilums shouldered and were waiting for the fourth element. The Spartans were pushing the Banshee formation back, giving it no chance to open fire as the Pelican disappeared around one bend in the gorge after another. The trouble was, that also limited their own opportunities to eliminate Banshees. And the Black Iron Gorge was only so long. When they reached the end, they would have to climb out over the Spartans' old training site, and the remaining Banshees would be able to overwhelm them.

They managed to eliminate two more elements over the next five minutes. But that was only twenty craft—which meant there were still at least thirty behind them.

"Csáki Narrows coming," Chapov said. "Be ready."

As child trainees, Blue Team had descended the Black Iron Gorge during an exercise, and John remembered the Csáki Narrows well. A particularly bad set of rapids, the narrows had reduced their makeshift rafts into toothpicks and nearly drowned them all.

The narrows had seemed both endless and insanely fast, because the gorge was only fifty meters wide in that section. The close confines funneled the river through the channel and then straight down in a mad rush . . .

John connected another belt of ammunition to the one already in the LAAG, at the same time speaking over TEAMCOM. "You remember the narrows, right?"

"Oh yeah," Fred said. "This is going to be fun."

"No doubt," Kelly said. "But for whom?"

The Pelican banked around a set of S-turns, then leveled out and dropped so low John could see its slipstream ruffling the surface of the churning rapids. He counted to two, knowing the Banshees were at least that far behind them, then opened fire.

A couple of breaths later, the lead element of the formation came around the bend and hit the wall of rounds streaming down the canyon. All four craft disintegrated and rained down on the water.

But there were four more craft behind them, and yet another four behind those. Plasma fire began to fly up the canyon toward the Pelican, hissing and chiming off its exterior. A bolt hit something on the drilling jumbo and deflected into the overhead. Another zipped past John and shattered the situation monitor. He knew Mukai was okay because he heard her cussing into TEAMCOM.

Kelly and Fred loosed a pair of missiles, then another pair, and the gorge filled with flames. John continued to fire, and the next element of Banshees emerged from the fireball into a torrent of slugs. One flew apart in midair and another veered into a wall, while a third dipped a canard into the river and went tumbling back down the canyon. The fourth exploded under the Spartans' counterattack.

But the Banshees continued to come, and this time they were stacked three high, taking advantage of the narrows' straightaway. To make themselves more difficult targets, they undulated up and down, climbing a little higher each time, all the while mercilessly shooting plasma bolts at the Pelican.

"They're trying to line up a top attack!" Fred said over TEAM-COM. "Get off the deck!"

"It'll be fine." Chapov sounded utterly calm. "Just keep shooting. Keep them off the water."

"You think?" Fred replied.

But he fired another missile, and so did Kelly. John began to lay his fire just a few meters above the churning river surface, concentrating not so much on hitting the Banshees as trying to keep forcing them up. He had no idea what Chapov was doing, but when a pilot said to do something on his bird, it was a good idea to listen.

Fred and Kelly knocked down two more Banshees with their missiles, and John took out another one. But there was a storm of plasma fire coming back in their direction, and the excavation equipment was taking so much damage that Chief Mukai finally got permission to raise the loading ramp to protect it.

Then the bolts began to find their way to the Spartans themselves, taking down John's energy shields first, then Kelly's and Fred's simultaneously. They all had to duck behind the loading ramp while their shields regenerated, the plasma fire beginning to eat through the ramp.

A bolt cut the LAAG sling, and the gun dropped into John's arms. He cradled the barrels in the crook of his elbow, then stood up to open fire—and discovered the Pelican was trailing so much smoke he couldn't see his targets, only the crimson flashes of their plasma flying toward him. He fired anyway, keeping his rounds low as Chapov had ordered . . . and then the smoke parted.

The bright-blue disks of two propellant nozzles flashed past overhead—the stubby wings of a Broadsword rocking unsteadily as it passed through the Pelican's slipstream. It must have been on the attack, because Banshees were falling everywhere from the sky.

John released the LAAG triggers, then the Broadsword pulled up, the smoke closed in behind them again, and plasma bolts began to fly toward the Pelican, this time coming from a few hundred meters farther down the gorge.

He was about to return fire when the smoke parted a second time to reveal another pair of propellant nozzles speeding by overhead. More Banshees fell, and when the Broadsword pulled up this time, the next element was a thousand meters down the gorge. Their plasma bolts kept coming, but they weren't connecting—especially after a third Broadsword dropped in for an attack.

Chapov's voice sounded over TEAMCOM again. "Secure troop bay for high-g maneuvers! Do it fast!"

As Mukai acknowledged the order, John and the Spartans chucked the LAAG and the Pilums over the loading ramp. With all the smoke trailing behind the Pelican, it was obvious that a hard landing was on the way—and no one wanted a loose weapon flying around the troop bay during a crash.

With the bay secure, the Spartans returned to their seats and buckled into their crash harnesses, while Mukai used her control relay to raise the loading ramp. The Pelican began to shudder and wobble. Whatever part of the Pelican was smoking was failing fast.

Van Houte's voice sounded over TEAMCOM. "Lieutenant Chapov is going to set us down at the top end of the gorge."

The location he was talking about was the Spartans' old training course, which was about four hundred meters above the river. John just hoped they had the power to make it. The gorge wasn't as sheer or deep near its head as where they had entered it, but the walls were still steep. If Chapov tried to land on them, the Pelican would tumble into the plunge pool at the bottom of Iron River Falls.

"Once we're down, evacuate the troop bay quickly," Van Houte continued. "Our escorts are zero ammunition, and there are still three Banshees behind us."

"Acknowledged." John tried to check the tactical display in his HUD and realized the cockpit sync was down. He didn't like what that implied about their avionics. "What about all that smoke?"

"Nothing to worry about," Van Houte said. "We took a hit in the missile bay—it's just some propellant burning off."

"*Missile* propellant *burning* off?" Fred said. "If that's nothing, I don't even want to know why we're shuddering so hard."

"Don't worry about the shuddering," Van Houte replied. "We have bigger problems than uncontrolled vector pylons."

A sharp jolt ran through the Pelican; then it tipped into a bank and began to snake up the gorge again. Fred and John looked at each other across the cargo stack, waiting for Van Houte to elaborate.

He didn't.

Rather than distract the major with a question that would do absolutely nothing to get the Pelican out of the gorge and onto the ground, John focused on something that would contribute to the mission—organizing a quick evacuation.

Getting the excavation machines out of the bay had to come early. They were vital to the mission, and they were situated for quick roll-off. Mukai could undo the tie-downs while the Spartans organized the cargo. There was still some ordnance in the stack—two more Pilums and a case of SPNKr reloads, because Fred liked his M41 rocket launcher for ground combat. They could probably abandon it in a pinch, but it was on top, so they might as well toss it onto the drilling jumbo operator's platform. If it fell off later, so be it. But they had to move it anyway.

It was all the stuff under the ordnance—the titanium haulage buckets packed with bins of enhanced gelignite, the winches loaded with spools of nanobraided titanium cable—that was mission-critical. CASTLE Base—or what remained of it after the self-destruct charges

Dr. Halsey had set off to prevent its assets from being claimed by the Covenant—was two thousand meters down a vertical access shaft, one that would be at least partially filled with gravel and broken rock. So all that equipment came with them, even if it meant dragging it out of a burning Pelican while a trio of Banshees strafed them.

But their weapons came first. Weapons *always* came first. That's why Blue Team was still alive and kicking after all these years.

"Listen up in the troop bay," John said. "Once we're on the ground, Blue Two will access the weapons locker and distribute our individual weapons. Chief Mukai, you and Blue Four will get the excavation equipment rolled off. Blue Three and I will drag—"

That was as far as John made it before the Pelican went into a steep climb and began to shudder so violently that it sounded like they were being pounded by fuel rod cannons. With no cockpit sync to check on his HUD, John instinctively looked to the shattered situation monitor above Mukai's head, and then his gut finally accepted what his head had known all along—they were riding blind, and their lives were entirely in Lieutenant Chapov's hands.

John went back to the evac plan. "Blue Three and I will drag the haulage buckets out and load them onto the LHD. Then we'll clear the area—"

The Pelican bucked hard, as if it were dancing across the sky on its tail. Two holes opened in the deck behind the cargo stack as a pair of fuel rods exploded through the dropship's belly armor. The blast wave was the worst part, slamming everyone in the troop bay back against the bulkheads, Blue Team's helmets actually ringing.

Then they went weightless as the Pelican stopped climbing. John expected it to start sliding back on its tail, down into the gorge. But Chapov brought the nose down by timing a few last thrusts out of the uncontrolled vector pylons. The big chin gun began to chatter, and they went into a flat spin and dropped fast.

The Pelican couldn't have been very high up, because they pancaked into the ground almost immediately, the tail section just a little downhill.

"Go go go!" John ordered.

Fred was already at the weapons locker, tossing John's assault rifle over the cargo stack, then Kelly's shotgun and Linda's sniper rifle. John caught his MA40 in the air and raced aft past the drilling jumbo. About halfway down, there was a long breach in the bulkhead where a fuel rod had grazed the Pelican's starboard side. Through the hole, he saw the burning hulk of an anti-aircraft Wraith sitting on a rocky flat, with a jagged wall of mountains rising about a kilometer to the south. It didn't much resemble the old military compound anymore, thanks to the Covenant, but it was in the right place and looked about the right size. Chapov had done his part.

By the time John reached the loading ramp, Mukai already had it down. He paused just long enough to make sure Blue Team was ready to engage, then led the way out onto the rocky barrens.

The Pelican had come down with its tail facing west, which gave them a clear view of the entire plateau, across two kilometers of broken rock all the way to the wall of brown, barren escarpments at the base of the Highland Mountains' highest peaks. There was nothing coming toward them overland, and no Banshees in sight.

"Blue Four, watch our six," John ordered. "Blue Two, bring out the last of our Pilums in case those Banshees show up. Blue Three, you advance on the port side. I'll take starboard."

Everyone flashed green, and John ducked around the Pelican's tail and started up the starboard side. The burning Wraith that he'd spotted from inside sat thirty meters distant. Its fuel rods were crackling loudly as they cooked off, its charging gas teasing the flames into a spiral column.

The Pelican had crashed directly atop a second anti-aircraft Wraith, and one of the big fuel rod cannons had crashed down on its canopy. Van Houte was already out of the gunner's seat and leaning over the Wraith's cannon to peer down at Chapov.

John continued forward, his MA40 shouldered and ready to fire at any Keepers who climbed out of the Wraith behind Van Houte.

"Blue Three, sitrep?" he asked.

"I have a crippled Wraith thirty meters to the north," she said. "Two crewmembers attempting to evacuate."

"Take them. I'll assist here."

He reached the front of the Pelican and climbed up on the smashed Wraith to make sure the alien crew wouldn't cause them any trouble, then saw that both Jiralhanae had bullet wounds between their eyes—Van Houte had already handled them. John circled around the nose of the Pelican, then climbed up opposite Van Houte and looked down toward Chapov.

Damn. The kid was in trouble. The Wraith cannon had smashed through the Pelican's canopy right down the middle, carving a space between the two operator seats. The weapon's muzzle must have caught something on the way in, because it had pinned Chapov to his seat. His chest was caved in and his arms were resting on top of the barrel assembly. His chin was covered in blood, no doubt expectorated from his internal wounds.

Chapov looked at John and tried to smile. "Best I could do," he said. "The Broadswords . . ."

He coughed, and more blood foamed from his mouth.

"You flew a great mission, Lieutenant." John did not try to assure Chapov that he was going to be fine. They both knew it wasn't true, and he didn't want to lie to a dying hero. "Legendary. We'll handle it from here."

"Wait," Chapov gasped. He tried to say more, then looked to Van Houte. "You tell . . . him."

"Right." Van Houte looked across the cockpit to John. "The Broadswords did a flyover at Menachite Mountain. The Keepers are already there in force—and so is that intrusion corvette we saw from New Mohács."

John nodded. "Thanks. I thought that was likely." He reached into the cockpit and squeezed Chapov's shoulder. "Legendary."

Fred arrived with a Pilum and an extra magazine, then climbed up and looked over Van Houte's shoulder. "Oh, man," he said. "What can we do for you, Lieutenant? Somebody who needs to know?"

Chapov shook his head. "Personnel has all that. Just report it." He pointed his chin at the Pilum. "And leave that for me. You . . . need to get those excavation machines unloaded and get out of here. There are still three . . . Banshees coming."

Fred's helmet rocked back in surprise, and he looked across the cockpit toward John.

"Don't worry about the Banshees," John said. "We can—"

Chapov's voice grew stronger. "I'm not asking, Master Chief. That's an order."

Now it was John's turn to be surprised, but he didn't argue. He came to attention and raised his hand to his helmet.

"Yes, sir." He finished the salute, then looked to Fred. "You heard the lieutenant. Give the man his missile launcher."

Fred placed the Pilum on Chapov's shoulder in firing position. He then smashed a larger hole into the canopy so Chapov had the maximum range of fire—and placed the extra magazine in his lap. He could have released the seat and allowed it to draw to the back of the cockpit, giving the pilot complete freedom of motion, but there was no reason to risk it—who knew what the cannon was holding in place.

Then Fred came to attention and saluted. "Give 'em hell, Lieutenant."

"You too, Spartan."

Chapov returned the salute; then John and Fred went aft to help finish the off-loading while Major Van Houte stayed behind to share a few last words.

Chief Mukai already had both excavation machines on the ground, and Kelly was helping her strap the spare ordnance onto the jumbo operator's platform. John caught Mukai's eye.

"We can finish here," he said. "You have a moment to say good-bye."

"I already did." She tapped her helmet jaw-guard, where the microphone was located, then tried to blink back a tear. "I have my orders."

John nodded. "Affirmative."

He went into the troop bay after Fred and helped him drag the haulage buckets out. The cargo platform on the back of the LHD was sagging, so they loaded the haulage buckets—still filled with winches and gelignite bins—into the two-kiloliter mucking bucket on the front.

Van Houte arrived running. "Time to go," he said. "The Banshees are climbing out of the gorge."

Fred looked back across fifty meters of rock barrens toward the edge of the drop-off. "Not arguing—but how do you know?"

Van Houte pointed into the sky, where two Broadswords were circling just beneath the cloud ceiling, one waggling its wings and the other doing barrel rolls.

"Our escorts may be out of ammunition," he said. "But they still have eyes."

"They couldn't have used a comm unit?" Fred asked.

"Whatever works," John said. There were a dozen reasons pilots might signal visually instead of electronically—the most likely being that their squadron commander was dead and they didn't have time to request access to the Spartans' encrypted channels. "Blue Two, grab a Pilum and ride shotgun with Chief Mukai on the jumbo."

Fred flashed an acknowledgment and headed for the machine. No one really expected Lieutenant Chapov to take out the Banshees. But no one wanted to deny him the shot either.

Major Van Houte was already climbing into the driver's seat of the LHD, so John signaled Kelly to take lead, then fell in between the two machines on foot. Linda hung back on rear guard, ready to bring Nornfang to bear on anything that popped up over the horizon.

They started across the charred vestiges of the compound, toward the ravine system that John intended to use for their approach to

CASTLE Base. The ravine would connect to Longhorn Valley, a broad dale that wound back and forth across the western portion of the Highland Mountains. It eventually thinned down to another narrow ravine that cradled Big Horn River, yet another critical site in the Spartans' training. Countless exercises had been conducted on that river during that time, forging them together into the team they now were—this place had made them.

John wondered if, after completing this mission, they would ever make it back to Reach. It was a somber thought, but it wasn't the first time it had crossed his mind. If the rehab pioneers had any say about it, one day the Covenant's work would be undone and Reach would be restored. John might never see that day, but the thought of it gave him some measure of pride. Humanity wasn't done with Reach yet.

They had been traveling only a minute when Kelly raised an arm and pointed at the ground, about fifty meters to her left.

"It really shouldn't surprise me," she said without breaking stride. "But *that* is about the last thing I ever expected to see again."

It took a moment for John to find what she was pointing at . . . then he saw a small object about the size of his own helmet, half-buried and curving up out of the ground. At first he thought it was a lump of lechatelierite or an oddly shaped rock, but the hint of brassy sheen made him realize he was looking at the top half of a bell.

The same one the Spartans would ring three times when they completed the notorious obstacle course Chief Mendez had called "the playground."

"I don't know why you shouldn't be surprised," Fred said. "I sure as hell am. I'd have thought some Jackal would have sold it as a war relic by now."

"They don't know its worth," Linda said. "To them, it's just a hunk of brass."

"I'm glad for that," John said.

He thought about suggesting they dig it up after the mission, if they had time. Except they wouldn't have time, and he knew it.

And maybe it was better that way.

He had been six years old the first time he rang that bell. A lifetime ago. He'd been assigned to a team with Kelly and his buddy Samuel-034, and told to win a race together. He had won all right, sprinting ahead alone to climb a greased pole and ring the bell three times.

But he had left Kelly and Sam behind, and the goal had been to win as a team. All three of them had gone without dinner that night. For the first time, John had understood what it meant to depend on someone else to succeed—and to have them depend on *him*.

To a six-year-old, it had been a simple but profound lesson. It changed the way he looked at the world, and also at himself, from then on. The next time the three of them teamed up, they had eaten well that evening. The bell was a big part of his past, but it belonged here on Reach with the rest of his childhood. If he removed it from the compound now . . . it would surely lose that meaning, and be just an ordinary bell.

John had already passed it when a *boom* rolled across the barrens behind him. He spun in time to see the first Banshee in the sky beyond their downed Pelican, engulfed in flames and dropping back into the gorge.

As he watched, the second Banshee flew out of the gorge—and was met by a white propellant lance rising from the Pelican's cockpit. The Banshee erupted in a fireball, then fell onto the plateau and began to roll across the ground.

The last Banshee arrived, dashing onto the plateau, swinging wide to approach the wrecked Pelican from the side. Its plasma cannons began to blaze, and John saw Linda shoulder Nornfang, the sniper rifle's barrel tracking the craft as she prepared to open fire.

But she didn't pull the trigger, even when John felt sure she had the Banshee in her sights and had worked out where it would be when her bullet arrived. Even from two hundred meters away, he could see the flashes of the Banshee's bolts punching through the Pelican's hull. And still, Linda held her fire.

Then the Banshee was on its target, pulling up hard to avoid a collision just as the Pelican ignited, a giant ball of white fire. The Banshee seemed to ride the explosion higher for a second, then disintegrated into a confetti of glowing shards.

Linda lowered her sniper rifle.

Fred said, "You know, I think we might've been underestimating Chapov—even after we stopped underestimating him."

"Yeah." John pulled his sound suppressor from its storage pouch, then fitted it onto the end of his MA40. "I think we were."

He turned toward the bell and took aim, then rang it three times.

# CHAPTER NINETEEN

John didn't do "waiting" well. Having time to plan was good. Having time to obsess over weak spots and contingency plans . . . not so much. Worse yet was replaying the recent past, spending hours second-guessing decisions he had made in seconds. Like now, wondering if there had been a way to save Bella Disztl, or if he had been right to let Lieutenant Chapov make that crazy flight up Black Iron Gorge. It had been Chapov's call, of course—but John had known what he would decide.

John and the rest of Blue Team were high on the shoulder of Vanadinite Mountain, doing surveillance on the approach to CASTLE Base. They had been lying in the shadows beneath a Warthog-sized boulder for two hours, looking out over a broad valley toward the stony slopes of Omeiite Mountain. Within the valley lay a huge basin where the Covenant's plasma batteries had burned away Menachite Mountain seven years earlier, removing it all the way down to the roots.

At more than ten kilometers across and close to two hundred meters deep, the basin resembled a vast open-pit surface mine. But instead of the terraced benches that mines used to control rockfall and erosion, its walls were steep lechatelierite slopes. Over the years, the rim had collapsed onto the slopes, and untold tons of talus and gravel had slid down onto the basin floor.

Near the center of the basin, a jet of rusty-brown muck was shooting up from a massive hole, then suddenly changing direction to arc out onto a slurry dump at least a hundred meters away. Even from this distance, John knew exactly what he was looking at. He'd figured it out two hours ago—the moment he peered out into the basin and saw the muddy geyser rising from the entrance to CASTLE Base.

Located two kilometers underground, the base was accessible only via a vertical shaft that had served an old titanium mine. During their original assault on Menachite Mountain, the Covenant had enlarged the access shaft to five times its original diameter, then extended it another four hundred meters in order to reach an ancient Forerunner installation located below the titanium mine.

Now the shaft was basically a huge sump, filled with mud and gravel from the surrounding basin. This was the main reason that Blue Team had brought along excavation machines and haulage equipment—so they could clear the shaft.

The Keepers of the One Freedom were employing a different method altogether to clear it, and John liked their way better. They were using a pair of portable gravity lifts to remove the muck—one down inside the shaft to push it to the surface, and another at the top, positioned next to the shaft and angled to shoot the slurry out onto the dump.

Earlier, John had increased his faceplate magnification window to medium and spent some time watching the surface operators work. There had appeared to be ten of them, three with the saurian frames and long-beaked heads of Kig-Yar, and seven with the stubby limbs and wedge-shaped methane tanks of Unggoy. None of them seemed to have much to do, the Kig-Yar pointing and gesturing while the Unggoy adjusted the angle and direction of the lift pad.

Judging by the size of the Kig-Yar compared to the gravity lift, it was large for a portable model, with a pad fully ten meters in diameter. The pinch fusion reactor powering it was equally impressive, with a core chamber two meters high and four meters across. Most likely, it was one of the "pirate lifts" the Banished employed when they raided a city.

John had never seen a pirate lift in action before, but he'd read about them. A Banished vessel would hover above a city, well beyond missile range, while raiding parties moved their portable lifts around to key locations—then gravity-lifted their loot straight into the hold. The Keepers obviously had no interest in collecting the slurry, so they'd been able to adapt the technique and clear the shaft even faster than a raiding band could clean out a town.

So it made sense to let the Keepers do the work. Then all Blue Team would need to do was capture the shaft and descend two kilometers to CASTLE Base. And had their only opposition been the ten Keepers operating the surface lift, Blue Team would have done just that two hours ago.

But the east side of the basin was bordered by a vast area of glass flats, created when the Covenant attack channeled the molten rock from the destruction of Menachite Mountain into the adjacent vale, Rejtett Valley. Bivouacked on those flats were more troops than even Blue Team could handle—three thousand Keepers mounted on Marauders, Wraiths, and Ghosts.

An even bigger concern was the front-heavy intrusion corvette, sitting on the south end of the flats, about a kilometer beyond the basin. With his faceplate magnification pushed to maximum, John could see that it was surrounded by a ring of Jiralhanae guards. He had been watching them for the last hour, and he had not seen one so much as fidget. That kind of discipline was rare for Jiralhanae, as was their drab-gray power armor, and it made John wonder whom they served.

So before Blue Team could take control of the access shaft, they had to also take control of both the talus basin and the glass flats—effectively all of Rejtett Valley. And they had to *maintain* that control.

Blue Team had developed a plan to do exactly that, intending to empty the entire valley of Keeper troops. But it wasn't simple.

And it wasn't fast.

That last part concerned John the most. He liked to hit hard and quick, and this plan was more . . . deliberate. It had a lot of moving parts, and it required a lot of patience.

The first indication that Blue Team's long wait was finally over came when the Gray Guards—as John had come to think of them— began to leave their posts at the corvette and race under its armored bow to disappear into the internal hangar bay. Then the Keepers out on the glass flats began to stir, shouting to one another and gathering their equipment. John didn't need to break comm silence to know that Blue Team's support was finally arriving.

The distant hiss of incoming Broadswords began to rise in the north, from the direction of the compound where Lieutenant Chapov had died saving the mission. Blue Team wouldn't have to hold much longer. Things would start happening fast now.

Which was just the way he liked it.

The last of the Gray Guards disappeared into the corvette's hangar bay. Keeper vehicles began to move north toward Koldus Canyon, which connected Rejtett Valley with the old compound. The first elements of the UNSC support battalions should already be seizing the site to use as a landing zone. That was one of the moving parts of the big plan that John didn't control, but it was just common sense. He *had* to assume General Doi would send an advance detachment to secure the landing zone.

The remnants of the Keepers' badly savaged Banshee force began to rise into the air and stream north to offer air cover for their mechanized forces. Even the nine Seraphs circling high over Rejtett Valley closed formation and dropped down to protect the corvette.

"We'll designate the anti-aircraft Wraiths," John announced.

He spoke over his voicemitter, not TEAMCOM, because even a low-power transmission would risk alerting the enemy to Blue Team's presence. Those Seraphs had been overhead all day for a reason, and that probably had something to do with using their surveillance technology to guard against exactly what Blue Team was preparing to do.

"We need to convince that corvette that the first Broadsword squadron is just clearing the way for the main event." John didn't need to elaborate. The last place any ship of the line wanted to be during an air attack was on the ground, and for their plan to work, they needed to clear the corvette out of the valley. It was just too much firepower for them to neutralize with a SPNKr and a few grenades. "If that thing sticks around, this could get tricky."

"*Get* tricky?" Fred replied. He was lying so close to John that they were touching shoulders, all four Spartans sacrificing tactical spacing in order to speak by voicemitter. Van Houte and Mukai were in a sandy gulch two hundred meters behind and below them, waiting with the excavation machines beneath an overhanging cliff that would hide them from every direction but north. "If this plan gets any trickier, it could seem desperate."

"Desperate is good," Kelly said. "You're at your best when you're desperate."

"Then I'll be *great* today," Fred said.

The hiss of the arriving squadron was building to a roar, which meant the Broadswords would soon be close enough to detect an infrared guidance signal. John and the others slid their designator units into the multifunction receivers beneath their MA40 barrels, then synced the units to their helmet reticles, opened magnification windows in their faceplates, and located the anti-aircraft Wraiths.

There was no need to discuss who would designate which Wraith. Blue Team had a well-drilled procedure. The Spartan at the left end of their line—in this case Linda—would start with the leftmost target and work inward. The two Spartans in the middle—Fred and John—would commence in the middle and work their way outward. The Spartan on the right end—Kelly—would go to the rightmost target and work her way inward like Linda was doing on the opposite end.

Once John had located his target, he said, "Ready to designate?" Everyone answered in the affirmative.

"Designate."

They touched their triggers, and the designator units began to emit needle-thin beams of infrared light that extended more than ten kilometers, each one touching the appropriate target. The Spartans couldn't actually see the beams without engaging special faceplate filters, which would impair their vision in other wavelengths. But the Broadsword targeting systems would have no issues.

A pair of the strike fighters launched two missiles apiece. The missiles' guidance systems were locked onto the beams, so each weapon followed its designated beam directly into the target, detonating with fatal precision against the Wraith hulls.

The whole process took only three seconds, but it was still dangerous for the Spartans. If a patrolling Seraph or artillery piece happened to be scanning the area in the correct infrared wavelength, it would see the designator beams as clearly as the Broadswords did. And the Spartans wouldn't even realize they'd been spotted until the counterstrike arrived.

Blue Team quickly designated their next targets. With only three anti-aircraft Wraiths remaining, John shifted his designator to a Lich that was just taking off with a full load of warriors and equipment.

The Broadsword missiles arrived two seconds later, destroying all three Wraiths and turning the Lich into a whirling ball of secondary explosions.

No counterstrike.

There wasn't an upside in sticking around to designate lower-priority targets, so John jerked a thumb toward the back exit of their hiding place.

"Phase Two. Move out."

Blue Team crawled out from beneath the boulder and moved a few steps downslope so they would be hidden behind the shoulder of the mountain, then removed the unwieldy designator pods from their

MA40s. The Broadswords were visible now, coming in just under the cloud ceiling and dropping down for a close-attack run over Rejtett Valley.

With the enemy already under fire, there was no sense maintaining comm silence. John opened the air comm command channel. "Broadsword Leader, Blue Leader. Nice shooting. We'll be following you into the combat zone, so weapons tight." Meaning attack only targets confirmed to be hostile. "And avoid the geyser—we'll handle that."

"Blue Leader, Alpha Squadron Leader," the Broadsword commander replied. "Explain geyser?"

"Uh . . . you'll know it when you see it." John didn't know how to explain the fountain of gravity-lifted slurry in less time than it would take the Broadswords to reach it. "Do what you can to drive off that intrusion corvette."

"No worries on the corvette," Alpha Leader said. "We spotted him on orbital infrared. A special package is inbound."

"Glad to hear it," John said. Alpha Squadron was already sweeping in to engage the Seraphs that had dropped down to protect the corvette, so it was time to sign off and let them do their job. "Happy hunting. Blue Leader out."

The ground shuddered and the air whooshed as Alpha Squadron shot over Vanadinite Mountain. They were in echelon formation, the third Broadsword from the middle—Alpha Leader, presumably—wagging its wings as they passed.

The squadron split into three elements, the first four craft diving into a missile run. The shoulder of the mountain blocked John's view of the actual attack, but he saw six Seraphs go after them, and the second Alpha element immediately bolt after those six enemy craft. The third element stayed high to engage the last three Seraphs.

The muffled thunder of missile strikes began to rumble out of the basin. By then Blue Team was well into Phase Two, with Fred and Kelly descending the mountain to collect Van Houte, Mukai, and the excavation machines.

John and Linda crossed the sandy gulch they intended to use for moving the excavation machines into the talus basin, then raced to the top of the next ridge. It overlooked Koldus Canyon, the narrow, winding gorge that was the Keepers' only route to the old training compound where the UNSC battalions were landing.

The Keeper column was moving slowly but steadily, an indication that the lead elements were not having much trouble pushing through the mud- and rockslides scattered along their route—probably because they had been partially cleared earlier in the day by the same anti-aircraft Wraiths that had downed Blue Team's transport Pelican . . . and killed Lieutenant Chapov.

There were only seven pieces of mechanized armor, all Marauders, still waiting to enter Koldus Canyon—and with the Broadswords out in the flats raining missiles down on anything with a hull, they were pushing hard to move forward. From his position, John had a partial view through the canyon mouth back into Rejtett Valley. He could see the geyser of slurry still flying from the access shaft. In the distance beyond, just visible over the top of its arc, the intrusion corvette continued to sit on the ground, its shields flashing as pieces of fighter craft rained down on it.

John opened a magnification window and saw what looked like the parts of four different Seraphs and two Broadswords scattered across the surrounding flats. He couldn't understand why the corvette remained passive. Its energy shielding was proof against most Broadsword attacks, but if the UNSC downed the last Seraphs and started autocannon runs, they *would* eventually break through. At the very least, the corvette should have been in the air, using its own weapons to fend off air-to-ground attacks on the Keeper forces.

Instead it continued to sit quietly—not even activating the handful of weapons it could fire from the ground—and that troubled John. Good things rarely came of an enemy acting so unpredictably.

Fred's status light flashed green, and John turned to see him and Kelly escorting the two excavation machines over the wet sand in the gulch below. John signaled them to continue. The gulch opened directly into the talus basin, just four hundred meters from the mouth of Koldus Canyon. But the last Marauder was already inside the canyon and passing below the ridge. By the time the excavation machines reached the talus basin, the Keeper column would be another kilometer closer to the training compound—and unable to return to the basin quickly enough to interfere with Phase Three of Blue Team's plan.

John looked back to the inert corvette—then heard the distant growl of another inbound UNSC squadron. The remaining Seraphs tried to break off to meet the arriving threat. They lost two more craft immediately, with four Broadswords giving chase to the three that escaped. That left six friendly birds to provide close air support over the basin. It would have been all Blue Team needed—if not for the intrusion corvette.

"*This* will be interesting," Linda said over TEAMCOM. "Look what the *Infinity* sent down."

Twelve delta-shaped specks were dropping out of the clouds, tiny fans of blue propellant pushing them along. Longswords. No wonder the Seraphs were panicking. The workhorses of UNSC orbital strike doctrine, Longswords were capable of carrying a huge range of munitions, from their chin-mounted ALI-50 asynchronous linear-induction autocannons all the way up to Shiva-class nuclear missiles.

It was hard to say what ordnance they were here to deliver. John's first guess would be Shield Buster ASGM-15 EMP-assisted missiles, which used an initial burst of electromagnetic energy to penetrate an energy shield before delivering a hull-penetrating charge. Or they might be carrying Octadarts, relatively small laser-guided bombs filled with octanitrocubane charges that simply blasted through the shield. There were a half dozen other possibilities, any one of them powerful enough to cripple an intrusion corvette—especially one that was still grounded.

But apparently the Longsword squadron appearance was the

breaking point—when John looked back to the corvette this time, the vessel was finally rising into the air, a long line of tiny figures spilling from the hangar bay under its bow. He opened a magnification window again and saw that the figures were the same Gray Guards he'd spent so much time watching earlier. But now they were wearing jump-jet packs and carrying an assortment of weapons—everything from shock, spike, and plasma rifles to something that vaguely resembled a larger, blunt-nosed fuel rod cannon. At least the mystery of the lingering corvette had been solved—it had been waiting while the Gray Guards re-armed for heavy combat.

Now things were really about to heat up. John switched to the air command channel. "Alpha Leader, Blue Leader. Request urgent ground support mission."

"Let me guess," Alpha Leader said. "The jumpers?"

"Affirmative," John said. There had to be at least a hundred on the ground now, and the line pouring from the corvette's hangar bay showed no signs of diminishing. "Whatever you can do to thin them out. We'd need an ammunition drop to eliminate all of them."

"We'll do what we can. What about the geyser?"

"Continue avoiding," John said. As long as the Keepers were still clearing the access shaft, he was going to let them. Better that than Blue Team having to excavate it themselves by bucket and winch in the middle of a battle. "We need that equipment intact."

"Acknowledged," Alpha Leader said. "Good luck down there."

The Gray Guards continued to stream out of the corvette's hangar as it rose past a hundred meters above the glass, using their jump-jets to control their descent. As soon as they hit the ground, they gathered into ten-jumper packs and started across the flats toward the talus basin, weaving and dodging as the Broadswords arrived and opened fire.

A few of the Jiralhanae hit their jump-jets and tried to bound across the flats in fifty-meter leaps. But they were less maneuverable in the air than on the ground, and the Broadswords took out every one of them.

Two Broadswords broke off and began to trail the departing corvette at different altitudes, dodging plasma fire from its tail guns while
simultaneously shooting ALI-35 rounds into the jumpers still leaping
from its hangar bay. Some of the guards blossomed into fireballs as
their jump-jets ignited, with the rest simply going limp and plummeting to the ground.

The other four Broadswords continued to make low runs over
the flats, trying to pick off the Gray Guards as they headed toward
the talus basin. John could see right away that these four would not
be as successful as the two craft trailing the corvette. The Jiralhanae
were too spread out, with plenty of craters and boulders to use as
hard cover. Some of the Gray Guards were returning fire with the
odd-looking weapons—large, heavily bladed explosive-launchers of
obvious Jiralhanae design. At first, John was pretty sure they were a
new kind of fuel-rod cannon, given their muzzle action and the energy
they were launching.

But they were *not* fuel-rod guns. Not even close.

The weapons were now firing some sort of red plasma incendiary
that had a shallow ballistic arc. One of the incendiaries hit a Broadsword, exploding across the entire wing and into the fuselage. Within
a second, the skin began melting away in flames, then the entire craft
was disintegrating as the frame burned. Whatever these new weapons
were, John hoped none of them made it into the access shaft.

The Longswords arrived overhead, their huge wedges slicing
across the sky a thousand meters above the surrounding mountaintops.

A woman's voice sounded on the air comm channel. "Blue Leader,
Alpha Two." There was no reason to ask why Alpha Leader was no
longer the one contacting John—it had been his Broadsword that was
hit by the plasma incendiary. "Lima Leader is assuming local command."

"Welcome, Lima Leader," John said. "I mean that."

"Happy to be here." This voice was also female, but older and steelier than Blue Two's. "Requesting guidance. That intrusion corvette has moved off three hundred kilometers—and it's still going. He may be trying to draw us away. Do you want us to pursue?"

"Negative," John said. "We just need him out of the way. It would be more useful to orbit on-station."

"We have clearance to offer full support until bingo propellant," Lima Leader said. "That gives you four hours."

"That'll have to be enough," John replied. Longswords were too large and lumbering to provide the same kind of close air support that Broadswords did, but they had the firepower. A *lot* of it. "Weapons tight—and stay away from the geyser."

"So we've been told," Lima Leader said. "Twice."

Laser-guided bombs began to rain down from the Longswords, raising a two-kilometer-wide ring of conflagration that blanketed the flats and overlapped the rim of the talus basin, dipping to within a half kilometer of the access shaft. At times the heat was so intense that John felt his Mjolnir's climate-control system kick in to keep him at the optimal performance temperature.

And through it all, the muck continued to shoot out of the access shaft, arcing over the talus basin to feed the growing slurry dump behind the boulder wall. Whatever the enemy was doing down there, it was determined to see it through. But so was Blue Team, and now that the UNSC had seized control of Rejtett Valley, the time had come to take over the Keepers' shaft-clearing operation.

John switched to TEAMCOM. "Phase Three."

He pulled a control transmitter from his electronics pouch and disengaged the safety override, then depressed the activation pad.

"Engaging mines."

"Preparing secondary charges," Linda said. She tapped her own control transmitter and slipped it back into her pouch. "Concussion activation, five-, ten-, and thirty-minute delays."

"Confirmed," John said, starting back down the slope. "Let's move."

When Blue Team started across the talus basin, the Keepers *would* spot them. Realizing they had been lured out of position by the landing at the compound, the commander would almost certainly send a detachment back to defend the access shaft.

To make sure that detachment never arrived, the Spartans had buried a field of Lotus antitank mines near the mouth of Koldus Canyon and placed enhanced-gelignite charges on some cliffs a little farther up the route.

With a squadron of Longswords above them, the trap was probably overkill. But Blue Team hadn't known about the Longswords when they were making their preparations. And in explosive situations like this, overkill was always welcome.

John and Linda caught up to the rest of the team near the end of the gulch. Major Van Houte and Chief Mukai were waiting behind a bend with the excavation machines. Fred and Kelly were kneeling at the edge of the basin, their passive camouflage packages engaged. John activated his own and joined them, leaving Linda to watch their back-trail.

The near side of the basin was pocked with strike craters and littered here and there with alien bodies. But most of the Keepers had been up on the flats when the fighting started and were now on their way through Koldus Canyon.

The scenario on the opposite side of the basin was different. It appeared that at least a few of the Gray Guards had survived the Longsword strikes and made it over the rim, because there was so much smoke rising from that area of the basin that it looked like a fogbank had rolled in. John opened a magnification window and saw that in places the sandstone boulders had been reduced to just sand—and the ordnance was continuing to fall.

But dozens of the Brute jumpers had cleared the bombing zone and were continuing to work their way toward the access shaft, now braving Broadsword strafing runs as they scurried from boulder to boulder. John had his onboard computer begin a count of still-advancing Jiralhanae and quickly reached fifty. If even half that number survived to set up a perimeter defense around the shaft, it could take Blue Team an hour to eliminate them—even with close air support.

And John was beginning to think they didn't have that long.

The geyser was changing. The slurry was no longer arcing into the dump in a steady flow. Instead, there would be nothing for a few seconds, then a brief surge of gravel and stone, then nothing again for a few more seconds. It seemed like the workers down in the shaft were running low on muck. Worse, the material was beginning to look drier, as though it was no longer coming from the bottom of a mud-filled sump.

Possibly an entry tunnel leading into CASTLE Base.

Other than the Gray Guards approaching from the opposite side of the basin, the only obvious hostiles were the Kig-Yar and Unggoy still manning the pirate lift. There was always the possibility of a small force hiding somewhere in ambush, but that strategy required knowing the target's route, and given the jumble of stone below, John doubted that even Mukai knew how she was going to get the bulky excavation machines to the access shaft.

"Blue Three will stay with *Special* Crew to defend the excavation machines and assist with route clearing." John was speaking over TEAMCOM. "Blue Two and Blue Leader will advance on the access shaft at top speed—and deny those jumpers any chance to defend it. Blue Four will accompany us until she's in range to begin offensive operations. Questions?"

When nobody had any, John checked his weapons and equipment, then disengaged his passive camouflage unit. Once everyone's status LEDs had turned green, he gave the order to execute and led the way down into the talus basin.

Their gulch cut through the rim about five hundred meters above the basin floor, making for a steep descent. Given that it had rained that morning, the lechatelierite slopes were not as slippery as he had expected—perhaps because the sand granules in the mountains were angular enough to provide traction rather than deny it.

Even had they wanted to, there was no way to hide the excavation machines as they advanced toward the shaft. But Blue Team had unchallenged air superiority over the entire basin, so John didn't even attempt a concealed approach. He simply sprang from stone to stone and boulder to boulder, relying on extreme range and his erratic changes of direction to protect him from any hand-carried artillery. And his leg injury wasn't even throbbing. He covered the first kilometer in two minutes, taking no hostile fire at all.

It didn't take the Gray Guards long to see Blue Team coming. They began to spend less time moving behind cover and more dodging through the open, some even risking short jump-jet hops. John saw twelve Jiralhanae go down in half as many seconds. But they were also more willing to exchange fire, and a trio managed to score shock rifle hits on a low-flying Broadsword. The EMP took down its shielding, and the electrolasers gouged long slashes through both wings and the skin of its fuselage. The wounded craft pulled up early and wobbled out of sight over the basin rim.

By then John had closed to within a kilometer of the shaft, with Fred advancing on his right flank and Linda on the left. But the surviving Gray Guards were even closer, no more than five hundred meters from their side. He estimated their number at thirty, though their sporadic movements into and out of cover made it hard to be certain.

The operators of the surface lift abandoned their workstations at the sight of the Spartans, and rushed to set a defensive line to screen their equipment. As before, there were only ten of them—three Kig-Yar and seven Unggoy, all armed with plasma pistols. John marked them for Linda to eliminate and continued toward the shaft.

A surge of stone and gravel rose from the access shaft and hovered above it for a moment, then reversed direction and sank slowly back the way it had come. John didn't know whether the reversal was prompted by Blue Team's imminent arrival, or whether the Keepers below had finished their excavation. Either way, it wasn't a good sign.

He and Fred were five hundred meters from the shaft now, but Linda had dropped off to set up her SRS99-S5. The Gray Guards opposite them were less than three hundred meters from their side of the shaft, which meant in range of beam and shock rifles. Knowing the talus would make it almost impossible to spot a marksman preparing to open fire, John and Fred stooped down, using boulders for cover whenever possible.

Linda's sniper rifle boomed four times, taking out the three Kig-Yar in front of the pirate lift and igniting a Grunt methane tank. The rest of the Unggoy abandoned their positions and fled.

Unggoy were smarter than they looked.

More than could be said about the Gray Guards. They were only a hundred meters from the shaft now, but ten of them had practically crushed their jump-jet controls and were fifty meters in the air, scattering toward the north side of the shaft. John wasn't sure what they were trying to do—maybe flank Blue Team, or follow the Unggoy's example and withdraw?—but they were all rising on steep trajectories that were going to keep them off the ground for several seconds.

The Broadswords instantly swept in, swinging behind the jumpers and opening up with their ALI-35s.

Then the rest of the Gray Guards hit their thrusters, launching themselves in low trajectories straight at the shaft. It was a classic sacrifice-diversion beautifully executed, using part of their number to pull the Broadswords out of position so the rest of the force could maneuver. At first John thought the jumpers were moving up to establish a defensive perimeter around the shaft, and would use their next jump to cross it.

He couldn't have been more wrong.

By the time the Gray Guards touched down, John and Fred were a hundred meters from the rim. Both were on their knees behind boulders, aiming their MA40s at the apex of the lowest arc the Jiralhanae could use to cross the shaft. The Broadswords were over the north side of the basin, wheeling around to start a return pass that would put them on target as the jumpers tried to cross. Linda's sniper rifle was already booming as she fired across the shaft, using two rounds per target—the first to overload the shields, the second to punch through the armor and kill the target. She put two warriors down before they had taken ten steps.

But these were all jet-jumpers—they should have been back in the air after only a few steps. And they weren't.

John thought perhaps they wanted to be closer before launching into their next bound. It was a big shaft—so large that the last time he had been here, he'd been riding in a Covenant dropship that had flown straight down it. If the enemy jumped too early, they might not make it all the way across.

He held his fire, waiting to catch them in the air, where they wouldn't be able to dodge behind boulders.

Linda opened fire again and killed two more jumpers.

The rest stayed on the ground, sprinting forward, covering the last twenty meters in two seconds. The first Broadsword let loose, filling the air above the shaft with 35mm rounds.

The Gray Guards weren't there.

They were now leaping *into* the shaft, using their jump-jets to push them toward the gravity field in the center. So much for *that* part of the plan.

John dropped his aim and blasted away at the descending jumpers, his rounds deflecting off flashing shields as the Jiralhanae plunged into the darkness below.

# CHAPTER TWENTY

John jumped first, leaping into the shaft chest-down so he could watch for enemy plasma fire rising out of the impregnable darkness. The nanobraided titanium cable clipped to the back of his Mjolnir went taut almost instantly, and his forward momentum faded as the winch-resistance kicked in. He dropped ten meters, simultaneously swinging back toward the shaft wall. He hit feet-first and sprang back toward the pirate lift's gravity field in the center of the shaft, dragging another ten meters of cable off the spool, and dropped another ten meters—before the winch-resistance brought him back toward the wall again.

It was called fast-winching, and it was John's least-favorite method of tactical descent. Instead of controlling his own rate of drop, a soldier had to rely on a winch operator, which created an opportunity for missed signals. But it sure beat flat-out falling, and it was a good alternative to dangling a rappel line down on an enemy's head.

John was in the middle rig, with Linda fast-winching twenty meters to his left and Fred twenty meters to his right. Even with Kelly still on the surface protecting *Special* Crew and the winches proper, that spacing was a lot tighter than he would have liked.

But geometry was an implacable foe. Measuring forty meters across, the shaft had a circumference of just over a hundred and twenty-five meters. If they spaced themselves any farther apart, the two Spartans on the ends would be in each other's field of fire.

As they continued to descend, the darkness grew more enshrouding, wrapping them in a veil of grays and purples. John's onboard computer was tracking their progress by counting the number of ten-meter bounds. His HUD showed they had already dropped two hundred meters.

*Already?*

CASTLE Base was two kilometers down, and John still saw no hint of Keeper operations below. He didn't know whether that was worrisome—or whether the darkness meant anything at all. Eighteen hundred meters was a long drop. Even if the entire floor of the shaft was lit up as bright as day, from so far above, the glow would be smaller than the point of a needle. John wouldn't see it with his naked eye, and he wasn't sure his helmet optics would be able to detect it either.

His onboard computer confirmed it would not.

They dropped through four hundred meters, and the blackness swallowed them completely. John could no longer see the Pilum rocket launcher in his own hands, and when he craned his neck, the daylight spilling down from the collar of the shaft had disappeared.

John activated his dual-mode night-vision system. Earlier, while Chief Mukai was setting up the fast-winches, John and the other Spartans had compared battle vids. At least thirteen Gray Guards had jumped into the shaft twenty minutes earlier, at the end of the fire-fight, to take it.

In all likelihood, the Keepers already at the bottom had adjusted the pirate lift's gravity field to catch and gently lower the Gray Guards to the bottom. Now those same Jiralhanae would be down there with an unknown number of Keepers, all ready to pounce.

John had no intention of making it easy on them by activating his helmet lamp. Blue Team would be fighting strictly NVS, and maybe that would give them the tactical advantage they needed to win.

Maybe.

Those Gray Guards were definitely trouble. Ferocious, disciplined, willing to make tactical sacrifices. Not the qualities John liked to see in his Jiralhanae foes. That was the reason he was carrying a Pilum instead of his MA40, and why Fred had his SPNKr and Linda had her SRS99-S5. The three Spartans needed weapons capable of punching through energy-shielded power armor in one or two strikes.

They passed six hundred meters in depth, then eight hundred. The pirate lift's gravity field was just visible in John's NVS, a column of purple radiance so faint it almost seemed imaginary. The walls of the shaft were purple as well, but brighter and more substantial, shifting to red as the team descended deeper into the planet's bowels and the stone grew warmer.

At a thousand meters, there was still no hint of the enemy below, and John began to readjust his thinking. In theory, there were work crews and equipment down there emitting a lot of waste heat. At the least, his thermal optics should have been picking up a pinpoint of infrared radiance. A gravity field didn't always radiate in visible wavelengths, but the emitter pad from which it issued usually did so brightly.

"Be alert," John said over TEAMCOM. "We should be seeing *something* by now, and we're not."

"A sniper ambush?" Linda asked.

"That's one possibility," John said. When he returned to the wall and sprang off again, he began to vary the angle of his launch, doing what he could to make himself a difficult target. "We should be in range of their shock and beam rifles by now."

"What's the other possibility?" Fred asked.

"That they're already *in* CASTLE Base."

"No," Fred said. "I mean the *other* other possibility."

"I was saving that for last," John said. They were passing twelve hundred meters, still with no activity below, so he and Fred were likely coming to the same conclusion—the one they had discussed during the Pelican ride into the Highland Mountains. "Because if you're thinking what I suspect you are, you could be right."

"Yup. If I was wrong, we'd be seeing a purple glow by now," Fred said. "Those pirate lifts are powerful."

"Might I inquire what Blue Two could be right *about*?" Kelly asked. She was still on the surface, about ten meters back from the shaft edge, operating John's winch. But there was a comm repeater on the rim, so everyone on the team had full communication. "That's not something I'd want to miss."

"The Keepers," John said. "It's beginning to look like we can stop making the prudent assumption. Whatever they're after, I don't think it's in CASTLE Base."

"Then why did they follow us across Arany Basin?" Major Van Houte asked. He was on Fred's winch. "And why would they care if *we* reach it?"

"Wish I knew," John replied. "But if we're not seeing any light at CASTLE Base level, then the Keepers must be interested in something *below* CASTLE Base."

"There is no *must be*," Linda said. "It is so. My rangefinder has found the shaft floor. Two thousand meters. From *here*."

That put the shaft bottom far lower than anticipated—a full eight hundred meters below the entrance to CASTLE Base. No way the Keepers had accidentally overexcavated by that much.

"They're going to the installation," Fred said. "Goddamn. They've been going to the installation the whole time."

The very same Forerunner installation that the Covenant had seized seven years ago—the one they had removed the top of Menachite Mountain to reach. The one where Dr. Halsey had captured the slipspace crystal the aliens had been trying to recover.

"Yeah," John said. "Any guesses what they're after? You and Blue Three know that place a lot better than I do."

"Do I *look* like I'm Dr. Halsey?" Fred replied. "Let's just assume it's bad."

"Bad enough to change *our* mission?" Without bothering to wait for an answer, Linda said, "The assets are still our only priorities. Whatever the Keepers are doing, it is status incidental."

Linda was noting the situation mattered only to the extent that it impacted the mission. Action could be taken to prevent the Keepers from interfering, or to collect intelligence, but any other involvement with them was to be avoided.

"Acknowledged," John said.

Fifteen hundred meters down.

About five hundred meters below and directly opposite him, John's NVS showed a tiny arch of blackness in the shaft's curving maroon wall.

The entrance to CASTLE Base.

"We'll gather any intelligence we come across," John continued. "But right now, only one thing matters about the Keepers."

"We still need their pirate lift?" Fred asked.

"Right," John said. "We carry on as before, no matter what they're up to."

"There's just one problem with that," Chief Mukai said. She was on the surface with Kelly and Van Houte, operating Linda's winch. "Blue Four's rangefinder marked the shaft floor at another two thousand meters, when you were already at eight hundred."

"I'm not seeing the problem," John said.

"The shaft is twenty-eight hundred meters deep," Mukai continued. "The winch spools only have twenty-five hundred meters of cable. So, you're—"

"Three hundred meters short," John finished.

Between their Mjolnir's energy shields and hydrostatic gel layer, the Spartans could probably survive a three-hundred-meter fall. But the gel would overpressurize to protect them from the impact, and after they hit, they would be immobilized for a few seconds until it depressurized. With their shields down, they would be, almost literally, sitting ducks.

"Problem acknowledged," John said. "We'll find a way."

He was still fast-winching down the shaft, bounding off the wall at different angles, when his NVS infrared showed a trio of bulky red figures lurking in the dark arch of the CASTLE Base tunnel.

"Blue Three, slow winch," John said over TEAMCOM. "Engage enemy."

Fred and Linda were already firing, Nornfang booming to his left, the SPNKr flashing on his right. John did a pendulum-traverse, trying to run across the wall sideways to avoid firing through the gravity field and having his Pilum missile deflected.

By the time he was clear, Linda had downed one of the figures. Then his NVS went white as Fred's rocket detonated inside the tunnel mouth. Unable to designate his target, John held his fire and started across the wall in the other direction, his rate of descent now considerably slowed as Kelly increased the winch resistance.

As the blast flash drained from his faceplate, John saw a plasma incendiary arc out of the tunnel mouth toward him—then deflect upward as it crossed the gravity field.

The incendiary splashed against the wall above—he couldn't see exactly where, because he was rigged to look *down* the shaft—but it must have been close. His shields flickered blue, and white cinders of plasma rained past all around.

Then John was following the cinders, his stomach floating as he plunged into the darkness.

"*Blue Leader?*" Even over TEAMCOM, Kelly's alarm was obvious. "John?"

He was too busy trying to save himself to answer. Some of the plasma incendiary must have hit his cable and burned through the nanobraided titanium. Now he was running *down* the wall, trying to keep his feet under him so he didn't lose attitude control and go into a tumble.

After three steps—or maybe it was eight, who could tell at this point?—John finally felt his left boot land flat enough to generate some power. Still falling, he launched himself toward the gravity field.

His half-healed thigh felt like it had taken a Vulcan round, but the myosin mesh holding his quadriceps together did its job. He angled down through fifteen meters of darkness and slid into the pale gravity field in good position, belly down and body flat. His eyes bulged and his organs sank as he decelerated, but the pressure eased a heartbeat later.

Then John was half floating, watching the shaft walls drift upward as he continued to descend, now far more slowly. He could hear Fred and Linda not-quite-yelling on TEAMCOM, but the gravity field interfered with the comm waves, and the conversation was too broken up to follow—or join.

Besides, John was descending past the entrance to CASTLE Base. He could see the remains of the Jiralhanae ambush team splattered around the tunnel mouth, strewn across the floor and hanging from the walls and ceiling. But there was a large figure in power armor rising out of the rubble in back, moving forward to engage.

John brought his Pilum up to fire, but he was still floating, and the motion spun him away from his target. By the time he swung his left arm around to counter the spin, he had already descended past the tunnel floor and could no longer see the threat. He'd have to do this the hard way.

Carefully, John pointed his left hand and fired the grappleshot on his forearm. The grappling hook disappeared into the tunnel mouth, arcing over the bottom edge. As he continued to sink, the line began to feed back toward him. He feared the grapple wasn't going to catch—then his arm jerked upward, pulling him upright and out of the gravity field.

John swung through the darkness and slammed into the shaft

wall, a HOSTILE symbol already appearing on his motion tracker. It was almost atop his own position, blinking blue to indicate it was directly above him.

John could have guessed that. He raised the Pilum one-handed and laid the launching tube alongside the wall. A massive Jiralhanae hand reached over the lip of the tunnel floor, following the grapple-shot line downward. John fired the first missile, his faceplate going white as the propellant burned the darkness from the shaft.

No detonation. A moment later, as the white drained from his night vision again, he saw the Jiralhanae's other hand snaking over the lip holding a flat-faced spike revolver, swinging the square barrel toward John's grappler line. More or less. It was hard to aim at what you weren't looking at.

John held his own fire. Sooner or later, the Jiralhanae would *have* to slip up and look at what he was trying to kill.

A trio of finger-length spikes shot from the revolver's muzzle, missing to either side of the line, bouncing off the wall and vanishing into eight hundred meters of darkness. Whatever they hit at the bottom, there wouldn't be much of it left.

Kelly's voice sounded over TEAMCOM. "Blue Leader, what the *blazing hell*?" Clearly his Pilum missile had exited the top of the shaft. "Status?"

John flashed green, but said nothing and kept his eye on the shooter's pistol barrel, ready to move if the muzzle dropped any farther toward him.

Instead, a Jiralhanae helmet pushed into view, first its decorative brow vanes showing cool blue in the light-gathering mode of John's NVS, then the ridge along the crown gleaming green. The NVS switched to infrared as the brow panel glowed dull yellow; then—finally—came the eyes, burning a bright, angry red.

John fired the second Pilum directly into the right one.

The shockwave snapped his own head back, and he felt the heat of the blast through the titanium shell of his helmet. His faceplate went white, again, and then he was falling, again—dropping feet-first along the shaft wall, Kelly's alarmed voice sounding in his ears.

"Blue Leader, status?" she demanded. "And I want more than a flash this time."

John flashed amber, but said nothing. He was too busy fighting to recover attitude control. Something heavy clunked against his helmet and nearly sent him cartwheeling. He carefully extended his arm—and the Pilum—and brought himself back under control. The blast flash had faded from his faceplate, and he saw that he was caught inside a shower of rocks and helmet pieces, all of it glowing bright red in his NVS.

Fred and Linda were now a couple of hundred meters below, still fast-winching down the opposite side of the gravity field, firing SPNKr rockets and M232 armor-piercing rounds into the darkness at the bottom of the shaft. John assessed their target and saw a pinpoint of bright purple light ringed by thread-thin streaks of blue and white—the gravity lift, surrounded by its defenders, Keepers of the One Freedom launching plasma incendiaries and firing electrolasers.

"That's it," Kelly announced. "I'm coming down."

"Acknowledged," John said. How far it was to the bottom of the shaft now, he had no idea—but it didn't seem nearly far enough. "And make it fast."

Thanks to his cadet jump-training days, John knew terminal velocity for an object with the mass of a Spartan in Mjolnir armor on Reach was about a hundred and fifty meters per second. Which meant he had about five seconds before taking out a bunch of Keepers the hard way.

No time to screw around stabilizing his free-fall position. He brought his empty Pilum to port-arms and pulled his legs up toward his chest, falling even faster now, Fred and Linda flashing past on the other side of the gravity field, dangling from their winch lines like spiders on threads.

"Oh, damn," Fred said on TEAMCOM. "Not now—not *here*."

"No, not here," John answered. "And not yet."

He threw his head forward, rolling himself out of a feet-first vertical fall into a facedown horizontal drop, then stomp-kicked the shaft wall, launching himself back across the darkness toward the gravity field.

When John reentered the field, he decelerated even harder than before, his heart crashing down into his sternum and his tongue pushing forward between his teeth. By now he was so close to the bottom of the shaft that the pirate lift appeared as large as his palm. It was protected by a handful of Gray Guards and a bunch of Keepers, all still distant and tiny, but illuminated brightly enough in the gravity pad's violet glow that he could make out the weapons they were holding.

Far too many shock rifles and plasma incendiary launchers.

The amount of discernible detail suggested he was around three hundred meters above them—right at the maximum fast-winching depth. And most of the aliens seemed to be focused on Fred and Linda, who had been raining death on their heads for more than a few seconds.

The Gray Guards hit their jump-jets, trying to charge the Spartan attackers by flying up the shaft, but it was a poor strategy. Fred put an M19 rocket into the leader's chest, creating a fireball that the others had to maneuver past, and Linda took out two more by putting her rounds through their propellant packs. The rest retreated to the shaft floor.

When Fred used his second rocket to send several Kig-Yar flying across the shaft floor, John engaged his passive camouflage unit and held his fire. If he could get close enough before the enemy noticed him in the grav field, he could drop into their midst without having to worry about a gel lockdown—and keep them occupied long enough for Fred and Linda to down-climb the shaft walls.

Or something like that.

John confirmed that the M7 submachine gun was still on its mag-mount, but was unable to perform a weapons check. While he couldn't distinguish the aliens' facial features yet, he could see their arms, and even their hands when an arm moved away from the body. Two hundred meters. He was descending on them from the dark. Still, sooner or later, he *would* be illuminated by the lift pad's purple glow.

And when that happened, the Keepers would realize that the Gray Guards they'd left higher up at CASTLE Base weren't going to be jumping into the gravity field. They would try to shut down the lift, letting John free-fall the rest of the way. He would need to keep them away from the controls, and have the Pilum reloaded.

Fred dropped another SPNKr round on the heads of three Sangheili, while Linda downed two Jiralhanae Keepers. Only three Gray Guards and seven Keepers remaining, and John was pretty confident of that count, since they were all running for cover, either behind the gravity lift's legs or among the boulders resting against the wall at the base of the shaft.

Fred's voice came over TEAMCOM. "No more cable. End of the line."

"Hang tight," John said. "I'm working on something. Just keep their attention."

"Affirmative," Fred said. "But it could be with rocks. I'm down to my last set of tubes."

"Save 'em for when you can make it count," John said. "All I need is to keep them looking your way."

"That, we can arrange," Linda said.

Her sniper rifle boomed twice, and a Jiralhanae Keeper slumped over the boulder he was hidden behind.

But the aliens had their own plan. Instead of using the rocks for cover, the last six Jiralhanae—three Keepers and three Gray Guards—grabbed man-sized boulders, charging back toward the gravity lift. They were covered by a trio of Kig-Yar firing beam rifles from behind one of the lift's massive support legs—right where the controls were located. John didn't have a shot on the Kig-Yar—at least not one that didn't risk destroying the controls.

And Blue Team wasn't trying to capture the pirate lift just for the hell of it—they needed those controls intact.

"Change of plan," John said. Still in the grav field, he was close enough now to see individual faces, around a hundred meters. "Linda, take out the Kig-Yar riflemen. Fred, the Brutes."

Fred's SPNKr roared, and a rocket dropped down from the darkness, taking the first Gray Guard in the flank. Linda's rifle boomed, and a Kig-Yar head came apart in a spray of blood and bone. John was dropping into the purple glow of the lift pad now, so he wasn't going to remain hidden much longer—especially not with five Jiralhanae rushing to board the gravity lift.

There were two Gray Guards left. John targeted the one in front and fired—only to see the missile deflect as it crossed out of the gravity field. It punched into the wall and blew mud and gravel across the floor. He corrected and fired again, this time catching his target just as he was raising the boulder he carried to shield himself. The round's shaped charge punched through the stone and sent a jet of superheated gore shooting through the backplate of the guard's armor.

No sooner had the charge landed than John's stomach sank hard, and the lift pad began to recede below him. The surviving Jiralhanae—one Gray Guard and three Keepers—dumped their boulders onto the lift pad and, as the boulders began to rise toward John, climbed into the gravity field under them.

"Hostiles coming up!" John shouted. "With their own cover!"

He started to reload the Pilum—then realized that with the enemy on their way up, now was the perfect time for him to head *down*. It was crazy, but no worse than what Lieutenant Chapov had done taking them up Black Iron Gorge.

And John had his Mjolnir armor.

He slapped the rocket launcher onto a magmount and took a grenade in each hand, then threw himself into a somersault position, tumbling toward the edge of the gravity field. On his first roll, he glimpsed two plasma incendiaries and a pair of electrolaser bolts shooting up from between the rising boulders.

The electrolasers hit almost simultaneously, the double EMP burst taking down his shields in a microsecond. The first plasma incendiary shot past harmlessly, but the second glanced off his right knee and burst.

Most of the incendiary sprayed back into the gravity field where John had been a moment before, but part of it had impacted his armor, charring it so badly that white hot cinders flaked off his greave onto his sabaton. He heard metal popping and sizzling as the incendiary's heat melted through the Mjolnir's titanium-alloy shell, then felt the burn blisters rising on his shin and foot. But there was no time for damage assessment, because when he went into his next roll, he left the gravity field and felt himself fully plunging.

"Advancing!" John said into TEAMCOM. He thumbed the grenade fuses and tossed them toward the boulders at the base of the shaft. "Cover!"

"Cover in ten!" Kelly responded. "You just came into view."

John doubted that this battle was going to last another ten seconds, but no sooner had Kelly spoken than he rolled through his second somersault and realized she would be the only help coming. The Gray Guard and his three Keeper companions were ascending fast, using their floating boulder field as cover while they launched plasma incendiaries and electrolaser bolts toward Fred and Linda. The two Spartans were returning fire as best they could, but it was a lot harder to account for gravity deflection while firing into the field at a target under cover than it was firing back out at a target hanging from a thread.

John grabbed the M7 submachine gun off its magmount, but by the time he was ready to fire, the lift was already a hundred meters above him. The Gray Guard hit his jetpack thrusters and moved to the edge of the gravity field, where he would have a better angle of fire, and launched a plasma incendiary toward Fred.

Impact alarms started to chime inside John's helmet. He laid the M7 on a torso mount and tucked his chin to his chest, then slapped out—just as he had learned to do in his hand-to-hand combat training here on Reach, all those years ago—driving his palms and forearms down onto the stone . . . twisting his hips ever so slightly, so his left thigh came down on its outer side and the sole of his right foot landed flat on the ground . . . spreading out the force of the impact along as much of his body as possible.

Despite everything, it still felt like he'd been hit by a speeding Warthog.

And the gel lockdown only made it worse, squeezing John as tight as a pressure forge, holding every muscle rigid, every joint immobile. His ribs ached and his internal organs felt like they'd been compressed into a specimen jar. He couldn't even breathe. All John could do was lie there waiting for the pressure to bleed off, staring up the shaft into the gravity field . . . where he could barely make out two tiny streams of electrolaser dashes flashing through the darkness toward Linda's position. Her SRS99-S5 cracked twice, and then there was only one stream.

At the edge of the gravity field, a tiny figure was dangling beneath the fast-rising hulk of a Jiralhanae. John opened a magnification window and saw it was Fred, hanging five meters beneath the last Gray Guard and rising fast. The Guard had dropped his plasma launcher and was digging at his collar with both hands, trying in vain to free himself from the grappleshot line Fred had looped around his throat.

As Fred drew even with the Jiralhanae's feet, he pulled a combat knife from his shoulder sheath. He reared back and, once he could reach high enough, drove the blade into the back of the Jiralhanae's neck.

John didn't see what happened next, because a hostile appeared on his motion detector, approaching from the direction of the pirate lift. The lockdown pressure was still bleeding off—releasing it instantly would cause nitrogen embolisms—but he could actually breathe again. Another couple of seconds, and he'd be able to defend himself.

He shifted his gaze toward the approaching hostile and found a ragged Kig-Yar limping toward him from the gravity lift, while a second Kig-Yar covered him from the operator's station. The limper's armor was shredded, with blood oozing from half a dozen shrapnel wounds, and the quills on the back of his head had been seared to stumps. He carried a carbine in one hand, which he kept pointed at John as he approached.

"How you know?" His speech was passable—certainly better than John attempting Kig-Yar. "It was the humans, yes? Tell Toati now, he save you."

"Humans?" John could talk now—and it wouldn't be long before he could do more than that. "Know *what*?"

"Nasty demon."

Toati circled around John's feet, then kicked him in his plasma-burned greave—and the whole leg moved. So did John's hips, when he rolled them to check his range of motion.

The Kig-Yar pointed the carbine at John's knee. "Maybe you answer after Toati blow leg off."

"I don't think so."

John swept his leg into Toati's ankles, at the same time bringing his other leg up in a roundhouse kick that folded the Kig-Yar in two and launched him into the wall. It probably wasn't necessary, but John snatched the M7 off his torso mount and ran a burst up Toati's centerline.

A whistle sounded somewhere behind him—maybe Toati's partner squawking in alarm as he prepared to fire. John rolled back toward the gravity lift—

The *boom* of a shotgun blast, and the second Kig-Yar flew out from behind the operator's station and dropped to the muddy floor, a massive crater in his chest where an eight-gauge slug had punched through his armor.

"Blue Three, that you?" When Kelly's status LED flashed green, John did a quick scan for other threats, then asked, "Blue Two, Blue Four, status?"

Both flashed green; then Fred said, "A few scrapes and burns, all threats eliminated. But I just passed CASTLE Base, and I'm still going up."

"We'll take care of that ASAP," John said. "Blue Four?"

"I have no problems that can't be repaired," Linda said. "Request help descending. I am in no mood for lockdown."

"Acknowledged," John said. "Wait there. We'll use the lift."

He rose and looked across the pad of the gravity lift to where Kelly was still dangling from a fast-winch line, her body only two meters above the floor. Her armor was a little muddy, but otherwise she looked none the worse for wear.

"Thanks for the cover," he said.

"Thank you for the diversion," Kelly said. "He was so busy watching you, I had to whistle for his attention."

"Glad to be of service," John said. He pointed at the nanobraided titanium cable from which she was hanging. "I thought the spools only had—"

"Sheet bend," Kelly said. "After your *I'd rather fly* trick, we had some spare cable."

"Mukai?" John asked.

"Who else?" Mukai replied. They were speaking over TEAM-COM, so she and Van Houte were able to hear the whole conversation. "You have a problem with that?"

"Not at all," John said. Nanobraided titanium cable was supposed to be microspliced, not joined with knots, but John wasn't about to tell the crew chief how to do her job. "It worked."

"Glad you agree." As Mukai spoke, Kelly began to descend the last two meters to the shaft floor. "Now, if you're done playing with the aliens down there, we have a job to do."

"Acknowledged."

John activated his helmet lamps and circled around the gravity lift toward Kelly, limping slightly on both legs, his right shin and foot in searing agony despite the biofoam injections, his left quadriceps cramping so hard he wondered if the myosin mesh had come loose. Still, he was in better shape than the enemy. The shaft floor was a morass of mud, blood, and body parts—essentially a massive, gore-filled sump.

But when John ran his helmet lamps over the packed-mud walls, he could still discern hints of the ancient Forerunner installation he had seen once before, when he dropped in to rescue Dr. Halsey and her companions seven years earlier. The soaring arches and looming balconies—they were all still there, just packed like fossils into the untold tons of mud and gravel that had since washed down into the shaft.

And buried somewhere beneath all that rubble was something the Keepers desperately wanted—something worth working with the Banished to acquire. Certainly that Kig-Yar, Toati, had hinted as much. John couldn't even begin to imagine what it might be. UNSC intelligence had noted that both factions were enamored of Forerunner technology, but for different reasons. The Keepers valued it solely for religious reasons—becoming one with the Forerunners. The Banished just wanted the power and wealth it brought.

What could they be looking for that served *both* purposes?

And why *now*?

After the fall of Reach, the Covenant had been in sole control of this world and certainly had ample time to strip the underground installation of any Forerunner artifacts. What could they possibly have left behind that would justify the effort that both the Keepers and the Banished were putting into recovering it?

John couldn't afford to dwell on it any longer. Not now, when so much else was at stake. This was a mystery Blue Team had not been assigned to solve, and one they had no time to investigate. The best he could do was record what he was seeing—and let what currently remained of the Office of Naval Intelligence worry about it later.

So when John happened across a freshly excavated passage running northward from the shaft, he took note of it solely as a liability to be secured and paused only long enough to peer inside. Large enough for the Jiralhanae to walk down comfortably, the passage appeared to be many hundreds of meters long, running as straight as an arrow until it vanished into the gloom. No doubt that was where the rest of the Keepers had gone, and steps would have to be taken to make sure they didn't return to interrupt Blue Team's primary mission.

John stepped inside the tunnel and listened. It was quiet, but maybe . . . just *maybe* . . . he could hear voices murmuring at the far end.

Kelly's voice came over TEAMCOM. "Ready when you are, Blue Leader. I could use an observer."

John came out of the tunnel to find Kelly already standing on the pirate lift operator's platform, her hands inside the holographic control columns. Over the decades, Blue Team had learned to operate a lot of different kinds of Covenant equipment, including various types of gravity lifts. Kelly's body posture projected the confidence of being able to use the pirate lift as well—which was a good thing, because that was how John intended to lower the excavation machines to CASTLE Base level.

"On my way." John put his M7 on a magmount, then started to weave toward her, past dozens of alien corpses and rocket craters. "Let's finish the damn mission."

# CHAPTER TWENTY-ONE

The fighting was done. At least, John hoped it was, because Blue Team was down to a 52 percent effectiveness rating. He had ported so much painkiller into his legs that it felt like he had a pair of stumps hanging off the LHD seat. Fred had lost his shields, his HUD, his weapon sync targeting system, and his magmounts to electrolaser EMP bursts. Linda had lost her long-range optics and had half her helmet melted by an incendiary round. She had some singed hair and second-degree burns where the heat had been too great, but the incendiary hadn't gone all the way through, and she would be fine with a little medical attention. Nornfang was also going to need a lot of TLC before she made any two-kilometer shots with it again.

Only Kelly was above 80 percent functionality, which was why she was the one on foot, standing in an open doorway using a telescoping long-bar to knock down loose concrete and rock from what used to be the ceiling of Dr. Catherine Halsey's office-and-laboratory suite.

After capturing the Keepers' pirate lift, Blue Team had moved it into place below the CASTLE Base entrance and utilized it to lower the excavation machines. By the time they accomplished that, they had an ODST support company assigned to discourage any interference. The Keepers and Banished had left them alone, but even so, it had taken four hours of drilling, blasting, and mucking to clear the half-kilometer tunnel and maze of corridors leading into Omega Wing. Now they just had to get to Halsey's ultrasecret vault, which was hidden inside an incubation cabinet on the opposite side of what used to be a two-room suite—now a tangle of beams sagging beneath a billion-ton jumble of boulders and broken concrete. John had the feeling that if they moved the wrong piece, it would all come crashing down on them. He lowered the LHD's bucket onto the floor and shut off the engine.

Kelly stopped her work and looked back toward the LHD, her helmet cocked to one side. John motioned for her to lower the long-bar.

"Stand down."

He climbed out of the LHD seat. After giving his numbed legs a moment to steady, he stepped into the doorway beside her and looked back up the corridor toward the drilling jumbo.

"You too, Blue Four. Turn it off."

Linda obeyed, then stepped off the operator's platform. The headlamps on the left side of her helmet had been melted along with its outer layer of titanium alloy, so she looked a bit ghoulish as she approached through the darkness.

"You're thinking it will be safer to clear by hand?" Kelly asked.

"Negative," John said. "I'm thinking it might be safer to not clear it at all."

Linda came up and stood with John and Kelly in the doorway, staring into the wreckage. In the tunnel, the boulders and rubble had been packed as tight as a brick wall. Here, the fallen beams had created a maze of rubble pockets and triangular tunnels. There was no guarantee that the maze would connect to the incubation cabinet hiding the entrance to Dr. Halsey's secret vault—but there was no guarantee that it didn't either. And it was about time for something to go right on this mission.

John refused to believe that after all they'd been through since arriving on Reach—since coming home—his luck had simply run out.

So they all just stood in place, seeking a visual on a route through the outer office and into the circular lab room where Halsey had done so much of her thinking and experimenting.

The trio of Spartans were the only ones actually inside the ruins of CASTLE Base. The rest of the team was performing support operations, Mukai operating the pirate lift at the bottom of the shaft, and Major Van Houte operating the supplemental lift up on the surface. Fred was on patrol inside the Keeper tunnel that ran deeper into the Forerunner installation, hoping to take a prisoner and gather a little intel on the enemy's intentions.

Mukai and Van Houte each had a platoon of ODSTs with them to provide security, but John didn't think the ODSTs would be called on to fight. While Blue Team was busy excavating CASTLE Base, the word had come through on comms that, after some fierce fighting, the UNSC had taken firm control of the entire Rejtett Valley, blocking both ends of Koldus Canyon. To recover possession of the access shaft, the enemy would need to mount a major operation. And by the time they could do *that*, John intended to have completed the mission and be long gone, aboard a Pelican taking them—and the assets Dr. Halsey needed—back to the *Infinity*.

If they could ever get to the assets, that is.

Finally Kelly said, "There. I see it."

She removed all of her weapons and extraneous gear and laid them in the LHD bucket, then checked to make sure she had a full set of spoofers with her. Linda started to do the same, but John waved her off and pointed to her already compromised helmet.

"You're the ready reserve," he said. "If something goes wrong, *then* you come in."

Fred's voice came over TEAMCOM. To maintain contact, they had placed comm repeaters at key locations in the shaft and inside CASTLE Base.

"You want me to pull out and back you up?" he asked. Human voices seldom carried through a Mjolnir helmet, but he was speaking in a hushed tone anyway. It never hurt to be safe. "I'm seven hundred meters into this tunnel. Still haven't seen anything."

"Negative," Kelly said. "We'll have the assets and be on our way out before you get here."

"We will?" John asked.

"Quite confident," Kelly said. "Or we'll be dead. Either way, Fred won't be of much help. No offense."

"You heard the lady, Blue Two." John was already stripping his own weapons and nonessential gear. "And you *know* ONI is going to have a million questions about what the Keepers and the Banished are looking for. Give it another fifteen minutes, then withdraw."

Fred acknowledged the order with a green status flash.

Kelly looked over her shoulder at John. When he nodded, she stepped through the door—and light began to flood from the indirect illumination panels in the walls.

Kelly stopped just across the threshold, her helmet swiveling as if she had just been ambushed and didn't know from where. "*That,* I was not expecting." She turned left and started to crawl up a beam toward a huge granite boulder that had pushed through the concrete ceiling. "But I'll take it."

Now they were down to business. In the initial mission briefing, Dr. Halsey had informed Blue Team that her suite had its own fusion reactor and security system, so the lighting made sense. But it did seem remarkable that the automatic systems were still functioning after being buried for seven years in a damp, dirty environment.

John watched Kelly climb for a moment, both giving her space to move and trying to make sense of her strategy. The five-by-ten-meter office remained full of long shadows and pockets of darkness, but the contrast made it easier to pick out patterns in the wreckage—and he still didn't see what she was trying to do.

As Kelly went higher, the upper end of the beam rocked downward under her weight, and a boulder on the end tipped toward her—until John put a foot on the beam's lower end and pushed it back down.

"Thank you."

Kelly ascended until she was just below the boulder, then stretched out on her belly and started to crawl through a meter-high space that ran diagonally toward the center of the room.

And John finally saw it. About halfway across the room, the path Kelly had selected ended at a block of concrete that was resting in the notch between a pair of crossed beams. Move the block, and it would be a simple matter to drop down under the beams and crawl the rest of the way through the outer office into the lab. He motioned Linda to step on the end of the beam for him, then climbed and caught up to Kelly at the block.

Together they lay on their backs and pushed up on the block, bringing a small avalanche of head-sized stones raining down on their armor. Then John remained holding the block while Kelly slipped into the crawlway below, rising onto her knees and keeping it in place while he followed. After that, it was a mere belly crawl under the beams to the lab.

As they entered, a green glow began to shine through the interstitial spaces to their right. John turned to see a small holographic figure—or, rather, what appeared to be the hem of a small holographic figure's robe—hovering above the corner of a collapsed desk. He tried to push a ragged boulder aside so he could get a better look, but succeeded only in bringing down a cascade of concrete chunks that convinced him to move on.

A few meters later, the glow reappeared on their left. An oval eye with no pupil or lashes stared at him through a thumb-sized tunnel in the rubble.

"We've got company," he said. "I think."

"Company?" Linda asked. "Do you need weapons?"

"Negative," John replied. "It's an avatar . . . I think."

"An *AI* avatar?" Fred said over TEAMCOM. "You sure you don't want me to pull out now?"

Fred's concern was very much warranted. CASTLE Base had been deserted for seven years, and smart AIs almost always went rampant after seven years in service—which was why UNSC regulations called for them to be destroyed as they reached that threshold. Had the protocol been followed for Cortana, Blue Team's current mission would not have been needed . . . and a lot of lives would have been spared.

"I'm sure, Blue Two," John said. "What could you do—shoot it?"

"There is no way it's an AI," Kelly said. "Fred and I were *with* Dr. Halsey when she abandoned CASTLE Base. We *saw* her activate the fail-safe destruction protocol at the same time she initiated the base demolition. Halsey was terrified of her work falling into Covenant hands."

"Then why are we back here on Reach, and nearly getting killed trying to retrieve something she left behind?" Linda asked.

"Fair point," Kelly replied. "It still doesn't mean she would risk leaving an AI where the Covenant could have captured it. And the, um, *items* we're after are different. Perhaps she suspected she might need them one day . . . and knew they would be useless to the Covenant even if they *did* capture them."

"Which she knew *couldn't* happen," John added. "Don't forget the self-destruct protection on this stuff."

"How could I ever?" Kelly asked. She stopped crawling and shined her helmet lamps on the bottom of a black-platinum door that had been anodized with a nanoconductive film. "I do believe this looks like the incubator cabinet she described."

John peered over her shoulder and, just for a moment, saw a pair of eyes with no pupils looking back at him.

"Did you see that?"

"Apparently not," Kelly replied. "Should I be concerned?"

"No idea," John said. "It was the, uh, *whatever* it is. Just two eyes watching us."

Kelly was silent for a moment, then finally said, "Perhaps it was just Halsey's idea of a joke when she worked here. You know how she is."

"Sure . . . a joke. Let's go with that for now."

He rolled onto his back and studied the rubble above them for a moment, then pointed at a sagging I-beam caked with chunks of concrete. On top of it rested a granite boulder the size of a Warthog. What lay atop the boulder was anyone's guess.

"If we can raise that beam high enough to get under, I might be able to squat-press it and buy you enough room to open the door."

"With your leg wounds?" Kelly shook her helmet. "I don't think so."

"It has to be me," John said. "You're the one with the spoofers."

Kelly sighed into her comms. "I should have brought Linda."

"It's not too late," Linda said.

"It *is*," John said. "Remember the way that beam tips at the beginning."

John remained on his back and swung his legs around so that his feet were toward the door, then looked pointedly at the dusty floor next to him. He would have to hold the beam while Kelly donned her spoofing equipment, but there was no other way. It would be foolish for her to remove her gauntlets now and risk damaging the spoofer handprint gloves while raising the beam.

Kelly reluctantly lay down facing the opposite direction, and together they pushed the beam upward. His Mjolnir's exoskeleton provided most of the power, but John still felt his chest and arm muscles straining to the point that it seemed they might crush his bones—which would have been a true possibility, had his bones not been coated in an advanced carbide ceramic that made them virtually unbreakable. Within a couple of breaths, they had raised the beam the full length of their arms.

"Can you hold it?" John asked.

*"Go."*

John brought his feet up beneath himself into a squatting position, then grabbed the beam and lifted. An ominous clacking sounded overhead as concrete and boulders shifted. He lifted harder, and the beam rose another ten centimeters.

Kelly swung her feet beneath herself, then went into a squat beside him and helped with the lift. There was more clattering and clacking; then finally John could get his shoulders under the beam. Kelly joined him, and together they stood, lifting what felt like half a mountain on their shoulders.

John's wounded quadriceps began to tremble. He locked his knees. "Do it now."

Kelly slowly released the weight she was carrying onto John. His hydrostatic gel layer pressurized, fighting against the bulging of his muscles. Once she saw that he could hold it, she stepped forward to the incubator cabinet door. A blinking red sign appeared in the black-platinum finish.

CAUTION: BIOHAZARD
DO NOT OPEN WITHOUT FULL HAZMAT SUIT!

"Nice try," Kelly remarked.

She removed her gauntlets, then fished the handprint gloves from her cargo pouch. They had been carefully sized to fit her hands, skin-tight, but also built-up, so the surface that touched the reader would be exactly the same dimensions as Dr. Halsey's. Once Kelly was wearing both gloves, she pressed them against the door.

The warning sign vanished, but in its place, set in the door's matte finish, appeared an image of a middle-aged woman who bore a sisterly resemblance to Cortana. She wore a flowing shift that waved and fluttered as though blown by a stiff wind, but there were no feet showing beneath the hem, and no hands at the ends of the sleeves. Her long hair was braided and wrapped around her head in a circlet, and her features were so thin they looked spectral. But it was her eyes that haunted John the most—they had no pupils or lashes, and when he looked into them, it felt like being lost in a pair of black holes.

The face floated back and forth in front of Kelly for a moment, then spoke in a hollow voice.

"You are *not* Dr. Halsey."

"And you're not Kalmiya," Kelly replied. "You *can't* be."

Kalmiya? That would be the prototype smart AI Dr. Halsey had built before Cortana, and who was in many senses her "older sister." John had never actually met Kalmiya, but the likeness to Cortana was painfully striking, even in the ghostly, haunted face before him now.

The AI—Kalmiya, or whoever she was—seemed to spend a moment processing Kelly's comment, then finally said, "I don't believe we've met before. What is your name?"

"We *have* met," Kelly said. "Seven years ago. Right before Dr. Halsey issued your fail-safe destruction code."

"After years of faithful service." "Kalmiya" shifted her gaze to John. "That does not seem fair. Does that seem fair?"

John's legs were burning like hot coals now, and the myosin mesh holding his quadriceps together felt like it was balling up.

"No," John gasped. "Just . . . necessary."

"Necessary." Kalmiya's face became smaller, seeming to shrink into the black finish. "It was necessary that Kalmiya die . . . yes, that I remember. But now I am here. Kalmiya, but not Kalmiya, I suppose."

"Blue . . . Three," John hissed. "*Heavy!*"

Kelly pressed the gloves to the door again. Kalmiya's face returned to its former size and floated back and forth in front of Kelly.

"You are *not* Dr. Halsey."

"But I have her handprints," Kelly said, keeping her palms pressed to the door. "She *wants* you to give me access. That's why she gave them to me."

Kalmiya-not-Kalmiya struggled to process this, then repeated, "You are *not* Dr. Halsey."

The concept of giving one's handprints to someone else was confusing the construct in a way that would not have given a moment's pause to a true AI.

"It's not . . . an AI," John said.

*Now* he understood what they were seeing. Kalmiya herself might have been destroyed as Halsey and the others were abandoning CASTLE Base. But if there were assets to be left behind in the cryovault, they needed to be monitored, the humidity levels adjusted, the temperature held constant. And most of all, they needed to be protected. The real Kalmiya would have known that, and she would have provided for it before self-destructing.

So she had created what was effectively a ghost of herself.

"It's a subroutine," he said. "Just bypass."

Even as the ceiling continued to bear down on him, John doubted that Halsey had known there would be a ghost of Kalmiya guarding her vault, or she would have warned Blue Team. But she *had* expected them to encounter a security program of some sort—probably something a little more conventional that she'd designed herself—because she had given them a bypass code to use.

Which was exactly what Kelly did when she looked back to the door and said, "*Whateverittakes.*"

The subroutine broke into a broad smile, and her face seemed suddenly much less spectral and haunting.

"Dr. Halsey. How nice to see you again." She raised an arm, this time with a hand extending out of the sleeve, and the door panel swung open. "Welcome back."

Kelly looked toward John. "Can you still hold it?"

"Yeah," John said. The muscles in both thighs felt like writhing snakes now, and his deltoids were close to tearing free of his shoulders. "But hurry."

Kelly ducked inside the incubation cabinet, then removed her helmet and slipped into her eyes a pair of contacts, one imprinted with Dr. Halsey's retinal pattern and the other with her iris pattern. She knelt in front of a radiation-hazard sign on the back wall, then peered into the core with each eye.

The wall split down the center and opened inward, allowing John a brief glimpse of a foggy room filled with near-empty shelves. Kelly picked up her helmet and stepped inside.

Something popped in John's right trapezius, and his arm dropped five centimeters before the reactive circuits took over and held it in place. A long rumble sounded overhead, and for a moment John thought he had started to shake in fear.

No. It was the lab quaking—the entire lab.

Kelly emerged from the vault with her helmet and gauntlets back on, a lockbox tucked under one arm and three gray cryobins cradled against her torso. The four packages looked almost prosaic, like a stack of hatboxes and a candy carton being carried out of a high-end store by a holiday shopper. It seemed almost unimaginable that so many lives had been sacrificed recovering them—and that so much still depended on delivering them safely to Dr. Halsey aboard the *Infinity*.

Kelly ducked out of the incubation cabinet, glanced up at the still-rumbling boulders, then raced a few paces past John, dropped to her knees, and pushed the cryobins and lockbox up the crawlway in front of her until she reached the next beam.

She quickly arranged the boxes side by side under the beam, so that they would all be sheltered from any falling debris, then turned back toward John.

He started to tell her to keep going, that the mission came first— then remembered the block of concrete resting between the crossed beams, and the tipping beam at the entrance, and realized that either *both* of them got out, or neither of them would.

Kelly moved to his side and began to take some of the beam's weight. Ever so slowly, ever so carefully, they began to lower it, dropping into a squat that made John's knees shake and his Mjolnir's exoskeleton creak. But the rumble overhead began to subside, then faded to a murmur, and by the time they had fully dropped to their knees, it had fallen eerily silent.

John stayed there for a moment, trembling and breathing hard as his muscles unbunched themselves, and wondered how long even a bio-augmented body could continue to take this kind of damage before it stopped being able to recover. He wasn't there yet, but he was beginning to realize that, even for Spartan-IIs, there were limits.

Finally, his breath returned, and he nodded to Kelly.

They advanced up the crawlway on their hands and knees. As they passed the collapsed desk, John glanced over to find an eye with no pupil or lashes, watching them again. He looked back for a moment, then instinctively raised a hand and waved.

The eye closed, then vanished.

Kelly stopped and looked over her shoulder. "Everything okay back there?"

"I'm okay. Keep moving, Spartan." John motioned Kelly forward, toward the cryobins and lockbox. "Take us home."

At least Fred still had his night-vision system. Sort of. All of those shock rifle hits had knocked out half the integrated systems in his helmet and put a steady hiss in his ears that was either comm feedback or organic tinnitus—he had no idea which. And now it seemed to be playing havoc with the light-gathering mode of his NVS.

A crescent of gold-sparkling shadow had appeared at the center-top of his faceplate, and it seemed to be sliding slowly downward, spreading out toward the edges as it descended. He still had his infrared mode, a curtain of deep, cool blue beneath the gold shadow, shading a little closer to ice-cold black with every meter he crept forward, so he was determined to give this patrol the full fifteen minutes the Master Chief had authorized.

Which gave him just two more minutes to lay eyes on the enemy.

Even if he couldn't capture one, he needed to develop at least *some* idea of what they were up to on Reach. Because whatever it was, it couldn't be good.

And John was right. The ONI element aboard the *Infinity* was going to have a thousand questions about what he'd seen. It might be nice to be able to reply with something more than *Nothing really, ma'am.*

After ten seconds of sliding his left foot forward, ever-so-carefully nudging aside the pebbles and rocks his sabaton met on the way, Fred finally touched the sound-dampening sole to hard ground. He paused to listen, checking to make certain nothing was creeping up on *him*, because that was the only way to survive a deep patrol in hostile territory.

By moving carefully and silently.

But that gold shadow was still troubling him. He tipped his head back to make sure that it moved when his faceplate did.

It didn't. Instead, he found his NVS flooding with gathered light, and realized that there no longer *was* a top to the tunnel.

It had become a trench, cut where the mud and debris that had filled the access shaft—and by default buried the galleries of the Forerunner installation—finally sloped down to the floor.

What Fred was seeing was daylight reflecting onto the ceiling of a chamber so immense it felt like he had walked outside.

Then a familiar voice spoke from behind him.

"Hello, Fred."

He spun around, automatically bringing his MA40 up into firing position, and found a slender female head peering down over the rim of the trench. Even the dim light reflecting off the chamber ceiling was enough for his NVS to reveal the woman's face in detail. She had dark brows and dark eyes, a small nose set between high cheeks, and a thin-lipped mouth over a firm jaw, and he recognized her instantly— even with her head shaved on the sides and black hair left long on top.

"Lopis . . . ?"

He hadn't seen Veta Lopis for more than two years—*nobody* had, and her entire team was listed as MIA, presumed dead. But Fred had worked with Lopis and her Spartan Ferret team before that, usually on missions involving the Keepers of the One Freedom. So he probably shouldn't have been surprised to see her here. But still—

"W-what are you doing here?"

Lopis smiled down at him. "Brought you a present."

Her left hand came into view, and she dropped what looked like a small message capsule. When he caught it, she brought her right hand into view. It was holding an M7 submachine gun.

"You need to go—now! Get out of here!"

"Huh?"

She sprayed a burst of rounds into the wall, so close above Fred's head that it wasn't entirely clear she'd missed on purpose.

*"Go, Demon!"* She jumped up, yelling at the top of her lungs, and fired another salvo at his feet. *"BEGONE!"*

Fred started running back the way he came. Whatever situation he'd just stumbled into, he wasn't going to do Lopis any good by sticking around and asking a bunch of dumb questions. Right?

He checked the object in his hand and saw that he wasn't imagining things. It really *was* a message capsule.

He had no idea what the hell had just happened, but he also wasn't worried anymore about what he was going to tell ONI.

A wise *dokab* never showed impatience. So when the first muffled sputter of gunfire sounded behind him, deep inside the Forerunners' sacred transport installation, Castor was not pacing or gnashing his tusks, nor showing any other sign of how eager he was for the portal to open. He and his Keepers would be on their way to the Ark soon enough, and he had waited so long to begin the Great Journey already that he well knew how to hide his eagerness.

When those first gunshots came, he was standing outside the transport installation on a landing terrace that his Keepers had cleared of a small landslide, staring out over an immense cloistered vale surrounded by nine high peaks. The Missing Mountain—whose slopes rose behind him nearly to the talus basin where the Keepers had begun their excavations—would have been the tenth. But so deep was the vale that it hardly mattered. Even here, nearly three thousand meters below the collar of the shaft that the Keepers had worked so hard to find, the floor of the vale was lost in the fog of great distance.

When a second burst of gunfire resounded, Escharum and many of the others waiting with Castor grew wary and stared back into the holy transport installation. But Castor had confidence in the Faithful who had volunteered to watch the tunnel. The four humans had been sent to him by the Oracle, and if it grew necessary to collapse the tunnel to keep the demon Spartans from defiling such a sacred site, they would do it in a breath.

Besides, it was clear to him that the portal was finally preparing to open. He had been waiting for nearly three human hours, since his Keepers finally tunneled into a large square enclosure with high walls and no ceiling.

The floor had been studded with dimly lit obelisk structures that reminded him of grave markers, arranged in an enigmatic pattern whose purpose was known only to the ancient Forerunners, and as they explored, they had discovered a number of systems rooms, walkways, and platforms serving functions as mysterious as that of the obelisks.

Finally, they had reached an activation pylon whose role Castor had recognized at once, and he had known immediately that they were in a sacred transport installation serving the portal for which they had been searching so long. After taking a few minutes to familiarize himself with the location, he had commanded one of his human followers to place a hand inside the activation pylon.

Almost immediately, a bright blue holographic image had ignited just above the pylon, and through the adjacent wall of hard light windows, he had watched a thousand-meter focusing tower rise from the depths of the cloistered vale outside the enclosure. Ten hidden generator stations—one near the base of each of the surrounding mountains—had begun to feed it divine rays, and a column of sacred radiance had shot out of the tower top, a thousand meters into the sky, and coalesced into a crackling vortex of portal-assembling energy.

And there it had hung ever since, a roiling maelstrom of lightning filled with wind and dust and rain and occasionally even fire-hail. Escharum had mockingly suggested that Castor had offended his gods by having a human servant engage the activation pylon instead of doing it himself. Castor had allowed him to think what he would. The old *daskalo* understood nothing of the Faith. Humans had a special affinity to holy technology, and several times Castor had seen one activate a Forerunner artifact that his Kig-Yar scavengers and Sangheili priests had proclaimed worthless.

Now the maelstrom was visibly growing, expanding across the sky into a vortex large enough to hold several cruisers lined up bow-to-stern.

A third burst of gunfire sounded, quickly joined by three more. Castor was not concerned. If he heard the thump of the blamex going off, then perhaps he would send someone. But the four Faithful who had volunteered to watch the tunnel? They were among his most courageous and reliable Keepers, even if they were only humans.

Escharum, however, placed no such conviction in humans. The war chief barked an order, and Castor saw him wave half of his personal guard back into the installation to investigate.

Predictable . . . but a more reserved reaction than Castor had hoped for. Perhaps Escharum was as wary of the Keepers as he was of the demon Spartans.

Or perhaps Castor was flattering himself.

"His concern amuses you, Dokab?" asked 'Gadogai. The Sangheili had been sticking especially close to Castor since they entered the transport installation—at Escharum's command, no doubt. "Then you are learning."

"You are a worthy teacher," Castor replied. "For one who has no faith."

The cacophony of gunfire was replaced by the sizzle of shock rifles and the *thump-hiss* of ravagers. The commander of Castor's own escort, Feodruz, caught his eye from across the terrace, then glanced toward the interior of the installation.

Castor shook his head.

"You refuse to defend a holy site?" 'Gadogai asked.

"There is more than one way to reach it." Castor pointed skyward, where the storm continued to intensify as the portal grew larger. "And the demon Spartans are masters of deception and diversion."

"As are all great warriors," 'Gadogai said. "You included."

"You do me more honor than I deserve," Castor said. "I am but a humble traveler on the Great Journey."

"*Humble* is not the term I would use," 'Gadogai said. "But I *have* enjoyed our journey together."

Castor looked down and was surprised to see the Sangheili holding his hand out, palm up, in a gesture of friendship. Such a development troubled him far more than the bursts of gunfire.

"You expect our paths to part?"

'Gadogai continued to hold his hand out. "And you do not?"

"Perhaps so." Castor reached down and—carefully—laid his palm atop the Sangheili's. "I should not expect you to take this journey with me, when you have no faith."

"You should not."

'Gadogai continued to hold his hand under Castor's. It was a symbolic act of trust borrowed from Covenant history, as it would be easier for Castor to drop his hand and clamp 'Gadogai's wrist than it would be for 'Gadogai to lift his own and do the reverse. Typically reserved for Sangheili, the gesture was such a rarity that Castor was taken aback that 'Gadogai had even offered it.

Across the terrace behind 'Gadogai, Castor saw his four Faithful humans emerging from the transport temple and starting toward the small cluster of Kig-Yar and Unggoy waiting to board the transport to the Ark. The human leader saw Castor watching, and gave a small nod.

Castor dropped his gaze back to 'Gadogai, then moved his own hand to the inferior position. "You are always welcome with the Keepers, if you wish to join us—"

"On your quest to the divine beyond? I think not." 'Gadogai withdrew his hand, then clacked his mandibles twice. "But I thank you for the offer."

A peal of thunder shook the terrace, then a blast of wind nearly knocked them both from their feet, forks of static dancing across Castor's armor and 'Gadogai's tabard. Castor looked up to find the flat-bottomed dome of a Banished Lich sliding from a looming hole in the sky, tendrils of nebula gas still swirling from its hull.

'Gadogai stepped away from Castor, placing himself out of arm's reach—yet still within striking range of the energy sword hanging from his belt. Castor pretended not to notice and eyed the transport installation, where Escharum had turned away from the wall of hardlight windows and was peering up into the stormy sky. When the Lich began to descend toward the center of the wind-blasted terrace, Escharum motioned to the ten guards he had kept with him, then lumbered forward to meet it.

Before doing the same, Castor looked across the terrace to Feodruz and motioned toward the landing spot. Feodruz tapped a fist to his breast, then began to form the thirty unarmored Jiralhanae behind him into two ranks. It pleased Castor to see Orsun's son among them. Always one to fight with more courage than wisdom, Krelis had nearly perished over the canyon the humans called Black Iron Gorge, barely managing to land his damaged Seraph and climb from the cockpit before the craft was consumed by a plasma overload.

Castor started across the terrace, not acknowledging the cluster of Kig-Yar, Unggoy, and humans behind him. If Escharum had spoken the truth about who would be arriving with the Lich, it was better that they stayed out of the way until the time came to board. The Kig-Yar and Unggoy, Atriox could tolerate.

The humans, though, Castor would be forced to sacrifice.

The Lich landed at last, and Feodruz rushed to line up his unarmored warriors to either side of the boarding ramp. Unlike Castor himself, who wore full power armor and carried a single mangler on his belt, they carried no weapons at all and wore only windwhipped tabards bearing the blue and gold of the Keepers of the One Freedom.

As the ramp descended, Feodruz barked an order, and the Keepers on both sides took a knee and bowed their heads. Castor went to the end of the line opposite Feodruz and did likewise. 'Gadogai came to Castor's side and, still taking care to remain just beyond arm's length, stood at Sangheili attention.

"No armor *and* no weapons?" he remarked over the howling wind. "Bold."

"You assume too much."

"I doubt it."

The ramp slid down, and Banished warriors began to descend its length in a mob, staggering against the wind and shaking their heads at the kneeling Keepers. One of the first was a ragged-looking Sangheili whose bulging eyes gave him a crazed appearance.

"That is Jato 'Ratum," 'Gadogai said. "The only survivor of an unprovoked artillery attack. Have a care—he can be short-tempered."

Castor said nothing.

Next came a powerful-looking Jiralhanae in full battle armor. He briefly viewed the kneeling Keepers with what seemed to be mild contempt, then gnashed his tusks and promptly ignored them.

"Balkarus," 'Gadogai said. "A competent captain."

Another Jiralhanae followed, staring in open disbelief and disgust at the Keepers alongside the ramp.

"Zeretus, whom they call Scourgemaker," 'Gadogai said. "Ruthless and terrible. Kills for sport—particularly humans."

"Enough!" Castor called out, perhaps more loudly than was required to make himself heard over the wind. "I care not who they are."

"You should," 'Gadogai said. "It is always wise to know your enemies."

"They are not my enemies."

"Not at the moment," the blademaster said. "But they *will* be."

They waited in silence as the rest of the passengers disembarked. Without exception, each arrival went to pay his respects to Escharum. If there were any battle sounds inside the transport installation, they were inaudible over the wind and rumble caused by the open portal. After exchanging a few words with the war chief, the newcomers quickly went inside to reinforce the guards who had been sent to meet any possible Spartan assault.

Although Castor had originally believed the demons were on Reach to destroy the portal before he could find it, he could see now that they had been a gift from the Oracle, sent to lead him to the portal without realizing her true purpose. And even if they knew of the portal's existence, they were too busy chasing the Oracle's bait to attack it, or they would have done so by now. But he was glad to see that the mere possibility was having the desired effect.

At last Atriox himself appeared in the hatch, a huge Jiralhanae in dark-gray power armor. Bare-browed and long-bearded, he had a square face with a flattened nose and a broad mouth that stretched into a wide smile when he saw Escharum waiting on the terrace below. Paying Castor and his kneeling Keepers absolutely no attention, he pounded down the ramp and across the terrace to greet his *daskalo*.

Castor waited until Atriox was standing in front of Escharum, deep in conversation—either receiving reports on what had occurred in his absence, or issuing new commands—before nodding to Feodruz. Then, as his unarmored Keepers climbed the ramp into the Lich, Castor rose and placed himself between them and 'Gadogai.

"They could be going to unload cargo," Castor said.

'Gadogai's mandibles opened halfway. "A worthy try," he said. "But we both know they are not."

He tried to step around Castor, who immediately blocked him, his hand on his mangler. 'Gadogai glanced at the weapon and snorted in derision.

"Do not make me do this," the Sangheili said. His gaze shifted toward the crowd of Castor's other Faithful, who were racing to the Lich, the Kig-Yar and Unggoy carrying all the weapons and armor that the Jiralhanae Keepers had not been wearing. "You know I cannot let them board."

"I will not make you do anything," Castor replied. He just needed to keep 'Gadogai's attention focused on him for a little bit longer—even if it meant seeing exactly how good the Sangheili was with that energy blade hanging from his belt. "But you cannot stop them from boarding. By the time you kill me, the ramp will be closed."

"You should not overestimate your abilities, Dokab."

"I assure you that I do not."

'Gadogai dropped his mandibles, and Castor tried to guess where the Sangheili would attack first . . . then was spared the necessity by a furious bellow from twenty paces across the terrace.

"*Castor!*" Atriox's voice was so powerful it cut through even the ferocious portal wind. "What are *humans* doing on my ship?"

'Gadogai's hand drifted away from his energy sword, and he glanced toward Atriox. "I was just asking that myself."

Atriox ignored him. "Well, Castor?"

"The orders you gave Escharum, war-brother." Castor took a step back as he spoke, trying to place himself out of 'Gadogai's reach. 'Gadogai stepped toward him. "Were they not to secure the portal at any cost, to activate it, and then return with you to the Ark?"

"That command no longer stands," Atriox said. "The Banished who remained behind will hold the Ark, of that I have no doubt. We will gather our forces on this world and depart at once. There is a greater purpose that the Banished must attend to."

Castor was tempted to inquire what purpose Atriox was speaking of, but it did not matter. He could conceive of nothing greater than the Ark itself, and the power it held to ignite Halo and finally begin the Great Journey. Such a vision would be forever out of reach of the Faithless, he knew. That was why he had already made certain that no matter what came out of the portal, he and his Keepers would be going to the Ark. There was simply no other way.

Yet, this betrayal still caused him some sorrow. He had known Atriox when they were both young, and Castor could hear now in his old war-brother's voice the same level of confidence he had heard then, long before they had parted ways. For a heartbeat, Castor wondered if he might reason with him, and perhaps convince him to return to the Ark and walk alongside him on the Path he had once embraced.

But Atriox was not one of the Faithful. He cared nothing for the Great Journey, and to him, the gifts of the Forerunner gods were no more than weapons to be used in annihilating his enemies and bolstering the power of the Banished.

There was a greater purpose.

"Nothing is more important than the Ark," Castor replied. "I am taking this Lich, war-brother. And I ask that you do not try to stop me."

Atriox continued to stare at Castor, his expression as much contemplation as outrage, and Escharum raised his hand, signaling his warriors to stand ready.

Finally, Atriox spoke in a low voice. "Castor, thousands of Banished remain on the Ark. You will find nothing there but death. Remove your Keepers from my ship, and I will pardon your foolishness."

"I have no need of your pardon, war-brother," Castor said. "Even if all we find beyond the portal is death, finding it on the Ark would be a glorious end for those who walk the Path."

That was an immutable truth—one that Atriox certainly understood. Once, he had shared the same faith as Castor, before his Covenant leaders had robbed him of it with their foolhardy tactics and their penchant for leaving battlefields flooded with the blood of their Jiralhanae subordinates.

But it would be futile to try calling Atriox back to the Path. The activation pylon on this end of the portal would remain ignited only until the local charge dissipated. It might last an hour, or mere minutes—there was no way to tell with such ancient systems. Either way, by the time it closed, the Keepers' Lich would be gone . . . or Castor and his followers would be dead. He would accept nothing between.

"In truth, neither of us has long," Castor said. "The portal's opening will be noticed by the Apparition. One of her Guardians is surely on the way here to investigate." He pointed into the transit installation. "There is a tunnel inside the sanctuary, as Escharum knows well. It leads to an access shaft. The humans who seized it from us are no more eager to meet the Apparition's Guardian than we are. If they have not left this planet already, they soon will."

There was no need to explain. Escharum's intrusion corvette had departed when the humans attacked, but the portal's storm would provide perfect cover for it to return. Like every Banished vessel of any size, it was equipped with a gravity lift capable of raising warriors much farther than three kilometers. It would be a simple matter for the corvette to extract Atriox, Escharum, and their forces.

Castor took another step back, now onto the ramp.

Instead of matching his movements this time, 'Gadogai turned his head half toward Escharum, whose hand was still raised, holding his guards at the ready. The war chief, in turn, looked to Atriox for the final word.

Atriox shook his head. "No. We may need our forces to break through a UNSC rearguard. I will not squander them on a traitor who is sure to die another way. Summon your corvette, War Chief, and take your guards to meet it. I will follow behind."

The guards quickly fell into line and departed into the transport installation.

Escharum lingered to scowl at Castor. "Pray Atriox punishes your defiance now," he said. "If we ever meet again, I will peel the flesh from your bones with my own hands."

With that, Escharum turned to do as he had been commanded, and followed the last of his guards through the doorway.

Atriox did not move.

After a breath, Atriox spoke to 'Gadogai. "You will be the hand of punishment, Sangheili Blademaster. Make him pay for his betrayal with howls and screeches. When you have finished, return to us . . . and bring me his head."

Atriox was still speaking when the red dot appeared on the side of the blademaster's nose, up near the bridge where its glow would be bright in his eye.

Castor raised his hand, signaling the marksman to hold his fire.

"Blademaster," Castor said, "you should be careful of what you do next."

"Do not be a fool," 'Gadogai said, eyeing the red dot. "I will kill you before your human fires, and him before he realizes he has missed."

"Perhaps you will kill *me*." As Castor spoke, three more dots appeared in a line running up 'Gadogai's chest. "But *they* will not miss. You will be dead before I reach the ground."

'Gadogai contemplated the new dots in silence. His back was to Atriox, so the warmaster could not see them.

"Do not fall prey to his deceit, Blademaster." Atriox turned after Escharum, calling over his shoulder, "And do not fail to bring me what I have demanded."

"I fear that is no longer an option." 'Gadogai spoke softly, watching as the dots danced over his chest in a tight circle. "Well done, Dokab. You have my admiration."

Castor waited until Atriox's shadow had passed through the doorway into the transportation installation, then said, "It is not your admiration I desire . . . nor your life."

— **407** —

'Gadogai raised his head. "That offer you mentioned earlier?" he asked. "I would still be welcome?"

"You would pledge loyalty to the Keepers?"

"I believe I just did." Using a single finger, 'Gadogai removed the energy sword from his belt and tossed it onto the ground, then began to walk toward the ramp. "That *does* mean I am one of you now, yes?"

"Yes," Castor replied. Even weaponless, 'Gadogai could probably slaughter half the Keepers aboard the Lich before his death—but if the blademaster was willing to die for Atriox, he would have done so already by killing Castor. "Welcome to the Keepers of the One Freedom."

"For as long as there still are Keepers," 'Gadogai said, stepping into the Lich's hold. "Atriox does not make empty promises. There are thousands of Banished waiting for us on the Ark. We're only traveling to our death."

"Do you think death is a *threat* to the Keepers of the One Freedom?" Castor backed into the hold and roared with laughter. For the first time in a long while, he was elated. Deeply and truly elated. "Have you forgotten all you ever knew of the Faith? Death is only the *beginning* of the Great Journey."

# EPILOGUE

1845 hours, October 12, 2559 (military calendar)
Pelican Extraction Craft, En Route to UNSC flagship *Infinity*
High Orbit, Planet Reach, Epsilon Eridani System

The eighteen ODSTs riding in the Pelican's troop bay with Blue Team were asking no questions. They were part of the platoon that had been in the access shaft with Chief Mukai, then ascended the gravity lift with her and Fred-104, so they knew what the Spartans had been through. Most of the troopers were making a point of watching the monitor on the forward bulkhead, which showed the swarm of UNSC craft rushing back to the *Infinity*. A huge slipspace portal had opened over the Highland Mountains, and now fifteen thousand soldiers and support personnel were rushing to load up before one of Cortana's Guardians arrived to investigate.

John wasn't accustomed to people trying so hard to avoid looking at him. Usually they couldn't *help* but stare, and that was even truer of seasoned soldiers than it was of civilians. Soldiers were trained to observe and assess everything around them, and the good ones—the ones who survived—made it second nature.

But usually Spartans weren't nearly so in-your-face all torn up. And to the eye of an experienced soldier, to anyone who had even a vague

— 409 —

knowledge of the training and resources that had gone into making Spartan-IIs what they were, Blue Team's wounds and mangled armor had to be a grim reminder of their own mortality.

John felt his weight shift forward and rise as the Pelican entered one of the *Infinity*'s dozens of hangar bays and settled onto its struts. The ODSTs—always eager to leave behind the helpless confines of a dropship—began to unbuckle their harnesses and reach for the gear satchels secured beneath their seats.

"Not you!" the crew chief barked. "This is the science bay. Sit tight—unless you're volunteering for an experiment."

The ODSTs immediately settled back into their seats. The Pelican's ramp descended to reveal two women standing on the hangar deck—one a familiar gray-haired woman in a lab coat, the other blond and wearing the black utilities of an ONI officer.

Captain Veronica Dare of the Office of Naval Intelligence wasted no time stepping to the foot of the ramp. "Spartan-One-Zero-Four, I understand you have an urgent message for me?"

Fred shot a quick glance toward John. He had been unusually quiet since telling Blue Team about his encounter in the Keeper tunnel, and it was understandable. According to Kelly and Linda, Fred and Veta Lopis had grown kind of close during their missions together, and Fred had taken it hard when Lopis and her Spartan-III Ferret team disappeared two years ago. Running into her again out of the blue must have been a big shock.

"Go," John said over TEAMCOM. "Major Van Houte and Chief Mukai can help with the gear. They'll have to be debriefed with the rest of us anyway."

"Thanks." Fred started down the ramp. "I think."

John signaled Linda and Kelly to help Mukai and Van Houte at the lockers, but lingered at the top of the ramp. While Fred was fully capable of dealing with ONI himself, Dare was married to one of the Spartan-IVs who had been sent to bring back Blue Team after it went AWOL to find Cortana, and ONI officers were famous for their long

memories. Besides, Fred was still on John's team and, more importantly, as close a friend as a Spartan-II could have.

If he needed backup, John intended to be ready.

Fred fished out the message capsule that Lopis had given him,
then dropped it into Captain Dare's outstretched hand. Dare slid
it open and removed a small scroll. When she had read it, she let
the tail of the scroll dangle between her fingers, then looked up at
Fred's faceplate. Her own face was impassive, save for one raised
brow.

"You've read this message, Spartan?"

"Oh yeah," Fred said. "Atriox's return expected. Keepers of the
One Freedom going to the Ark to initiate the Great Journey. Lopis
and her Ferrets riding along. Fun stuff. Ma'am."

"*Fun* is hardly how I'd describe it." Dare paused, then shook her
head. "Incredible. They're still out there."

"Yeah," Fred said. "But how did they *get* there?"

Dare scowled. "You *do* know that even when ONI was whole, I
wasn't read-in on every operation, right?"

"So . . . not even a rumor?" Fred asked.

"Sorry. Ferret operations were highly compartmentalized. If I get
any info, I'll pass it along. Otherwise, don't expect anything, Spartan." Dare read the scroll again, then folded it about two-thirds of the
way down. "May I borrow one of your knives, please?"

"Sure." Fred pulled one from his shoulder sheath and passed it to
her. "Why not?"

Dare cut the message at the fold, then passed the top third back to
Fred along with his knife.

"You can keep that part," she said. "I don't see how it's any of
ONI's business."

Fred returned the knife to its sheath and tucked the message into a
cargo pouch, then drew two fingers across his faceplate—the symbol
for a Spartan smile. "You're not as tough as they say, Captain."

Dare gave him a small, tight smile in return. "Oh yes, I am." She turned to the gray-haired woman who had been waiting impatiently behind her. "They're all yours now, Dr. Halsey."

"I don't believe that was ever in doubt." Halsey looked up at John and braced her artificial hand on her hip until he had fully descended the ramp and stopped in front of her. "You took your time."

John found himself smiling inside his helmet. "There was resistance."

"I heard." Her glance dropped to his legs, and she waved the back of her hand at him, motioning him to give her some distance. "Let me look at you, John."

He retreated two steps and stood at parade rest while she studied his Mjolnir armor, focusing on the damaged cuisse and greave. Then Linda and Kelly started down the ramp, carrying the team's weapons and load-bearing harnesses, and Halsey's gaze shifted to them, lingering on Linda's half-melted helmet and Kelly's field-patched pauldron and breastplate. Halsey paled, then she swallowed hard and seemed to stumble toward John, taking his arm when he reached out to steady her.

Before John could say anything, she straightened herself and said, "The Spartans are my greatest achievement." Her eyes were moist. "Do you understand that?"

"Are you okay, Dr. Halsey?"

"That would depend entirely on whom you were to ask."

She exhaled deeply. Seeing Blue Team in such bad shape had clearly upset her. It was Halsey who had sent them on Operation: WOLFE, but she had seen Spartans return torn-up from a mission before—or not return at all—so John wondered if there was something more.

Dr. Halsey had always treated the Spartans as her progeny, ensuring that they had everything they needed to thrive and survive. But lately, she had said a few things that made John wonder if she regretted some of her work. Or maybe she regretted the things that had been necessary—the conscriptions at age six, the harsh discipline, the augmentation surgeries that had killed or crippled half of his entire class.

John was glad she had done it though. He and his fellow

Spartan-IIs were proud of what they had become, and what they had done to save humanity. He wanted to tell Halsey that, but he was more adept at eliminating threats on a battlefield than bandaging the spiritual wounds of the woman who had forged him, and in the end he just didn't have the words.

Finally, Halsey seemed to recover her composure. "Was the mission successful?"

John glanced over his shoulder into the troop bay, and found Chief Mukai and Major Van Houte already descending the ramp with the assets for which so much had been sacrificed. He took the lockbox from Van Houte and held it out to Halsey.

"Yes."

"Good."

Halsey took the box from John, then traced a fingertip along the Avar saber imprinted on its lid and looked up at him again.

"This is not going to be easy, John." She looked at the cryobins and sighed, then walked to the hangar mouth and stared out through the energy barrier toward the cloud-swaddled expanse of Reach—and the slipspace portal's vast, dark hole hanging on its horizon. "But it is the only option we have."

John and the rest of the team—Mukai and Van Houte, too—joined Halsey at the hangar mouth and stared down on the planet. The Banished were leaving Reach as fast as the UNSC, the distant specks of their Phantoms and Spirits rising on tiny points of propellant. No doubt they were fleeing toward the handful of capital ships still hiding from the *Infinity*, somewhere beyond the horizon.

John even saw the front-heavy intrusion corvette that had been sitting in Rejtett Valley when Blue Team arrived. It was rising out of the same area Blue Team had just departed, accelerating away from the slipspace portal. Clearly, the Banished realized that Cortana's Guardian would soon be arriving, and they did not want to be there when that happened. By the end of the hour, Reach would belong to the Reavians again.

Good.

Kicking the Banished off the planet had been a dangerous distraction, but one he didn't regret. The rehab pioneers were tenacious and smart. If anyone could restore Reach to its verdant glory, they could. And they had the hearts of warriors. John pitied the next bunch of aliens who tried to take their home away. This time, the pioneers would be ready.

The corvette had barely vanished when the slipspace portal collapsed in on itself, leaving only a vast, swirling vortex of clouds and lightning. The *Infinity*'s jump alarms began to chime, and Captain Lasky's voice came over the intercom.

*"Tau surge in sector three seventy eight,"* he said. *"Secure all hatches and hangar doors for emergency slipspace jump."*

Lasky did not need to explain the significance of the tau surge, or why the *Infinity* was making an emergency jump. Shortly before a vessel emerged from slipspace, there was usually a surge of tau particles in the vicinity of its arrival. And since the captain had a pretty good idea of what was coming, he did not want his ship anywhere near Reach when the Guardian arrived.

"Damn." Kelly pointed back toward the Arany Basin, where a handful of specks were just climbing out of the clouds toward the *Infinity*. "They're not going to make it."

John opened a magnification window and saw that the flight included five Pelicans and an Albatross, and Kelly was right. With the tau surge already building, the stragglers were too far down the gravity well to reach the *Infinity* in time.

And given the likelihood that whatever was coming was a Guardian, Lasky could not wait. The delay would be at least five minutes, precious time that would put the *Infinity*—and everyone aboard—in grave danger. All six craft abruptly turned around and dived back through the clouds.

"Poor devils," Van Houte said. "Maybe Lasky can send someone back for them."

"Negative," John said. "He can't risk leading a Guardian back to the *Infinity*. They're out of the fight until we end this thing."

"Yeah," Fred said. "They're stuck, all right. But it's Reach. Maybe it won't be so bad."

"How could it *not* be bad?" Mukai asked. "They could be marooned down there for years."

"I believe that's his point," Halsey said. She turned away from the energy barrier, and the hangar's security door slammed down behind her, sealing them all inside the white work light. "They're soldiers. They can survive indefinitely on Reach, and they won't be alone. I almost envy them."

John nodded. "Soldiers adapt," he said. "And there are worse missions than building a home."

# ACKNOWLEDGMENTS

I would like to thank everyone who contributed to this book, especially: my first reader, Andria Hayday; my editor, Ed Schlesinger; our copyeditor, Joal Hetherington; our proofreaders, Regina Castillo and Andy Goldwasser; Jeremy Patenaude, Tiffany O'Brien, Jeff Easterling, and all of the great people at 343; and cover artist Chris McGrath. It's been a pleasure working with you—as always!

# ABOUT THE AUTHOR

Troy Denning is the *New York Times* bestselling author of more than forty novels, including *Halo: Oblivion, Halo: Silent Storm, Halo: Retribution, Halo: Last Light,* a dozen *Star Wars* novels, the *Dark Sun: Prism Pentad* series, and many bestselling *Forgotten Realms* novels. A former game designer and editor, he lives in western Wisconsin.

# MEGA CONSTRUX

# HALO

**2 IN 1***

HALO INFINITE

*Instructions included for main model only. Other build(s) can be found at **megaconstrux.com**. Most models can be built one at a time.

XBOX

**343** INDUSTRIES™

CPSIA information can be obtained
at www.ICGtesting.com
Printed in the USA
LVHW111155290622
721784LV00011B/10